SIDEWINDER

A sequel adventure to
Copperhead

R.P. DEISS

CONTENTS

From the Author   1

Chapter One   5

Chapter Two   9

Chapter Three   13

Chapter Four   22

Chapter Five   25

Chapter Six   34

Chapter Seven   42

Chapter Eight   49

Chapter Nine   51

Chapter Ten   60

Chapter Eleven   65

Chapter Twelve   74

Chapter Thirteen   83

Chapter Fourteen   101

Chapter Fifteen   108

Chapter Sixteen   126

Chapter Seventeen   134

Chapter Eighteen   143

Chapter Nineteen   153

Chapter Twenty   163

Chapter Twenty-One   186

Chapter Twenty-Two   201

Chapter Twenty-Three   211

Chapter Twenty-Four   225

Chapter Twenty-Five   243

Chapter Twenty-Six   271

Chapter Twenty-Seven   279

Chapter Twenty-Eight   304

About the Author   321

Other Books by R.P. Deiss   322

SIDEWINDER

A sequel adventure to
Copperhead

From the Author

F irst of all, I'd like to say this book is a work of fiction written for your pure reading enjoyment. This is the second book about my two star FBI agents and the eleventh book I've written so far. In order to set the stage for the story contained within these pages I'd like to take a few minutes to introduce you to the world of cryptids and supernatural beings.

Cryptid is the modern day word to describe beings that many do not believe exist. But there are many that have seen them and were either already believers or became believers because of what they witnessed.

Native Americans from all tribes have deep seated beliefs surrounding cryptids. For them their folklore going back to where their memories dim in the distant past is a fact of life that is believed by all and not doubted by many as they are in our modern society.

Hairy man, booger, skunk ape, Grassman, Honey Island swamp monster, sasquatch and fifty different names given by a hundred different tribes describing what we today call bigfoot. Seven to as much as twelve foot tall, flattened nose, squared teeth three times the size of ours. Huge sunken eyes and a protruding bridge above the eyes and a coned head. Arms longer than humans hanging down to their knees. They are bi-pedal and their color variations run from reddish brown to black, blond and white.

They are heard, seen and smelled. They do tree knocks and clack rocks together. They throw rocks, logs and sticks to warn people away. They give out whoops, whistles and cry like a woman or a baby to draw you to them. They build nests and blinds for hunting and have a stench described as musky and a cross between a wet dog and rotting garbage.

From the vast wilderness of Alaska to the swamps of Florida. From the Texas hill country to the mountains and volcanoes of Washington, Oregon and California. From the Pine Barrens of New Jersey and the river bottoms and woods of Ohio to the mountains of Colorado and all points in between they live. Many people every year see and either report them or keep their sightings to themselves to avoid ridicule. Bigfoot can be an aggressive creature. Sixteen thousand people have disappeared in the Alaskan triangle in the last three decades or so. Sure, some are lost because of injuries suffered in the wilderness. Some are killed because of the harsh climate and still others are killed by moose and bears. But can it explain the loss of sixteen thousand souls? Some believe there are two subspecies of bigfoot. One is meek and does what it can to remain hidden. The other one is aggressive. The aggressive one has a huge bulge between its shoulder blades and a large bald spot on its head.

Werewolves are another cryptid. From the Rougarou of the Louisiana bayou country to the Beast of Bray Road in Wisconsin, skinwalkers and shapeshifters. These are humans that can take the form of an animal that can walk on two legs. Like bigfoot they can be aggressive and should be avoided at all cost.

Dogman is different from a werewolf. It does not change form from man to beast but is a beast all of the time. The Michigan dogman is one such being. It is taller than a werewolf reported to be seven to seven and a half feet tall. It too can be aggressive.

Thunderbird is a huge bird that is said to make a sound like the clap of thunder when it beats its wings. It is said to be able to pick up a full grown cow and fly away with it. In the 1880s two cowboys were reported to have shot one. They said the wingspan was eighteen feet and had a head like an alligator. Later on it was thought they had shot the last known pterodactyl. Pictures have circulated on the internet of people in eighteenth century garb posing with a pterodactyl. I don't know if the two are related or not. Thunderbird sightings still happen today.

Mothman of West Virginia folklore is said to measure seven feet tall with massive wings and glowing red eyes. A group of grave diggers in the 1960s spotted something strange and are the first to have reported the cryptid. Said to be able to fly at a hundred miles an hour it was reported by many groups over a period of several years. Once spotted sitting on the superstructure of a bridge over the Ohio River only days later the bridge collapsed killing many travelers. It is said the mothman is the harbinger of death and destruction.

Chupacabras were first reported in Puerto Rico. Either they found a way to migrate to the mainland or perhaps just the legend did. They are a smaller cryptid, the size of a coyote. They suck out the blood of their prey. Several years ago a woman rancher in Texas received a phone call from a neighbor who told her a weird animal was lying dead at the end of her ranch road. She went and collected the animal and had it mounted by a local taxidermist. The animal was the size of a coyote and totally bald with bright blue eyes. People thought it was just a coyote with a severe case of mange. But no animal in the area or anywhere else had bright blue eyes. When the DNA was tested the test result said the DNA was a cross between a mexican wolf, a coyote and an animal not in the DNA database.

Cattle mutilations are reported every year. Cattle cut with surgical precision, drained of blood. Extra terrestrials have been blamed for these acts but have never been caught in the act. Is it aliens doing it or is it an unknown cryptid?

Wendigo, is a humanoid monster with fangs, and glowing red eyes. The Algorquian Wendigo either devours its victims or possesses their spirit and turns them evil.

As the tale goes, the Wendigo was once a hunter that was lost. During a brutally cold winter his intense hunger drove him to cannibalism. After feasting on another human's flesh, he transformed into a crazed man-beast, roaming the forest in search of more people to eat or curse with his own fate.

There are also cryptids in our waterways. To name a few, Sinkhole Sam in Kansas, Tizheruk in Alaska, Michigan merman, the Loch Ness monster, Bessie of Lake Erie. Other than brief sightings not much is known. Very few people have ever been reported being attacked by them. Who knows, maybe it's just because there were no witnesses.

Poltergeists, demons, ghosts and shadow people. Supposedly the Amityville horror was based on an actual event. Some priests are actually trained to do exorcisms and perform them. You won't catch me messing around with a Ouija board, I saw too many shows where families had to seek out help because they inadvertently summoned something into their home they didn't want.

Those of us who have the ability to sense or see what is around us know there is an afterlife. Shadow people, I see them occasionally usually but not always at night. You see them moving past you out of the corner of your eye. I lost a favorite pet fifteen years ago and from time to time I see his shadow go past me letting me know he is still with me.

My father died some thirty years ago. A few months after his death I had two couples over to play cards. We were telling anecdotes about my dad. Funny stories about interactions with him, just remembering fonder times. All harmless and nothing mean. Well he must not have liked it much. A deer head I had hanging on my wall for several years leaped off the wall, bounced off the aquarium and landed in the middle of the living room floor. Nothing like that has ever happened before or since that night. You might think it's just a coincidence but I have my own opinion. I have many other stories of things I've witnessed over my lifetime but those stories are for another time.

Now you have a somewhat working knowledge of cryptids and supernatural beings so we'll start our story. The first book in this series was called Copperhead so keeping with the series name this is Sidewinder.

Enjoy the adventure,
R.P. Deiss

Chapter One

"**H**ow is your breakfast?" I asked my partner Connie as I looked up from my plate of bacon and eggs.

"The potato pancakes are a little bit over cooked. Remind me next time we come here not to order them," she said as she poked them with her fork.

We'd just gotten back to Washington DC after a case in Wisconsin. We'd tracked down a serial killer who was preying on coeds in the University of Wisconsin system. The case had taken several weeks to complete. By the time it was over one of our lab techs was dead and another one wounded. We had taken time off of work after finishing the case.

My name is Ben Hawk. Connie sitting across the table from me is my partner. We work for the FBI and our specialty is tracking down serial killers, it's all we do. Everyone knows we are the best at what we do including the killers we hunt for. We gained our fame when we tracked down a pack of killers in the Chicago stock yards a little more than a year ago. From there our careers skyrocketed. Our status was now higher than that of any SAC in any city. SAC stood for special agent in charge. There was some envy from other agents who had been doing the job far longer than we have but they kept it well hidden. Some thought we'd just been in the right place at the right time. Both Connie and I had gotten bloody by the time the first case wrapped up.

"I talked to Bill's wife last night. She said the family had laid Todd to rest in the cemetery. She also said Bill was back at work again," Connie reported.

Bill was the local sheriff and his brother turned out to be the serial killer. Connie and I had killed him in a kill or be killed confrontation.

"That's good. Going back to work will be the best medicine for him. It's better to keep your mind busy instead of letting it dwell in the past," I replied.

"I sent flowers to the funeral home from us for Larry's funeral. You owe me half of the cost of the flowers sport," Connie said as she eyed me waiting for me to complain.

"I totally forgot about the tech's funeral being tomorrow in Chicago. Thanks for taking care of that for us," I said gratefully.

Connie's eyebrows unfurrowed after not seeing me complain about it. My phone picked that moment to ring. I looked at the called ID before answering it.

"It's the director's office," I told her as I hit the button on the phone. "Special Agent Hawk."

"Good, I'm glad I reached you. The director would like to see you and special agent Sanchez in his office right away," said his executive secretary.

"We're still on vacation until next monday Sue," I reminded her.

"First of all, are you back in Washington yet or still in Wisconsin?" She asked.

"We got back late last night," I told her.

"The director told me to tell you the rest of your vacation is cancelled. Report to his office in one hour," Sue told me.

"It must be important if he is cancelling our time off," I said with a sigh.

"Everything you have assigned to you is important, Agent Hawk. I still have to contact Agent Sanchez and give her the message," Sue said.

"Save yourself the phone call. She is sitting across from me having breakfast."

"Good, I'll let the director know you are on your way," Sue said as she hung up, ending the call.

"I'll pay for breakfast this morning Connie, seeing as you sprung for the flowers," I said magnanimously, grabbing the bill.

"Nice try sport but those flowers cost me eighty bucks. You're not getting off that cheap you tight wad!" Connie said as her eyebrows furrowed again.

"Eighty bucks! Why the hell did you spend so much?" I asked

in surprise.

"Ben, he was a co-worker and died helping us solve the case. You don't go cheap at a time like this," Connie growled, scolding me.

"It's been so long since I bought flowers I forgot how much they cost," I tried explaining.

"Truer words were never spoken. You sure haven't spent any money buying flowers for me," Connie hinted.

After we finished the Wisconsin case we somehow ended up in bed with each other. Well to be honest it was probably in the making for a long time. It just took this case for it to happen.

"I guess that I didn't know you were expecting any," I said, trying to defend myself.

"Save your money Ben. As often as we are at home they would just wither away in the vase and die with no one home to admire them, Connie said letting me off the hook.

"We better finish eating breakfast. The director is expecting us in his office in an hour," I informed her.

"I suppose we need to stop back at home and change clothes for the office," Connie thought out loud.

"No, I don't think so. After all, the director knows we are taking time off of our vacations to meet with him. He won't be expecting us to be dressed in business clothes while still on vacation," I said.

"That works for me," Connie said as she munched on her overcooked potato pancake and washed it down with coffee.

I looked at my watch. "We'll be lucky to get to his office at the time he wants us there. The beltway is bad this time of day and finding parking is going to be almost impossible," I said.

An hour and twenty minutes later we were getting onto the elevator that would take us to the director of the FBI's office. The elevator doors opened on the top floor and we exited right into Sue's office.

"You're late," Sue said looking up from her computer.

"It couldn't be helped Sue. You know how traffic is this time of the day and then trying to find a parking spot was nearly impossible," Connie explained.

"Why didn't you park in your newly designated executive

parking space?" Sue asked us.

"Since when did we have our own designated parking space?" I asked in surprise.

"Ever since director Burns decided you were high enough on the food chain to deserve one. You both have to share one but it's right next to my spot," Sue informed me.

"Sweet! The only problem is we are hardly ever in town so we can use it," I said.

"Well you're here now. Go right into the director's office. He is impatiently waiting for you," Sue said as she hit a hidden buzzer unlocking the director's door.

Chapter Two

"Ben, Connie, thanks for breaking away from your vacations and meeting with me," Director Burns said as he motioned us to chairs in front of his desk.

"No problem director, it goes with the job," Connie said as she took a seat in front of his desk.

"When people are being killed, vacations unfortunately have to take a back seat. We can't allow it to happen while we are recreating now can we?" the director said with a sad smile.

"No sir, we can't," I said, agreeing with him.

"I haven't heard of any new cases on the news," Connie admitted.

"That's because it's happening on the Navajo Indian reservation. Not too much news ever escapes outside their reservation boundaries," the director replied.

"That's a whole lot of country to search director," I said in shock.

"You're right, agent Hawk. The Navajo Indian reservation is by far the largest in the United States. It's 27,413 square miles in area and spills over into the states of Arizona, New Mexico and Utah," the director informed us.

"We just came from Wisconsin and if my calculations are correct that would be half the size of the entire state we just left," I said in awe.

"You're just about right Ben. It's a lot of area to search," the director admitted. "But you just searched for a killer in Wisconsin and like you said Wisconsin is twice as big as the Navajo Nation."

"Yeah but Wisconsin had towns and roads criss-crossing all over the place. The Navajo Nation is going to be a whole lot of empty space with just an occasional small community or ranch,"

I said.

"What's going on there director," Connie asked, trying to get us back on track.

"People are dying, Agent Sanchez. Five have died so far. Terrible, horrible deaths from what I've been told and shown by the Navajo sheriff."

"I'm surprised he even reached out to us. It's not typical for reservation police to do that. They prefer the feds to stay the hell away from them and leave them be," I said.

"You're right Ben. In all my years in law enforcement this is the very first instance that I can remember where we were asked for help. That just goes to show you how bad it is."

"What can you tell us? What have they shared with you so far?" Connie asked.

"Look at my big screen TV and be prepared to be shocked," the director said as he picked up a remote and turned on the TV before turning back to his computer.

The TV came on and the director hit a few keys on his keyboard. The grizzly image of what looked like half eaten remains came onto the screen.

"It looks like a bear attack to me, director. What makes them suspect a killer is involved?" I asked him.

"Look closer Ben. The body looks to have been skinned first before being eaten. What kind of animal would do that?" Director Burns asked.

"Good Lord! How many have been killed so far?" Connie asked.

So far they think the number of victims is five," The director said, Repeating himself.

"They think?" I asked.

"It's a huge area, Ben. Much of it is very remote and not everything gets reported. A lot of sheep ranchers live in remote areas alone by themselves. If anything happened to them it might not be reported for months if at all," the director explained.

"The way the body was left almost seems inhuman," Connie whispered with a shudder.

Ben gave his partner a sharp look before turning back to the director. "Give us the rest of the news director. I can't help but feel the other shoe hasn't dropped yet," Ben said guardedly.

"Connie hit it on the nutshell. The Navajo sheriff by the name of Joe Longbow thinks it's a being from Native American folklore. Now the Navajo Nation has a special police force that does nothing but investigate what we today call cryptids. They are called the Navajo Rangers. There is a captain in charge of the unit and has many years of experience dealing with the unknown," Director Burns said.

"You know something about cryptids don't you Ben?" Connie asked me.

"I've had dealings with some of them over the years. Especially back in my youth when I would spend summers with my grandparents," I admitted.

"I guess I don't know what the two of you are talking about," the director admitted.

"I'm half Sioux director. My grandfather is an Oglala Sioux healer. I used to spend my summers with my grandparents in the Dakotas learning about my heritage and the lore of my people," I explained to him proudly.

"You might just be the right man for the job then Ben. You'll be able to communicate with the Navajo not as an outsider but as a fellow Native American," the director said.

"Modern man started calling things they didn't understand, cryptids. But the stories of them are a part of our culture. Where you have many disbelievers we have none. We know of their existence and respect them and give them their space. There are areas we do not enter because we know to do so would anger them and they would seek out their vengeance. I don't know if this is what happened in the Navajo Nation. But if it was, depending on what is angered, there may not be a way of killing or stopping it until it is satisfied," Ben warned.

"Come on Agent Hawk. Do you actually believe all this bunk?" Director Burns said in astonishment.

"See director, this is what I mean. Too many disbelievers in the modern world. These beings exist and that is a fact. Look at Hairy man or what you would call bigfoot. From Alaska to Florida and in every state in between Native Americans all have legends about them. Fifty different names given by a hundred different tribes describe the same creature. It is impossible for that to have happened long before we even had ponies unless they truly existed? Even today there are dozens of reported sightings and who knows how many unreported sightings," Ben said.

"You know Ben is right director," Connie said, agreeing with me.

"There are many many more beings than just bigfoot. Some swim, some fly, some crawl and some are fleet of foot. Living in a city like Washington you are blind to what is out there. You need to go out into the country, into the wilderness. You need to open up your mind, your heart, your ears and your eyes to discover what most cannot see. Most can't do it. Those who see bigfoot become instant believers even those who were doubters before. Those who see a dogman or a shapeshifter are forever changed," Ben said.

"So you think this thing might be a bigfoot?" the director asked in shock.

"No director, I think this thing is much much worse than that. I think it will kill until its thirst for death is sated," Ben said looking miserable.

"I have a plane waiting for you at Andrews Air Force base. It will fly you to Arizona where the SAC will be waiting for you with a car. Keep me regularly informed agents. Contact me anytime you need anything, 24/7 my phone will be answered."

The director got up and ended the meeting. Connie and I walked out of his office and I'll admit that I was in a daze.

Chapter Three

"Y̶ou don't look too well Ben. Are you feeling alright? You look like you saw a ghost," Connie said, looking worried.

"We should be so lucky if that is all it is, Connie. Maybe you should sit this one out and stay in Washington," I told her shakily.

"No way, partner! You have my back and I have yours. What the hell is wrong with you even suggesting that? Connie said angrily.

Sometimes Connie's temper shines through like now. "You have no idea what you're getting yourself into. You have no knowledge of what we are up against and may be easy prey for what we are going to be going up against. Hell, right now I'm not even sure we can kill it," I admitted openly.

"Ben, I could never forgive myself if something happened to you because I wasn't there watching your back. You're stuck with me like it or not."

I inhaled a shaky breath and nodded my head silently. "Alright Connie but don't say that I didn't warn you."

"We got to pack and get moving Ben. Drop me off at my apartment and go get your things."

We were planning on moving in together but the move hasn't happened yet. We were going to do it before heading back to work but our plans just got changed.

"Don't pack any of your work clothes you normally wear in the office. Pack for the backcountry. Shorts, jeans both long sleeve and short sleeve shirts and sturdy boots preferably hiking boots if you got them. Don't bother bringing anything with any sort of heel. We might be spending time in the saddle. If you have any weapon bigger than your .40 caliber bring it along," I instructed her.

"Ben, I don't own a bazooka or a grenade launcher," Connie said with a grin trying to ease my mind.

"Connie, by the time this is over with you might just wish you had a bazooka or a grenade launcher."

The ride to our apartment complex was silent the rest of the way. Each of us thinking our own thoughts. We lived in the same complex but in different buildings. I dropped her off and drove to my building.

I unlocked my gun safe and started throwing boxes of double aught buckshot onto the kitchen table. I followed that up with a weapon I thought I would never use in the line of duty. It was a twelve gauge auto feed shotgun with a drum magazine that held fifty rounds. They call them a streetsweeper. Fifty rounds with nine pellets the size of a thirty two caliber bullet in each shotgun shell was the equivalent of 450 bullets. I grabbed extra clips for my .40 caliber and started taking the bullets out of the clips. Next I dug into my ammo compartment looking for specialized rounds for both the handgun and the shotgun.

I found two boxes of five shells each for the shotgun. The rounds were called dragon's breath. They shot out a white phosphorus flame up to one hundred feet and lit anything on fire it came into contact with. The .40 caliber ammo was designed to rip apart on contact ripping through your target and causing maximum damage. Whatever this cryptid was, these would hopefully give me the edge we needed.

I emptied my Sig and put in the new .40 caliber rounds and jacked one into the chamber before reupholstering it. I would get the shotgun magazine set up on the flight to New Mexico.

I packed my clothes and headed back out of the door to pick Connie up. She was already waiting out front when I got there.

Connie tossed her stuff into the trunk and slammed it shut before climbing in beside me.

"What's in the gun case Ben?"

"Hopefully what we need to survive," I said, pulling out of the parking lot.

"I didn't even know you owned a bazooka," Connie grinned

trying to lighten the situation.

"What are you packing for a weapon?" I asked, ignoring her attempt at humor.

"Just my .40 but I traded out the ammo for something special. I also have a back up .40 on my ankle."

"When we get on the plane I'll give you better ammo for your main weapon. It's designed to destroy anything it hits. Way more lethal than hollow points."

"You weren't kidding were you Ben? You really are worried about not being able to kill what we will be hunting for."

"No, I wasn't kidding Connie and I wasn't kidding about you sitting this one out either. If we run into what we will be hunting I'm worried about us surviving the encounter."

Connie pulled off one of her patented moves, looking out the side window so I couldn't see the expression on her face.

"It's not too late to back out of this. Trust me, I won't think any less of you if you did. You'll be walking into the unknown. You have absolutely no idea what is out there waiting for us," I said gently.

"Then you better damn well teach me Ben. The more you can teach me, the more help I will be."

"We'll talk more on the plane. You know you have a stubborn streak about a half mile wide."

"Yeah, what can I say except you're starting to rub off on me," Connie said finally looking away from the window.

I pulled into Andrews Air Force base and parked next to a government owned corporate jet. The two pilots were standing next to the stairway waiting for us.

"Agent Hawk, Agent Sanchez it looks like we get to fly you again. Arizona this time around instead of Wisconsin. Good job on the last case by the way. I read you got your man," the pilot said with a grin.

"We did, but we got hurt doing it guys. One of the lab techs was killed and another one wounded," Connie said.

The smile slid off the pilot's face. "We heard about that too. Wish it could have been avoided."

"Not as much as we do. How long will it take to fly to Phoenix?" I asked.

"We'll have you there in just under four hours," the co-pilot said.

"Good, then let's get this show on the road," I said as I lugged my gear up the stairs.

The plane left the runway and leveled off at cruising altitude fifteen minutes later. I grabbed my gun case and pulled out the drum magazine.

"What the hell did you bring along, a Tommy Gun?" Connie asked in shock.

"No, it's better than that. A twelve gauge streetsweeper with a fifty round magazine."

"You really think you need all of that fire power?" Connie asked incredulously.

"I'm just hoping it will be all we need. If it isn't Lord help us," I said looking up at her conveying my seriousness of the situation.

"What are you loading it with?"

Hush, I'm counting as I put in the rounds. First I'm loading thirty rounds of double aught buckshot. Then ten rounds of dragon's breath and then another ten rounds of buckshot."

"Isn't dragons breath those rounds I saw on Youtube that shoot a flame about a hundred feet out the end of the barrel?"

"Yep, I'm loading so my first ten rounds are buckshot. That will put ninety pellets into our target. If the target is charging us and closing in, the next ten rounds will be at close range and burn him up. The next thirty rounds will hopefully finish him off or at least get him to move away from us."

"You really are serious about this aren't you?"

"You should know me by now Connie. I don't kid about stuff like this."

"You better show me the rounds you have for my .40 Ben."

"These aren't quite as good as DumDum rounds but they are a close second."

"What are DumDum rounds Ben?"

"DumDum rounds explode on contact. They have an explosive built into them. Upon contact when the projectile starts to mushroom the charge detonates, tearing out chunks of flesh. These rounds are like shrapnel flying in all directions tearing up the flesh."

"I'll use these for my back up magazines. I'll keep the mag I have in my weapon for now."

"These are better than hollow points Connie."

"I said I had hollow points along but I didn't say that was what was in my weapon."

"Okay, what do you have in your Sig?"

Connie ejected her magazine and showed it to me. "I got these little beauties."

I looked at her clip and the rounds had a sharp point on them that were red in color. Unlike what hollow points look like.

"Okay, I give up. What the hell are they?"

"I think for the most part they are illegal to own now but I'm not sure, they're cop killers. The tips are tungsten steel and they are ceramic and teflon coated. The design makes them able to penetrate a bullet proof vest. I'm thinking if this thing even had armor these little beauties would get through and cause some major damage."

I handed them back to her with an impressed look on my face. "Good thinking Connie, it's one more weapon in our arsenal."

I finished by changing out the rounds in my Sig and it was time for me to teach Connie what I could about cryptids and the dangers they posed.

"Alright Connie, let's spend the rest of the flight talking about cryptids so you have a working knowledge about them."

"Anything you can tell me will help," Connie said as she settled into the seat across from me.

"First of all let me start by telling you I don't know everything there is to know about them. I can only pass on the knowledge passed on to me by my grandfather when I stayed with him during my summers growing up."

"That's way more knowledge than I have, Ben. My knowledge is confined to seeing a couple of shows about bigfoot on TV when there was nothing else to watch."

"Let's start with that then. Did you believe what the people in the show were telling you or did you think it was a bunch of crap?"

"To tell you the truth I didn't form an opinion one way or the other. The TV was just on because I didn't have anything better to do," Connie said honestly.

"Well, to start off with, I'm telling you bigfoot is real. There are many skeptics out there that became believers after an encounter. Bigfoot can come in just about any size from baby bigfoot to beings over ten feet tall. They can be any color from brown, reddish brown, black, blond and white. They can be docile and timid or aggressive and deadly. They can cry like a human baby or scream like a woman to try to draw you away from the fire so they can attack you. They do wood knocks, clack rocks, throw logs and boulders, whoop, whistle and have a chattering language all their own.

"This is for real Ben? You're not just trying to scare me are you?" Connie asked with a half grin of disbelief on her face.

"No I'm not. I'm trying to teach you enough to survive. I have to teach you to be aware of your surroundings at all times."

"Alright Ben, go on."

"They have a stench you wouldn't believe. When they are around, you are very likely to smell them long before you ever see them. I'm not sure if they secrete the smell from a gland when they are frightened or sense danger or if they are just that dirty. The best I can tell you is that it's a musty smell and a cross between a wet dog and rotting garbage."

"You talk like you've seen and smelled them before Ben."

"I have, four times growing up and spending time with my grandparents. Three times I had eyes on them. Once I saw a group of three and once I just smelled them but never spotted them. They are experts on keeping hidden when they don't want to be seen. You would think as big as they are they'd be easy to spot, but they're not. It seems like they have an extra perception ability to sense danger and people. They are normally bi-pedal but they can run at great speed on all fours and just bulldoze through brush."

"They are omnivores. They eat anything from nuts and berries and grass to meat, fish and clams."

"Have you ever felt frightened by one of them?"

"Once, I was out squirrel hunting and it was getting close to dark. All I had with me was my little .22 rifle. I was walking along the river bottom headed back to my grandparents. I knew I was being followed but I couldn't see it. Once in a while I caught a whiff of a smell like I already described to you. It was walking parallel to me and once in a while I could hear it Just out of sight. I have to tell you it gave me the willies. It followed me all the way home. It never attacked me or threatened me. I felt like it was just escorting me home and letting me know I wasn't welcome, that I was trespassing in his home."

"Did you ever go back hunting there again?"

"No, grandpa said let it be. There were other places to hunt and we should respect and honor their privacy. Grandpa didn't know I was going to hunt there that day or he would have warned me to stay out of there. He said there was a whole clan of them living there and had been for years. They never bothered the people of our tribe and we returned the favor and left them in peace."

"So, so far I need to listen for them, smell for them and look for them," Connie said, ticking the items off on her finger tips.

"Not just them, Connie but a whole lot more. We're just getting started here."

"Okay Ben, what's next?"

"Seeing as we will be in the southwest the next cryptids will be shapeshifters and skinwalkers. I need to add the word cryptid is a modern man's word to describe something he doesn't under-stand or more often than not believes to exist."

"I kind of got that from our conversation in the director's office."

"Shapeshifters have the ability to go from being a man to being an animal or even from one type of animal to another. Some cryptozoologists think they are a form of a werewolf but I don't agree with that."

"What is a crypto whatever ist you're talking about?"

"Cryptozoologists, there are people who study cryptids that refer to themselves as cryptozoologists. I don't know if there is an actual area of study in a university somewhere or if it is a self proclaimed title by people who are just crypto enthusiasts."

"I guess I haven't been that interested in the field to have even heard about them before today," Connie admitted.

"The reason I don't think shapeshifters are werewolves is they have never been reported walking on two legs like a werewolf while in animal form."

"Do you believe in the supernatural Ben?"

"Just because you never saw it doesn't necessarily mean it's supernatural. Some things are like demons and poltergeists. But things like bigfoot and shapeshifters are living breathing beings."

"Back to shapeshifters and skinwalkers. Have you ever seen one and are they something dangerous that we need to be worried about?"

"I only saw one, one time. We were at tribal ceremonies, a powwow and one appeared on a hill just at dust. It was hard to see in the half light with the fire burning but I could see a man climb to the top of the hill and transform into a coyote just as he topped the hill. Grandpa said the shapeshifter was at our powwow and left just before it ended. I never talked to it. I don't even know if they can talk in a language we understand but it gave me pause."

"Gave you pause? It would have scared me silly to know something like that could have been standing right next to me or worse behind me," Connie said with a shiver.

"Shapeshifters are rather shy; they will do what is necessary to stay undetected. I have never heard of one attacking a human. I'm not saying they won't if given a chance to do it and not get caught."

"Alright, but why are we even talking about shapeshifters if they can't do what we saw done in those photographs?"

"Like I said they are not known to, but we are entering lands renowned for having shapeshifters and skinwalkers and you need to be aware of them."

"What's next Ben?"

"Let's talk about thunderbirds for a minute. They have been known to pick up a full grown man. To this day they are seen from time to time. They have a wingspan maybe as wide as twenty feet and are said to make the sound of thunder when they beat their wings.

"By the look on your face in Washington Ben you don't think it was a bigfoot, shapeshifter or thunderbird. What do you really think we'll be facing? You brought enough firepower to start a war and still think we might be out gunned."

"There is a slim chance it could be a werewolf but there are other things out there in other dimensions that could be far worse. Grandfather talked about them but I have never seen them myself. But just because I haven't seen them doesn't mean they don't exist."

"Do you care to give me a list of things they might be?"

"There is an endless list of things they might be Connie. Pigman, Sheepsquatch, wood devil. The beast of seven chutes, hoop snake, mothman, cactus cat, silver cat, shunka warakin, the beast of Bray road, the windigo, wapaloosie and a lot more we don't have time to cover. When we get it narrowed down we'll talk in more detail of what it is and how we need to deal with it."

"You know Ben, this isn't what we signed up for when we took this job. I don't even like spiders and then you throw all this crap at me?" Connie said shakily.

"Still not too late for you to stand down Connie," I said looking at her with no sign of judgement in my eyes.

"Forget it, sport. I'll just buy a big can of bug killer when we land in Phoenix."

"Speaking of which, I can feel us decelerating and dropping in altitude."

"We'll be landing in fifteen minutes if you want to buckle up," the pilot's voice came over a speaker.

Chapter Four

The plane landed and taxied off the runway and shut down on the tarmac near a gate in the chain link fence. I could see a couple of men standing off to the side next to a pair of chevy Tahoes.

The co-pilot let down the stairs and stepped off to the side so we could exit the plane with our bags.

We put our sunglasses on to protect us from the blinding sunshine reflecting off of the concrete surface and walk down to meet the local FBI agents.

Good afternoon agents Hawk and Sanchez, I'm the Phoenix SAC, Colin Sands and this is my second in command, Brian Thompson, welcome to Arizona," he said from behind a dark pair of sunglasses. The four of us shook hands all around.

"Here are the keys to your transportation," Brian said, handing over two sets of keys.

"Thanks for meeting up with us. Do you have any more information on the case we are here to work on?" I asked the two.

"No sir, nothing. The Native Americans on the reservations are normally tight lipped. They don't share much information with the outside world. For them to do this is very rare," Colin said.

"We have been instructed to help you in any way possible by the director. If there is anything, anything at all you need from us we are available twenty four seven. Here are our business cards. They have both our office numbers and our private cell phone numbers on them," Brian said, handing us each two business cards.

"You can help us out already. We need a handheld FLIR and three pairs of night vision goggles to start out with," I said.

"Why three pairs and not two Ben?" Connie asked me.

"Because I figure we'll have a guide on our hunt for the killer and we better have a set for him too."

"You better make it four sets so we have a spare set just in case we take someone else along or one of our sets breaks down. Add an extra FLIR to the list too," Connie said.

"I don't know if we have all of that at our field office or not. We might have one FLIR but probably no goggles. We'll reach out to the local army base and see what they can lend us," Colin said.

"Get it out to us just as soon as possible. We'll be operating blind without the equipment," I said.

"We could have had the equipment waiting for your arrival if we would have known about it," Brian said.

"Six hours ago we didn't even know we were coming out here. Hell, six hours ago we were still on vacation until the director canceled it on us," Connie said.

We'll fly it out to you by helicopter just as soon as we can get our hands on it. Where will you be staying?" Colin asked.

"Their main town is Window Rock Arizona so we'll set up shop there," I said.

"If we're lucky we can beat you there with your equipment. Give us your cards too so we can contact you when we get there," Colin said.

"We made sure you had a real spare tire underneath and not one of those cheap vinyl ones. Also we put a second spare tire in the back. You get moving off road and there are a lot of sharp rocks that can take a tire out," Brian said.

"Good thinking, we really appreciate that," I said.

"We better get hoofing Ben. It's 284 miles to Window Rock. It will be almost dark out when we get there," Connie said looking at her watch.

We tossed our stuff into the Tahoe and set off.

"I'll have us there in under three and a half hours Connie," I said as I spun our tires out of the gate.

We got out of the city and I hit our lights and sped up to a little over ninety miles an hour.

Thirty miles outside of Phoenix we flashed by a state trooper who turned his lights on and started following us.

"Who might y'all be that just flashed past me at a high rate of speed?" The trooper asked over his radio.

"I'm busy Connie, you answer him," I said, looking in my side view mirror.

"This is the FBI, Special Agents Hawk and Sanchez."

"What are y'all doing speeding in my state?"

"Trooper, we are on our way to the Navajo reservation to investigate a series of murders. The sooner we can get there the sooner we can try to prevent another one from happening," Connie said.

"Y'all those two agents that just last month caught that killer in Wisconsin?"

"Yes sir, that was us and before that, the band of killers in Chicago," Connie replied.

"Y'all have yourself a good day and good hunting. I hope you get the killer," he said as he turned off his flashing light and pulled off to the side of the road.

"He'll radio ahead now and let any other troopers and country mounties know that we are headed for Window Rock. We should have a clear pathway now," I said.

Four times we passed squad cars as we hurried to our destination. As we passed each one of them they flashed their red and blue lights and gave us a short blast on their siren to show their support and to let us know they knew why we were there.

True to my word we entered the town of Window Rock Arizona a little over three hours later.

Chapter Five

"T he sign says the town has just over twenty two hundred people, Ben. It shouldn't be too difficult to find the sheriff's office."

"There's a squad car parked up ahead on the right. Either that's the cop shop or the local donuts shop," I said with a grin.

"Speaking of donuts, we haven't eaten since breakfast. I could use some food. When we get done talking to the sheriff, um Joe Longbow we need to find a diner," Connie said looking up the name in her notebook.

I parked the car and the two of us walked into the adobe southwest style building.

"What can I do for you?" A deputy asked from a desk behind the counter.

"We're FBI agents Ben Hawk and Connie Sanchez. We were sent here to help you out with what's been happening here. Is Sheriff Longbow still here?" I asked while flashing my credentials.

"No sir, he went home for the night. But he told me he was expecting you to show up and to give him a call when you did."

"Where is your dinner in Window Rock?" Connie asked.

"Out on the other end of town. It's a truck stop with a motel alongside it," the deputy said as he listened for the sheriff to answer the phone.

"Once we see the sheriff we need to get a room and then get some food," Connie said again.

"Our equipment should be showing up anytime too," I reminded her.

"Sheriff, the two FBI agents showed up. Yes sir, I'll let them know, sheriff," he said, hanging up the phone. "He's on his way and will be here in a couple of minutes."

"The sheriff came into the office and yanked his sunglasses off. "I'm Sheriff Longbow."

"I'm Ben Hawk and this is my partner Connie Sanchez," I said as we shook hands.

"Come on back to my office and we'll talk," he said, leading the way.

The sheriff closed the door to his office after we were inside to keep our conversation private.

"First I'd like to thank you for getting here so quickly."

"Our director knew it was important to respond right away and pulled us off of vacation," Connie said.

Sheriff Longbow nodded his head silently. "People are dying gruesome deaths. We have never seen anything like it."

"No need to apologize, sheriff. Working serial killer cases is what we do. When one comes up we have to drop everything and respond. To not do so could result in more unnecessary deaths," I said.

"I wasn't apologizing, just stating facts."

"When did you find the first body and where was it located?" Connie asked.

The sheriff walked over to a wall map that had stick pins in it. "These are the locations of where we found the five bodies. Who knows if there are any unreported bodies anywhere. Most of these areas are very remote. So far the only reason we know they were dead is because they were reported missing. They didn't come home at the agreed upon hour. There are people on the reservation who live alone with no one around to report them missing. As of right now I have no idea if any of them are missing. I have deputies checking on their well being but it's a lot of territory to cover and I don't have a very large force to work with."

"The director was surprised when he received your call, sheriff. It's a rare thing when reservation police departments reach out to the federal government for help," I said.

"We like to handle things ourselves and keep the outside world outside of our business. But like I just said, good people are dying and I have to do everything in my power to end this."

"We understand, sheriff," Connie said.

"Are you a Native American, Agent Hawk?"

"I'm half Sioux. My grandfather was an Oglala healer and I spent my summers in the Dakotas learning from him," I said with heartfelt pride.

The sheriff nodded his head approvingly. "You will have an easier time talking to the tribe. They won't feel like they're talking to an outsider. The director was wise to send you to help."

"Serial Killers is our specialty sheriff, it's what we do," I said.

"Being a tribe member I'm sure you know what we fear is happening here," the sheriff said with a small amount of fear showing in his voice.

"When we saw the pictures of your last victim I sensed what you were up against. I too fear what may be waiting for us in the darkness," I said.

"We are going to be spending a lot of time together, call me Joe," the sheriff said.

"You can call me Ben and this is Connie," I said as we dropped the formalities.

"How long ago was the first killing Joe?" Connie asked.

"It was just two weeks ago and like I just told you there might be more people dead than we know about."

"Have all the victims been in the same condition as the one we saw the photos of?" Connie asked.

"Yes and a couple of them were even in worse shape. Whatever is doing this is not an animal. Animals don't skin their kills like humans do and humans don't do what's been done to these people.

"I have to agree with you Joe. When I heard the circumstances and saw the pictures I knew we had a huge problem. I don't yet know what creature is out there preying on your people but we'll find out. I can already knock off hairy man and a shapeshifter. Whatever is doing this is far worse and far more deadly and dangerous than either one of those," I said.

"I heard you had a couple of deputies that specialized in dealing with harry man, shapeshifter and spirits on the reservation," Connie said.

"Yeah we do, the Navajo Rangers and they're stumped too. Our most experienced one retired last year."

"First thing in the morning I'd like you to take us to see him, Joe. It might be time for him to come out of retirement," I said.

"I've been out to see him a couple of times since this started and he told me he is stumped too."

"He might not know the specific being we are facing but he might know the best way to fight it and survive," I said.

"We'll want one or both of your rangers to assist us in the hunt. They'll know the area better than we do and the extra firepower will be welcome," Connie said.

"Do you want to go out tonight already?" Joe asked.

"No, we'll be operating blind. I have some needed equipment being flown in by helicopter. It should be here anytime now," I said.

"We have some handheld FLIR units and night vision goggles coming," Connie explained.

"As far as I know all of the attacks have happened either at night or just before dark so the equipment will definitely come in handy."

"Tomorrow morning I'd like to start out by talking to the families of the victims. Maybe someone will have an important detail that can give us an edge," I said.

"Are the killings age related? Are just old people or younger people being targeted?" Connie asked.

"No, we've had young men just starting their families killed and we've had old men who probably should leave sheep and cattle herding to younger folks killed. The killings are definitely not age related."

"It was just a thought. How big an area on your wall map are we talking about for the killings?"

"That's got to be close to five hundred square miles," Joe said with a little bit of thought.

Connie gave a low whistle at the thought of such a large area.

"That's not as big of an area as you think it is Connie. Five hundred square miles is only an area twenty by twenty five miles in size," I told her.

"You explaining it like that makes it seem smaller but that's still a lot of country to cover Ben."

"How long has it been since the last killing?" I asked.

"Only three days Ben. But there has been no rhyme or reason on the timing. They've been a week apart and two days apart."

"But that's just the ones you know about. Like you said there might be others."

"There might be others," Joe agreed, nodding his head.

Connie's phone rang and she answered it. "Hello, Agent Sanchez," Connie said with her finger in her other ear to help hear better.

"Is our equipment here?" I asked her.

She nodded her head still listening. "Sheriff, where can our helicopter land?"

"Have them land next to the truck stop. It's all open land and you have to go there and get a motel room anyway."

"Land next to the truck stop and we'll come out and meet you."

"Okay, how do I find the truck stop?" Agent Thompson asked.

"I don't know, it's supposed to be on the edge of town and the town isn't very big. If I was you I'd probably look for a parking lot with a lot of stopped trucks in it," Connie said grinning into the phone.

"Dah, no kidding Mrs. Obvious," Brian said with a groan.

"If you didn't want a smart ass answer you shouldn't have asked a dumb question."

"And here my third grade teacher told me the only dumb question was an unasked one. Wait until I see her again."

Connie turned to me still grinning. "Well that was fun. We better get going Ben."

"Meet us at the truck stop at seven for breakfast Joe, my treat. We can go and talk to some of the family members after breakfast," I said.

"You better take him up on it, because Ben is normally a real tightwad."

"Alright, I'll see you in the morning then," Joe said as he stood to walk us out.

We got to the truck stop just as the helicopter landed.

"I got everything you asked me for. Four sets of night vision goggles and two sets of handheld FLIR. I also had the army give you extra batteries. If there is anything else you need from us give me a call.

"Thanks Brian for getting these to us so quickly," Connie said.

We shook hands and got into the car before the helo started kicking up sand.

"We better get our motel room first, Ben. Who knows how many vacancies they have and they might fill up while we're eating," Connie said.

I drove to the motel and parked. "Not much of a motel is it?" I said looking at the flat roofed single story building with only ten rooms in it. The front of each room held an air conditioner mounted in the wall below the single window.

"Beggars can't be choosers Ben,"

We walked into the office and an old man was sitting behind the counter watching the news on a small wall mounted TV.

"Can I help you folks?" he said as he rose with a little bit of difficulty.

"Yeah, we need a room preferable with two queen sized beds in it," I said.

"I only have one room left but it does have two double beds in it if that helps you out."

"It does and we'll take it," Connie said with a kind smile.

"Will you be just staying for the night?"

"We don't know how long we'll be here for sure. It could be a couple of weeks," I said.

"Not too many people stay for more than a day or two."

"We're with the FBI. We were asked to come and help you catch the killer."

"Good luck with that. People are getting spooked and not going out after dark."

We signed for the room and got our old fashion room key before heading over to the cafe. We entered the restaurant and sat in a booth in the back.

"I'm really hungry Ben old buddy and it's your turn to buy," Connie said as she looked hungrily over the menu.

"Hold the phone el cheapo! I bought breakfast if you would remember!"

"But you still owe me for the flowers so pay me my fifty bucks and I'll think about buying supper."

"Wait a minute, the flowers were only eighty bucks, remember?"

"It came out of my pocket and I charge interest after the first notification and payment wasn't met," Connie said with a wink.

"Since when? Are you making up the rules as you go along?" I said grinning at the banter. When we are on cases like this we joke around and pull things on each other to help ease the tension we feel from the danger.

"I'll cut you some slack just this once. Hand over two twenties right this minute and I'll treat you to dinner and a pine float," Connie said magnanimous.

"What the hell is a pine float?" I asked suspiciously.

"Why, it's a glass of water with a toothpick floating in it," Connie said grinning widely.

I handed her two twenties to her delight before opening the menu and ordering a ribeye and a thirty two ounce beer. "Here's mud in your eye partner!" I said grinning widely while taking a big drink of my beer.

"You'll pay for this one bucko! Tomorrow you get to buy breakfast and supper."

"Your turn to buy breakfast, remember?"

"You invited the sheriff and told him it was on you, remember?" Connie said with an evil grin on her face.

Connie can be such an asshole. We finished eating and drove back over to the motel and parked in front of our room. While it was true we were sleeping together it was also true we didn't while working on a case. Our occupation was extremely dangerous and we couldn't afford to have our minds on anything but the job we were there to do. That was the reason for having two beds instead of one.

Connie entered the room first. The stale heat was oppressive. "You would have thought the motel owner would have the air conditioning on for us. It must be a hundred and ten degrees in here," Connie complained.

"I walked over to the air conditioner and pushed every button on the unit and nothing happened.

"I'll go and talk to the old guy and find out why the air isn't working," I said after opening the window as wide as it would go.

I walked into the office and the old guy was back watching TV again. "Our air conditioning doesn't work," I said.

"Yep, it's been broken for a week now. I have a new one ordered but nothing gets delivered very fast in these parts. I expect the unit to get here in oh, a week or two."

"Can we get a different room? One that has working air conditioning," I asked.

"Nope, not right now. They're all taken because the air conditioning in the other rooms works, sorry."

"If one of those rooms becomes vacant I want it."

"That probably won't be happening."

"Why is that? Didn't you tell me earlier that most people don't stay for more than one day?"

"That's folks that are traveling. These other rooms are being lived in by permanent residents."

"See if you can't hurry the delivery of the air conditioner up a little bit. If we don't get air we'll probably have to find somewhere else to stay."

"There isn't anywhere else to stay within forty miles of us," the old guy said with an apologetic smile.

"Then I guess we'll have to figure on commuting back and forth," I said as I walked out the door.

I walked back to our room. Connie had pulled a chair outside and was sitting where she could get a little bit of a breeze. "Well, what did he tell you?"

"He has a new unit ordered but doesn't think it will be here this week and maybe not next week either."

The only saving factor was there was a ceiling fan in the room. About all it did was move the hot air around but at least it did that.

I got into the shower and got my body wet and then toweled off. I lay my damp naked body on the bed and let the ceiling fan blow on me and cool me down.

"That's the first good idea you had all day Ben," Connie said as sweat dripped off of her chin. She followed suit and lay down on her bed next to mine.

"The trick will be falling asleep before our bodies dry completely off and we get hot again," I said with my eyes closed.

We got up the next morning and showered before driving back over to the cafe. We got there a half hour early so we could enjoy the air conditioning.

Chapter Six

J oe walked in and we waved him back to the table we were sitting at in the back of the room. We had a pot of coffee at our table with an extra cup and he helped himself.

"Good morning Joe," I said as he settled in his chair.

"Good morning Ben, Connie," he said as he tried his coffee.

"Where do you want to start out this morning?" the sheriff asked.

"Let's start out with your Navajo Ranger that just retired. After that we can interview the widow of your last victim. Everything will be freshest in her mind and we might pick up a clue that can help us. After that we can work backwards through the victims," I said.

Our food came and we dug in. The waitress gave us a friendly smile as she set down our plates of food. "Thanks Sadie," the sheriff said as she walked away.

"You're welcome Joe," she said as she turned away.

"I don't seem to be very hungry this morning," I said as I watched Connie out of the corner of my eye while trying not to laugh.

"You shouldn't be after sticking me with that bill last night. He ate a twenty ounce ribeye with all the fixings and two thirty two ounce glasses of beer Joe!"

"It was a long day and we hadn't eaten since breakfast, way on the other side of the country," I said, defending myself.

Joe looked between us and could see this was our normal behavior, the way we bantered back and forth.

"So Joe, how long have you been in law enforcement?" Connie asked.

"Sixteen years. I was a deputy for the first ten years and then got elected sheriff."

"You were saying yesterday you have a couple of Navajo Rangers that work cases beyond the norm," I said.

"Yeah deputies Sid Canyon and John Stillwater. John replaced Jeff when he retired last year and Sid has been doing this for six or seven years now."

"Does Jeff have a last name? We just like to know who we're talking to, sheriff," Connie asked.

"Yeah, it's Longbow. Jeff is my uncle."

Sadie came back by and refilled our empty coffee pot.

"Seeing as you have special people to handle special circumstances, do you have a lot of those situations happening here?" I asked.

"More than I'd like for sure. There are hairy man sightings on a fairly regular basis. Especially in the backcountry. Skinwalkers, shapeshifters and ghosts are common events. As far back as anyone can remember we've never had a situation like we're having now though."

"I've never seen any of those, but Ben has. I'm looking forward to seeing my first one actually," Connie admitted.

"Some of the areas you need to go into you might have to go by horseback," the sheriff informed us.

"I looked at Connie with a grin on my face. "Sure you're up for this partner?"

"Are you kidding Ben? I'll ride circles around you. I'm from Oklahoma. I grew up with horses and used to barrel race in high school. Don't worry about me, sport." Connie grinned seeing the look of disappointment on my face.

"Well, if we're done eating we better get a move on if we want to get anything done today. My uncle is expecting us," Joe said looking at his watch.

Joe's uncle lived in town so we only had to drive about a mile to get to his place. Jeff Longbow was sitting out front on his porch waiting for us.

"Good morning Uncle Jeff. These are special agents Ben Hawk and Connie Sanchez," Joe said making the introductions. We all shook hands and sat down.

"I heard Joe was calling for outside help with this. I've heard about the two of you. I just read about the killings that were happening in Wisconsin, that was good work," Jeff said.

"We heard you're the man with the most experience dealing with these situations so we figured we needed to talk to you first," I said.

"Not ever a situation like this one Ben, no one has as far as I know. This is different and to be honest with you, it has even me scared. I don't have any idea what kind of creature you're dealing with. But I can tell you this, the last man it killed was very very good. He knew it all, the backcountry and the animals that lived there, both natural and supernatural. There was no one better with a rifle or a horse. If whatever this thing is took him out I don't know anyone or anything that can stop it."

"Do you want to come out of retirement and give us a hand?" Connie asked him.

"No I don't. Like I said, Jeremy was the best and it took him with no problem. When they found what was left of him there was no blood, other than his own, no sign that Jeremy was able to defend himself at all. The time might come when I don't have any choice but to help you but today isn't that day. "I'll try to help you out if I can by searching through tribal records and seeing if anything like this has happened in the past."

"That would help, I'll give you one of my cards," I said, handing him one.

"If you hear any rumors of anyone else who is missing, let us know Uncle Jeff," Joe said as he stepped off the porch.

"I will Joe, and you be careful. As far as we know so far this thing only attacks in the darkness or near darkness so make damn sure you're not out in the open and vulnerable at night," Jeff warned him.

"Yeah that's the rub now isn't it? If we aren't out hunting for him when he is hunting for us how are we ever going to find him?" Joe asked.

"I'm not worried about you finding him, Joe. I'm worried about him finding you."

Joe nodded his head silently before leading the way to our car.

"First stop is to talk to Jeremie's widow. Show us the way Joe," I said as I slid behind the steering wheel.

"It's about twenty miles in that direction. Once we get close we'll have to traverse a pretty rough dirt road for the last four miles or so," Joe said pointing out of the windshield.

"I'm starting to get a bad feeling about this Ben. We just talked to a man that has been dealing with these things, for lack of a better word, that goes bump in the night for nearly thirty years. Even he is at a loss on what it can be," Connie said in a worried tone.

"You're not the only one worried Connie. I started getting worried if you remember before we left the director's office in Washington DC."

With the rough roads it took us the better part of an hour to get to the sheep ranch. There were roughly a hundred head of sheep in a fenced in pasture a distance away from the buildings.

A woman in her late thirties was sitting on the front porch with a shotgun leaning up against the wall. Two twin boys around ten or twelve were sitting on the edge of the porch watching us as we got out of the car.

"Joe, do you have word for me on what killed my Jeremy?" The woman asked in a voice still filled with pain.

"I'm afraid not Clara. "I'm here with the FBI to ask you some questions that might help us figure this thing out," Joe said.

"I'm not real fond of you bringing outsiders onto my land, sheriff. We don't like airing our dirty laundry in front of strangers."

"These are special circumstances, Clara. I don't know if you got news about the killer that was just caught a couple of weeks ago in Wisconsin but these are the two who caught him."

Clara eyed us but didn't show that she was accepting the news any better. "Strangers are still strangers."

"You don't want Jeremy"s killer to go free do you? You need to tell them what you heard and saw the night that Jeremy was killed. Ben here is an Oglala Sioux. He knows the old ways, Clara. He is our best chance of ending this so talk to him!"

Clara gave out an exasperated sigh. "Come on into the kitchen and I'll get us a pitcher of lemonade to drink. Boys get the lemonade and some glasses out while we sit down to talk. Then go back outside so you can't hear us. I don't want either of you to go no farther than the edge of the porch, understand?"

"Yeah ma," they both said as they got up to do their ma's bidding.

We sat in her small but neat kitchen and waited for the boys to get out of ear shot.

"My Jeremy has only been gone for three days now," Clara said the pain was clear to hear in her voice.

"We know ma'am, but it is freshest in your memory right now. It's best if we get your story from you before you have a chance to forget key details," Connie said gently.

"Trust me agent, I will never forget any details from that awful night if I live to be a hundred and one," she said as a single tear slid down her cheek.

"There was nobody better than my Jeremy in the outdoors. He could ride and shoot better than anyone around. Ask Sheriff Joe if you don't believe me. He had a knowledge of the unknown and a respect for things in this realm and the other realm the outside world has no knowledge of. When anyone had a problem with a rogue bear or wolf my Jeremy was the man they asked to help track it down and kill it. He could track a bear across bare rock and never lose the trail."

"Joe's uncle Jeff told us your husband was the best there is. He said after what happened to Jeremy he was scared for the tribe and he has no idea of what could have killed him," I said.

"If Jeff doesn't know what it could be then no one does," Clara said as she blew her nose and wiped her eyes.

"Can you tell us about what happened that night? Why did Jeremy leave your house in the middle of the night?" I asked.

"We used to have two herding dogs that stayed with the sheep."

"What do you mean by had?" Connie asked, interrupting her.

"I'm just getting to that. We were sitting playing a board game like we do at night sometimes. The dogs started barking ferociously. I never heard them acting up like that. Jeremy knew instantly that something was in the pasture with the sheep and grabbed his gun. There was yelps of pain from our dogs and then dead silence other than the bleating of the sheep," Clara paused as she sobbed.

"I know this is difficult Clara, take your time," Connie said, laying a gentle hand on her arm.

Clara nodded her head silently as she wiped her face with the sleeve of her blouse.

"Jeremy ran out the door with his lever action rifle. He always kept it loaded and hanging on the wall where he could get to it easily. Five minutes later I heard Jeremy shooting out by the sheep, four or five shots just as fast as he could work the lever. Then came the most God awful screams from where Jeremy was."

"Was it your husband screaming Clara?" Ben asked.

Clara shook her head no. "It was whatever that creature was. I never heard anything like it in my life. It was a terrible sound that bounced off the rocks and the cliffs."

"Can you describe the sound you heard?" I asked.

"It was like this SKREEEEE! SKREEEEE! It did it four or five times and then dead silence. When Jeremy didn't come back home after a half hour or so I called the sheriff's office and a patrol car came out to investigate. At first light they found my Jeremy in the pasture. That's pretty much all I know. I don't know how that can help you."

"We'll at least now we know the sound it makes. Maybe that will help us with our research to find out what this creature is," I said.

"I was sitting out on the porch waiting for the buyer to come, sheriff. I'm selling out and moving into town. I'm not staying way out here with my two boys alone with that thing on the loose."

"I don't blame you for a minute Clara. When you get ready to move into town let me know and we'll get some of the tribal men to come out here and give you a hand," Joe promised her.

"Thanks Joe, I'll give you a call later this afternoon. I should know by then if the place is sold or not."

"So what are you thinking?" Joe asked as we got back into the car.

"I'm thinking I was right about being worried about what we might be facing. "Lets head back to town and you can introduce us to Sid and John from your Navajo Ranger unit," I said.

By the time we got back to the sheriff's office it was past noon. Joe called ahead and the two officers were waiting for us when we got there.

"Sid Canyon, John Stillwater, meet special agents Ben Hawk and Connie Sanchez of the FBI,"

"Joe told us he was hoping it was the two of you the FBI was sending," Sid said with a grin while shaking our hands.

"Has anything new developed today while we were out of town?" The sheriff asked his deputies.

"We have a lead on another missing ranch hand sheriff. Carl Whitelaw was supposed to be getting back to the ranch where he works after spending three days checking the rancher's line fence and is late getting back in. The rancher said this has never happened in the past. Either his horse came up lame and left him afoot or something worse," John reported.

"Can you show us on the map where this is?" Connie asked.

"Yeah, it's right about here. The ranch is around sixty thousand acres in size. There is a line cabin in this area where men checking the fence can sleep."

"That's right on the outer edge of where the other people have gone missing," I said looking at the stick pins on the map.

"Is the area reachable by vehicle or only by horseback?" I asked the two.

"Parts of it can be reached with a four wheel drive but others are too rocky and you'll need a horse," Sid said.

I pulled out my phone and called the SAC in Phoenix, Colin Sands. "Colin, this is Ben Hawk. I need a helicopter at first light tomorrow morning. Yeah we have another missing man and the terrain is pretty rough. We should be able to cover the area in a few hours by air."

"We'll be there at first light."

"Bring a body bag with you too. I have a bad feeling about this."

"Tell him to make sure he brings a helicopter large enough for six to eight passengers," Connie said.

"Why that big Connie?" I asked.

"There are the five of us and the pilot and the SAC and the body we fear we are going to find."

"Did you hear that Colin? Make sure the bird is big enough for us."

"We'll bring the Bell Ranger this time around. We'll see you in the morning Ben." he said, ending the call.

Chapter Seven

W e spent the rest of the day talking to townspeople. The sheriff came with us to break the ice. It seemed the locals were a might standoffish. We started off at the local barber shop. You will never find a better place than a barber shop for gossip.

"Jake, this is Ben and Connie with the FBI here to help us with our problem," Joe said to the barber and the two old timers sitting in a couple of chairs talking.

Jake looked at us over his glasses as he trimmed the hair of a young boy. "You think bringing in outsiders will help solve our problem, do you Joe?" he asked with an impish smile on his face.

"I'll tell you what Jake, it sure can't hurt. We sure as hell aren't getting anywhere on our own."

"Non believers aren't going to do anything but get themselves killed, I'm telling you it's not the right answer."

"Jake, these are the two that caught the killer a couple of weeks ago in Wisconsin. They're the ones that took out the Chicago stockyard satan worshipers."

"But they were flesh and blood beings, Joe. What we're dealing with here isn't flesh and blood and you know it."

"Ben here is an Oglala Sioux Jake. He spent his summers with his grandfather learning the old ways. His grandfather was a healer."

Jake took a sharp look at Ben and nodded his head in approval. Maybe, just maybe you have a chance after all. Don't get me wrong Mr. and Mrs FBI agents, I don't have anything against city people or people not from the tribe but I figured non believers would just be this creature's next meal."

"No offence taken Jake. Have you heard anything helpful from your customers that could help us?" I asked talking for the first time.

"Lots and lots of speculation on where it might be hiding. Some people claim to know what the hell we're dealing with but I don't buy it. I think some folks are just bragging and looking for attention."

"Where do they think it's hiding?" Connie asked.

"There are a bunch of canyons out that way," he said, nodding his head and pointing with his scissors in the right direction while he continued to cut the boy's hair.

"Do you know where he is talking about Joe? I asked.

"Yeah about twenty five miles out the country gets real rough. Box canyons, slot canyons washed out stream beds and arroyos. There are quite a few small caves in the area too. Many of them are unexplored and probably not even discovered because the area is so remote. Not much lives out there but jackrabbits, rattle snakes, scorpions and Gila Monsters."

"Yep, that's the place folks are saying the creature lives, sheriff," Jake said as he whipped the barber's cape off the boy and shook it out.

"What's the gossip on what the creature is?" Joe asked.

"Folks are coming to the opinion it might just be a werewolf. I don't know why they think that. Maybe one fella came to that opinion and it just caught on with the others."

"From what I've seen from the pictures it would have to be a whole pack of werewolves to do that much damage in only a few hours," I said.

"I don't know the details of what happened to the men who were killed. That information hasn't been shared with the tribe."

"We have five dead so far, right Joe?" Jake asked.

"I don't know Jake, there might be a sixth one now," Joe admitted.

"Really, who?" Jake asked in surprise.

"I'm told that Carl Whitelaw is the man . He rode for the Circle R ranch. He didn't come back in after riding the line fence. We're heading out tomorrow to look for him."

"I'm glad no one has been killed in town yet," Jake admitted.

"That might be coming. If people start taking precautions and not go outside at night he might start looking for better hunting grounds like in town," Joe said.

"If you get any information that could help please call right away," Connie said, handing him a card.

We walked out of the barber shop into the bright sunlight and put on our sunglasses.

"Where to now?" the sheriff asked us.

"Let's go out and talk to the rancher. We can get the lay of the land and go over maps with him before we search by helo tomorrow," I said as we walked to our car.

We drove the first twelve miles on paved roads before turning off on badly maintained dirt roads. After another six or seven miles we turned off the goat path of a road and through the gate announcing we were on the Circle R ranch. Another five miles and we reached the ranch itself. The ranch was comprised of a main house, bunk house, grub house, barns, grain silos and corrals.

"Pull on up by the main house Ben. Mr. Goodearl has his office there," Joe said.

I parked in front and waited for the dust to settle before we got out of the Tahoe and walked up the steps.

Joe banged the large knocker several times before a woman of around forty answered the door.

"Sheriff, do you have word about our missing ranch hand?" the woman asked.

"Ben, Connie, this is Silvia Goodearl, Mr. Goodearl's eldest daughter," Joe said, making the introductions.

"Silvia, this is Ben Hawk and Connie Sanchez of the FBI."

"Sorry, I forgot my manners while worrying about Carl being missing," she said, apologizing.

"We understand completely. Is there a chance we can have a word with your father?" I asked.

"Sure, come on in and follow me. He is sitting in his office doing paperwork."

Silvia showed us to a large office with double doors that stood open. "Dad, the sheriff and the FBI are here and would like to talk to you."

Mr. Goodearl was a man in his mid sixties, his face was lean and weathered from a lifetime outdoors. "Please have a seat," he said as he rose to shake our hands.

"John these are FBI agents Ben Hawk and Connie Sanchez," Joe said making the introductions once again.

"I know I've seen you someplace before," John said, trying to jog his memory.

"You might have seen them on the national news when the Wisconsin serial killer was brought to justice John," Joe said.

John snapped his finger in recognition. "Yep, that's where I saw you. You were on a few breaking news reports during the case."

"Yep, that was us. We do nothing but hunt down serial killers. We go wherever killings are happening and bring them to justice," Connie said.

"I'm afraid what you've been sent here to hunt isn't a serial killer. This being isn't a flesh and blood human. You may be up against something you're not equipped to deal with. "Do either of you know anything about Native American legends? About beings not human that many don't believe even exist?"

"Yes sir, I know much about them but there is much that I don't know too. I spent summers with my Oglala Sioux grandfather in the Dakotas learning about our culture and our legends," I said.

"His grandfather was a healer John," Joe informed him.

"Then you do know about the old ways and you still came anyway?" John said in surprise.

"Yes sir, it's what we get paid to do."

"You don't earn enough to go willingly and get yourselves killed. If I was you I'd hop on the first plane going back to wherever you came from and don't look back," John said bluntly.

"As of right now we don't have a handle on what kind of creature we're dealing with. We know it hunts after dark and we know the sound it makes and that's all. We don't know what we need to use to get rid of it either," I said ignoring his suggestion about leaving.

"It's my opinion this will end when whatever this is has its fill and disappears on its own," John said.

"We can't in good conscience let this thing kill indiscriminately until its hunger is sated. We will take our chances and search for it," I said.

"I hope the hell you know what you're doing Ben, it's your funeral," John said.

"Can you show us the boundaries of your ranch and where your ranch hand Carl might be holed up?"

"Sure, let me show you on my wall map," John said, standing up and walking to a framed map.

"This is a map of my ranch, fifty nine thousand acres of it. We have line shacks here and here where a ranch hand can spend at night while out checking fences," he said pointing to the spots on the map.

"Have you ever had a ranch hand not shown up when he should before?" Connie asked.

"It's happened a couple of times in the past. Usually it's because they either found a big break in the fence that took time to fix or his horse came up lame and couldn't be ridden."

"But you don't think that's what happened this time?" Joe asked.

"No I don't. Hell, I didn't think there was any danger of Carl running into trouble with this thing. Like I said we have line shacks for them to stay in. I figured as long as he was inside somewhere safe nothing could happen."

"You normally send out people when someone doesn't show up?" I asked.

"Normally we do it right away. If a hand doesn't return at the time he is supposed to I send out a pair of riders with extra horses in both directions looking for them. But with what is going on I didn't think it wise to do that."

"First thing in the morning we're going out looking for him by air in a helicopter. Hopefully we find him with a lame horse and he is alright," Joe told the rancher.

"Do you have any speculation on what we might be dealing with?" I asked him.

"I built this ranch forty three years ago Ben and I have never heard of such a thing happening. I talked to my parents who are still alive and living in Window Rock and they are totally puzzled too.

"We'll let you know what we find tomorrow. Until then I think it would be wise to keep your ranch hands close by," I said.

"I plan on it, Ben. A few heads of cattle isn't worth someone's life," John said as he rose to his feet to escort us out.

We sat in silence each with their own thoughts about what we were facing and what John had shared with us. We didn't feel good about finding the ranch hand alive. It was late afternoon when we got back to Window Rock. After dropping the sheriff back at his office we agreed to meet with him and his Navajo Rangers at the diner for breakfast at six in the morning.

"We may as well eat dinner now Ben. Neither one of us has eaten since breakfast."

"Yeah and when we're done I want to stop at the convenience store and buy a cooler, some ice and a few beers. It's too hot in our room to be comfortable so we may as well sit out front and enjoy the evening."

"See, you do get a good idea every now and then. Don't forget it's your turn to buy too Ben," Connie reminded me.

We sat in the air conditioned comfort of the diner and picked up menus. "I think I'll just have a chicken sandwich and potato salad for supper," I said.

"You are a skinflint, do you know that Ben? If I were buying you'd be eating high off the hog!"

"I had steak last night Connie. I have to watch what I eat a little bit. Too much red meat isn't good for you," I reminded her.

"You're absolutely right Ben. I think I'll have broiled shrimp."

"Now you're talking," I said pleased with myself.

"Also I think a ten ounce tenderloin to go with it and a nice garden salad," Connie said closing the menu.

I nodded my head unhappily.

"Also a nice cold blended strawberry margarita," Connie said, grinning at my unhappy look.

"Is that it? You're not going to have a couple of desserts too?"

"I'll have to wait and see if I'm still hungry or not, Ben. But I probably should save a little room so I can help drink the beer you're buying us," Connie said grinning widely.

"We better enjoy tonight Connie because shit could be hitting the fan very soon," I said, ending the light atmosphere.

"Do you think it's really going to be that bad Ben?" Connie asked as the grin slipped off of her face.

"I think it's going to be way worse than we have ever faced in the past Connie. I think we're going to have to be at our very best to stand a chance of survival."

My large frosted beer and Connie's margarita arrived and we took grateful drinks. It had been a long hot dusty day and the drinks were just what the doctor ordered.

I took a bite of my chicken sandwich and watched Connie sawing into her steak. "I should have gotten a steak. The chicken is alright but it's not a steak."

"Like I said before Ben ole buddy, you're too cheap to buy yourself a steak," Connie said with a wink.

We finished eating and walked over to the store attached to the truck stop and bought a styrofoam cooler, ice and beer before driving back to our hotel room. I got a couple of chairs out of our room and we relaxed out front. I had the streetsweeper leaning up against the wall of our room by my right elbow.

"You really think that's necessary Ben?" Connie asked, nodding at the shotgun.

"You heard what Joe's uncle and the rancher said. You were there when we talked to the barber and the Navajo Rangers. From this moment on the shotgun stays by my side unless I'm in a crowded room."

As the evening passed it became cooler. Sometimes in the desert it could get unbelievably cold out. It could be well over a hundred degrees during the heat of the day and then down into the thirties or lower at night. Around ten we called it a night and went into the room. The room wasn't as hot as the night before because we had the window open and the fan on all day. Once again I slept naked on top of my comforter. It was still around eighty in the room. Connie ended up following suit.

Chapter Eight

"Baaa, Baaa, BAAA!! Moo, MOOO!! Something has the livestock spooked Sandy. I better go out and make sure they're safe," Kyle Cloud told his sleepy wife as he swung his legs off of their bed.

"Make sure you take your rifle with you Kyle. It might be a bear, wolf or coyotes bothering them," Sandy said without opening her eyes.

Kyle grabbed his loaded rifle from above the fireplace and stomped into his boots before heading out. The livestock was still acting scared. Kyle had never heard them act up this badly before. Kyle walked behind the barn to where the nearest sheep was struggling. The black faced sheep they'd named Betsy was tangled in the barbed wire fence. Its rear leg was twisted around two of the strands and she was bleeding. Kyle grabbed the sheep around the middle and tried to untangle her but she was struggling too hard for him to handle alone. Her terror knew no bounds and he couldn't both hold the sheep and work the barbed wire. He would have to get Sandy out of bed to help him out.

Kyle leaned his rifle against the wall of the barn and ran back to the ranch house as fast as he could. He knew the longer that Betsy struggled the more injured she would become.

"Sandy, you need to get up. Betsy is tangled in the barbed wire fence. I can't hold her and untangle her at the same time, I need your help,"

Sandy was instantly awake. The sheep and cattle were their only livelihood. She slipped on her bedroom slippers and rushed out of the door behind her husband Kyle. Betsy was still sounding like she was in total terror. The animals they couldn't see in the dark pasture were echoing the terror they could see in

Betsy.

I'll get hold of Betsy while you spread the barbed wire apart so I can slide her leg out," Kyle grunted as he grabbed the sheep around her middle.

"She is really tangled in the wire honey. What is causing the animals to act this way?"

"Baaa, BAAA!!, BAAA!" Betsy yelled out in terror as she thrashed around frantically.

"I don't know Sandy but can you hurry a little bit. She already kicked me in the head once."

"There, she's loose. You can let go of her now," Sandy said as she let go of the wire.

Kyle let go of the sheep and it knocked him off of his feet in its hurry to distance herself from them.

"OOOF!" Kyle grunted as he landed on his backside.

"Stampede, stampede," Sandy laughed out seeing Kyle laying on the ground. She saw the look on his face change to one of terror before spinning around to see what Kyle was seeing.

In front of them was a being seven and a half feet tall. Its head was devoid of flesh and the translucent skin was stretched tightly over the animal-like skull. Its eyes glowed a bright eerie red and its bone white antlers towered above its head. They knew immediately they were seeing the creature responsible for the deaths on the reservation. It was a creature from Native American folklore but a creature they knew nothing about.

"SKREEEEE! SKREEEEE!" the creature screamed out. The noise was so loud Kyle could feel it reverberating off of his breast bone.

"Sandy run!" Kyle shouted as he made a grab for his rifle. He never stood a chance. The creature easily stepped over the wire fence and swung a massage claw at Kyle's head, instantly crushing his skull and killing him before turning to Sandy. Sandy let out a blood curdling scream and was dead before she had a chance to even turn towards the house.

Chapter Nine

A round five in the morning I heard something plop on the floor followed by the unmistakable sound of a rattlesnake's rattle. Connie's light came on and she let out a scream before diving back onto her bed from ten feet away.

"Watch it Ben! That sneaky bastard crawls sideways!"

I looked down at a five foot sidewinder rattlesnake. "How the hell did that get in here?" I asked as I heard the sound of a vehicle kicking up gravel as it left the parking lot.

"I think someone left us a gift," Connie said as she crouched naked on her bed.

I stood on my bed looking at the snake that was looking back at me still rattling his rattles.

"What are you going to do Ben?" Connie asked excitedly.

"I'll tell you what I'm not going to do. I'm not going to stay standing on my bed until someone comes along and rescues our naked asses. We'd be the laughing stock of Window Rock!"

I threw my comforter over the snake and wrapped it up tight. Walking over to the window I tossed the comforter out and hung onto a corner of it and shook the snake out of it. The snake hit the gravel and hurriedly slithered away.

"I didn't know snakes could climb into windows, Ben."

"He didn't climb in Connie. Someone who doesn't want us here threw it into our room."

"If the motel owner doesn't have a room with AC in it for us we are moving to a different place. I don't give a damn how many miles we have to drive back and forth," Connie said with a shudder.

After the incident with the snake, sleep was out of the question. We had to get up in an hour anyway.

Connie showered first. I grabbed my bath towel before she showered. She had a bad habit of using all the towels and leaving me with nothing but a loin cloth sized hand towel.

We got to the cafe a half hour early and sat drinking coffee waiting for the others to show up. The three of them came together in a squad car and parked next to our car.

We had grabbed a round table that was large enough for the five of us.

"Good morning guys," I said over the rim of my coffee cup.

"Good morning," Joe said as he grabbed the coffee urn and filled up their three cups.

"You have a strange wake up alarm in this town Joe," I said.

"Yeah, you do! Someone tossed a sidewinder rattlesnake into our open window this morning," Connie said, still excited about the experience.

"Someone tossed a snake in your room?" Joe asked in surprise.

"Our room doesn't have a working air conditioning unit so we kept the window open. I guess it was an open invitation for someone to pay us a visit," I said angrily.

"Do you have any idea of who might have pulled off a stunt like that?" Connie asked.

"The three locals looked at each other. "I can think of a few guys who would think something like that would be funny," John said.

"After we heard it plop on the floor and start rattling I heard a vehicle spitting gravel as it left the parking lot of our motel," I told them.

"We are either getting a room with AC so we can close the window or moving to a different motel," Connie stated.

"The next nearest place is forty five miles from here," Joe told us.

"So we've been told by the motel owner," Connie grumbled.

"When I find out who did it I'm going to flatten his nose for him before arresting him for assaulting a federal law enforcement officer," I growled angrily.

We all ordered breakfast and asked for two pots of coffee for the table. I had simple fare this morning, bacon and eggs. An hour later we were done eating and headed outside to wait for the helicopter to show up.

I looked at my watch when I could hear the approaching bird and saw it was right on time. It landed a hundred feet from the parking lot and we waited for the rotors to stop and the dust to settle down before we walked over to it.

Brian, the second in command of the field office in Phoenix, got out of the helicopter and met us.

"Good morning Ben, Connie, I brought what you asked for."

"Brian, this is Sheriff Joe Longbow and Navajo Ranger deputies Sid Canyon and John Stillwater," I said making the introductions.

They all shook hands with each other before walking over to the helicopter.

"Joe, why don't you ride up front with the pilot. You know best where to have him go and the rest of us will take seats in the back," I said.

We all got into the bird and buckled in. The pilot started throwing switches and slowly the rotors started to spin. Once the rotors were at full power he pulled back on the cyclic and the helo lifted off of the desert floor.

Joe directed him to the outer perimeter of the ranch. We were flying at only a few hundred feet.

"There's the barbed wire fence. Head north and keep following it wherever it goes," Joe said into his mic.

Following the fence by air was tremendously faster than doing it over uneven terrain on horseback. It took less than an hour to reach the first line shack. We weren't flying at high speed because we needed to search the terrain as we flew along. There were too many places in the rocks that could hide a body if it was there.

"Land over by the corral and we'll check to see if we can tell if anyone has stayed here recently," I said.

The helicopter landed and I jumped down holding my streetsweeper with the muzzle in the air. The sheriff eyed the drum magazine that was attached to its underside.

"You know what we're dealing with as well as I do Joe. As far as I'm concerned you can't have too much firepower," I said.

"Amen to that brother," he mumbled under his breath as he followed me to the shack.

There were signs that someone had been here recently. There was a plate and a couple of pans sitting on a drain board. Everything was dust free. It was agreed that if the dishes were there for any length of time there would have been some dust on them. The chair also looked sat in. There was a bare spot where someone's butt had sat in it.

"I'd say he was definitely here recently but he moved on," I said.

"That's what I'd say too," Sid said after a brief examination of the inside of the cabin.

We loaded back up into the helicopter and continued the search for the ranch hand.

"Pretty rugged country you have around here Joe," I said looking down at the rock and cactus filled landscape.

"You don't think the government would have put us here if the land was good for anything, do you Ben?"

"Well, you got the last laugh anyway. I spotted all of the oil wells on the way in."

"Yeah, they found oil a couple decades ago. It's been a big help."

We got to the second line shack finally. I could see a horse in the corral.

"It looks like we found the missing ranch hand. Land the helo way over there so we don't spook the horse," Joe said.

We got out of the helicopter. From where we stood I could see the door was totally destroyed. Even the frame of the door was laying in splinters. I examined the strike plate on the door frame and saw it wasn't damaged though.

"Lead the way Ben," Joe said as everybody armed themselves.

"Why me?" I said, glancing over at him.

"You're the one with the autocannon. You got more firepower than the rest of us combined."

"The day may come when you're glad I have this shotgun,"

"You mean besides today?" John asked as he followed me while holding his handgun in a two hand grip.

I walked towards the line shack cautiously. The other five were spread out behind me.

I put my back to the wall next to the door and listened for any sound. I smelled for any scent that would indicate death. I looked as well as I could into the dim recesses of the shack. All the things I told Connie she needed to start doing when we were flying here from Washington.

I had a flashlight mounted under the barrel of the streetsweeper and I clicked it on. I flipped up my sunglasses and quickly stepped into the shack before the sun could screw up my vision in the dim interior.

I could see something had happened inside. The table and chair were laying shattered in a pile on the floor. There was blood but not as much blood as I would have expected. The photos we saw of the last victim had great swaths of blood sprayed and splattered everywhere. Here we were inside a structure with hardly any blood at all.

"Come on in," I called out to the others.

The others came in and surveyed the wreckage.

"The dishes are dusty so whatever happened here happened before he had a chance to make his meal," John said after wiping his hand on the plate.

"There is hardly any blood here either. Do you think whatever attacked him captured him and took him away alive?" Connie asked.

"With the other five they have all been grizzly deaths. Blood was splattered everywhere. The attacks were very vicious. But here we have a little bit of blood and some broken furniture."

"I don't get it either Joe," Sid said as he looked around for any clues.

"Am I right in thinking no one has ever been attacked inside a building?" I asked.

"All of the attacks have happened outside so far, at least until now that is," Sid said.

"Here's what I think happened guys. The ranch hand got here and the inside of the line shack was unbearably hot from being closed up. So he had the windows and door open. The open door was an open invitation to whatever this creature is to enter the building and attack him," I said.

"That makes about as much sense as anything I can think of," Joe said.

"Joe, can one of your rangers ride the horse back to the ranch house? We'll continue searching for him by air. He might be hiding out in the rocks nearby," I said.

"How long will it take you to reach the ranch?" Connie asked him.

"Damn little time. I'm not taking any longer than I need to. That horse is going to be tired when we get back to the ranch. I won't be out here anywhere near dark by myself, you can bet on that!"

"From here moving at a good clip he should reach the ranch in three or three and a half hours. There is a pretty good trail that runs along the fence from other line riders," Joe said.

"Once we search the area thoroughly we'll follow along in the helicopter and keep an eye on you until you get to the ranch. Then we'll land and pick you up," I said.

"Eyes from the sky would be greatly appreciated, Ben. I better get saddled up and moving."

"Make sure the horse has its fill of water. There is a creek next to the shack. If the horse has been in the corral and couldn't get to water he'll be thirsty," I said.

"I'll walk the horse over so it can get its fill of water while you gather up the saddle and blanket," Connie said as she reached up and grabbed the horse's halter and led her over to the creek where she drank thirstily. You're a thirsty girl aren't you?" Connie said gently as she patted the horse's flank affectionately. The horse came up with water dripping off of her muzzle and stood licking her lips nodding her head before going back down for more.

"Connie knew enough to not let her drink too much and led the unwilling horse back to the corral fence. The horse whinnied and nudged Connie gently. She knew the horse was happy to have human company once again.

"I found Carl's lever action rifle still in the saddle scabbard. He never had a chance to get it out to protect himself," John said.

"He was definitely taken by surprise," the sheriff said.

John saddled up the horse and left the line shack at a brisk trot. He didn't want to wear the horse out before he reached the ranch. We watched as he disappeared over a ridge before climbing back into the helicopter to avoid spooking the animal.

The helicopter rose into the air and hovered about a hundred feet over the terrain.

"Alright, everybody keep your eyes peeled for anything out of place. Watch for clothing, blood or a fresh trail leading away," I said.

We circled in ever widening circles, widening our search. A few hundred yards from the shack Connie spotted something in the rocks.

""Ben, I think I see something, it looks from here to be a cowboy hat," Connie said as she pointed out the window.

"Find a place nearby where you can land so we can have a look," I said as I looked to where Connie was pointing.

The pilot landed and we scrambled over a hundred yards uphill over broken rocks and boulders. I got to it first and reached down for the old battered mouse colored stetson. I turned it over in my hands and saw a small blood stain on the brim of the hat. You couldn't see any trail over the rocky landscape.

"So whatever it was that took Carl headed off to the northwest from the shack. Why don't we head on in that direction and see where it leads us," Joe said.

"We can't spend too much time looking, Joe. We have to keep an eye on John, remember?" Connie said.

"We can take a quick look though. It's been two days since he went missing so we probably won't see the creature out in the open but we might spot where he was headed," I said.

We hurried back to the helicopter and the pilot rose up off the desert floor a few hundred feet and turned to the northwest to go in the direction the creature was headed.

"What's all the trees up ahead sheriff?" Connie asked.

"It's the Cinnamon River. It's not very wide or very deep but there is always water in it. The ranchers who have land alongside the river use it for watering their cattle and growing hay."

"Down in this river bottom would definitely be a good place to hide with all of the trees and brush growing alongside it. It would also have a good supply of water," Sid said.

I looked at my watch. "We'd better head on over and keep an eye on John. He's been on his own for over an hour."

The pilot circled around and gained altitude as he dipped the nose of the helicopter down and gained speed rapidly. It didn't take long to catch up to John. He waved at us as we passed by him on his flank. We were high enough to see the ranch in the distance. It was probably still seven miles off but at the speed John was traveling he would reach the ranch in under an hour.

Once John was within sight of the ranch after crossing the last ridgeline we powered ahead of him and landed behind the ranch house so we wouldn't spook the ranch animals. The rancher hearing us came out to meet us hoping we would have good news about Carl.

"We didn't find Carl. We did locate his horse at the second line shack. That's John Stillwater riding his horse back now," I said, breaking the news.

"Do you have Carl's body in the helicopter?" the rancher asked.

"We found the horse in the corral and something big and powerful busted down the door, frame and all. The table and chair are laying on the floor in splinters and a small amount of blood was found but no Carl," Joe said.

"Where the hell did Carl go? Did you do a search for him?" John Goodearl asked.

"We searched by air all the way to the Cinnamon River. We found his banged up stetson several hundred yards away in the rocks. Whatever took him was headed northwest. Any idea where he could be headed?" Connie asked.

"That's his hat alright." John said, turning it over in his hands.

"There is a small amount of blood on the brim of the hat. This crime scene isn't like the other ones the sheriff has investigated. There isn't nearly the amount of blood there was at the other crime sites," Sid said.

"What can you tell us about Carl? Where is he from and how long has he worked for you?" I asked him.

"Carl claims to be from up Montana way. He claimed to be part Blackfoot. He says he cowboyed all his life but doesn't like the snow so he moved down here to get away from it. He's been working for me for nearly four years now and has always been very dependable. If Carl is missing, trust me he didn't go willingly."

"We're just getting started with our investigation. We'll keep you up to date with any new information we have on your ranch hands' disappearance," Connie said.

"Y'all just be careful, you hear? Don't take any unnecessary risks you don't have to. We have no idea what you're up against," the rancher warned.

"You're right we don't know what we're up against but whatever it is, it isn't good," I said.

The rancher walked back to his ranch house. We kept the stetson because it was evidence in our investigation. We boarded the helicopter once more and it took us back to the truck stop where we got off before it left taking Brian back to Phoenix.

"So what's next Ben?" Joe asked me.

"I guess we're done for the day Joe. We have to check out of our motel room and find a different place to stay. Brian will turn the stetson over to forensics and see what they can find out. See if there is any microscopic evidence and check the blood for blood type."

Chapter Ten

W e checked out of the motel after the owner told us he still had no idea when the new air conditioning unit was coming. We told him about the episode with the snake and that we were checking out. He wasn't very happy to hear he was losing business because of a stunt like what was pulled on us.

We left town in the opposite direction in which we arrived at Window Rock from. We found a Best Western hotel where the highway we were on met another larger highway. We pulled into the parking lot and parked by the front door under the overhang and walked to the front desk.

"Welcome to the Best Western," said a smiling girl in her early twenties.

"Hi, can we get a room with two queen sized beds in it? Preferably not on the first floor," Connie asked.

"Certainly, are you just staying for one night?"

"We aren't sure how long we will be here yet. It could be a couple of weeks," Connie said, showing the girl her FBI credentials.

"Yes ma'am, I'll put you in a suite, room 204. The room has two beds plus a larger sitting area with a table and chairs plus a balcony."

"That will be a big improvement over the last place we stayed," Connie said with a smile as she accepted the electronic room keys.

"We dragged our things to the elevator. "Why did you want a second floor room?" I asked her.

"If anyone, anyone wants to drop off any more visitors into our room they're going to have to work for it!" Connie said as she remembered the snake again.

I grinned at her. The expression on her face was priceless. "So you think we're snake charmers now? Last case was the Copperhead killer and now we have the Sidewinder?"

"I don't know Ben but if the next one is the King Cobra or the Cottonmouth, I'm going to retire!"

"It could be worse, partner. It could be spiders or scorpions," I said, grinning once again at the look she shot me. We dropped our bags and my streetsweeper on our beds before heading back down stairs to the bar and restaurant the hotel had.

"Not funny Ben, not funny at all!"

"Well, I have something to take your mind off of snakes."

"You do huh? What's that?" Connie asked me suspiciously.

"It's your turn to buy tonight," I said grinning at her once more.

"It's not anymore, sport. Now that we're staying in a hotel with decent amenities we'll put our daily food and drink expenses on our room bill. The FBI can pick up the tab."

"You take all the fun out of giving you a hard time. If you don't learn how to loosen up when we have a few hours of rest from a case, that white streak you put in your hair is going to be permanent."

"You're a real comedian Ben, I don't have a white streak in my hair. Hell, I'm just barely thirty years old!"

"You mean to tell me you didn't put that white streak in your hair as some sort of fashion statement?" I asked as the smile slid off of my face.

"Very funny Ben! What are you trying to do? Get even for writing asshole on your forehead when we were on the Wisconsin Case?"

"If you remember I got even for that when I dowsed you with the bucket of water."

The bartender brought us frosty mugs of beer and set them down in front of us. We told him our room number so he could charge them to our room.

"Let me ask you a question. Do I have a white streak in my hair?" Connie asked the bartender.

"Yes, but it looks good on a woman so young," he said, trying to compliment Connie.

Connie shot me a look of horror before she bolted off her bar stool and ran to the ladies room. I could hear her shrieks all the way from the bar room. She came running back with a look of terror on her face.

"I have a white streak in my hair! I'm too young for this to be happening Ben," Connie said as she grabbed me by the collar and shook me.

Tears were running down my face. I was laughing so hard. "I suppose now I'll have to start calling you Petunia," I said howling with laughter.

"Why Petunia Ben?" Connie asked as her eyes narrowed. She still had a firm grip on my collar.

"Because that's the name of Pepe Le Pew, the skunk's girlfriend. She has a white streak down the middle too," I said, laughing all the harder.

"This white streak is all your fault Ben! It's all this supernatural, cryptid bullshit, you dragged me into!"

"Hey, I asked you not to come if you'll take the time to remember!" I said still grinning widely.

"You had better wipe that smile off of your face buster! I'm armed with teflon coated rounds. They'll go right through your bullet proof vest if you're wearing one," Connie threatened.

"I'm not worried about you shooting me Connie. If you shoot me, who will let you know when your hair turns whiter?"

"In the morning we could have stopped and got some, just for men hair gel but you can't use it. After all it's just for men," I said, grinning even more.

"I know a woman who did four tours in Iraq. The same thing happened to her. She has a white streak in her hair just like yours."

"What did she do about it?" Connie asked me, thinking I was just stringing her along.

"She kept it Connie. She considers it a badge of honor for what she did for her country, for what she had to go through," I told her honestly.

"You're not kidding right now are you Ben?"

"No, I'm as serious as a crutch. Maybe the two of you can start an exclusive club. After all, very very few women get a white streak like that in their hair because of what they went through for their country. She even works in Washington DC. You can call yourselves the Petunias'," I said winking at her.

"You can start an exclusive club too, Ben. You can call yourselves the "I got shot in my ass by my angry partner club.""

The bartender came back around to refill our mugs. "By your reaction the white streak is new huh?" he asked with a grin.

"Ben here is going to start a new exclusive club. How would you like to be a charter member of it?" Connie asked with a glare.

"I think I'll pass for now," The bartender said, the grin sliding off of his face, having heard her comment about shooting me.

We took our beers and moved to the dining room. A waitress brought us menus before walking away.

"There is a difference between supernatural and cryptid Connie, just so you know," I said.

"So go ahead and tell me the difference," Connie said grumpily.

"Supernatural beings are like shapeshifters, ghosts and werewolves. Cryptids as modern man calls them are flesh and blood beings of this realm such as hairy man, the Loch Ness monster and Dogmen. They don't change form."

"So do you think we're chasing something that is a cryptid or is supernatural Ben?"

"Definitely something supernatural Connie. Look, beings like bigfoot don't do things like what is happening here. Yes, a bigfoot or hairy man will kill you if he is angry enough. But they will not carry you off alive or leave you like the victims we saw in the photos."

"So are there ways to kill all cryptids and supernatural beings?" Connie asked as her plate with her pork chop and potato was placed in front of her.

"Not always. First of all we don't know which one we're dealing with. Then there is the fact that there are many of them that have no way of killing them attached to their legends. Some of them might not be living breathing beings so there is no life for you to end."

"That's just great Ben!"

"For instance, look at werewolves and vampires. Werewolves

according to legend you need a silver bullet. Vampires are the undead. You can keep them at bay with garlic or crosses and kill them with a wooden stake. No amount of small arms fire will kill them according to legend."

"So you're saying that your streetsweeper might be useless?"

"Yes, it is possible that we have no weapons that can protect us from whatever this thing is," I admitted as I started eating my pork chop.

"I think from this moment on you need to have that streets-weeper with you at all times. We've had a snake tossed into our room so there is no telling what else they have planned for us. They could screw around with your shotgun. Take out the firing pin or change out the rounds you have loaded into it," Connie said.

"You're right. I can carry it in a gun case when in the hotel or restaurant."

We finished eating and headed right up to our room. Just to be safe I checked out the shotgun and its rounds to make sure it wasn't tampered with. We'd have to get an early start in the morning. It would take us almost an hour to get back to Window Rock.

We undressed and crawled into our beds. It was nice having a room cool enough to be able to cover up in bed.

"Good night Ben," Connie said with a yawn from the bed next to mine.

"Good night Petunia," I said as I grinned in the dark.

"It's bedtime, Ben; you can quit being such an asshole now!" Connie said angrily.

Chapter Eleven

"**I**t wasn't a bad dream!" Connie shouted from the bathroom, waking me up.

"What wasn't a bad dream?" I called out as I swung my legs out of the bed.

"The white streak in my hair!"

"Nope it wasn't. Like I told you last night you need to wear it like a badge of honor. Look what you were willing to do for your country," I said, trying not to laugh outright.

"Ben, I can't see you but I can hear you grinning from here! You better wipe that grin off of your face if you know what's good for you buster!"

"Before we head out we'd better call Director Burns and give him an update on the case," I said to change the subject.

Connie came out of the bathroom combing her hair. "Ben, is the white streak wider than it was yesterday?"

"I don't think so. I think it looks that way because it's still wet. I think it looks good on you though," I said, trying to calm her.

"That better not be a smirk I see!"

"You know, it wouldn't be so noticeable if you had blond hair instead of black hair," I said before disappearing into the bathroom.

I came out of the bathroom ten minutes later still dripping wet. "Damn it Connie, you used all of the bath towels again!" I said angrily.

"My hair needed an extra towel this morning to inspect the white streak sport!" Connie said with a smug look on her face.

I hurriedly got dressed. My shirt was sticking to my back. I could feel the water trickling down the middle of my back. It's hard to dry your back with a washcloth.

I phoned the director's office number. He was two hours ahead of us.

"Agents Hawk and Sanchez, I was hoping to hear from you on the case today."

"Yes sir, there is another missing cow hand."

"He is missing but not dead?"

"We found out a local rancher had sent him out on a three day route to ride the line fence and check it for breaks. It's a normal ranch job. When he didn't return at the normal time Sheriff Longbow was contacted."

"I see, go on. You said you didn't locate a body."

"We visited with the rancher by the name of John Goodearl and talked to him about the lay of the land. His ranch is nearly sixty thousand acres. We arranged for a helicopter the next morning and searched along the fence following the route Carl the cowboy would have taken."

"There are two line shacks at intervals around the ranches' perimeter so the cowboys have shelter for the night. We found the cowboys' horse in the corral at the second line shack. The door to the shack was laying in splinters and the furniture was all busted up. Very little blood was found at the scene."

"Did you search by air and try to locate the body?"

"Yes sir. All we found was his cowboy hat several hundreds of yards away from the shack in the rocks."

"So if the door was broken down are you expecting it to be a bear that did it?"

"No sir, a bear would have torn him up and there would have been far more blood. A bear might drag him off into the brush to hide the body to consume later but not haul him off while still alive."

"So if you eliminate bears there are no other animals that could have done it. Coyote and Wolves couldn't have busted down the door like that," The director reasoned out.

"No sir, they couldn't have."

"So what do you think you're dealing with Ben?"

"Something a man who works in Washington DC and was raised in New York City wouldn't understand sir."

"You're talking about that cryptid mumbo jumbo you were

talking about before you left again, aren't you?"

"No sir, I don't think it was a cryptid. What modern man would call a cryptid is like a bigfoot or the Loch Ness monster. This is something far more sinister and deadly than that sir. We are talking about a supernatural being of immense strength and intelligence that might not have a chink in it's armor for us to use to kill it."

"So what you're telling me is you might not be able to end the killing that is happening on the Navajo Reservation?"

"Yes sir, that's what I'm saying. Hell, we don't even know what we're dealing with yet. It's a being that can slaughter at will and devour a body rapidly in only a matter of a few hours. So far as far as we know, no one has been able to harm it."

"I don't know if I can buy into all this supernatural hooha Ben."

"As a man who was raised learning Native American lore I totally believe it. We will do what we can to stop it sir but the time may come where we bail on this case. If we get to the point where we know we can't kill it and if we stay we are likely to die ourselves, we will be pulling out."

"What does Agent Sanchez think about the case?"

"She is right here listening in."

"Sir, Ben is right. From everything I learned in the last few days I don't think we are dealing with a flesh and blood being. I didn't realize how stressed out this case has gotten me in only a few days," Connie said.

"I don't think I quite understand that last part," Director Burns said.

"Connie's hair has turned white sir. She has a two inch wide white streak in her hair from the stress of the situation she is going to have to live with."

"I know someone else that happened to. She did four tours in Iraq and the stress and tension put a white streak in her hair."

"I know who you're talking about and told Connie about it. I told her to wear the streak like a badge of honor."

"Agent Sanchez, do I need to pull you from this case and put someone else in your place?" Director Burns asked.

"No sir, I'll find a way to deal with it," Connie said glaring at me.

"What can I get you that will help you out?"

"Nothing right now sir. Once we find out what we are dealing with I'll come up with a plan if possible. We have a lot of creatures talked about in our folklore and not all of them had a method of killing them attached to the legend."

"Like I said a couple of minutes ago. I'm having a hard time wrapping my mind around what you're telling me. Keep me posted agents. I will get you any resources that I can to help you bring this to an end."

"Oh, one more thing as a footnote, someone tossed a sidewinder rattlesnake into our motel room. We ended up moving to a hotel forty five miles from Window Rock. We're staying at a Best Western now. The other motel didn't have air so we had to sleep with the window open and someone saw it at an open invitation to give us a present," Connie said.

"Any idea of who or why they did it?"

"Not yet sir but if I learn who did it I'll arrest him for assaulting a federal officer right after I flatten his nose for him," I said.

"I'm on call 24/7. You need anything, anything at all, don't hesitate to call me."

"We won't, sir," I said, ending the call.

"I read they have a continental breakfast here. We just have time to grab a bagel or a muffin and some coffee," Connie said while holstering her side arm and attaching her spare to her ankle holster.

We grabbed pastries and coffee and headed out to our car for the nearly hour long ride to Window Rock. I tossed the streetsweeper onto the back seat and we were off.

We pulled up in front of the sheriff's office. Joe was standing out front watching for us to arrive. I knew instantly something had happened while we were away for the night.

"Good, you're finally here," Joe said.

"Something happened Joe?" Connie asked.

"I received a call first thing this morning from the postmaster. Lots of folks just come to town once a week to pick up their mail and any groceries they need for the week. Sandy and Kyle Cloud were two of those people.

"They didn't come into town Saturday. The postmaster finally called me this morning when he saw they hadn't picked up their mail from their post office box inside the post office all weekend."

"Has this ever happened before?" I asked him.

"According to the postmaster they stop regularly as clockwork. The only thing that would keep them home would be the weather and you can see we haven't had any bad weather to speak of."

"How far from town do they live?" Connie asked.

"They're only about seven or eight miles out but some of it is a pretty rocky road."

"We'd better go and check on them then," I said as we climbed into our car.

"How do the Cloud's earn a living Joe?" Connie asked.

"They own a mixed herd of sheep and cattle. I think they run about sixty head in all."

"We got to their run down ranch yard and everything was still except for some chickens running around and a dirty looking scrawny dog that scurried away with his tail between his legs.

"That's strange, old Blue is usually very friendly," The sheriff said as he cautiously got out of the car.

"Something has him scared, Joe. A dog doesn't tuck his tail between his legs unless he is scared of something or someone," I said.

I grabbed the streetsweeper and took it out of its case. Connie and Joe armed themselves with their handguns.

"Suddenly I feel over exposed and under armed," Connie admitted.

"Don't worry about it, partner. I have the streetsweeper and feel the same way," I said as we scanned the yard.

"I smell something and it isn't Sandy's flower garden," Joe muttered.

We walked around back behind a small barn and two vultures jumped up and flew away. It scared the hell out of me. I almost wasted buckshot on the birds.

In the uncut brush behind the barn lay the married couple. I could tell they'd been laying there for a few days but the way they looked couldn't have been because of the vultures.

"Aw hell, they were good people," the sheriff said as he turned away sickened by the sight of them laying there.

"It looks like whatever did this to them also took down some of their livestock," I said pointing to the bodies of sheep and cattle laying in the pasture.

"We should have a forensic examination of the remains, Ben," Connie said.

"Get your people out here with body bags, sheriff. I'll call Phoenix for a helicopter to collect the remains and take them for autopsies."

"Alright Ben, I'll get my people on their way."

I pulled out my phone and called the SAC, Colin Sands. "Colin, I need a helicopter sent to my location to pick up a couple of bodies, or what's left of them to be autopsied."

"I'll get it moving right away Ben. It should be there in under two hours."

"Good, use my cell phone for the GPS coordinates," I said, ending the call.

We walked out to the pasture to examine the dead livestock. I couldn't tell for sure why they were dead. They certainly didn't suffer the same fate that Sandy and Kyle had.

"You better get the local vet out here too to see what killed these animals," I said as Joe made a second call.

A half hour later we could hear the approaching sirens of the other squad cars and the local doctor/medical examiner.

"They're over behind the barn Glen," Joe told the medical examiner.

"Do a quick examination and get them into body bags. I have a helicopter coming to take the bodies to a state crime lab," I told Glen.

Twenty minutes later the veterinarian showed up. "There are dead livestock out in the pasture. We need to know what killed them. There are no apparent wounds to their bodies," Connie told him.

"Thanks for dropping everything and coming out Jim," Joe said, slapping the veterinarian's shoulder.

The four of us walked out into the pasture. Anything was better than being by Sandy and Kyle, but not by much. The dead livestock were bloated to the max having been laying in the hot desert sun for days.

"You're right. I don't see any exterior wounds on the animals either. Let's see if we can flip over a couple of the lighter animals and check the other side," the vet said.

We flipped the animals over so the vet could examine them. "Huh, no exterior signs of injuries here either."

"Is it my imagination or does something look out of place with the way they're laying there Jim?" Joe asked him.

"You're right. They appear to be all hunched up funny." Jim grabbed one of the sheep by its neck and twisted it back and forth. We could hear a grating sound.

"Well I'll be forever damned!" the vet said in a shocked voice.

"What did you discover?" I asked, looking at him sharply.

"This animal's neck is broken." He checked all of the sheep and came to the same conclusion. He couldn't lift the head of the bull and cow high enough to check they were too heavy.

"They're all broken," He whispered in shock.

"What could have done this doc?" Connie asked.

"Nothing I can think of. A grizzly if any were around here might break the neck of a sheep. But not take a bull down and kill it without any bite or claw marks. I can guarantee you it wouldn't be able to break its neck."

"What about some escaped exotic animal from let's say Africa? Connie asked.

"An African lion would take one down maybe with some help. But there would be bite marks on it and its neck wouldn't be broken."

"So you can't explain what could cause this?" Joe pressured him.

"I can explain what caused this and so can you Joe. It was caused by one of the beings we heard folklore about all of our lives. One of the ancient ones, said to have walked this earth in the past. Something or someone has caused it to reappear and come back."

"Ben, is it too late to get that bazooka? I really want one now!" Connie said fearfully.

It was after noon when the helicopter appeared over the horizon. It landed on the other side of my car and the rotor blades wound down. Colin jumped out of the helo and walked over to us.

"I need what's left of the bodies taken to the state crime lab Colin," I told him.

"I'll take them right there, Where are they?"

"Over by the medical examiner's car," I said as we walked over.

"Jesus Ben! If we weren't a thousand miles from the ocean I'd say the shark from Jaws had a go at them. There isn't much left of them."

"No, they're two thirds gone. When we got here the vultures were feeding on them but they can't account for all of this damage."

There was so pitiful little left of them that Colin grabbed a body bag in each hand and carried them effortlessly to the helo.

"What the hell happened to them guys?" Colin asked Connie and I. I could tell he was shaken up.

"We don't know yet. Hell Colin, I'm not sure we even want to know," I said as I still kept my attention on our surroundings scanning for danger.

We entered the ranch house to look for clues of what happened. I saw where Kyle kept his gun above the fireplace. We walked into the bedroom and saw the unmade bed.

"I would guess they heard the animals out in the pasture being attacked and went to investigate only to get killed themselves," I said pointing to the bed.

"Yeah, they were sleeping with the windows open so they could catch a breeze," Joe said, nodding towards the open windows.

"So Kyle thought about the safety of the herd and rushed out to see what was spooking them," Connie said.

"Then Sandy joined him to help with the herd. We saw blood on the barbed wire fence near their bodies. Maybe it wasn't their blood but the blood of one of the animals that got caught in the fence," I said.

"Kyle would have had to get Sandy to help get the animal untangled. It would have been panicking and fighting to get free," Joe said.

"There isn't a rancher worth his or her salt that wouldn't have rushed out to aid an injured animal," Connie said.

"That was their demise. Do we have to think this thing is smart enough to harm their animals to draw them out of the house so they can themselves be slaughtered?" Joe asked.

"I can say one thing for sure, Joe. I'm not going to underestimate this creature from here on out," I said.

Chapter Twelve

We stood by my car and watched as the helicopter and the other cars that responded to our call headed out.

"What do we do now Ben, Connie? The sheriff asked us.

"Let's head on back to your office Joe and figure out our next move," I said as I scanned the area one last time before climbing behind the wheel.

"We walked into the air conditioned sheriff's office and closed the door for privacy.

"It would appear people are taking risks they shouldn't be taking. I think Sandy and Kyle would still be alive if they hadn't gone out in the dark."

"But what rancher wouldn't rush out of their house if they thought their herd was being attacked?" Connie asked.

"We need to have a town hall meeting, Joe. We have to warn people about this thing. We might just save a few lives," I said.

"When do you want to have it?" Joe asked.

"Now, today, the sooner the better. It has to be before nightfall so it doesn't find another victim tonight unaware," I said.

"The only place we have big enough for a town hall is the gymnasium at the high school."

"Let's plan it for four o'clock today, right after school lets out. Have the schools hold their kids over for the meeting so they all hear about it. Have the squad cars go down the streets in town announcing over loudspeakers for people to come to the meeting," Connie said.

"Do you have a TV station in town?" I asked.

"No, all we have is a radio station that plays mostly country music and oldies."

"Call them and have them start announcing the meeting every fifteen minutes. Have them broadcast the meeting from the school too, so people living out of town have a chance to get the news," I said.

"We only have a couple of hours before it will be time for the meeting, Ben," Joe said.

"I wish we would have more time but we'll have to work with what we have for now."

We made the calls to the schools. The kids in the elementary school would be bused to the high school for the meeting. The squad cars were going slowly up and down the streets announcing the meeting. Soon it was time for us to head to the school.

We entered the gym and the bleachers were full. Folding chairs had been set up for the overflow and they were mostly full too. Everyone was scared of what was happening on their reservation. They wanted information about what was being done to solve the problem.

A large tv screen was set up so we could share pictures with the tribe. The shock of what they were about to see might save a life.

The sheriff went up to the microphone first. "Good afternoon my people. We have called you into this meeting to give you news about the murders that are happening here. With me from the FBI are FBI Agents Ben Hawk and Connie Sanchez. You might or might not have heard of them. They are the ones who solved the serial killer case in Wisconsin a couple of weeks ago. They do nothing else but hunt down the worst of killers."

"Those are flesh and blood beings, sheriff. How good can they be with something they don't understand," shouted someone from where the folding chairs were.

"I'll let them answer that question for you," the sheriff said as he stepped away from the microphone.

"I'm Ben Hawk and I'm here to help solve your problem. So far I can tell you hairy man isn't responsible for what has been happening here. Neither is a skinwalker or a shapeshifter doing this thing to your people. But it is a supernatural being of immense strength and intelligence."

"What do you know about it? What would a city boy know about hairy man?" yelled out the same voice.

"I spent my summers with my grandfather in the Dakotas. He is an Oglala Sioux healer. I learned many things from my summers there."

"So you do know about the old ways," stated an elderly woman from the first row of bleachers.

"I know much but not all. I have seen a hairy man several times. I have seen skinwalkers but I do not pretend to know all there is to know. I know I still have much to learn and hopefully we can fix what is happening here."

"What about your partner? She has no knowledge of what can be out there. She would be nothing more than a snack for what waits for her," the old woman said.

"I have to teach her to hear. Teach her to listen to her surroundings. Smell what might be a danger and see trouble before it arrives. I have spoken to her and she knows the dangers we face. All you need to do is look at the white streak that is in her hair. It wasn't there two days ago. The situation we find ourselves in has put it there."

"She is wise to realize the terrors that are out there and to show that she fears the unknown is wise," the old woman nodded approvingly.

"So far seven people have been killed and another one has gone missing," Connie said.

"We thought the number was only five and who is missing?" one of the teachers asked us.

"Carl Whitelaw, from the Circle R ranch disappeared while riding the line fence," Joe informed them.

"He was in a line shack when the creature busted down the door and took him," Connie said.

"So we aren't even safe in our own homes?" shouted out a frightened mother.

"You are much safer there than you are outside. Being a line shack it might be that the creature didn't associate it with being a house but just a shed," I said.

"We think he had the door open to cool the inside off and the creature walked through the open door," Connie said.

"Who else was killed?" Someone asked from the bleachers.

"We found the remains of Kyle and Sandy Cloud this morning behind their barn," the sheriff said, breaking the news.

"Good heavens, I just saw them a week ago Saturday!" cried out a woman in her forties.

"We speculate their herd was being attacked by this creature and they went out to protect it and were ambushed and killed. Do not underestimate the intelligence of this creature or its strength. Those of you listening to this broadcast who live out of town heed this warning. No matter how much danger you think your animals are in, do not, I repeat do not go out in the dark to investigate. You are far better off losing a few heads of stock than you are your own life," I said.

"We are going to show you a few pictures of some of the victims now. Their remains are unidentifiable because of the damage done to them. We will not tell you who the victim you are looking at is out of respect for their families and friends," Connie said.

A picture suddenly appeared on the screen. There was a collective gasp of shock from those seeing it for the first time.

"The damage you see on this victim is estimated to have been done in less than four hours. You can see the creature that killed this person consumed most of the body in only a few hours. We think the reason more wasn't consumed is daylight was approaching and we feel the creature doesn't like the sunlight," Joe said.

The DJ was describing the picture for his on air audience. We waited for him to finish before we continued.

"This second victim was killed either going to or from his outhouse. We aren't sure how long the victim was being fed on for sure," Connie said.

"I have an outhouse sheriff!" yelled out a panicked older man.

"If I were you, Clem, I'd get me a bucket to use at night and empty it in the daytime," Joe said. The statement would have normally gotten a lot of chuckles but not today and not here.

"I think these pictures have sickened everybody enough. We aren't going to show you anymore. Hopefully you are shocked enough to keep yourselves and your kids from becoming easy meals," I said.

"What we think we know about the creature so far is minimal at best. It only feeds in the dark or near dark. You parents who tell your kids to be in the house when the streetlights come on better not be doing that for now. The streetlights come on at near dark and the creature might be already hunting for its next victim while your kids are still outdoors," Joe warned them.

"They aren't going to be outdoors until this is over with," a mother shouted out.

"Aw mom!" complained an unhappy ten year old.

"I'm not going to hear any complaining Sam. You can stay in the house and play your video games until this is over with. If I catch you sneaking out of the house I will blister your hide for you! Do you hear me young man?"

"Yes mom," said the embarrassed young boy. At least he would be able to play with his games.

"In the next day or two the Navajo Rangers, Sid and John along with Connie and myself will start to search for the beast. Hopefully we can end this before anyone else is killed," I said.

"Do you know of a way of killing it?" asked a man.

"We don't even know for sure what we are dealing with yet sir. Until we do know what it is we can't come up with a plan of attack," Connie answered.

"I'm putting a curfew into place until this is over with. All businesses will close by seven at night. No one is allowed outside from eight at night until an hour after daylight. We will jail anyone found violating the curfew for their own safety. If there are no more questions the meeting is over," Joe said as the DJ walked up to us for some follow up questions.

"Can you share with our listeners the area where you expect to concentrate your search in?"

"We have a wall map at the station in my office. You're more than welcome to see where the seven victims were found. We will focus the search within the bounds of where they were killed," the sheriff explained.

"You said you have no idea yet of what creature you're dealing with. So you don't know what you'll need to do to end this. How do you face the unknown not knowing if you can survive the first encounter?"

"Now that's a damn fine question. Hopefully it will be from a far distance away so we can escape the encounter if needed," I said.

"I want your listeners to heed our warning. No matter if it's a favorite family pet or your entire herd do not go out in the dark thinking you can save them. The best thing you can do is make sure all of your pets are in your house well before dark. Your ranch animals will just have to fend for themselves," Connie said.

"One thing we forgot to share in the town hall meeting that I just remembered. This creature broke the necks of four sheep, a cow and a large bull. According to your local veterinarian we know of no animal on the face of this earth that is powerful enough to have done that. Don't underestimate this beast's potential to do harm," I said.

"Only a fall off of a high cliff could have broken the neck of that bull and there are no cliffs in the area where the dead animals were located," Connie added.

"I want to thank the FBI and our sheriff for your time in cautioning our listeners to the danger. Folks, pay heed and don't venture out after dark. This is KNAV ending this public service warning. This transmission will be broadcasted on a regular basis to warn our listeners. This is Brett Morning signing off, back to you in the studio Bob."

"Well, we did all we could to warn the folks. I guess now it's up to them to stay safe," Joe said.

"You need to talk to your deputies about not taking any unnecessary risks. If someone calls about someone not showing up when they're supposed to they are not to search outside their vehicles at night. Fuel the squad cars up during the day and other than going into and out of the police station they are to stay put in their vehicles with the windows rolled up," I told Joe.

"For the time being it would be best if they don't venture out of town either," Connie tossed in.

We went back to the sheriff's office and he told his dispatcher to call in all deputies both on duty and off duty for a meeting.

"Have the ones on duty now fuel their squad cars up on the way to the station," I told her.

The area covered was large so we needed to wait for the furthest cars away to show up. It was nearly seven o'clock before we started the meeting.

"Listen up and pay attention. Until further notice you don't leave your vehicles after eight o'clock at night to investigate anything. If someone calls in about a missing person you can go around looking from inside your squad cars. But I don't want anyone outside of their units exposing themselves. Do you understand me?" the sheriff asked his deputies.

"If we hear someone calling out for help we can't aid them?" asked a young deputy.

"We don't know what this creature we are facing is yet. For all we know it would be the creature calling out to lure you away from your vehicle," Connie said.

"Do you really think this thing is capable of doing that?" asked a second deputy in surprise.

"You were out at Cloud's ranch earlier today Bob. You saw the dead livestock. We totally believe the creature attacked the livestock to lure Kyle and Sandy out of their ranch house," Joe said.

"If the creature can lure the Clouds, don't you think it could also find a way to lure you to your death?" I asked them.

The deputies looked at each other in shocked silence.

"From this moment on, the night shift will have two deputies in each patrol car. No one rides alone," Sheriff Longbow said.

"We will only have half the units we normally have out patrolling at night patrolling," an older deputy said.

"Your math skills haven't deteriorated much Virgil. But it will also afford each squad car with two sets of eyes while doubling the manpower and firepower. Each squad car is to be carrying an M4 carbine and a shotgun loaded with buckshot," Joe told them.

"Will they kill this thing?" Virgil asked.

"Hell, we don't even know for sure if it will even piss it off. We don't know if this creature is killable. No living person other than Carl has ever seen it and he's missing," Joe said.

"We want you to make sure the squad cars you will be using at night are fueled up no later than seven at night. The only time you leave your vehicle is when you're parked in front of the sheriff's office. Bring a thermos along because there will be no stopping at the diner for coffee," I said breaking the news to them.

"The parking lot of the diner is well lit. It wouldn't attack us in a well lit parking lot would it?" asked the youngest deputy.

"Two trains of thought on that Louis. First of all, is a cup of coffee really worth risking your life for? Secondly we are imposing a curfew until further notice. All businesses will be closed down at seven PM to give their workers time to get safely home. That means all bars, restaurants, grocery stores, filling stations and any other business used to being open past supper time will be closed down to protect our citizens. If you see anyone not abiding by the curfew you are to arrest them and jail them for the night so they have a chance to think about the errors of their ways," Joe said.

"What about the radio station Joe? They normally broadcast 24/7." Virgil said.

"I made an exception for the radio station. It might have to broadcast warnings if anything happens. Their broadcast booth is on the second floor of the building. The bottom floor is all sales and management space. They know they have to stay on the second floor for the entire night and the doors going into the building need to be secured for the night."

"They are also using black out pull down shades so no one from the outside knows anyone is upstairs," Connie said.

"You're really giving this thing a lot of credit," one of the deputies chuckled.

"I won't get someone killed because we got careless or stupid, deputy. The front door of the radio station is ninety percent glass. I won't have him passing by and deciding to pay them a visit because he saw the lights were on upstairs," I said angrily.

"I didn't think about the door being all glass," the deputy said looking down sheepishly.

"Are there any questions about patrols?" Joe asked.

"Who is going to be partnering up tonight sheriff?" Louis asked.

"Oldest with youngest and the two middle experienced deputies will be together. So Louis you will be with Virgil. You already have shotguns in the squad cars. Pick up the M4 carbines out of the armory before heading out on patrol. Stay close to town unless you receive a call. Remember not to leave your vehicles under any circumstances." the sheriff said, ending the meeting.

Chapter Thirteen

O nce the meeting was over at the sheriff's office we got into our car for the ride back to our hotel. Our hotel was out of the area where the creature was hunting for its prey and in a different county. It was nearly eight thirty when we left Window Rock and the town was locked down tight. Not single business was left open out of fear of the creature they'd learned about at the town hall meeting.

I parked our car and took the streetsweeper out of the back seat and removed the drum magazine so the shotgun would fit into its case. There was a separate pocket on the case for the drum magazine to fit into.

We walked into the bar and sat down. I leaned the shotgun against the bar between us. After ordering drinks our conversation turned to our case.

"So what's on the agenda for tomorrow Ben? We aren't going to find this thing by staying in town."

"Yeah I know. I've been dreading having to go into the back country at night hunting for it."

"This case could easily turn real ugly," Connie said.

"Hell, it already has partner," I said, taking a sip of my cold beer.

"So where do we start from? Where the Cloud couple died or somewhere else?"

"I'm thinking we can begin at the Circle R ranch to start with. We can call the rancher in the morning and get him to loan us some horses. There are a couple of high ridges a few miles apart north of the ranch. We can put Sid and John on one ridge line and you and I can be on the other one."

"What are we going to be using for bait to draw it into us?" Connie asked.

"I hate to tell you this Connie, but we are the bait."

We ordered simple fare tonight, burgers and fries and stayed sitting at the bar while we ate.

"So watching for the creature from the ridge tops takes care of tomorrow night. What are we going to be doing all day long?" Connie asked.

"I'm not sure yet but we still have witnesses to talk to and who knows something might pop up in the meantime."

We finished eating and went up to our room. I turned on the news to see what was going on in the outside world. A Phoenix television station had picked up the broadcast from KNAV radio and were in Window Rock interviewing the sheriff. We just caught the tail end of the broadcast where the sheriff told them he would get them back safely into their van for the ride back to Phoenix.

The reporter chuckled at the thought of having an escort to walk twenty feet to his van.

The sheriff opened a three ring notebook and showed the reporter one of the crime scene photos and the reporter's face turned white.

"We'd appreciate you escorting us out, sheriff," the reporter said shakily.

"It's ten o'clock! The sheriff shouldn't have left his house to meet with them. He put himself at risk," Connie said as she watched the sheriff pick up a shotgun.

We went to bed right after the news and I fell into a fitful sleep. The events of the day and what was to come were spinning through my head. I could hear Connie in the bed next to mine suffering from the same thing.

Four o'clock in the morning my phone rang and I felt for it blindly on the nightstand.

"Yeah, Ben Hawk here," I said groggily.

"Ben, we've had a development. How soon can you get back to the sheriff's office?" Joe asked.

"We'll be there in an hour Joe," I said as I swung my legs out of the bed.

"What's going on Ben?" Connie asked sleepily.

"Something happened at Window Rock. They want us to come now."

"Five minutes for a shower first and then we can go," Connie said with a yawn.

"Good idea Connie," I said, stripping off my nightwear and bolting for the shower ahead of her.

"Ben, you're an asshole!"

"You aren't getting my towel this morning!" I called out through the open door.

Fifteen minutes later we were on the highway. I hit the lights and siren and pushed down on the gas pedal. We made the forty five miles in under thirty minutes. As we hit the edge of town I shut down the siren and lights.

There were a group of people in front of the sheriff's office standing around one of the squad cars.

We walked over to the squad car and could see the trunk and roof of the car were caved in at least a foot.

"What the hell happened?" I asked.

"Let's go inside so we aren't out in the open and talk," Joe said.

"So who was driving this squad car?" Connie asked.

"Virgil was driving and Louis was riding shotgun. Tell them your story Virgil," Joe said.

"We were staying close to town like the sheriff told us to when we received the call from dispatch. A woman and her daughter were six miles out of town and they ran out of gas. Could we go out to assist her. Well we had orders to not get out of the squad car except here at headquarters but we figured we could at least go out and give them a ride into town." Virgil said.

"Yeah, so we drove out to the stranded car and Virgil drove past it and turned back around so we were facing back towards town before picking up the two. I had my spotlight shining back on the stranded vehicle to make sure nothing was close by we needed to worry about. I rolled down my window a couple of inches and told the frantic woman to get into the backseat and to hurry," Louis said.

"We heard this God awful noise. It was so loud it seemed to shake the whole car. It sounded like this SKREEEEE,

SKREEEEE! But it was a thousand times louder than that and very, very close to us," Virgil said as his face paled, remembering the event.

"The woman yanked her kid out of the car and threw her across the back seat before diving in herself. I saw a blur of motion as the creature tried to grab hold of the door frame and missed. It slammed down on the roof of the car and again on the trunk before we could outdistance it," Louis said with a shudder.

"Did you get a good look at it?" I asked hopefully.

"Sorry, but it all happened in a blink of an eye. I saw this blur of off white and a streak of red as we sped away. But I could tell that it was big! Seven or eight feet tall at least." Louis said.

"Where are the woman and the girl?" Connie asked.

"I have them sitting in my office," Joe said.

"Bring them out Joe. they might have noticed something your deputies were too busy to notice," I said.

The two walked out and joined us. I could see how shaken up they were from the experience. The woman was in her mid thirties and the girl was probably around seven or eight years old.

"Did you see anything that might help us identify what attacked you?" Connie asked gently.

"After I tossed Gail into the car I dove in face first and didn't see anything but the car seat. I didn't even have time to shut the door before the deputies sped off," the mother said.

"Yeah after we were a quarter mile down the road the force of the wind from our speed shut the door for us," Virgil said.

"It was an ugly monster!" the little girl said tearfully.

"Did you get a look at it?" Connie said gently.

"I saw it just for a second. It had bright glowing red eyes and looked like it was dead for a long time."

"What do you mean that it looked like it was dead for a long time?" I asked quietly so as not to frighten her.

"It was like the animals you see dead along the side of the road that have been laying there for a few days."

"Do you mean the creature looked like it was rotting?" Connie asked in a shocked voice.

"Something like that. I want to go home!" the girl said as tears sprung into her eyes.

"Where is home mom?" Connie asked.

"We live here in town. I was out visiting my elderly mother and forgot to get gas before leaving town. I thought I had enough to get back."

"Once it's light out we'll get you to your home. Gail, would you like a can of soda?" Connie asked with a smile.

The girl nodded eagerly without saying anything as she wiped the tears from her cheeks.

Once Gail got her can of soda she sat clutching it tightly, her mind on her frightening experience.

"Don't worry Gail, nothing can hurt you while you're here with us," Connie said, giving her a reassuring smile.

"You know the monster might have been an alien!" Gail whispered loudly to Connie.

I turned around sharply and looked at the young girl while she spoke. The thought of what she was saying never crossed my mind.

"Mom, you remember last Saturday night when you and dad were watching that late movie. I was supposed to be sleeping and you caught me up? I was peeking around the corner watching it too."

The mother's face paled at the thought of what her daughter thought she had seen.

"What movie were you watching?" Connie asked, dreading the answer.

"We were watching the original Aliens movie where they were on the spaceship with the alien creature killing everyone."

Connie and I made eye contact with each other across the room. The thought of facing something like that was frightening, be it alien or a supernatural being from Native American legend.

"Is your husband home wondering why you're not back from your visit yet?" I asked.

"No, he's an over the road truck driver. He won't be home until Friday night," the mother said.

"Once it's light we'll get you home and then go out and bring your car back into town," Joe told her.

"Mom, do I have to worry about the monster coming to look for me? I saw what it looked like and it might want to kill me because of it!" Gail wailed as she started crying again.

"You'll be safe Gail. The monster doesn't know where you live. He is miles away from here," I reassured her.

"If he's miles away from here why do we have to wait until daylight to go home?" Gail sniffed.

Connie looked at me with a raised eyebrow waiting to see what I'd come up with for an answer to ease the girl's fears.

"Because the truck stop doesn't open until six and We're taking you and your mom out for a pancake breakfast. You like pancakes don't you Gail?" Ben said with an easy, carefree smile.

"They're my favorite! Can I have chocolate chips in mine?" she asked as she smiled through her tears.

"You sure can. You can even have whipped cream on them too if you'd like."

"Yum!" Gail said as she forgot all about the monster.

"Very smooth Mr. Hawk," Connie whispered to me, nudging me in the ribs.

"Who do you have for a crime scene investigator Joe?" I asked.

"Everything gets sent out, Ben. We can dust for fingerprints and take DNA samples but we have no actual CSI investigator in our small town."

"I want crime scene tape to be put around the damaged squad car so no one can get close enough to touch it and contaminate the evidence. I'll get a person here from Phoenix to collect the evidence if any exists."

"That's a good idea Ben. I wouldn't even know where to look or what to do if I did find anything so it wasn't compromised," Joe admitted.

I pulled out my phone and called Colin, waking him up. "I need you to fly a crime scene investigator to my location. Make sure he has all of his testing equipment with him," I said.

"What's going on Ben?" Colin asked with a yawn.

"One of the squad cars was attacked last night and heavily damaged. We need to see if any DNA was left behind by whatever did it."

"We'll be in the air inside the hour," Colin promised.

"Land by the truck stop. We'll be going there for breakfast once it becomes daylight."

"Alright Ben, I better get going. We'll see you in about three hours," Colin said, ending the call.

The sun came up and I watched as they taped off an area large enough to keep curious spectators far enough away to protect the crime scene.

"Alright Gail, climb into the sheriff's car and we'll go and get you those pancakes," I said as I put my streetsweeper back into the back seat.

Gail had her chocolate chip pancakes and followed it up with hot chocolate. Even with all the caffeine she was yawning sleepily from being up most of the night.

"I think it's time to get her off to bed mom," Connie said with a warm smile.

"Sheriff, why don't you take them home and then come back. We might as well have another cup of coffee while we wait for the helicopter to arrive," I said.

"Let's get you home and to bed so you can get some sleep Gail," the sheriff said as he pulled out her chair for her.

"I'm still scared Sheriff Joe. Can you look in my house first to make sure the monster isn't waiting for me?" Gail asked in a small scared voice.

"I just remembered, my keys are still in the ignition of my car. There is a spare house key under the ceramic frog though," mom said.

The sheriff gave the house the once over before walking back out to his squad car.

"There isn't anything in the house but your pet cat Gail," Joe reassured her.

"Did you look underneath my bed?" she asked in a small voice.

"I sure did and I looked in your closet too."

"Thank you Sheriff Joe," Gail said, giving him a tight hug.

"I'll get a therapist appointment set up for Gail. She is going to be needing counseling," Joe said quietly while hugging Gail.

"Thanks Joe, let me know when and where we need to be," she said, giving Joe a brief hug of her own.

Joe got back to the cafe and told us about looking through the house. We sat drinking coffee waiting for the helicopter to arrive. Time always seems to go by slower when you have to wait and after only getting six hours of sleep it seemed even longer. Finally we heard the wop, wop, wop of the approaching helicopter. I paid the bill and we went out to meet it.

Colin and his crime scene investigation tech got out of the helo and walked halfway and met us.

"Jimmy, these are Agents Hawk and Sanchez of the FBI and the local sheriff Joe Longbow," Colin said making the introductions.

"It's good to finally meet the two of you. Congratulations on wrapping up the Wisconsin case," Jimmy said while shaking our hands.

"Thanks, that was a difficult case for sure," Connie said.

"Colin, tell the pilot to stay here with the helicopter while we investigate part of the crime scene here. When we are done here we have to investigate the other part of it out of town," I said.

Colin relayed the message to the pilot.

"Is it alright if I get some coffee while I wait for you to get back?" the pilot asked.

"Sure, but get it in a to go cup and stay outside by the bird. I don't like the idea of leaving the helo unguarded. Someone already dropped a rattlesnake into Ben and Connie's motel room."

The five of us got into our car for the short two mile trip to the sheriff's office. A small group of curious onlookers were already gathering a safe distance from the damaged car.

"What the hell happened to your cruiser sheriff!" Colin asked excitedly.

"We don't know for sure. That's why you're here. They were attacked by a creature. We need you to help us identify what the creature might have been."

"Do your thing Jimmy. See if you can get any prints or DNA off of the damaged areas," Colin said.

Jimmy put on a pair of latex gloves and swabbed different spots for DNA before dusting for prints. Other than a few smears from the creature's contact with the vehicle he didn't come up with anything.

"We'll take you back to the helo now. I want you to follow us by air to the other location where the abandoned vehicle is. Once we arrive on site I want you to do a thorough aerial search a mile out from us to make sure this thing isn't still lurking around. We don't want any surprises. After giving us the all clear, go ahead and land on the road and examine the other vehicle.

"Alright, Ben. How far from town is it?"

"I think the deputies said it was about seven miles. Sheriff, can you contact the local towing service to follow us out to the scene. We'll have the car towed back to town. We won't let the family have the car back until we get results on the test Jimmy is going to be doing to their car," I said.

The sheriff called the local towing service. " Buck, Sheriff Joe, can you grab your tow truck and meet us by the truck stop? Plan on making a day of it. I don't know right now how long this will take."

"Does this have anything to do with the people being killed, sheriff?" Buck asked.

"It has everything to do with that Buck so if I were you I'd bring along a gun or two."

"I don't go anywhere unarmed anymore, sheriff. Not since this business has started up with the killing. A man can't be too careful can he?"

"No Buck, he sure can't," Joe said ending the call.

"He'll meet us at the truck stop," Joe said as he got into the car.

We dropped Colin and Jimmy off by the helicopter just as the tow truck showed up.

I explained what we were planning on doing. Performing an aerial survey of the area before getting out of our vehicles for safety reasons.

"I saw the squad car by the sheriff's office this morning. Tell your pilot to take his time with the survey and be damn sure we're alone," Buck said.

"What the hell is that cannon you got strapped to your waist?" I asked him.

"This baby is a fifty caliber with hollow points. If I don't put this damn thing down I'll at least slow him up a mite."

"What the hell kind of a machine gun are you carrying?" Buck asked me, seeing the drum magazine.

"It's a streetsweeper. I have forty rounds of double aught buckshot in it and ten rounds of dragon's breath."

"I never heard of dragon's breath," Buck admitted.

"They throw out a flame of white phosphorus one hundred feet from the barrel. Guaranteed to light anything they touch on fire," I explained.

"Damn, that could end up being useful."

"I sure as hell hope so because as of right now I don't know if this thing can be stopped."

"Get your helicopter in the air and follow us Colin. We're ready to head out. Buck, follow behind us and don't approach the stranded vehicle until we tell you too," Connie said.

"Roger that," Buck said, tossing us a salute.

We traveled out to the scene. The helicopter followed behind like a kite without a string. We got to the abandoned car and could see it was extremely damaged before we got near it.

We stopped fifty feet from the wreckage and waited for the aerial search to be performed. Twenty minutes later the helo landed in the road a hundred yards from the vehicle so they wouldn't blow away any evidence that might still exist on the car.

"All clear Ben," Colin shouted from the helicopter.

"I figured it would be. It seems like this thing only hunts at night. But there is no such thing as being too careful," I yelled back.

We walked up to the car. The windshield was crushed into the front seat. The hood, roof and trunk all had huge deep dents in them.

"I think they pissed this thing off for sure Ben. It looks to me like it had a temper tantrum," Joe said.

"I have a feeling it did all of this damage in only a few seconds. I think it started at the hood over the engine and slammed it only once. Then it moved to the windshield and hit it only once. Then did the exact same thing to the roof and the trunk."

"The strength of this thing must be incredible. I've seen full grown elk get hit by a car at highway speeds and not go through a windshield any further than this and they are eight hundred pound animals," Joe whispered in shock.

"Call out your Navajo Rangers. I want them to see what they're going up against," Connie said.

"If they're smart they'll resign on the spot," Joe said as he looked their numbers up on his phone and called them.

"Jimmy, it looks like there might be some skin and hair in the cracks in the windshield," I said pointing at what I saw.

Jimmy put on a new pair of latex gloves and grabbed a pair of tweezers and two small glass vials with rubber stoppers from one of his kits. He slid a pair of magnifiers over his eyes and bent down close over the windshield. He used the tweezers to choose and collected samples for testing.

Next he chose white fingerprint powder to use on the dark grey car to look for prints.

"Are you going to check the rest of the car for DNA?" The sheriff asked Jimmy.

"No Joe. If the DNA exists we have it from the samples I pulled off of the windshield.

"If you stand back and look at the windshield from this angle you can see a single huge handprint. I think the creature only slapped the glass with one hand!" I said in surprise.

"I would have thought it would have raised both arms over its head and slammed down with both fists," Joe said.

"If that is a single hand print, look how huge it must be!" Connie whispered horsely.

"Do you have anything for us on the autopsies from the bodies you took yesterday Colin?" I asked him.

"Preliminary results show both of their skulls were crushed first. Kyles was crushed face first and Sandy's was struck from the side as if she had started to run but didn't get anywhere."

"Were they able to collect any DNA from the beast feasting on their bodies?" Connie asked.

"DNA has been collected for testing but that takes time. We don't know yet if the DNA we collected is from only the victims or also the attacker."

Sid and John pulled up and got out of their car. Sid gave a low whistle when he saw the damage to the car.

"Our creature did all of this?" he asked in awe.

"We believe so. His next two victims escaped by only a wisker. He got angry at missing out on his meal and took it out on the car," I said.

"Do you still want to go out with us on the hunt tomorrow night?" Connie asked.

"It's what we signed up for Connie," John said unconvincingly.

"Well Ben, our chances of surviving just doubled," Connie said as she winked at me.

"What do you mean by that?" John asked.

"Well, the creature will have more than one choice on the menu. If it chooses you instead of us we get to live another day," Connie said, unable to not grin after seeing the looks on their faces.

"That isn't even funny!" Sid said.

"Remind me to put a nice juicy steak in her saddle bags Sid," John said unhappily.

"Does that mean we are going hunting tonight?" Sid asked.

"No, not tonight. We'll give the lab a chance to get us some answers on what we're dealing with. We'll put it off until tomorrow night and see if they can get a DNA match off of the windshield where they took skin and hair samples from," I said.

"Buck, go ahead and hook up to the car and tow it back to town. Park it next to the damaged squad car in front of the sheriff's office. Joe, can you get the vehicles covered with tarps and strapped down? We want to preserve any DNA that might still be on the two cars," I said.

"I'll call one of my deputies to get working on that right away," Joe said.

Buck hooked up the car and pulled up even with me when I waved him down.

"Go slow Buck, keep it under thirty miles an hour. We might lose a little evidence but we can keep the loss to a minimum."

"Will do Ben," he said, giving that off hand salute once again.

"Joe, call your uncle Jeff and have him meet us at your police station. Let's tell him what we know so far and see if it jogs his memory. Let's see if he has any idea now of what we're dealing with," Connie said.

"That's a good idea, I'll call him right now so he is waiting for us when we get back to town."

We passed up the wrecker a mile down the road and sped off to town. We couldn't afford to drive thirty miles an hour all the way back. We had an investigation to keep on track.

We pulled up in front of the sheriff's office. A deputy was busy unwrapping a large tarp to cover the cruiser with. Joe's uncle Jeff was sitting on a bench out front waiting for us.

"Thanks for meeting with us again Jeff," I said, shaking his hand.

"No problem Ben. I was just looking at this squad car. Did your mystery creature do all this?"

"He sure did. Virgil and Louis were on patrol and got a call about a disabled car. They pulled up next to it to rescue the woman and her little girl. They could hear the creature and it was close. They yelled for the two to jump into the back seat and sped off just as the creature reached them. It grabbed for the door frame and missed. Then it hit the roof and trunk of the car as it sped off."

"So this thing only hit the car twice and did all of this damage?"

"That's what the two officers reported and we have no reason whatsoever to doubt them," Connie said.

"We have their car being towed in now. It was heavily damaged by the creature. It looks like it had a temper tantrum because it lost its next meal," Joe said.

Buck showed up with the car and pushed in against the curb next to the damaged police car.

"Send the bill to the office Buck and I'll make it right with you," Joe promised him.

"Will do Joe," he said as he climbed back into the wrecker.

"Now if you stand over here at this angle and look at how the light hits the windshield you can see his giant hand print where he one handed smashed the glass and caved it in," I said.

Jeff gave a low whistle when he moved over to see what I was looking at.

"It would take incredible power and strength to do what this thing did. Did the officers get a look at it?"

"No, they were too busy trying to stay alive to get a good look. All Louis got was a blur out of the corner of his eye. But the little girl saw it and said it was a monster. She said it was over seven feet tall with a skull for a head. She said it kind of looked like the alien from the movie Alien," I said.

"Does that give you a hint of what we might be dealing with Jeff?" Connie asked him.

"It's nothing I've ever heard of or dealt with on the reservation. I started to look at Navajo folklore and haven't seen anything that can help yet but I'll keep looking."

"We'd appreciate any insight you can give us. The FBI crime scene investigator captured skin and hair samples off of the windshield. Hopefully we'll have a clue of what we're dealing with tomorrow," I said.

"Seeing the damage that was done to these two cars you might want to call the army and borrow a bazooka or a rocket launcher," Jeff said.

"I told Connie she might want one before we even left Washington the other day."

"When he said it I thought he was kidding. I don't think that anymore," Connie admitted looking at the wreckage.

"We still have five hours until the curfew shuts Window Rock down. If you're not going out tonight, what do you want to do with the time you have left until dark?" Joe asked us.

"We can talk to another one of the families who lost a loved one to the creature," Connie suggested.

"It was a part of the job I hated most. The only thing worse was having to notify a family about someone's death.

"Just as a footnote, I have some of the tribal men helping Jeremy's widow Clara and her boys move her things to town today. She sold her spread after we saw her the other day. She said she can't leave the place fast enough," Joe reported.

"I can understand her not wanting to stay out there alone with no close neighbors with her two boys," Connie said.

"Who do you have for us to talk to next Joe? Preferably someone not way out in the boonies." I said.

"We have one about eight miles out just off the main road. We can probably get there in ten or twelve minutes."

"Are they ranchers?" Connie asked.

"No, they're farmers."

"Farmers? Out here in all the cactus, rocks and sand. What on earth could they be farming?" I asked in surprise.

""They own land along the Cinnamon river bottom. The river is longer than you think. Yes, this time of year there isn't a lot of flow but it still always has water in it. Along the river bottom out a ways the land is pretty fertile," Joe said.

"So what do they farm?" Connie asked.

"They have several acres of vegetables they sell here in town and they raise hay to sell to the local ranchers. During the winter months the ranchers need all the extra feed they can get."

"Is it just the farmer that was killed and his wife living there?" I asked as we got into our car.

"No, they had four kids too. They're mostly grown up now. I think only one of them is still in school."

We drove out to the farm. The man of the house had been killed two weeks ago. He was the first one killed.

We turned down the farm lane. Someone was cutting hay on an older John Deere tractor. I parked by the house and the three of us got out of the car. An older woman came out of the house when she heard the car doors shut.

"Sheriff Joe, did you catch whatever killed my Tom?" She asked, her bottom lip trembling.

"No, not yet Karen. These are FBI agents Ben Hawk and Connie Sanchez. I asked them to come here and help us figure this thing out," the sheriff said gently. He could tell by looking at her she was still suffering greatly at the loss of her husband.

"We're trying to get as much background information on the killings as we can Karen. It could help us in the hunt for the killer," Connie said softly.

"Come on into the kitchen and I'll get us some coffee," the widow said.

"We sat in her spotless kitchen while she put water and coffee into her coffee pot before sitting down with us.

"We were told your husband was the first one that was killed. Can you tell us what happened that night?" I asked her.

"We had finished eating dinner. We always sat at the table and ate together as a family. After the dishes were done we sat in the living room and watched tv. About nine thirty our chickens started making a racket and our old dog Goldie started barking something fierce. Tom figured there must be a coyote after the chickens again and went outside with the shotgun he kept leaning in the corner of the kitchen by the door. Every now and then a coyote comes around looking for an easy meal." She paused and got up to bring the coffee to the table and poured it before sitting back down.

"So it was dark outside when all of this happened?" Connie asked.

"Yes, it had been dark for about forty five minutes or so. Tom went out the door and I heard Goldie start yelping in terror. Suddenly all of the chickens went silent and I heard Tom's shotgun being fired three or four times. Then there was a terrible screeching sound the likes I've never heard before and then dead silence."

"Did you go out to see what happened to your husband?" I asked gently.

"After whatever made that screeching sound we were afraid to venture outside. Then about twenty minutes later something slammed the back wall of the house three or four times. By then we'd already called the sheriff's department asking for someone to come out and find Tom."

"Two cruisers were sent out, Ben. They discovered Tom's remains out back behind the chicken coop. Their dog Goldie was also dead," Joe told us.

"Was there any damage done to your house where the creature hit it?" I asked, thinking of the damage done to the two cars.

"Come on out back and I'll show you," Karen said as she got back up again.

We walked around back behind the house. "Look up high, about ten or twelve feet up. Do you see those broken planks? They weren't like that before he came around."

"It looks like the plank siding is broken and the two by fours underneath are cracked too!" Connie said in shock.

"We measured it from the ground. Those broken boards are up ten and a half feet. This creature must be very big," Karen stated.

I thought back to the little girl, Gail saying the creature was over seven feet tall and knew she wasn't exaggerating.

We thanked her for talking to us before we got back into the car for the ride back to town.

"I didn't want to say anything in front of Karen but her husband was two thirds devoured. If what she says is true, that thing ate him in only twenty minutes before hitting the house on his way out of the yard," Joe informed us.

"He was probably pissed that nobody else came out to investigate. He had to cut his meal time short," I said grimly.

"Oh," Connie moaned, holding her head.

"What's the matter Connie?" I asked worriedly.

"I think I feel my white streak growing wider. This thing ate most of Tom, bones and all in twenty minutes or less! What the hell did you get me into Ben!"

"I warned you to stay in Washington, but you wouldn't listen to me. Now see what you got yourself into?" This was one time I didn't grin at her because there wasn't a damn thing funny about our situation.

"Where to now?" Joe asked us.

"Let's head on back to your office and get things planned and set up for tomorrow night," I said.

We sat down in the sheriff's office. "I think we can start searching by the Circle R ranch tomorrow night. We know the creature has operated in the area already so there is a chance he might come back there," I said.

"Yeah, we know they have the one major food group that will draw him to them, people," Connie said straight faced.

"Let's call John Goodearl and see if he'll loan us four saddle horses and four sets of hobbles," I told Joe.

Joe used his desk phone and put it on speaker. "John, Joe Longbow here. Can we borrow four saddle horses with hobbles for tomorrow night? We're going to go out hunting for this thing."

"Borrowing the horses is no problem Joe. But going after this thing after we've seen what it can do makes me think you're going out a little short handed to me."

"You might have a point John but we have no idea of what we're dealing with yet. The two FBI agents along with our two Navajo Rangers will be the ones going out after it."

"Well, they're either the bravest people I've ever met or they're complete fools. Seeing as how I've talked to them I don't think they're fools."

"Trust me we know what we're getting involved in. Did you notice the white streak in my hair? It wasn't there before I got here. It's got me scared to hell," Connie said.

"What did John Wayne say in that war movie? It's not about being afraid. It's about doing what's needed no matter what, that's bravery. All brave men have fear but they face it and fight through it."

"They also say a brave person dies but once and a coward dies a thousand times over," Connie shot back.

"Whatever I have is yours. We really need to find a way of stopping this."

"We'll be there a couple of hours before dark so we have time to get set up before this thing goes out hunting again."

"I'll have four good horses saddled up for you. I'll pick horses that are gentle and won't spook."

"Thanks for your help John. We'll see you tomorrow afternoon," I said as we ended the call.

"We might as well head on back to our hotel for the night Connie. Sheriff, can you get us some canteens for tomorrow so us and the horses have water?"

"I'll get you water bags. They hold more water and the water will stay cooler."

"We won't get here before late morning unless something comes up and you call. It's been a hell of a long day and we won't be getting any sleep at all tomorrow night. Tell John and Sid to rest up so they're ready for tomorrow night. Have them pick their weapons of choice carefully. Remind them we don't know what we are dealing with so try to think outside of the box on weapon selection," I said.

"You got it. I'll see you tomorrow," the sheriff said, getting up to walk us out.

Chapter Fourteen

W e woke up the next morning around ten o'clock to the sound of rain hitting our hotel room window. Rain was a rare thing in the desert this time of the year. I turned on the tv to watch the weather report while Connie was showering. According to the report it should be ending shortly.

"The shower is all yours Ben," Connie said as she opened the door and let a cloud of steam escape.

"From now on I get to shower first," I said.

"Why should you go first, sport?"

"Because I leave the door open when I shower so I can actually see my face in the mirror to shave when I'm done showering, that's why."

"You always find something to complain about don't you!" Connie said unhappily.

"Besides that, If I shower first I get to actually use my own towel instead of a couple of hand towels. You took my towel again!"

"Waa, waa, waa, Complain, complain, complain. Would you like me to call you a wambulance?" Connie said, grinning wide.

I looked at her, my eyes narrowing. "Okay, just remember when it happens you brought it on yourself," I warned her.

"Come on partner, can't you take a little joke?" Connie asked, grinning nervously.

My phone rang and I answered it without looking at who was calling.

"Ben, Colin here. We have the DNA and hair results off of the windshield and you're not going to like the results."

I put the phone on speaker so Connie could hear too. "Alright Colin, I have you on speaker so Connie can hear too. What did you learn?"

"The DNA results from the skin shows twenty seven percent human DNA and seventy three percent unknown.. The hair sample is not in any known database worldwide. You are dealing with a creature that is part human and a whole lot of something else."

"Is there a chance the DNA is cross contaminated. Could a human have touched the windshield either before or after the creature did?" I asked hopefully.

"I thought of that too, Ben. But the scientists tell me it's a single double helix DNA strand. So that means the DNA is from a single being and not two."

"How the hell am I to process that information!" Connie shouted out agitated.

"I don't know what to tell you Connie. I can only report the truth so you have accurate intel."

"This doesn't give us any kind of an edge over it. We still don't know what the hell it is. All we know is that it's big, strong, smart, incredibly destructive and unbelievably deadly," I said.

"I'll contact you as soon as I have any new information. Maybe the DNA from the bodies will show something different," Colin said hopefully, ending the call.

"Maybe we need to pull the plug on this Connie. We are incredibly exposed dealing with this unknown entity. All we know is whatever is doing the killing isn't human. We have no known means to kill it and if it gets close enough to us it will more than likely kill us," I told her after much thought.

"We need to call the director and update him, Ben," Connie said as she hit his speed dial.

"Agent Sanchez, you have an update for me on your case?" Director Burns asked.

"Yes sir. I have you on speaker. Ben is here listening in. We got hair and DNA results off of the windshield just now Sir. The hair sample does not exist in any database worldwide. It is an unknown creature. The DNA results show twenty seven percent human and seventy three percent unknown."

"I'm having a hard time wrapping my mind around that. You're telling me whatever is killing out there is unknown?"

"I warned you before we left Washington that we were going to be either dealing with a cryptid or a supernatural being. I'm sad to report that I was right sir," I said.

"Sir, we are dealing with a being of incredible strength, intelligence, speed and size. It's over seven feet tall. It has proven itself to be savage and totally deadly," Connie said.

"What do you propose to do?"

"I'm thinking of pulling the plug on the case sir. All we can accomplish here is getting ourselves killed. We have no known means of killing it."

"You seem to be the resident expert Ben. If you think that's best then do it."

"No, not yet Ben," Connie said to Ben's surprise.

"What, you want to stay now Connie?" Ben asked in shock.

"I'm just thinking about the next little boy or girl like Gail, Ben. If we bail from this case, who will keep the next one from being killed."

I saw the earnest look on her face and knew how much she'd struggled to get those words out. Most of Connie wanted to fly just as fast as possible back to Washington. But there was a small part of her that wouldn't let her abandon these people. I nodded my head in understanding.

"For now we're going to stay director. We want to at least get eyes on this thing so we have an idea of what we are up against," I told him.

"If this becomes too dangerous for the two of you to handle I want you to pack your bags and get the hell out of there. At the end of this case I want two live agents, not two more dead bodies."

"Yes sir. Tonight we are going hunting for the first time by horseback with the Navajo Rangers," I said.

"Call me tomorrow and let me know what happened overnight."

"We'll call as soon as we come back in director," Connie promised as she ended the call.

"Are you absolutely sure about this Connie?" I asked her. I could see the conflict waging a war in her mind.

"For now Ben. Go ahead and shower. We'll eat breakfast and then let Joe know we have more information and to have the Navajo Rangers come in for a meeting," Connie said.

After our phone calls with the director and the SAC the steam was off of the mirror and I could see my reflection. I don't know if it was my imagination but I seemed to have aged since we got here.

We got to the sheriff's office and the sheriff and the two deputies assigned to the Navajo Rangers were waiting for us in a small conference room. The sheriff's office was too small for the five of us to sit in.

I leaned my streetsweeper in a corner close to where I was sitting.

"You said over the phone you had results from the car's windshield?" Sid asked.

"We do, and it's not good news guys. The hair sample is in no known database. This creature has never been documented. The DNA shows twenty seven percent human and seventy three percent unknown," I informed them.

"Could the DNA have been cross contaminated?" John Stillwater asked.

"We asked the same question John and the answer we got was no. It is a single double helix strand." Connie said.

"So we don't know anything about the creature then?" Joe said.

"We know how big it is, how strong it is, and how deadly it is. We don't know if we have a way of killing it though."

"I just want to warn everybody here that the day might come where we have to pull the plug on the case. If we can't figure out a way of ending this without ending up dead ourselves," I told them regrettably.

"To tell you the truth, I'm surprised you haven't run off already," Sid said.

"We were close this morning when we got the test results. But Connie and I decided we wanted to get eyes on this thing before we called it a day. We want to at least know what the hell this thing is."

"We'll meet at the truck stop at four and eat before we head on out. We are borrowing horses from the Circle R ranch tonight," I said.

We have two water skins for each horse so the horses have water to drink. The two of you need to go buy stetsons today."

"Why do I need a cowboy hat?" Connie said, thinking they were pulling her leg.

"We have two skins of water each Connie. Your horse is going to have to be watered while we're out. How is your horse going to be able to drink if you don't have a stetson to pour the water into?" I asked her.

"Oh yeah, I didn't think of that."

Horses drink by slurping water, sucking it in. The sound they make when drinking sounds like they are sucking it through a giant straw.

"Let's go over what we're bringing along for protection," I said.

"I'll have my Glock and an AR15 with a bump stock so it will be like an automatic weapon. I'll have two thirty round clips and the ammo will be steel jacketed," John said.

"I also have my Glock with hollow points and a shotgun with an extended magazine so it will hold eight rounds with the one in the chamber. I'm thinking outside the box like you said. I'm loading it with rock salt. When dealing with the supernatural a lot of times salt and sage is used. The rock salt should be similar to buckshot," Sid said.

"My secondary weapon is on my ankle and is a .40 caliber. It is loaded with hollow points. My main weapon is also a .40 caliber but I have it loaded with teflon coated rounds," Connie said.

"Why teflon coated rounds? Sid asked.

"They'll go straight through a bulletproof vest. Not knowing what we're dealing with I thought it couldn't hurt," Connie said.

"My main carry weapon is a .40 caliber Sig and I have it loaded with hollow points. The streetsweeper holds fifty rounds. I have forty, two and three quarter inch shells loaded with double aught buckshot and ten rounds of dragon's breath," I said.

"What the hell is dragon breath? Joe asked.

"They are white phosphorus rounds. The flame shoots out of the barrel up to one hundred feet and will start anything they touch on fire instantly. My first ten rounds will be buckshot. The next ten will be the dragon breath followed by thirty more rounds of buckshot," I explained.

"Let's figure out where we are going to set-up for the night. There are two ridges here and there," I said pointing at the wall map.

"Yeah, you can see them off in the distance from the ranch house," Sid said.

"Right, You and John set up on this ridge and Connie and I will take the other ridge,' I said.

"We have some electronics to help you out tonight too. You'll each have a pair of night vision goggles and a handheld FLIR unit to share between you. We had them flown in by helicopter when we came," Connie said.

"That will help out a lot Connie. I sure hate the thought of this thing being able to sneak up on us," John said.

"The rancher is also supplying us with hobbles so our horses can't run off on us," I added.

"We'll meet with you at the truckstop to eat at four o'clock. So if there is nothing else Connie and I need to buy some hats."

"Window Rock will pay for you supper tonight Ben. Hell it might be the last one you ever get," Joe said.

"Not funny, not funny at all Joe!" Connie said, giving Joe her patented look.

"Hey, I was just trying to break up the tension a little bit," Joe said with a grin.

We went to the local hardware store where we were told they sold stetsons and looked at the selection.

Connie put one on and stood in front of a mirror admiring herself. "I'm a rootin tootin cowboy," Connie said while grinning into the mirror.

"You look more like a short little fat Mexican girl," I said laughing out loud at the look on her face.

"This short little fat Mexican girl is just about to unload a case of whoop ass on you! I have a gun and I'm not afraid to use it, Tex," Connie said with a Texas drawl.

"Do you think I should buy these spurs Connie?"

"Why would you be that cruel to your horse Ben?"

"I wasn't going to use them on the horse Connie. I was thinking once this case is over with and we can have sex again. I'd put them on and ride you like an unbroken colt," I said with a lopsided grin.

"You put those on before play time and the only thing you'll be doing is visiting the proctologist!" Connie said while giving me her patented look.

"Yeah, who needs spurs anyway. I can still stay on till the count of ten," I said grinning as I set them back down again.

"Wow, so you're going to up your game are you," Connie said grinning as she walked away with the hat as the grin slid off my face. Connie can be such an asshole!

We bought our stetsons. Mine was a light brown and Connie went with a medium brown.

"Well Tex, in another hour we'll have to sashay on down to the cafe," Connie said as she hooked her thumbs into her belt and showed off her sashay step.

"I have to say Connie, the hat pretty much hides the white streak in your hair."

"You're an asshole even with a cowboy hat on Ben."

I slid my sunglasses on and grinned before glancing at my watch. In a few short hours we would be out in the darkness either the hunter or the prey.

Chapter Fifteen

W
e pulled in front of the truckstop at the agreed upon time. The sheriff was already there ahead of us.

Connie tipped her hat to the back of her head. "This here town isn't big enough for the two of us, sheriff!" She grinned using her newly acquired Texas drawl.

"After tonight we might not have to worry about that, Tex" the sheriff grinned after seeing the new look on Connie's face.

""Y'all have a mean and nasty streak, a mile wide sheriff," Connie said, her grin turning into a frown.

"It pretty much matches the white streak you've been sporting in your hair Tex," Joe said, grinning wider.

"Time out, time out! You've been taking asshole lessons from Ben?" Connie said while the others laughed at her expense.

The talk turned serious after we ordered off of the menu. "Virgil and I will be stationed at the ranch. We will be able to respond quickly if you call for assistance," Joe said.

"How are you going to be able to do that Joe? That's pretty rough terrain," I said.

"I called in a favor and got an armored Humvee delivered to us this morning from a National Guard armory. It's ours for as long as we need it. Hopefully the Humvee can withstand an attack by this thing if it comes after us."

"The Humvee should be able to go just about anywhere a horse can go," I agreed.

"Hey, how come we aren't using the Humvee?" Connie asked.

"It's because we need to be out in the open where the creature can see us." I said.

"Oh great, so we are the bait!"

"Being on top of that ridge we might draw him to us like a

moth to a flame." I told her.

"More like a wolf to an injured rabbit," Connie mumbled.

"What was that?" I asked her.

"Nothing Ben. The rancher is supplying hobbles. What are they used for?" Connie asked.

"They're for when you are out in the rocks and desert where there aren't any trees or brush to tie off your horse to," Sid said.

"Yeah, you put them on the front legs of your horse. It can still move around enough to graze but it can't bolt and leave you stranded," John finished.

"Being stuck out in the middle of nowhere on foot would be bad," Connie agreed.

"Especially if that thing is still on the loose," Joe said.

"Yeah, especially then," Connie agreed.

We finished eating and those of us heading out on horseback left in our car for the ranch. Joe and Virgil went back to the police station to trade the cruiser for the Humvee before following us out.

We reached the ranch and as promised four horses were waiting for us. Connie walked over to hers and immediately started to adjust the stirrups for her height.

"She's done this before," Sid commented.

"Yeah, she grew up in Oklahoma and rode all her life," I explained.

"I'm glad Connie has riding experience and isn't a greenhorn. If anything were to happen and she was a greenhorn she wouldn't be able to stay in the saddle without falling off if we had to move fast," Sid said.

"John Goodearl walked out by us and shook our hands. "I hope you are successful tonight."

"This will be our first night hunt," I said.

"You can borrow the horses whenever you need them, Ben."

"We appreciate it, John."

"The hobbles are in the saddle bags. I see you brought water skins to water the animals."

The water skins were tied in pairs so you could throw them over the saddles to balance them out.

I handed John and Sid their night vision goggles and showed

them how to use them and then did the same with the FLIR.

Joe and Virgil pulled into the ranch yard and parked facing the ridges we were going to watch from tonight.

"The sheriff and Virgil are going to stay here in the ranch yard tonight. If anything happens they'll be able to reach us with the Humvee," Connie said.

"That's some pretty rough country you're heading into, Ben. Are you sure the Humvee can get there?"

"It'll get there John. When they designed it they made it part billy goat. The tires can't get a flat plus they are true four wheel drive. Also they have steel plates under them to protect the transmission and oil pan. There is power going to all four wheels all of the time. They even have a snorkel so they can go through six feet of water without stalling."

"The windows are all made up of bulletproof glass too," Connie said.

"Where are you going to be watching from?" the rancher asked.

"Sid and John will be on top of that ridge. Connie and I will be on top of that ridge over there. I figure they must be about five miles apart so we can cover a lot of ground."

"They're closer to six miles apart. They are far enough apart that if anything were to happen to either group the other group wouldn't have time to respond and come to help," John warned me.

"That's where the Humvee comes in. They might get the fillings in their teeth shook loose but they are faster than a horse and can respond to either location in about the same amount of time."

"Ben, we just decided to not post ourselves in the ranch yard. We'll give you a head start and then drive about three miles in your direction. It will shave several minutes off of our response time," Joe said.

"Make sure you stay in the vehicle Joe," I warned him.

"We will. There will already be four fools out in the open. No reason to add to that number," Joe said.

I gave Joe a look before turning away. "Alright, let's mount up and get into position," I said as I swung a leg over the saddle and grabbed my reins.

We left the ranch yard at a trot. Joe and Virgil were still talking to the rancher. We came to a fork in the trail after about three miles.

"Sid, you and John take that fork and Connie and I will take this one. I figure this is the spot where Joe will set-up for the night," I said.

We split up and rode the well worn trail. It took us another hour to reach the spot we would be setting up in.

I dug the hobbles out of the saddle bags and put them on our two horses. They must have been used to wearing them because they didn't put up a fuss at all.

"The rancher said he was giving us good gentle horses," Connie said as she rubbed the neck of her horse affectionately.

"Ben, after tonight I want a bigger gun," Connie said.

"You have two hand guns with specialized ammo in them now," I said.

"I'm the only one without a long gun. I need more than the penetration of my Teflon-coated rounds, Ben. I need something with some knockdown power."

It got dark out, it was a clear night and the stars were shining brightly. We were wearing our night vision goggles and watching with our backs together so we could watch all around us. From time to time one of us would pick up our FLIR and scan around the area. About two in the morning Connie began to yawn every now and then.

"Knock it off Connie, you're making me tired."

"Me too, Ben. Ben, can you turn around and look over where that dry creek bed disappears between the rocks," Connie asked me.

"What do you see Connie?"

"I might be imagining things Ben. But from here it looks like a man walking buck ass naked across the desert floor," Connie said.

I focused on where Connie was looking. It is a naked man walking barefoot across the desert. His feet must be shredded from walking across all that rock. Let's go and check it out Connie. It could be Carl wandering around lost," I said as I took the hobbles off of our horses.

"Hee haw!" I yelled out as I whipped my horse with the ends of my reins.

Connie being the lighter rider shot past me. I could see even in the darkness how at home she was in the saddle.

The naked man spotted us and started running away from us heading for the broken rocks of the wash wall.

"Why is he trying to avoid us, Ben?" Connie shouted.

"I think I already know but you have to see this to believe it," I said as my horse pulled even with hers.

The naked man disappeared in the rocks a hundred yards in front of us. Out of the other side bounded a wolf that zig zagged through the rocks and over the rise.

"Well Connie, you just saw your first shapeshifter," I explained to her.

"No I didn't, Ben. He's in the rocks hiding somewhere," Connie argued.

"Prove me wrong partner. Go after him and bring him out."

Connie dismounted her horse and handed me the reins before arming herself and following the footsteps of the naked man.

Twenty minutes later she was back, puzzled and alone. "I don't understand where he could have gone, Ben," she said looking up at me.

"Did we not see a naked man run into these rocks?" I asked her patiently.

"Yes we did, but..."

"Did we not see a wolf bound out of the rocks right where the naked man ran into them?"

"Yes we did, but..."

"Have I not proven to you in the past week there are things in this world we don't know about? Cryptids and things that are supernatural in nature?"

"Yes you did. But..."

"I told you when we started this case that I would have to do three things to you to keep you alive. I would have to teach you all over again how to see, how to hear and how to smell. Does your brain not believe what your eyes have shown you?"

"Oh my God, oh my God, I saw a shapeshifter!" Connie yelled out excitedly.

"I'm happy you're finally believing what your eyes have shown you. Now I need to work on your sense of smell and hearing to keep you alive," I said as I handed her the reins of her horse.

We rode back to our ridge and collected the hobbles. It was nearly five in the morning now and time to meet up with Sid and John. I radioed Joe and told him we were calling it a night. Sid and John echoed our message and we met at the trailhead by the Humvee.

"We didn't see anything but a pack of coyotes last night," Sid reported.

"We gave chase to a shapeshifter," Connie announced.

"You actually saw a shapeshifter?" Sid asked suspiciously.

"Connie spotted a naked man walking across the desert floor towards a dry creek bed so we gave chase. We thought it might be Carl lost and for some reason or another naked," I explained.

"When he heard and spotted us he took off running for the rocks. By then we were only a hundred yards behind him. He disappeared in the rocks and a big wolf bounded out the other side and zig zagged through the rocks and over the top of the wash," Connie said wide eyed.

"Connie was still a non-believer so I had her go into the rocks looking for the naked man. She came out empty handed."

"I saw a shapeshifter!" Connie attested still wide eyed.

"You saw a real shapeshifter," John agreed with her.

"A lot of people go their whole lives on our reservation and never see one. You were very lucky to have had the experience," Joe said.

"Are they dangerous? This one only wanted to get away and not be trapped," Connie said.

"We have never heard of one attacking anyone. But if they are one on one with someone defenseless, who knows," Sid said.

While we were standing by the Humvee we took off our hats and watered our thirsty horses before riding them back to the ranch.

We drove Sid and John back to town before heading to our own beds. We entered our room tired and dusty. I stripped down and headed for the shower and took a nice long cool shower to sooth my tired body.

"Hurry up in there Ben, You aren't the only one who wants to shower you know!' Connie called out.

I came out of the shower with my towel wrapped around my waist. "Your turn partner," I said with a grin of anticipation.

Ten minutes later Connie called out from the bathroom wondering where her towel was.

"When we left for the day yesterday I told housekeeping we would only need one towel from now on," I admitted with a wide grin.

"You did what!" Connie shrieked.

"I told them to only leave one towel from now on."

"What the hell Ben! Why would you even do something that stupid!"

"Waa, waa, waa, complain, complain, complain. Would you like me to call you a Wambulance?" I said grinning.

"Ben you are such an asshole!"

"I told you what goes around comes around. How is it when it's on the other foot?" I said as I watched Connie dance around with a small hand towel naked trying to reach her back.

"Connie, I think you missed a spot," I said, reclining on my bed.

"Watch it buster, I have a gun!"

"You'll have to show me where you are keeping it hidden," I said looking wantonly at the forbidden fruit of her naked body. Sex was off limits during an investigation. It made the time we had between investigations even more desirable.

"You look like you're in pain Ben, good!" Connie said as she saw I was starting to become excited.

We slept until around one when the phone in our room rang. Connie grabbed blindly for the phone before mumbling. "Connie Sanchez here."

"Sorry to bother you after being up all night but we've had another death," Joe said, yawning into the phone.

"Where?" Connie asked, instantly wide awake.

"Right on the outskirts of Window Rock," Joe reported.

"We'll be there at your office in an hour or so Joe," Connie promised before hanging up.

"Another death?" I asked, not opening up my eyes.

"Yeah, right in town too. Here we were last night, twenty five miles away and the thing goes hunting right in our backyard."

I swung my legs off the bed. "Well, at least we don't have to shower before we go, just brush our teeth. Connie, you still look slightly damp."

"Don't worry Ben, my memory is very, very long!" Connie threatened.

"If your memory is so long then you'll remember I was just getting even for you using all of the towels up yesterday."

I grabbed my streetsweeper and headed out of the hotel room to get the car. Connie was finishing brushing her teeth and soon followed. I parked under the overhang and honked for her. I could see her by the front desk talking to the girl working the counter.

"What was that all about?" I asked as I pulled out of the parking lot.

"What was all what about?" Connie asked me innocently.

"I saw you talking to the girl at the counter. What were you talking to her about?"

"Oh that. I just told her that we didn't need anymore towels left in our room by the housekeeping staff," Connie said with a smug look hidden behind her sunglasses.

"You did not either!" I said, looking at her sharply.

"Oh yes I did. I figured that if I didn't get a dry towel then you didn't either."

Connie could be spiteful and I couldn't tell if she was kidding or not.

"You can run naked up and down the hallway flapping your arms to get dry," she said smugly.

Connie can be such an asshole when she wants to be. The rest of the ride to Window Rock was pretty silent while I digested what she told me. Was she kidding or wasn't she?"

I slowed the car as we came to the speed limit sign for Window Rock before she relented.

"Actually I told her to have them leave three towels from now on, Ben."

"But I still get the shower first, so you can't steam up the mirror so I can see my face to shave," I reminded her.

"I don't know why you'd want to look at that ugly mug in the first place," Connie said as she got out of the car.

"Come on, Petunia, let's get the details on the latest death."

"Ben, you don't have to be such an asshole. We just got out of bed after only three hours of sleep."

"Hey, you started it cupcake," I said, leading the way into the building.

The sheriff and the Navajo Rangers were standing there waiting for us.

"What have you got Joe?" I asked as I slid my sunglasses up on my forehead.

"We had an older lady killed early this morning before sunrise. She went out into her front yard to pump some water."

"Everybody in Window Rock doesn't have city water and sewer?" Connie asked.

"No they don't, Connie. You'll discover especially on reservations the communities are very poor out here in the desert. The houses on the outskirts of town still use outhouses and a pump in their front yards."

"It's gotten better since they found oil on the reservation but we have a lot of catching up to do to join the modern world," Sid said.

"Everybody is being extra cautious with this creature roaming around. He's having a hard time finding a meal so he had to come to town to get one," I said.

"This is the first killing we've had in Window Rock," Sid said.

"Everybody knew the creature was in town too. This thing started screeching something fierce. It was so loud that it echoed off of the buildings we couldn't tell what direction it was coming from. I had patrols running all over the place trying to locate it but we couldn't," Joe said.

I called Colin and told him to bring the helicopter and a CSI agent for another victim before we left to see the latest body.

"Mrs. Hardwood is a widow. Her husband died three years ago," John told us.

"That might be a blessing for the husband. He doesn't have to witness this," Connie said as she got into our car to follow the sheriff.

There was a patrol car at the crime scene keeping people at a distance from the body, or what was left of it.

The pail was lying on the ground where Mrs. Stillwater had dropped it when she was attacked.

"Does she have any family in the area?" I asked.

"She has two sons and a daughter. The oldest son works for me," Joe said.

"He doesn't know what happened here?" I asked.

"No, yesterday was his day off. Otherwise he would have had to respond to the call," Joe said.

"Thank God for small favors. Make sure he doesn't find out about this until after we can get the body removed," Connie said.

"That's already been done. I have a gag order on the department. We just have to hope that no well meaning friend calls him and lets him know about his mother's death."

"I would hope most people would be reluctant to have to be the one to notify next of kin," I said.

"That's my least favorite part of the job, notifications," Joe said as he turned away from the body.

The sheriff's phone rang and he looked at the caller ID and grimaced. "It's KNAV radio, they must have heard about the killing," Joe said before answering the phone.

"Sheriff Longbow here," Joe said curtly.

"Sheriff, is it true that the widow Mrs. Hardwood has been killed?" the radio DJ asked excitedly.

The sheriff let out a long sigh before answering. "Yes it is Bob, but I'm asking you not to report it over the radio until the family of the victim can be notified."

"We at KNAV radio understand Joe. We wouldn't want to hear about a death in our family over the radio either."

"Thanks for understanding Bob. Once we are done at the crime scene and the relatives have been notified we'll come on over to the radio station. We need to talk to your audience and get more information out to your listeners. Give us four or five hours and we'll be over."

"Is it alright to just tell the listeners there has been another death but not who or where?" Bob asked.

"Sometimes a little information is better than none at all. You can tell them that, but only that. Like you said, don't tell them who or where. We'll be over to talk to you around supper time."

"Just who are we, that will be coming?"

"Myself, the Navajo Rangers and the two FBI agents here on the case."

"I can also report that we have an upcoming interview with you later this afternoon?"

"I encourage you to get the word out, Bob. The more people tuned in and listening, the safer everyone will be."

"Thanks, Joe. I'll start announcing the interview every twenty minutes or so. That will help so people will be telling their friends to listen in."

"Thanks Bob, you and the radio station are being a big help keeping everybody safe."

"We do what we can to help, sheriff," Bob said.

The doctor/medical examiner showed up with a body bag. Hell, a basting bag for turkeys would have been big enough I thought to myself as I looked down on what pitifully little remained of the old woman.

The helicopter from Phoenix flew overhead on the way to the truck stop.

"I'll go and bring them here Ben," Connie offered as she walked away. Anything to be away from the grisly remains of the poor old woman.

When Connie got to the truck stop the blades were still winding down.

"We need the pilot to stay with the helo again. I'll drive you to the crime scene. It's right here on the edge of town," Connie informed them.

The medical examiner was standing off to the side with us waiting for the crime scene investigator. We didn't want to take a chance of contaminating the evidence he would try to collect.

Colin came walking up. "This is Jody, one of our crime scene investigators working out of our Phoenix office. Jody, this is Ben Hawk, Connie Sanchez and Chief Joe Longbow."

"It's a real pleasure meeting the two of you and you too Chief," Jody said as he shook hands with the three of us.

"What's left of the body is over here next to the hand pump. I'll warn you now that there isn't much left of the body," I told him.

"Good Lord! Where is the rest of the poor woman!" Jody blurted out in shock.

"Probably in the stomach of whatever ate her. I'll tell you this, he has one hell of an appetite. A couple of days ago he ate two at once," I informed him.

"After feeding like that this thing should be sated for a long period of time. Perhaps longer than a week depending on its size," Jody said.

"I'm starting to think this thing might hibernate, maybe for years at a time like a cicada. Some species of them stay underground for seventeen years before emerging. It has to eat ravenously in order to stockpile calories for the long term," I said.

"That's not a bad thought at all Ben. Somehow that makes perfect sense that it would eat so often to stockpile calories before it disappears again. Then years later it comes out and needs to feed again to survive," Connie said.

"If that's the case then there should be a record of when it last appeared and killed folks," Joe said.

"You're right Joe. But maybe the last time he appeared it wasn't around here. Maybe it was in Canada or even Europe," Connie said.

"Colin, we need you to put some of your computer people on this. Have them do searches worldwide. See if anything like this has happened in let's say the last fifty years or so," I said.

"I'll get the right people working on it right away Ben," Colin promised us.

"I don't understand this at all. You're not talking about an insect like a cicada doing this. You're talking about some sort of huge creature with incredible power and speed," Jody said.

"Jody, we are talking about a being of supernatural origin. Something not of this plane or realm," I explained.

"Are you talking about cryptids?" Jody asked.

"No, cryptids are real breathing living beings. You might not believe in the Loch Ness Monster, bigfoot or shapeshifters but that doesn't mean they aren't real. This thing on the other hand isn't of this world as we know it. It might exist in another dimension other than our own. Or it might be an evil being from the netherworld," I said.

"You're talking this might be a demon? Something that has escaped from hell!" Jody asked as his eyes bugged out.

"Jody, the description of this thing is a being seven and a half feet tall with an animal skull for a head that is devoid of flesh. Tell me what you would gather from a description like that," Connie said.

I could see Jody was shocked and was having a very hard time dealing with something he didn't consider part of reality. He glanced around himself nervously.

"Relax Jody, this thing only hunts in the dark of night," Connie reassured him.

"Even so, I want to get this done and get the hell out of here," He admitted nervously.

"I can't blame you for that," Connie said.

"I'm in a turmoil. After your description I'm left to think about paintings in the Louvre museum that depict hell. Some of the beings in those paintings closely resemble what you describe what this being looks like."

"I haven't thought of that at all, but you're absolutely right," I said. I was glad my eyes were hidden behind my sunglasses so those there couldn't see the shocked look on my face.

The situation here was getting uglier and uglier. We could very well be dealing with something from the bowels of hell. Perhaps this wasn't a being of ancient Native American folklore afterall. I could feel this case slipping through our fingers into an area where we had no chance of winning. How could we ever explain to the director that we tucked our tails between our legs and ran because we were being chased by a demon from hell.

The five of us needed to sit down in private and have a quiet conversation. This thing was going sideways in a hurry and I didn't have a clue on if we stood a snowball chance in hell of stopping it, no pun intended.

Jody took his samples and put them in test tubes and snapped his case shut. The medical examiner bagged what was left of the body and we put it in the trunk of our car to transport back to the helo.

"Joe, we'll meet with you and the Rangers right after we drop Colin and Jody back off by the helicopter," I said.

"We'll be in the conference room," Joe said as he rubbed his tired face.

We unloaded the body and the agents by the helo and headed straight to the sheriff's office. The others were in the conference room talking quietly among themselves.

"Were you guys listening in on the conversation we were having with Jody?" I asked them after closing the door for privacy.

"No we were over by the medical examiner, why?" Sid asked.

"We gave Jody a description of what this creature looked like according to Gail. His response was that it sounded like the paintings of hell that are hanging in the Louvre museum. Here are depictions of Dante's inferno among other paintings there. Do you see any sort of resemblance?" I asked them after showing them the pictures on my phone.

I saw the same shocked looks on all of their faces. They could see how closely the paintings resembled Gail's description of the monster she saw.

"So the supernatural being that Gail saw might not be of Native American folklore at all?" John asked in shock.

"What if it's both?" Connie asked them, throwing them a curveball.

"I don't understand where you're coming from Connie," Joe admitted to her.

"See if you can follow my train of thought. I'm the only one in this room that hasn't grown up learning about and thinking of the Great Spirit with reverence, Right?"

"I guess that's true," I said.

"Okay, so hear me out. All four of you believe in some way in the Great Spirit, correct?"

"Yeah, it's part of all of our upbringing," Sid said.

"If you believe in the Great Spirit you believe good people will go to an afterlife, to be by the side of the Great Spirit?"

"Sure, good things happen to good people in the afterlife," Joe agreed.

"So what happens to the people who aren't so good, who are

evil?" Connie asked the group.

"They go to a place that's not so good. A place where they have to atone for their past transgressions," Sid said.

"It's the same with Christianity. We have heaven for the good people of the world where they will reside by the side of our Lord for all eternity. We also have a hell where the souls of the damned are tormented for all of eternity."

"We understand all of that Connie. There are those on the reservation who attend Christian churches just like everywhere else," Joe said.

"What if my God and your Great Spirit were one and the same entity? What if it were just two different names for the same God?"

There were looks of shock around the table.

"What if this supernatural being we are hunting is both of Native American folklore and a demon from hell? I'm not talking about all cryptids, just the supernatural beings."

"Who knew this thing would ever get to this point. What do you think, sheriff, is it possible?" John asked in a whisper.

"This is difficult for me to get my head wrapped around. We have the description of the beast by an eyewitness. Then we have paintings in an art museum on another continent that are identical to the description made by Gail. It's got to be more than a coincidence doesn't it Ben?"

I ran my hand through my hair wondering if I wasn't getting a white streak in it too. "I don't know what else makes any sense Joe."

"You told me when we came here Ben that you would have to get me to think like you. I needed to learn all over again how to see, hear and smell. It seems to me you might need to catch up to me a little bit now."

"I'm there partner, I'm there," Ben said with a dazed look.

"So if we go with the assumption that this is a beast from hell how do we send it back to hell? We can't kill it because it isn't alive," Joe said.

We all looked around the table at each other and no one was speaking their thoughts.

"Well gentlemen, that's the lesson for today. I'm ready to bail and go back to Washington now Ben. There is no reason to stay here and become its next meal if we have no chance against this thing," Connie said.

"You can go back Connie but I'm staying."

"Did you hit your head when you woke up this morning or something! Read my lips Ben, WE CAN'T WIN!"

"I'll have Colin come in the morning and pick you up in the helicopter so you can head on back."

"Sometimes you're a real asshole, you know that Ben? I'm not going to abandon my partner and not have your back, for all the good it's going to do us."

"How are we going to be able to fight this thing Ben?" Sid asked me.

"First of all, we need all the protection from this thing that we can get. I'll make a call to Colin and have him bring us six Christian crosses on chains we can wear around our necks. I know it's not part of our natural upbringing but if Connie is right then both our Great Spirit and the Christian God are one and the same."

"Why six of them Ben? There are only four of you," Joe asked.

"Don't forget that you and Virgil have backup rolls too. You'll also need protection."

"He'll have to bring them tomorrow, Ben. By the time he gets here with them it would be too late to go out tonight anyway," Connie reminded me.

I looked at the wall clock and saw she was right. "You promised Bob at the radio station an interview. We better go and do it before the curfew starts."

"When we talk to Bob we won't mention that this thing might be a demon from hell. The people here are already spooked enough. We don't need to make it any worse than it already is," Connie said.

We walked into the radio station and climbed the stairs to the broadcast booth. The on air sign was lit. Bob saw us and waved us into the booth.

"I've been promising you an interview about the recent loss of life. With me in the broadcast booth are FBI agents Ben Hawk and Connie Sanchez. Also here are our sheriff Joe Longbow and the Navajo Rangers Sid Canyon and John Stillwater. Welcome all and thank you for coming."

"We are always happy to share a little information if it helps keep people safe," Connie said.

"What can you tell me about the death that happened this morning?"

"Mrs Hardwood was murdered when she went for water from her hand pump before daylight," the sheriff reported.

"This is the first person to be killed in our town sheriff?" Bob asked.

"Yes it is, Bob. We speculate the creature came to town hunting because people are listening to you and not going out at night. The creature felt a need to come here to feed."

"If you live in town you are no safer than someone out on a ranch. You must heed our warning and stay indoors during hours of darkness," I said.

"We are trying to save lives here. We don't need people taking unnecessary risks and endangering the life of a police officer that has to respond to a call for assistance. Know this, the police have been ordered to not exit their patrol cars in the dark. Even armed we don't think they'll be any safer than the person they would be attempting to help," Sid said.

"Getting a bucket of water or going to the outhouse is a stupid reason to get yourself killed. If needed go to the hardware store and buy a bucket to pee in," John added.

"So if you're saying an armed police officer wouldn't be any safer against this thing than anyone else, how are you going to kill it?" Bob asked for his viewers.

"That's the rub Bob. We don't know how to kill it yet. We are still in the gathering information phase of the investigation," Connie said.

"Dead bodies haven't provided us with very much so far. No DNA or other evidence to help with the investigation," I said.

"We just need people to realize just because you live in Window Rock that doesn't automatically make you safer. Get inside before dark and stay inside until well after daylight just to be safe," the sheriff said.

"We will be back when we have more information to help the

public stay safe," I said before opening the door of the sound booth.

"This was a KNAV special public announcement. This announcement will be rebroadcast on an hourly basis for the rest of the day," Bob said as we exited the second floor.

"We'll meet with you for breakfast at eight tomorrow morning. The government will take a turn and buy," I said as our group split up and Connie and I headed for our hotel. We were operating on only three hours of sleep.

I cased the streetsweeper and carried it into the barroom, leaning it against the bar.

"No weapons are allowed in the bar and restaurant," the bartender explained.

I showed him my FBI credentials and he walked away to get our drinks without uttering another word.

"It's going to be an early to bed night tonight," Connie said with a big yawn.

"I hear you. I'm just glad we aren't out in the desert on horseback tonight."

"Yeah me too. What looks good on the menu today?" Connie asked.

"I don't know. I think I'll stay sitting right here and just have a grilled chicken sandwich and some fries."

"That sounds good but I think I'll have a salad with mine instead of french fries," Connie said as she closed the menu.

The bartender refilled our glasses when he brought out our food. A half hour later we were in our room crawling into bed and falling fast asleep.

Chapter Sixteen

I showered first the next morning, happy to have a steam free bathroom mirror. Connie showered next, happy to have a pair of towels for her use. I grabbed the streetsweeper off of my bed and we headed for the parking lot.

I walked around the car to open the back door so I could lay the shotgun on the seat. Connie opened her door at the same instant that I heard the snake rattle. Someone has tossed a rattlesnake into our car during the night.

"Connie, stop! There is a snake in the car!" But it was too late. The snake struck Connie right when she opened up her door.

"I've been bitten, Ben. A rattlesnake bit me, Help!" Connie screeched.

"Where is the snake?" I yelled as I ran around the back of the car.

"It crawled under the car after it bit me."

"Get in the car Connie. I think the closest medical help is still in window Rock, forty five miles from here," I said as I burned rubber out of the parking lot.

I hit the lights and siren before flooring the gas pedal. I was traveling down the highway at over a hundred and ten miles an hour. Twenty four minutes later I was pulling in front of their clinic. I rushed Connie into the building.

"Connie has been bitten on the arm by a rattlesnake," I yelled out.

"What kind of a rattlesnake was it?" the nurse asked as she rushed over.

"It was a damn big one!" Connie blurted out.

"It crawled under the car after it bit her and we didn't get a good look at it," I said.

"It was inside of your car?" the nurse said in surprise while having Connie sit in a wheelchair.

"Yeah, and it didn't open the door and crawl in by itself," I growled in anger.

The sheriff came rushing into the clinic. He heard my siren when I came into town and showed up to investigate what happened.

"Some asshole put a rattlesnake inside of our car and Connie was bitten," I growled out in anger.

"Is she going to be alright?"

"I don't know yet. The nurse just wheeled her back into the examination room."

Twenty minutes later a doctor walked out to talk to us. We gave her anti-venom and it should help soon but she is out of commission for the rest of today."

"Okay, thanks Doc. Joe, do you have someone who can stay with Connie at our hotel room until we get back?"

"Why, where are we going to be going, Ben?"

"The hotel has security cameras in the parking lot, Joe. We are going to find out who put the snake in our car. Then I'm going to beat the shit out of them before we toss them in jail for the crime of assaulting a federal law enforcement officer."

A half hour later Connie came back out of the examination room looking a little pale.

"I'm taking you back to our hotel so you can rest. Joe will have an officer stay with you until I get back to you."

"Why, where are you going to be Ben?"

"I'm going after the son of a bitches that put that snake in our car and beat the shit out of them," I growled.

The police officer that was going to stay with Connie showed up. I told him we'd be back as soon as possible and left.

"We need to see your parking lot security footage from last night Susan," the sheriff said. We fast forwarded through the footage until an old rusty white ford pick up truck pulled in next to our car. Two long haired men got out and grabbed a gunny sack out of the back of the truck and shook out its contents into the front seat of my car.

"Do you recognize who they are, sheriff?"

"Yeah, I know them. They live in an old run down shack out of town a mile or so."

"Let's go and pay them a visit. When we get there let me do the talking."

Whatever you say, Ben. It was your partner that was attacked."

Joe showed me the way to their shack. The rusty ford was parked in front so we knew they were there.

I knocked on the door hard and no one answered. I knocked again hard enough this time to shake the entire building before the door was answered.

"What do you want?" a greasy haired thirty year old man sneered at me. He was chewing on a toothpick.

"Do you think it was a wise decision to put a rattlesnake in my car?" I growled at him.

He was grinning at me and that really pissed me off! "You didn't let it go did you? It took us half the night to find and catch it," He laughed outright.

"I couldn't hear you with the toothpick in your mouth. Could you hear him sheriff?" I asked.

He pulled the toothpick out of his mouth. "I said....."

"My fist planted right in the middle of his face. I broke his nose and knocked out his two front teeth with the first punch. I grabbed him by the front of his shirt so he couldn't collapse. I hit him a second time and then with an uppercut the third time. With the third punch I could hear his jaw break. I tossed him in a heap off of the porch and went into the shack after the other man. The sheriff could hear the breakage of furniture as I attacked the second man. When I finally tossed him out of the door he was unconscious.

"Ben, there is hardly enough of them left to arrest," Joe said grimly.

"We'll take them to town and put them into a holding cell for now."

"But they'll need medical attention Ben."

"When Colin comes with the crosses he'll take them back to Phoenix with him and charge them with federal crimes. He'll make sure they see a doctor once he gets them back to the city and booked."

"Let's toss them into a cell then and go meet the others for breakfast. They're probably wondering why we're late."

"Ben, you have blood on your face. Where is your partner?" Virgil asked me as we walked into the cafe.

"It's not my blood," I said before heading to the bathroom to clean the blood off.

"Glen and Gene, the Storm brothers, decided it would be fun to toss a rattlesnake into Ben's car late last night," Joe told them.

"Connie isn't with you. Was she bit?" Sid asked.

"Yeah, as soon as she opened the car door it bit her arm. She got treated at the clinic and then Ben took her back to their hotel. I have Joey staying with her until Ben can get back."

"So why is there blood on Ben's face?" John asked.

"It's because Ben went and knocked on their door to thank them for the snake. It didn't go very well for the brothers. Glen has his front teeth knocked out, a broken nose and jaw. Gene didn't fare much better. He probably has broken ribs, nose and multiple lacerations."

"So where are the brothers now, in the clinic?" Sid asked.

"No, they're sitting in a jail cell as we speak."

"They will need treatment for their injuries," Virgil said.

"Ben is having them flown to Phoenix to face charges for assaulting a federal law enforcement officer. They will be treated at a hospital there. My guess is we won't have to worry about them again for at least three to five years," Joe finished as I walked back to the table.

"Is Connie going to be okay Ben?" John asked me.

"They gave her anti-venom. The doctor said she needs to rest until tomorrow."

Sadie, the waitress came with coffee for Joe and myself before leaving menus on the table.

"We won't be going out tonight because Connie is out of commission," I told them.

"Maybe instead of sending the Storm brothers to Phoenix to face charges we can use them for bait," Sid suggested.

"Yeah, we could be saving the taxpayers a lot of money if they were eaten," Virgil said.

"As much as I'd like to do that guys I wouldn't want to do the paperwork afterwards. I'd have a hell of a time explaining to the director how I let two prisoners in my custody get eaten by a demonic entity," I said.

"The sheriff can explain how they escaped from his flimsy jail. I'm sure your director would believe anything bad you told him about reservation cops," John said.

"I didn't get that vibe from the director guys. He seemed genuinely surprised you reached out for help. He said you don't like feds interfering with things happening on the reservation. In fact he said it was the first time he has ever received a call for help."

"Well he isn't wrong about that. We do like to handle things on our own," Joe admitted.

"I want to get back to Connie as soon as we get done eating, Joe. The helicopter will be here at one to drop off the crosses and take the prisoners. Can you make sure to get the crosses?" I asked him

"Sure no problem Ben. I have to be there to turn over the prisoners anyway."

"Our food came and all of the talk stopped while we ate. Everyone ordered steak and eggs with all of the fixings. It's amazing how hungry they were with the government buying. I ordered two muffins to go so Connie would have some food in her before heading back to our hotel room. By the time I got back to the hotel it was nearly eleven. It was going to be a long afternoon sitting around with nothing to do.

I called the director and reported to him that Connie was bitten by a rattlesnake left in our car.

"That's the second time something like this has happened Ben. Were you able to find the responsible party?"

"Yeah, the hotel has security cameras in the parking lot. I went and paid them a visit they'll never forget."

"I take it they resisted arrest?"

"Yeah, more than once too. Colin Sands will be transporting them to a Phoenix hospital for treatment before bringing them up on assault charges."

"Well at least that's one mystery solved. Now what can you tell me about the deaths happening there?"

"I don't know if you really want to know the answer to that question, director," I told him honestly.

"I don't understand Ben. Why wouldn't I want to know about your case?"

"First let me ask you a question. Are you a believer in the bible?"

"If you're asking me if I take my family to church the answer is yes. Maybe not every week but often enough to consider myself a regular church goer."

"Are you going to church to appease your wife or because you really are a believer in God and the words of the bible?"

"What are you getting at Ben?"

"I need to know the answer to that question before I tell you everything I know or else you'll just have to wait for the final report."

"I was sent to a Catholic school that was run by nuns, Ben. Is that good enough for you?"

"Well, sit down and hold on because I'm going to tell you a story that is going to set your head spinning."

"Hold on a second Ben while I secure the room," I heard a click over the phone.

"Alright Ben, let's have it."

"A lot has happened since our last report. The local police rescued a woman and her young daughter, but just barely. The creature just missed getting inside the squad car. The young girl gave a description of the creature. Seven to seven and a half feet tall. It had an animal skull for a head devoid of flesh with skin drawn tightly over it. Bright red eyes and what she thought were antlers. It gave off an awful screech when it attacked. Now I want you to do a search of the paintings in the Louvre museum in Paris. Look at the paintings depicting hell. Dante's inferno and the different levels of hell. Tell me what you see when you do the search."

"I see a creature just like you're describing, what the hell Ben!"

"This is going to get way worse as I tell you the story of what's happening, so hang on to your hat. We were sitting in the conference room at the police station after Colin flew off with the latest victim's remains. We started talking about the Great Spirit and Christianity and how they were so similar. We came to the realization that both Christians and Native Americans were maybe worshiping the same God but using different names for him. Both religions believe in life after death and good people get rewarded. They also believe in bad things happening to evil people. Now Native Americans have supernatural beings in their folklore. What if these supernatural beings were actually demons?"

The director sprung to his feet without realizing he did it. "You're saying this thing is a demon from hell!"

"It's a possibility director. We have Colin looking through the records trying to find where this happened in other places, in other times."

"I think I'm going to pull the plug on this and order you and Connie to come back to Washington."

"Hang on a bit, director. Let's talk about what else we know about the creature so far. We know its appetite is insatiable. It can't get enough to eat. It can devour more than one person at a time and do it multiple days in a row. I'm coming to believe that it, for lack of a better word, hibernates for long periods of time. It's storing calories for perhaps years of dormancy. It's super fast, super strong, intelligent, vicious and deadly."

"I haven't heard any sort of an argument for staying at the Navajo reservation Ben."

"If this thing is a demon from hell we don't know if it can be killed. Is it even considered to be alive? Do we need to seek out some sort of divine intervention to have a chance against it?"

"You're still not helping your cause, Ben. I haven't heard an argument for staying."

"It's all about keeping little girls like Gail safe and alive, Director. Making it so an old woman can fetch a bucket of water and not have to worry about getting back into her house alive."

"Ben, to me, to us in the FBI you and Connie are a valuable asset. I don't like exposing you like this. I want daily reports while you're on this case. If possible get pictures of this thing.

Being a religious man I'm extremely anxious to see a photo of this thing. If I tell you it's too dangerous you and Connie will be ordered to return to Washington. If and when that happens I don't want any arguments from either of you. I expect you to follow orders without hesitation."

"Alright director, I'm going to let you go now. Connie is starting to wake up and I need to check on her." I said as I ended the call.

"Welcome back partner, how are you feeling?" I asked with a worried voice.

"Ohhh, I feel like I got hit by a mack truck," Connie moaned.

"I brought you back muffins and coffee,"

"Ohhh, give me!" Connie said, holding and sipping her coffee two handed.

"I just got off the phone with Director Burns. He is concerned about this investigation and wants daily reports."

"You can be the daily report giver outer. I abdicate the duty to you," Connie said, her eyes still closed.

"I arrested the two brothers who put the snake in our car. Colin came and picked them up and took them back to Phoenix to stand trial after healing in the hospital."

"That didn't take you long."

"We had video of them putting the snake in our car. They thought it was really funny until I knocked their teeth down their throats," I growled, still angry.

"What time are we going out tonight?" Connie asked.

"We aren't going out tonight. The doctor ordered twenty four hours of rest for you."

"That's the best news I heard all day," Connie said before finishing her coffee and going back to sleep.

Our room had a balcony so I went out there to sit and read the local newspaper. The rest of the day passed slowly. I wasn't much for sitting around doing nothing.

Chapter Seventeen

Morning came and Connie seemed to be her old self again. Other than the bruising on her arm where the snake bit her she looked ready to go.

"I'm famished Ben, hurry up, I need to get something into my stomach."

I was wiping down the street sweeper while Connie was in the shower. I put my cleaning rags away and put the gun in its case. "Alright let's go and eat."

"Are we going to have the continental breakfast here or go into Window Rock to eat. The restaurant here doesn't open until eleven," I said.

"Let's compromise Ben. We'll grab coffee and a donut here. That will hold me over until I get some real food in me."

"I don't want a donut but I could sure use some coffee." We grabbed our drinks and walked out to the car. Connie was hesitant to open up her car door so I did it for her.

"You don't need to worry about any more snakes Connie. I'm sure by now word has gotten around about what will happen to you if you do shit like that."

I pulled in front of the truck stop's cafe. The sheriff's car was already there so we joined him at his table.

"How are you feeling today Connie?" Joe asked, concern showing in his eyes.

"I'm almost back to normal. Are we going hunting again tonight?"

"We'll get together later this morning and talk it out between us. The Navajo Rangers are busy right now but they should be free in a couple of hours."

"What are they up to?" I asked.

"There was a report of a hairy man raiding a hen house. The times being what they are, the person that owned the chickens wasn't going outside to check it out."

"That was a smart move. Are they sure it was a hairy man and not the creature trying to lure them out of the house?" Connie asked.

"She said yes. She has a yard light and she said it passed through the yard right at the edge of the lighted area."

"Still, if it was at the edge of the light it could have been our creature. It too is over seven feet tall and if the light wasn't very good..." I said not finishing my thought.

"Yeah I know Ben but like you said, it was smart of her to not go outside."

"Did Colin remember to bring the crosses along yesterday?" I asked.

"Oh yeah, here," Joe said as he took two crosses on chains out of his shirt pocket.

"Did the others get their crosses?" Connie asked as she put hers over her head.

"We all have them on," Joe said as he pulled his necklace out of his shirt to show us.

"Good, we don't know yet if they will offer us a level of protection but we do know it won't hurt to wear them," I said.

"If you go out tonight do you have any idea of where you want to set up," Joe asked as he put jelly on his toast.

"I haven't thought of it yet. But maybe we can set up near where that woman said a hairy man attacked her chickens. Maybe it was a hairy man but maybe it was our creature and it will come back for a return visit," I said.

"I guess that's as good of a spot as any. The last two attacks were twenty five miles apart so who knows," Joe said.

Connie wasn't a part of our conversation, Connie was too busy shoveling food into her face. She said she had a ravenous appetite and she wasn't kidding.

"Breathe Connie, Breathe," I said with a grin.

"Huh?" Connie said, finally coming up for air.

"Slow down a little bit or you'll start to choke."

"Shut up Ben and let me enjoy my food. I didn't eat anything yesterday except that puny muffin you got me."

"I got you two muffins."

"Did you not hear the puny part?" Connie asked as she went back to ignoring me.

"Don't reach for the salt Joe, you might just lose a finger or a hand if you get too close to her plate," I grinned.

"I must be feeling better Ben because you're back to being an asshole," Connie said, giving me her evil eye.

"Snake bites only rank one day of sympathy in these parts Connie. If you want it to last longer you'll need to lose an eye or a limb or something."

"I feel much better now," Connie said happily as she patted her full stomach.

"I'm glad to hear it, partner. Now pay for breakfast," I said with a grin.

"Huh?"

"Two days ago the sheriff paid for breakfast and yesterday I did. So now it's your turn."

"But yesterday I was bitten by a snake. I didn't get any breakfast when you bought it!"

"It's not our fault you're stupid enough to let a snake bite you. Do you see anyone else around here walking around with snake bite injuries?"

"Ben, you are such an asshole," Connie said as she pulled out a credit card.

"Is it always like this between the two of you?" Joe asked with a grin.

"Yep always, sometimes worse," I admitted.

"Yeah, like the time on our last case when I wrote, FBI asshole on your forehead and all day people were calling you an FBI asshole," Connie said as she howled with laughter.

"Or like when I got even for that and soaked you down with a bucket of dirty mop water," I said laughing at the memory.

"That part wasn't funny at all. My gun and credentials were soaked. I was drenched. I even had water in my shoes."

"We might as well head on over to the office to wait for Sid and John to get back,' Joe said as he pushed back his chair.

We got back to the office and sat down in the sheriff's office to wait for the others to get back.

Colin called me to inform me the two Storm brothers wanted to press charges against me for police brutality.

"They resisted arrest Colin and besides that, they threw a rattlesnake into our cruiser and it bit Connie," I said.

"They're claiming that you used excessive force during the arrest, Ben."

"They resisted arrest. They were whining that I let the snake they spent half the night finding, get away!"

"They actually said that to you?"

"Yep."

"Do you have any credible witnesses? I know Connie was recovering from the snake bite."

"The sheriff was right there and witnessed the whole thing. He even said after they finished resisting arrest that they were lucky I didn't kill them with my bare hands."

"Alright Ben, how did they go about resisting you?"

"Well, after they made their statement that they fully intended us to be snake bit, they resisted arrest by staying on their feet while I was beating the holy shit out of them. It's their own fault they stayed on their feet and didn't fall down."

"I saw the whole thing, Colin. Ben did everything humanly possible to arrest them peacefully," Joe said while grinning all the while.

"They even assaulted me with a pointy object," I declared.

"What kind of a pointy object did they assault you with Ben?"

"It was one of those wooden toothpicks."

"They assaulted you with a wooden toothpick? How did they use that to assault you?"

"He had it in his mouth and I had to ask him politely to remove it so I wouldn't stab myself with it when I flattened his nose and knocked out his front teeth."

I could hear Colin tearing up the paper over the phone while he was sighing loudly.

"We'll just go with the simple statement that they were resisting arrest. That while in the process of arresting them for assaulting a federal law enforcement officer. You and Sheriff Longbow had to use a limited amount of force to subdue them and carry out the arrest of the Storm brothers."

"Whatever makes it easier for you Colin. But if I had to do it all over again they might have stayed vertical a while longer."

"Yeah, I understand Ben. I would have been pissed if it had happened to my partner too. I'm going to offer them three to five years in a medium security facility. If they decide to fight the charges I'm prepared to go for ten to twenty years for attempted murder. They'll get back out when they're in their fifties."

"Are they still in the hospital or are they in jail cells now?" Connie asked.

"They're both in jail cells. Glen has his jaw wired shut because Ben broke it for him. Gene has five broken ribs and they both have to see the dentist to take care of broken teeth."

"I stick with my statement they resisted arrest," I said feeling very satisfied they were still suffering.

"Thanks for getting the crosses to me Colin," I said.

"I've been meaning to ask you why you needed them."

"I'll fill you in later over a beer when this case is over. You'll be wanting to see the looks on our faces when you find out the reason."

"Alright, Ben. If you need anything else you know how to reach us," Colin said as he ended the call just as Sid and John arrived back at the station.

"Let's move over to the conference room," Joe said as he stood up. His office was alright for small meetings but too small for the five of us.

"So how did the hunt for the hairy man go?" I asked the Navajo Rangers as I sat down.

"We got to the property. She only lives about three miles out of town. We could tell where the chickens were taken right away. There were feathers scattered everywhere. But the ground was so hard packed that we couldn't find any tracks," Sid said.

"How certain was she that it was a hairy man and not the creature that is doing the killing?" Connie asked.

"Well, that's just it. We questioned her about it and mentioned the creature. We asked just how certain she was that it was a hairy man and she suddenly was unsure and very frightened," John said.

"Yeah, we brought her to town with us. She is afraid to stay out there by herself now. We dropped her off at her brother's house. She is going to stay with him until this is over with. I promised her I'd stop over at her house and toss out some chicken feed every day or two," Sid said.

"When she gets back she is going to have a passel full of chickens though because we don't have the time to go and hunt for eggs," John said, grinning.

"What do you guys think about staking out her place tonight for the creature?" I asked.

"I guess that's as good a place as any. It's sort of like tossing darts or playing whack a mole. You never know where it's going to pop up next," Sid said.

"We'll meet at the cafe for supper at the same time and then go out and post for the night. Show us on the topographical map guys where her place is," I said, pushing back my chair.

"It's right here, right on the main road. Her driveway is only about a hundred yards long." Sid pointed out.

I looked at the map. The closer the lines on the map were the steeper the terrain was. "Why don't you guys post on this hill and Connie and I will post on this one. Joe, you and Virgil can you station yourselves in her front yard? That will put you about halfway between us."

"Is everybody wearing their crosses?" Connie asked.

Everyone nodded that they were.

"Are we using horses again tonight and if we are where are we getting them from?" Virgil asked.

"How rough is the terrain, Sid? Can we use our vehicles to station ourselves or do we need horses?" I asked him.

"Horses would probably be better Ben."

"Is it all open land like where we posted last time?" I asked.

"You see this thin line right here? That's a creek that flows down through her property. There are a lot of trees and brush along its banks," John said as he drew the line of the creek with his finger.

"Don't you have your own horses for when you're doing investigations?" I asked them.

"Yeah, but we don't have any extra mounts," Sid explained.

"Joe, can you call John Goodearl and see if he can bring us four mounts by trailer to her house? He can leave them in the yard and pick them up tomorrow morning," I said.

"I'll make the call," Joe said as he picked up his phone. After talking for a minute he hung up.

"He'll have them there in a couple of hours. He said that he would have them unloaded from the trailer and tied off in some shade."

"When we're on station make sure to pay particular attention to the creek bottom. That thing will probably use the trees and brush to hide its movements," I said.

"Make sure you have fresh batteries in your goggles and that the FLIR is fully charged," Connie said.

"I guess that's it. We'll see all of you at the cafe later this afternoon," I said as I got up.

"I'll have all of the water skins filled up so you have water for the horses tonight," the sheriff said as he sat down in the cafe.

"We forgot to ask you to do that, thanks Joe," Connie said.

The others showed up and we ordered off of the menus and ate our meal. No one was doing much talking. Everyone's mind was on the danger we would be facing exposed out in the open tonight. We finished eating and loaded up in our vehicles for the drive to the chicken farm. The sheriff had the Humvee with him tonight so he wouldn't have to go to the police station to trade out vehicles like last time.

We parked in the farmyard out of the way of where the sheriff and Virgil would be stationed. Grabbing the water skins we walked over to the horses and tossed the bags over the saddle horns.

"We'll see you in the morning guys," I told Joe and Virgil as I reined my horse around and headed for the summit of our hill. The streetsweeper was resting across my saddle horn.

It took forty five minutes to get on station. I put the hobbles on the horses so they couldn't run off. We could see a fair amount of the creek bottom. Looking over to where Sid and John were stationed I could see they had just as good of a view as we did.

"Connie, why don't you sit on this rock and use the FLIR to watch the creek bottom and I can stand behind you and look over your head and watch with the night vision goggles."

"Alright Ben, but we can trade off every now and then or my butt is going to get sore sitting on this hard rock."

"That's fair, an hour on and an hour off?"

"Alright, why don't you do a radio check to make sure the sheriff and the Navajo Rangers can hear us," Connie suggested.

"Joe, can you hear me in the farmyard?" I asked.

"Loud and clear, Ben."

"How about you guys on the other hill?"

"Crystal clear Ben," John reported.

I put the radio down on the rock Connie was sitting on and scanned the area. I wouldn't need the goggles for a couple of hours yet. Connie was using the FLIR even though it was daylight. It would still pick up heat signatures if something was hiding in the brush and vegetation along the creek.

An hour passed and Connie got up and rubbed her butt. "If we sit here again tomorrow we'll need to bring a cushion along to sit on. Time to trade places," she said as she handed the FLIR to me.

"Just before dark we watered our horses. We used two full water skins so we had two of them left.

Once again it was a crystal clear night, not a cloud in the sky. We only had a quarter moon though so we didn't have a lot of moonlight to help us out.

I looked at my watch and saw it was nearing two in the morning. I got up off of the rock and changed places with Connie again.

"Ben, something is going on in the farmyard. The chickens are acting up," Virgil reported.

"We don't see anything! Can you see anything from the other hill?" I asked.

"No, nothing Ben," Sid said excitedly.

"Whatever you guys do, stay in the Humvee and keep the windows up!" I yelled into the radio.

"We aren't getting out, trust us!" Virgil said.

"I just saw a shadow behind one of the hen houses," Joe reported.

We focused our attention at the three hen houses and watched for movement.

"Ben, I have something big crouching down behind the hen house on the right. The hens are putting off heat signatures too so I can't tell what it is with the FLIR."

I focused on the area Connie saw the heat signature with my night vision goggles. I could see what she was looking at and I stood still waiting for it to move.

Suddenly it stood up and left the farmyard in great ground eating steps. "Can you see it Connie?" I asked her excitedly.

"I see bigfoot! I see bigfoot!" Connie yelled out in excitement.

I moved behind Connie so I could see it in the FLIR too. "Connie is right, guys, it's a hairy man," I reported.

"We have eyes on it too," Sid said from the other hill top.

"We might as well wrap it up for tonight Guys. The lady was right, she saw a hairy man," I said.

We got back to the farmyard and tied the horses up in the same place we found them. We used the rest of our water to make sure the horses were well hydrated.

"Let's head for bed. We'll be back to town around noon," I said as we left the property.

Connie and I drove back to our hotel. After putting a do not disturb sign on the door we went to bed. It was now nearly five in the morning.

Chapter Eighteen

O nly four hours later at nine our phone rang and woke us up. "Ben here," I said half asleep.

"I just received a call from John Goodearl and he isn't very happy," Joe told me.

"Why, we left his horses right where we found them yesterday," I said with a yawn.

"He sent two ranch hands there this morning to pick the livestock up with a truck and trailer. When they got there two of the horses were dead and another one was so badly injured it had to be put down."

"Awe hell! We should have stayed until morning. But after we spotted the hairy man we figured the creature wasn't in the area."

"What did you say to him?" Connie asked.

"I told him what you just said. After spotting the hairy man we figured that was what the woman saw and it wasn't the creature we were looking for. I told him to figure out the price for the horses and turn the bill into the town."

"Give me the bill Joe and I'll have the FBI accounting department pick up the tab. After all, I'm the one who asked you to get the horses."

"I was hoping you'd say that Ben. I'm heading over to look at the dead horses now. Do the two of you want to meet me there?"

"Yeah, we'll see you in an hour or so." I said ending the call.

We threw on the same clothes we wore the day before and brushed our teeth before heading to the car. We stopped at a vending machine in the lobby and grabbed a couple of cold cans of soda to drink on the way.

We pulled onto the property. The rancher was standing there talking to Joe. The dead livestock were only a few feet away.

"Hell of a way to start the day Ben," the rancher said grimly.

"We wouldn't have left them here alone if we thought they were in any danger," I said.

"Hell, I know that Ben. I want that bastard gone more than ever now," John said angrily while looking at his dead horses.

"Come on over here John and I'll show you something," I told him.

"What have you got Ben?" he asked me.

"Look how the horse's neck seems all hunched up. Do you know what caused that?"

"I don't have the slightest idea," John admitted.

It's neck is broken, so is this one. The third one had its skull crushed in," I said pointing at the one they had to shoot.

"Good Lord! I have never heard of a horse having its neck broken. How is that even possible?"

"When we found the dead couple there was a big, big bull that had its neck broken too. The veterinarian said he didn't know of a single animal on this planet that could have done that. Sure a tiger, lion or a bear could maybe take him down and eat him. But they never could have broken its neck in the manner it was."

"How the hell are you going to be able to kill something that can do this?" John asked. I could see the shock in his eyes.

"That's the problem John, we don't know. Hell, maybe we can't."

"I have another trailer coming to haul off the dead livestock. At least one horse was lucky and came out of it unhurt."

"After this, are you willing to still loan me horses?" I asked him.

"I am if you're still willing to pay for any you get killed."

"I'll do my best to make sure this doesn't happen again," I promised.

"I sure would appreciate that Ben. Damn, those were really good horses. They didn't deserve what happened to them."

I felt really bad and responsible for what happened to them. Come hell or high water I was going to put eyes on this creature and get my shot at taking him out.

"Can you have four new horses here later this afternoon? I want to go into the creek bottom and hunt for it tonight."

"The livestock will be waiting for you," John promised.

"We might as well get some more sleep Joe. We'll see you in a few hours back at the cafe," I said as Connie and I turned away.

We got back to our hotel room. We'd forgotten to take the do not disturb sign off of the door so housekeeping didn't make our beds. I climbed back into my bed and put a pillow over my head to block out the sunlight and fell back asleep almost instantly.

We woke up again and finally showered and changed clothes before driving back to Window Rock. It was hot out. The thermometer at the bank said it was a hundred and two degrees. After dark it would start to cool down in the desert. People were surprised when you told them it got as cold as it did at night. After dark the snakes came out from under rocks and brush to hunt. Tarantulas, scorpions and gila monsters were roaming around looking for a meal. Seems like everything that came out at night was poisonous.

I mentioned this to Connie and my information was met with an icy stare. "Hey, I'm just trying to be helpful," I tried to explain.

"No you're not Ben! You're trying to be an asshole and you're succeeding."

I really wasn't but maybe, just maybe it was getting easier to get Connie's goat. I got a slight smile on my face as I slid my sunglasses over my eyes and walked out of the hotel carrying my shotgun. I looked good sporting my aviator sunglasses and stetson.

"Look who's the long tall Texan now Connie," I said as I shouldered the shotgun and struck a pose.

"Huh, looks more like an overgrown papoose with a mid life crisis to me. How long have you been sporting that gray hair Ben?" Connie asked as she grinned behind her sunglasses.

"I don't have gray hair Connie!" I said as I slid behind the steering wheel and adjusted the rear view mirror so I could see my reflection in it.

Connie peeked at me over the top of her sunglasses. "Still think you aren't turning gray in the temples Ben. Oh and you do have gray hair here and there on the back of your head too,"

Connie said as she slid her sunglasses back up and got a satisfied smirk on her face.

"You're way too good at being an asshole, you know that Connie?" I said unhappily. The gray in my temples shocked me to silence.

"Maybe you can get a white streak in your hair too, Ben. We can call ourselves Pepe and Petunia!"

"This would be a good time for you to shut up Connie!" Every time I looked over at her she had the same shit eating grin on her face. She is such an asshole!

We pulled in front of the cafe and were the last ones there again. We sat down and ordered iced tea like the rest of our group had.

"Where are we posting tonight Ben?" Sid asked.

"We'll get down in the creek bottom, at the edge of it. We'll stay under cover and look to the north across open country. Anything coming from that direction we should see a long way off."

"Yeah, but what if it comes from behind us out of the creek bottom?" Sid asked.

"You each have night vision goggles and the FLIR. One of you will have to be watching each other's six. Try to pick a spot where the trees and brush are thinned out so you can see a good distance around you."

It was so freaking hot out we all ordered BLTs and potato salad. No one wanted anything hot to eat. We finished eating and headed out to the chicken farm. The ranch hands were standing in the yard holding lever action winchesters.

"The boss said to stay with the horses until you got here, sheriff. He said he wasn't going to lose any more livestock to this thing," the older of the two ranch hands said.

"Thanks Owen. We'll stay with the horses until morning. Be back at day break to pick them up again," Joe said.

"Will do, Sheriff, we'll see you tomorrow morning," Owen said as he shut the back of the trailer and the two of them drove off.

I was busy putting the drum magazine on the shotgun and making sure there was a round in the chamber.

"Seeing as we're going to be inside the treeline tonight let's keep closer to each other. Let's stay within a couple of hundred yards," I said.

"It won't bother us to have back up closer in case it's needed," Sid agreed.

We left the farmyard in a single file headed towards the creek bottom. It wouldn't be dark for a couple of hours yet.

"Pull out your crosses and let them dangle outside your shirts. We want to make sure this thing knows we're wearing them," Connie said as she pulled hers outside her tee shirt. We all followed suit. No one was willing to say this wasn't a good idea or necessary.

Our horses waded through the creek. It was only about two feet deep. The tree and brush line was about a hundred feet wide on each side of the creek. The creek ran on for miles so it was a good way to travel unnoticed by anything that wanted to remain hidden.

"Sid, why don't you and John set up here and Connie and I will find a good spot a little further down," I said.

"Alright Ben, we can see almost all the way to the creek from here so nothing should be able to sneak up to us unnoticed," Sid said as he swung his leg over his horse and stepped down.

We continued on for a couple of hundred yards and found another spot just as good as the other one.

"Sid, we found a spot only a couple of hundred yards from your location. We are going to set up here," Connie said over her handheld radio.

"Roger that Connie," Sid said.

"We are on a slight rise and can see for a few miles," Connie added.

"Do you copy in the farmyard Joe?" Connie asked.

"We copy, stay safe out there tonight," Joe replied.

Just before dark the frogs started to croak and the crickets were chirping. It reminded me of simpler times growing up with my grandparents. Around two thirty in the morning the frogs quit croaking and the crickets went silent.

"Stay alert guys, something is disturbing the animal life because everything just went quiet," I whispered into my radio.

"Bcn, I can sense that it's close. Have Sid and John come to our location NOW! Connie yelled out.

I knew from past experience to trust Connie's instincts. "Get over to our location right now guys!" I yelled out as I dropped the radio and spun around so I could watch Connie's back. Our horses were becoming scared. If we hadn't tied them off to an oak tree they would have bolted for home.

I could hear the thud of hoofs as Sid and John raced for our location.

"It's here, it's close to us, get ready," Connie screamed out as she looked all around herself holding her weapon in a two handed grip.

John and Sid quickly tied off their horses before bringing their rifle and shotgun to the ready.

I took the safety off of the streetsweeper and scanned the area along the creek.

"One of you watch the open area to the north for it so it doesn't come up behind us," I yelled out.

"I don't see anything Connie! What did you see before we got here!" Sid asked.

"It's not what I saw, it's what I sensed. It's here, it's here, be ready!"

"I trust her instincts guys. If she says that it is close then believe her!" I said.

"SKREEEEE! SKREEEEE! SKREEEEE!" The creature screamed. The sound of it was so powerful that I could feel it shaking my entire chest.

"There it is guys, coming out of the creek," John shouted as he fired his first round of rock salt.

"Light it up guys!" I yelled out as I swung my shotgun into line with it. Sid had the bump stock and went through a thirty two round magazine in no time. It didn't seem to affect it at all. The rock salt seemed to make it hesitate a little bit.

Connie started hammering it with her teflon coated rounds and wasn't having any success. I brought up the streetsweeper and started hitting it with buckshot just as fast as I could pull the trigger. By the time I got to the dragon's breath rounds the others were using their back up guns. It wasn't looking good for us. The creature stopped thirty feet from us and continued to scream at us. I felt the crosses we were wearing were offering us some protection. Without them I think it would have been on us already.

I hit it with my first dragon's breath round and it lit him up something fierce! The first round hit him square in the face and his head was engulfed in flame. I kept pounding him with the rounds. Soon his entire body was on fire. It suddenly turned away from us and fled towards the brush along the creek.

"Let's get the hell out of here guys!" I yelled out as I grabbed the reins of our two horses.

"Why Ben, you have it on the run, don't stop now!" John shouted out to me.

"That was my last dragon's breath round. We don't have any more to use against it, so move your asses!" I shouted as I jumped on my horse and held Connie's so it couldn't bolt.

Sid and John didn't need any more encouragement. Soon we were riding pell mell for the chicken farm just as fast as our horses could run.

Joe and Virgil were sitting in the farmyard when we opened up on the creature.

"It sounds like world war three out there Joe," Virgil said as Joe started the Humvee and went bouncing towards the creek just as fast as he could over the rough ground. They met the others on their horses as they fled in their direction. Joe rolled down his window so he could hear us.

"We're headed for the farmyard. Stay behind us and if you happen to see that thing, run the bastard over with the armored plated Humvee!"

We shot past the sheriff and kept going. We didn't stop until we were back in the yard. The horses were out of breath from running so far but as scared as they were they would have run further.

The sheriff pulled into the yard and we all got into the Humvee to talk. It was the only place that offered any kind of safety out here in the darkness.

"Okay, let's hear it," Joe said, all business.

"It found us, is what happened," Sid said.

"Connie somehow knew it was close. How the hell did you know anyway?" John asked.

"It's just something I've been able to do all of my life."

"It's a damn good thing you could or it would have had us for lunch," John said.

"We fired everything we had into it and it didn't bother it at all, did it guys?" Sid asked.

"It got to within thirty feet of us and stopped. I think it didn't like the crosses we were wearing. At least that's my assumption," I said.

"I don't know if the rounds were bouncing off or going right through it for sure. I don't think it liked the rock salt but that still didn't slow it down much," John said.

"It didn't even blink when I hit it with rounds that can go through a bulletproof vest," Connie said.

"I fired sixty four rounds out of my AR15 hitting it center mass with every round and it just kept coming," Sid reported.

"So how did you escape if nothing you had could hurt it?" Virgil asked us.

"It was Ben and his streetsweeper Virgil. If he didn't have it along we would have been toast," John said.

"I fired off my first ten rounds of buckshot. By the time I got that far the others were out of ammo in their primary weapons. My next ten rounds were dragon's breath. They are a white phosphorus round that set him on fire. He didn't like that much and took off through the brush. We took that as an opportunity to get the hell out of there," I explained.

"You had him on the run, why did you stop?" Joe asked.

"I only had the ten dragon's breath rounds in the shotgun and I was out of them. We weren't sticking around for a repeat performance," I said.

"Oh boy, so now what?" Virgil asked the group.

"The dragon's breath turned him away from us. But as far as I could see it didn't harm it at all. It just didn't like being on fire," I said.

"We have no known method of dealing with this creature. I honestly don't know where to go from here. I can tell you one thing for sure though. I'm not going back out there until I have more dragon's breath," I said

"If you can't kill it and it doesn't like being lit on fire can that be a confirmation that it is a demon from hell?" Joe asked.

"To me it's just a confirmation that he doesn't like fire. The jury is still out on that. But it might have been my imagination but it didn't like us wearing the crosses," I said.

"I don't know what else it could have been that kept it from killing all of us, Ben. It stopped before you hit it with the first dragon's breath round and our other ammo didn't seem to affect it much," Connie said.

"I agree with Connie, Ben. If it wasn't for the crosses it would have been in our midst before you fired a single round of dragon's breath. I think that's what made it hesitate," Sid said.

"Yeah, it was almost like we had a force field around us guys. It could only get so close to us while we were wearing the crosses. It couldn't bear to be any closer to us," John said in agreement.

"I don't know if that's the answer for sure but I sure am glad we had them along," I admitted.

"That was a good call, getting the crosses Connie," Joe said.

Morning came with no more excitement. We were glad to see the ranch hands return with the trailer for the horses.

"Why don't we meet at the cafe for breakfast before we head off to bed. I don't think a bagel and coffee in the continental breakfast will do it this morning. "I'll tell you what, I'll even buy," Connie said.

"It must be the near death experience guys. She is trying to atone for all the times she was being cheap in the past," I said.

"Breakfast it is," Joe said as he started up the Humvee.

"I followed him in our car and ten minutes later we were at the cafe. We sat at the same table we normally took. It could seat six people easily.

"After we eat we better all get some sleep. Connie and I will have to call Washington and give the director an update. He isn't going to like what we tell him either," I admitted.

"You're not planning on going out again tonight, are you?" Joe asked me.

"No, we have to figure out a way of winning before we go out again. Right now all we'd be is an easy meal," I said.

"Ben will need to get more dragon's breath rounds for his shotgun too," Connie said as she put down her menu.

"You didn't do much with those teflon coated rounds, Connie," I said.

"Other than your dragon's breath rounds and the rock salt the only thing that kept us safe was the crosses. Before we go back out I want that grenade launcher," Connie said.

"I'll get right on that one Connie," I said dryly.

"I'm not kidding Ben. I've already looked them up and picked out the model that I want. It's a M320 grenade launcher. It has a drum magazine and can hold eight grenades. I want fragmentation grenades for it."

Our food came and all talk ended while we ate our breakfasts. Ten minutes later I was pushing back my empty plate.

"Get ahold of your uncle. Set up a time later this afternoon when he can meet with our group," I told Joe.

Chapter Nineteen

W e got back to our hotel room. Housekeeping had already come and gone. Connie and I picked up coffees at the continental breakfast bar and sat outside on the deck to have our talk with the director. The temperature was still tolerable at only eighty five degrees.

"Director Burns, I have you on speakerphone. Connie is here with us listening."

"First of all Agent Sanchez, how are you feeling after getting bit by the rattlesnake," the director asked, concerned for Connie's wellbeing.

"I'm back to normal, other than some bruising on my arm. Thanks for asking about it."

"Alright, tell me everything that's happened since I talked to you last and don't leave anything out."

"Well, that first day I really didn't do much with Connie being down and recovering. The next day we had a report of a hairy man taking chickens from a chicken farm."

"What is a hairy man?"

"It's a Native American word for a bigfoot," Connie told the director.

They couldn't see it but the director was pinching the bridge of his nose. To him all of this seemed to be impossible to grasp.

"We went out to the farm and saw where the chickens were taken by something. There were feathers scattered all over the place. We thought it might be possible she misidentified our creature as a hairy man. So we decided to look for it there that night."

"Ben and I were on one hilltop and the Navajo Rangers were on another one a couple of miles from us. We were overlooking a creek bottom that could provide our creature with cover. The sheriff and a deputy were stationed at the chicken farm as back up. They had the loan of an armored Humvee."

"About two or two thirty there was a commotion by the hen houses. We tried to identify what it was using a FLIR and night vision goggles. After a few minutes we spotted the hairy man carrying off a chicken," I said.

"You saw a bigfoot," the director said in a monotone voice.

"Yes, we did director. After spotting it we figured the woman who lived there actually saw a bigfoot and not the creature we were looking for. By this time it was around three or three fifteen in the morning and we called it a night," Connie reported.

"We tied up the horses where the rancher left them for us and headed to bed. About ten that morning we received a phone call saying two of the horses were dead and another one so badly injured it had to be put down."

"So Ben, you're telling me the creature was in the area all along?"

"Yes, that's what I'm saying. It must have still been hidden in the creek bottom and didn't appear until we left for the night."

"Oh yeah, you'll be getting a bill for three dead horses. We asked the rancher to provide them and they were killed. That makes us responsible for reimbursing him," Connie said.

We heard an audible sigh over the phone. "Is that your report?"

"No sir, we haven't gotten to the good part yet. We figured the creature must have come out of the creek bottom so we positioned ourselves on the edge of it looking across a wide expanse of open desert the next night. Connie detected that the creature was close by and called the others to come to our aid."

"How did you detect the closeness of the creature Connie?"

"It's just a sixth sense I have. I just somehow knew it was close and we were in danger. Do you believe in people having ESP director?"

"After the last week, week and a half I don't know what I believe anymore Connie," the director openly admitted.

"So anyway, back to our report. The others came running to our call for help just in time. The creature came out of the creek bottom behind us and attacked."

"You must have been successful in repelling it because you're still here."

"Yes sir. One of the rangers had an AR15 with a bump stock and fired off sixty four rounds into this thing. Another had rock salt loaded into his shotgun. Salt is a known substance to repel supernatural beings. Connie had her Sig .40 loaded with teflon coated rounds and I had my streetsweeper with forty rounds of double-ought buckshot and ten rounds of dragon's breath."

"You had all of that firepower and this thing still got away?"

My first ten rounds were buckshot followed by the dragon's breath. By the time I got to the dragon's breath rounds the others had run out of ammo and were relying on their backup weapons or reloading. I started hitting it with the dragon's breath rounds and it didn't like it much. It turned tail and ran back to the creek."

"As a footnote director. I had Colin bring six necklaces with crosses on them. The creature got within thirty feet of us and then stopped. The religious crosses could be the reason he stopped and we're still here," Connie said.

"It's true sir. That thing is so fast he could have been on us before I hit him with the first white phosphorus rounds."

"So, your group fired nearly point blank at that thing and missed it almost completely?"

"That's not what I'm saying. We hit it with almost every round but the rounds had no effect on it other than the dragon's breath."

"I'm going to send you more help. I can have a squad of Green Berets there by tomorrow morning."

"We don't want you to send them. Keep them the hell away and safe," I said.

"The last time I checked the FBI directory it said I was the director of the FBI and not you Ben."

"You don't understand what I'm telling you sir. They don't have the knowledge or the means of coming out on top. If you send them you'll be condemning them to their deaths. Unless they were raised by Native Americans they will be its next meal."

"Connie wasn't raised by Native Americans but she seems to be doing alright."

"I'm keeping Connie close to me so I can help protect her. Besides that she is starting to learn the old ways and learning all over again how to hear, smell, and see the way we do."

"I'm not going to pretend to know what you meant by that last part, Ben. But I'm sending you that help. I won't have you out there on your own. You have shown me you need more firepower."

"Best be ready to attend some funerals then because they aren't going to all come back alive. I can just about guarantee it."

"Small arms fire is useless. I think last night proved that. So if they come with 9mm handguns and M4 carbines all they'll be doing is ringing the dinner bell. If they come, have them bring along an M320 grenade launcher for me with fragmentation grenades loaded into it," Connie said.

"You want a grenade launcher, seriously?"

"We just told you small arms fire is useless against this thing. If Connie wants a grenade launcher to feel safe she should have one."

"Alright, is there anything else you need from me?"

"I need seventy five rounds of dragon's breath. Get it in three and a half inch magnum rounds if they make them. Otherwise get whatever you can in twelve gauge. Also I want fifty DumDum rounds in twelve gauge," I said.

"What are DumDum rounds Ben?"

"They're a slug that explodes on contact and are extremely devastating."

"Yeah, and send some body bags to haul away the dead green berets in too," Connie said.

"They are a highly trained army special forces unit."

"How much training did they get on killing demons 101? Who was in the top of their class director? What we've been trying to tell you is they are ill prepared for what is out there."

"Hold on a second director!" Connie said excitedly.

"What's the matter Connie?" I asked.

"I forgot when you had the creature running away I was able to snap a picture of it with my phone."

I watched as Connie pulled out her phone and opened the app that held her photos. The image of a fireball came onto the screen but the demon that was in the middle of the fireball was missing.

"Send the picture to the director," I told Connie.

"Why, Ben? There isn't anything there."

"That's why I want you to send it," I said. I could see Connie understood why now.

"I just sent you the picture I took last night," Connie told him.

"I don't understand, all I see is a ball of fire and nothing else."

"Exactly, the demon was fully engulfed by that fireball but seeing as it's a supernatural being it couldn't be photographed. Now do you understand what we are up against?" I asked.

"Surely you can see the folly of sending modern troops to combat a demon maybe thousands of years old. They will stand no chance against this thing," Connie emphasized.

"I'm sending them. Whatever you and Connie decide to use them for is up to the two of you. They will be under your direct command. They will be told to follow your orders."

"Make sure they bring more than pea shooters and spit wads because that's all their basic armament is against this thing," I said.

"I will make sure they are well armed. I will get your rounds to you as soon as possible along with Connie's grenade launcher."

"Until we get what we need to protect ourselves we won't be venturing back out into the field again," I said.

"You'll have to put them up in the Best Western where we're staying too," Connie told him.

"They'll have their army issued tents to sleep in."

"They need to be inside a building when they sleep. This demon won't be stopped by a synthetic tent wall, they won't be safe," Connie said.

"If you're determined to get them killed, make sure they have their own transportation. Humvees to start with and hearses for the return to their base. Oh and have them make sure their wills are updated too," I said bluntly, trying to get him to understand the real danger of sending troops.

"If they have to follow our orders and we are responsible for keeping them safe have them bring along their swim trunks too,"

Connie said,

"Why swimming trunks?" the director asked suspiciously.

"Because the only place around here to keep them safe is by the pool at our hotel. Out there on the reservation at night, even in town is not safe. The last one killed was right in town," Connie said.

"If you go out at night hunting for this thing they will go along with you. Do I make myself clear?"

"The only thing clear to us is that they are expendable. Why do you need to be so bull headed on this?" I asked.

"You and Connie are an extremely valuable asset to the FBI and I'm doing my best to protect that asset."

"Protect us by getting the equipment we asked for to succeed. Don't send troops to get butchered. You've seen the pictures of the victims. You know what this thing is capable of," I said.

"If that is all you have to report I'll let you get to bed," the director said curtly.

"One more thing, director. Say a prayer Sunday when you're in church for those you are about to sentence to death!" Connie tossed in just before the director ended the call in anger.

"Well hell, that went really well, didn't it?" I said, as I rubbed my tired face.

"What are we going to do, Ben? You're right about these troops being ill prepared to combat this thing. Even with your knowledge and having the crosses we were almost killed."

"I know Connie, I know. Let's try to get a couple of hours of sleep before heading back to Window Rock to meet with Jeff Longbow."

I lay on my bed with a pillow over my head but the events of last night kept me from sleeping. I was worried about the squad of Green Berets that were being sent to me. I was fearing for their lives and didn't know how to keep disaster from happening. We would have to wait and see what they showed up with for weapons before deciding their readiness.

Finally about noon thirty I heard the shower turn on. I knew Connie didn't do any better than I did sleeping. We both showered and grabbed soft drinks on the way out the door.

We got to Window Rock about two o'clock and pulled in front

of the sheriff's office. The two damaged cars were gone. The sheriff said he was going to store them inside until the results of the DNA tests on them were totally done.

We walked into Joe's office. He was sitting there with his uncle waiting for us. He looked as tired as I felt.

"The others will be here in twenty minutes Ben," he told us.

"Thanks for coming Jeff," I said.

"I wouldn't miss this for the world. Joe was just telling me all about last night when you came in."

"We explained to him our theory about supernatural creatures of Native American folklore and demons from the bible being one and the same.

"That's an interesting theory Ben and If you weren't a Native American I would take that opinion with a grain of salt."

"Connie came up with the idea first. But after we talked it out it made sense. We call our God the Great Spirit and they simply call him God. What if it is just a different name for the same God?"

"Joe told you about our fight with the creature last night and what he looked like?" Connie asked.

"He sure did. It sounds like he is describing a wendigo. But wendigos are more a supernatural being from the north. They are part of tribal legend in Chippewa tribes of Wisconsin and Michigan, Cree of Canada and the Blackfoot in Montana. They were never a part of the tribal legend of the southwest as far as I know."

"Connie, show them the picture of the creature you took last night," I said.

Connie pulled out her phone and opened up the app for her pictures. "In the excitement last night I forgot I tried to take a picture of it when it was running away after getting lit on fire by Ben," Connie explained.

Joe grabbed the phone eagerly wanting to finally see what was preying on the people he was sworn to protect.

"I don't see anything but a ball of fire!"

"When I took the picture it was of the beast totally engulfed by that fire. You can see the fire is surrounding something but you can't see what it's surrounding. This creature cannot be photographed," Connie explained.

Jeff was looking over Joe's shoulder at the image and had a stunned look on his face.

"Is this for real?" he asked quietly.

"Wait until Sid and John get here and ask them to verify it. They were there and saw the same thing we did," I said.

"Also we were all wearing Christian crosses Jeff. The creature got within twenty or thirty feet of us and stopped. I don't know if the crosses were providing us with a layer of protection or if he stopped for another reason," Connie explained.

I opened up my phone and brought up the pictures from the museum in Paris and showed them to Jeff. "This is the creature we saw last night. It is accurate in every detail. This is a masterpiece painted by Dante."

"That is identical to descriptions of wendigos. So are you saying that we are dealing with a demon and not a wendigo?" Jeff asked.

"Not at all. I'm saying both creatures are one and the same," I said.

"Has your research found anything helpful yet?" Connie asked.

"Something happened here on the reservation back in nineteen hundred and I'm still looking up information on it. Once I have it all compiled I will call you and give you a report."

"What kind of things were happening back then?" Joe asked.

"People were dying mysteriously. I'm still trying to uncover what happened. Eleven in all were reported dead in a three month period. But I'm still looking at old reports so there might be more yet. I still don't know what condition the remains were in when they were found though. You have to remember back in nineteen hundred we were still traveling on foot and horseback. Folks could have just come up missing with no remains located. It wasn't like it is today. No phones, no motorized transportation, no electricity, no radio or tv."

Sid and John arrived and the group moved over to the conference room. We showed them the picture Connie took last night and they were dumb founded.

"Jeff, we swear that creature was inside that ball of fire," Sid told his old boss.

"I believe you Sid. They've been bringing me up to date on what you all think this thing might be."

"We called our boss this morning and brought him up to date on the events of the last two days since Connie was bitten by the rattlesnake. He insists on sending us a squad of Green Berets to help take this thing out," I said.

"He is going to get them all killed," Jeff said bluntly.

"We know that Jeff but he got bull headed and insisted they come. He said they were under our command. We told him he was sentencing them to an early grave," I said.

"They're supposed to be here sometime tomorrow. We told him they needed their own Humvees for transportation here and a few hearses for their transportation back to their base," Connie said.

"What did he say to that?" Joe asked us.

"He said it was up to us to deploy the troops as needed and if we went into the field he expected us to have them in the field too," I said.

"What he is saying is if you deploy them wrong and they get killed it's all your fault and not his," John said.

"What an asshole!" Joe said.

"He has never been like this in the past. His city boy upbringing has him lost. He doesn't know how to respond to talk about cryptids and supernatural beings. We talked about the bible and he is a believer in it. He believes in demons too so he is on board about that part of it."

"I'm surprised he isn't sending us a priest. He is grasping at straws out of desperation. The last thing I told him before he hung up on us was to say a prayer in church on Sunday for the men he was about to kill," Connie said.

"When do you plan on going out into the field again Ben?" Jeff asked me.

"I'm not sure yet. The director complicated the whole thing. I have to wait for the troops and the ammunition I requested. Connie has her grenade launcher coming too."

"Did you order enough ammo so you can share with us?" Sid asked hopefully.

"I ordered seventy five rounds of dragon's breath and fifty rounds of DumDums."

"What are DumDums," Sid asked.

"They are a slug that explodes on contact tearing out great chunks of flesh."

"I just had another idea, Joe. You have silversmiths on the reservation, right?"

"Sure, our silver and turquoise jewelry are known the world over," Joe said proudly.

"I want one of them to mold very small silver crosses for us. I want them no larger than a dime," I said thinking as I talked.

"What do you want them for?" Joe asked in bewilderment.

"I'm going to take a few of my double aught buckshot rounds apart and load them with the pure silver crosses. If this thing really can't stand being close to a holy cross I want to give it a belly full of them."

"Make a couple for me too," Sid said grinning wide.

"Let's send this thing back to hell where it came from!" I said as I got up from the table.

Chapter Twenty

J oe took us to see a local silversmith and I explained to him what I needed him to make, what they were for and how many I needed.

"This necklace can wait until tomorrow. This project is too important to put off. I'll make a mold and start pouring them in the morning. It will take the rest of today to make the steel mold to pour the silver into," Greg, the silversmith said.

"Have a bill ready for us in the morning. I'll have to turn it into the FBI so you can be paid," I said.

Uh-huh, this one is on the house. Anything I can do to help you get rid of whatever is killing our people is free of charge," Greg said.

We went back to the police station and sat in the sheriff's office.

"I forgot to mention to you that the Storm brothers decided to take the plea deal. You won't have them around for a few years."

"Well, that's one less headache I have to worry about for a while."

"They decided it was in their best interest to not pursue the police brutality charges. They didn't want to risk twenty years of their lives," Connie said.

By now it was late afternoon and time to head back to our hotel before the curfew shut the town down.

"We'll meet you for breakfast at the normal place and time?" Joe asked us.

"Sure, eight o'clock it is. The Green Berets will be here some-time tomorrow supposedly," I said, shaking my head in disgust.

It was going to be a really nice night. One of those few nights where you wanted to milk every single minute you could out of it before going to bed. I got the styrofoam cooler out of the trunk we bought when we first got to town and loaded it down with ice and beer. Connie and I sat out on our patio enjoying the evening.

We called down to the restaurant and ordered room service to deliver cheeseburgers and fries. We sat making small talk while eating our food on the small table that sat between the two outdoor chairs. For at least one more night life would be good.

Morning came and I was woken by the ringing of my phone. My thoughts went instantly to the problem we were dealing with. Someone else was killed. I thought to myself as I grabbed the phone.

"Ben, this is director Burns. The Green Berets won't get to you until tomorrow."

"I still can't get you to change your mind on sending them?"

"No, my mind is made up. They won't get there until tomorrow because of the distance they will need to travel."

"You just remember one thing, director. When this is all over with, their deaths will be on you and not on us!"

"You're getting awfully close to being insubordinate, Ben!"

"When this is all over with you can have my badge if you want it. Even though this whole thing with the Green Berets falls squarely on your shoulders. Connie and I will have to live with it too. That makes you a real son of a bitch, you know that?"

"Ben, I'm warning you! You're certain that a highly trained military unit can't handle this?"

"That's what we've been trying to tell you all along."

"I'll tell you what. They are coming to your location. Keep giving a day by day report and If it is clear they are in over their heads and you can confirm it. I will have their orders rescinded."

"By that time you'll have bodies to collect."

"I have your ammunition, the dragon's breath and the dum-dums arriving tomorrow. Also Connie's requested M320 grenade launcher will be coming with the Green Berets."

"I'll let you know when the military unit arrives."

"The officer in charge is Captain Baker. He has been told that you and Connie will be in command of his unit."

"We won't be looking for the creature again until we have the ammo and Connie's grenade launcher on hand. To go out without those things would be suicidal," I said.

"So don't bother calling in another report until after you spend another night out or another person is killed," Director Burns said.

"Right, we have a couple of irons in the fire today that will occupy part of our day but we won't be going into harm's way."

"Talk to you in a couple of days," the director said, ending the call.

Connie came out of the shower drying her hair. "I left the door open when I showered so you wouldn't whine about the mirror being fogged up. Who was that on the phone?"

"Director Burns. We had words again about the Green Beret unit he is sending to their graves. They won't be here until tomorrow because of how far they have to travel."

"Are they bringing my grenade launcher with them?" Connie asked hopefully.

"Yeah, and my special ammo should be here tomorrow too. The director and I had words again. I offered to turn my badge in when we got back to Washington."

"What did he say to that?" Connie asked as I stripped down and headed for the shower.

He sort of tried to appease us. Said if they prove they are incapable of dealing with this he would rescind their orders."

"For them to prove they can't handle the situation there will have to be casualties."

"I agree totally. I told him that when that happens their deaths will be resting on his shoulders, not ours. Then I pretty much told him he was a son of a bitch for trying to make us be the ones responsible for their deaths."

"Get showered and shaved Ben or we'll be late for our daily breakfast meeting," Connie said as she pulled on her tee shirt.

Twenty minutes later we were going down the highway to the cafe for breakfast.

I'm glad we still have tonight off. I need to do some laundry. I'm running out of things to wear," Connie said.

"Yeah, so am I," I said, sipping on the coffee we'd gotten on the way out of the hotel.

"How many rounds do you still have in your shotgun, thirty?"

"Yeah, but they're all buckshot. Once the new ammo shows up all of the buckshot will be unloaded. It's proven to be ineffective against the wendigo."

"Is that what you're going to be calling it now?" Connie asked me.

"I guess either wendigo or demon would be correct according to what we have figured out about it."

"I guess you're right Ben. Wendigo it is."

We pulled up in front of the cafe, rolled up the windows and locked the doors. I left the shotgun on the backseat. Where I parked our car was right outside the window where we sat so I would be able to keep an eye on the car. Besides that, after what happened to the Storm brothers I figured nobody was stupid enough to mess with us again.

"Once again everyone was already there ahead of us.

"You're running late again Ben," Joe said with a friendly smile.

"We have to drive an hour to get here and none of you do," I said with an easy smile of my own.

"Good morning everybody," Connie said as she took a seat and helped herself to coffee.

"What do we have on the agenda for today?" Sid asked me.

"We have to check on the silver crosses and see how Greg is coming along with them. We need to have another interview at the radio station too."

"Why do we need to go to the radio station again?" John asked.

"Let the people know we met the wendigo in battle and barely survived the encounter. Give the people more information to help keep them safe," I said.

"Oh, and the Green Berets that were supposed to be here today won't be here until tomorrow," Connie added.

"So we're not going out hunting for this thing tonight?" John said with a relieved tone in his voice.

"Wendigo, demon, whatever you want to call it guys. But at least now we know what we're dealing with. We're still learning what we have to do to end this but at least we're making headway," I said.

"Didn't Jeff say the wendigo was a supernatural being that was part of northern tribe legends?" Sid asked.

"Yeah he did. But he also agreed the painting by Dante was an exact match to the descriptions he has heard of a wendigo. Like our conversation a couple of days ago, we now think the Great Spirit that we worship and the God worshiped by Christians are one and the same."

"But if this is a creature of legend in northern tribes what the heck is it doing way down here in the southwest desert?" Joe asked.

"Next time we see it Joe, I'll let you ask him why he is way down here instead of up north where he belongs," I said grinning over my coffee cup.

"You bring him over by my nice safe armored Humvee and I'll ask him," Joe said with a wink.

"I wouldn't want to bet my life on how safe you really are sitting in that armor plated tin can," Connie said.

"Do you have any idea of what the Green Berets are bringing for armament?" John asked.

"No, not a clue. But we told Director Burns their normal handguns and M4 carbines would be useless. All they would do with those is ring the dinner bell," I said.

"Yeah, that thing sure does have an appetite," Virgil said.

"Did you tell your director to make sure they had crosses to wear?" Joe asked me.

"I told him we felt the crosses offered us a certain amount of protection. I would hope he passed that message on to their officer in charge, Captain Baker."

"Having them here isn't going to be helpful. It could end up being a real hindrance," John said.

"We tried to convey that sentiment too but it fell of deaf ears," Connie said dryly.

Our breakfasts came and I got ham and eggs this morning. All conversation dried up while we ate our food. We finished eating and I picked up the bill today. The sheriff joined us in our car for the ride over to see the silversmith.

We walked into Greg's shop and saw he was hard at work pouring the crosses.

"Good morning. I won't be done pouring and trimming them until mid afternoon."

"They look exactly like what I asked you to make," I said, picking one of them up to inspect.

"I went onto the computer to get exact dimensions of the measurements. I wanted the proportions of the cross bar to be exactly what it should be to the dimensions of the upright beam. I figured if the dimensions were off, it might not do what you wanted it to do," Greg explained.

"The smallest intricate details could make all of the difference," Connie agreed.

"Yeah, if the dimensions aren't exact they might not have the desired effect on the wendigo," Joe stated.

"Do you think this thing is a wendigo?" Greg asked us in shock.

"We saw and fired on it two nights ago. The beast we saw is an exact match for descriptions we've heard of a wendigo," I said.

"No kidding? So if it's a wendigo, why the crosses?"

"Tune in to the radio station around two this afternoon and we plan on telling the whole tribe what we have determined. It's going to blow your socks off," Joe said as we left the shopkeeper with a perplexed look on his face.

We went back to the sheriff's office and Joe called the radio station.

"This is the bee bop Bob oldies show. Do you have a music request?" Bob asked.

"Bob, this is Sheriff Longbow. We want to meet with you again at two o'clock to update your listeners on the search for the creature. Start telling your listeners to tune in at two."

"Will do sheriff. I'll start making the announcements right away.

"Thanks Bob, see you at two."

"We break into our normal program for a special announcement. The Window Rock sheriff's department and the FBI will be joining us at two o'clock this afternoon for an update on the hunt for the creature that has been terrorizing our reservation. Tune in at two to stay informed. This was a KNAV special announcement. Now for your listening enjoyment, Hotel California by the Eagles!"

"How much do we tell them guys?" Joe asked us.

"During a normal investigation we give out information by the teaspoon full. We keep things to ourselves only the killer would know about in order to trip him up," Connie said.

I nodded my head in agreement with what Connie said before continuing on her train of thought. But this isn't a normal investigation. There is no human killer to trip up and capture. So we aren't trying to trip him up and capture him. We're trying to send him back where he came from.

"So we're going to tell the people everything?" the sheriff asked.

"We feel it's the surest way of keeping everyone safe. We won't hold anything back. The more information we give them the more precautions they will take," Connie agreed.

The sheriff nodded his head in agreement. "I have to agree with both of you. Better scared and alive than brave and dead."

"They don't have to be scared, just alert and cautious," I said.

"We have four hours until the meeting. What do you have planned until then?"

"I think we'll head back to our hotel for a while. I can start taking the buckshot out of some of my shells for the crosses to replace."

"Maybe we can stop back by the silversmith and take what he has ready now. Then you'll have some done and ready to go," Connie said.

"I'm a week behind on paperwork so I'll be right here when you come back to town," Joe said.

We walked into the silversmith's shop. He had display cases full of intricate silver and turquoise jewelry.

"I'm not nearly done yet," Greg said, lifting his magnifiers off of his head.

"We know Greg, we're not rushing you. I have a couple of spare hours before we have the press briefing at the radio station so I thought we could take the ones you have done and start assembling the shotgun shells we need," I said.

Greg handed me a sandwich sized zip lock bag with enough crosses in it to make maybe four or five shells with.

"I like the thickness you gave the crosses. They'll have some knock down power," I said looking through the clear bag.

"When you told me what you were using them for I figured I needed to make them thick, I couldn't take a chance of them shattering when they came out of the barrel of your shotgun."

"That's good thinking Greg. If they didn't stay intact as crosses they would be useless," Connie said.

We took the crosses and headed back to our hotel room. There was a small dish on the table in the room. It was for leaving tips on for the cleaning staff. I took the dish, a few shotgun shells and the crosses and went out onto our outside deck to work. Connie came into the room with cold soft drinks for us to drink.

I always kept a pocket knife in my pocket. From time to time it came in handy. I used it to pry open the crimped end of the first shotgun shell and poured the buckshot into the dish so they wouldn't roll off the table and all over the deck. I then placed the crosses one by one into the shell casing. The crosses wouldn't fit into the shell like round balls do so there was more air space between the crosses.

"Not being round the crosses don't fit as tightly together as I'd like them to," I told Connie.

"That's true but they are about as big around as a piece of double aught buckshot. They're still pretty thick but they're flatter," Connie observed.

After putting the crosses in the first shell I found out I could get nine crosses in it. I folded the crimped end back down on the shell. It didn't quite lay flat.

"Will it still work with the end not being completely flat?" Connie asked.

"As long as the crosses can't fall out and they can't. The shotgun will hold three and a half inch magnum rounds so the length is no problem."

I was able to make five shells with a few crosses left over for when we made the rest of the shells later today.

"We may as well head on back to Window Rock Ben. The news conference is in an hour and a half. That will give us time to go over everything with the others before we meet with Bob."

I grabbed my sunglasses and the shotgun and we headed back out again for the second time today.

We entered the sheriff's department and we could hear voices coming from the conference room so we headed there. The others were already there so we took chairs and sat down.

"I was just explaining to Virgil, Sid and John how the news conference was going to be playing out," Joe informed us.

"I don't see why Sid, John and I need to even be there, Ben," Virgil said.

"It's because we are taking phone calls after this one. There are callers that might want to ask a specific individual a specific question," Connie explained.

"I'm going to feel about as uncomfortable as a porcupine in a balloon factory for a fact! I just don't like being put on the spot with a bunch of dumb questions," Virgil admitted.

"It won't be a dumb question if it keeps someone from losing their life Virgil," Joe said.

"I guess that's true Joe," Virgil sighed, becoming quiet again.

"We may as well walk to the radio station. It's only three and a half blocks from here," Joe said as he got up and led the way out.

We were quite a group walking down the street together. The six of us walked, I had my shotgun over my shoulder. We stomped up the steps of the radio station to the second floor where the broadcast booth was located. The on air neon sign was lit just like last time. Bob motioned us into the booth through the glass sound proof wall.

"Thanks for coming. I'll let this song end and then we'll get right into the interview.

"This is a KNAV special announcement to keep our people safe and informed. This is Bee Bop Bob coming to you from the KNAV radio headquarters with our special guests. With us are Sheriff Joe, Sid and John, our Navajo Rangers, Sergeant Virgil and FBI Special Agents Ben Hawk and Connie Sanchez. Welcome to the KNAV sound booth. After this informative interview we will be opening the lines for questions from our concerned listeners."

Bob had lined up chairs for us to sit in during the news conference today. He had a boom mic suspended over our heads so the audience would hear the entire conversation. We all took seats and the conference began.

"It's been a few days since our last news conference with you. It was that day that poor Mrs. Hardwood was killed."

"After the FBI and the CSI investigator left we went back to the sheriff's department to talk things over. The CSI investigator said the description of the creature sounded like the masterpiece painting is the Louvre Museum. He said we should look at Dante's hell masterpieces.

"Refresh our memory, sheriff. Tell our listeners the description of the creature," Bob asked.

"It was reported to be between seven and seven and a half feet tall. Its head was the skull of an antlered animal. The skull was devoid of flesh with skin stretched tightly over it. Its clawed hands were huge and it had hoofed feet. Its eyes are a bright eerily lit bright red."

"We looked up the paintings that were mentioned to us and discovered they were nearly an exact match for the creature we are hunting for," Joe explained.

"So are you telling our listeners we have a demon killing our people and not a being of Native American legend?"

"Yes and no Bob. We discussed this situation in length and came to the following determination. We know there are going to be people violently against our reasoning but if you have a better answer call in afterwards. We would be eager to hear your opinion," I said.

"Okay Ben, you have our listeners' attention. Tell us your thoughts."

"Okay, we Native Americans talk about the Great Spirit with reverence and Christians do the same thing with the one they simply call God. What if our Great Spirit and their God were one and the same? We think this thing is a wendigo. What if a wendigo and a demon from hell are one and the same?"

"That would be an astonishing revelation Ben. Are all of you in agreement with this?"

Everyone nodded their heads in agreement.

"This is radio people not tv, you actually have to talk."

"Everybody was in agreement after everything was laid out Bob," Sid said.

"So call this thing whatever you want. If you call it a wendigo or a demon you would be correct," Connie said.

"Forgive me if I'm wrong but aren't wendigos from the far north and not the southwest?" Bob asked.

The Chippewa of Wisconsin and Michigan. The Cree of Canada

and the Blackfoot of Montana all have legends of the wendigo," John agreed with him.

"Yes, a lot has happened since the day Mrs. Hardwood died, Bob. The lady who lives out of town that everyone affectionately calls the egg lady called the sheriff's department to tell us a hairy man took a couple of her chickens one night. We thought it might have been a misidentification and she actually saw the creature we were hunting," I said and let Connie take over the narrative.

"We borrowed horses from the Circle R ranch for the night and positioned ourselves on hilltops between the chicken farm and the creek bottom. Ben and I took one hilltop and Sid and John took another a couple of miles away. The sheriff and Virgil were posted in the farmyard in an armor plated Humvee."

"Around two or two thirty we heard a disturbance by the hen houses and called the two teams to notify them. We detected a disturbance by the right side henhouse. The two groups on the hilltops had night vision goggles and FLIR units to help see at night," Joe said.

"Tell our listeners how night vision goggles and FLIR units work."

"Well, night vision goggles bathe everything in an eerie green glow so you can see at night. FLIR units detect heat signatures so you can see objects even if they're hidden behind trees," I said.

"We finally spotted the creature disturbing the chickens. The egg lady was right, it was a hairy man. Thinking she didn't misidentify what she saw the night before we ended the hunt for the night," John said.

"We got a call the next morning that two of the horses that were lent to us were dead and another one so badly injured it had to be put down. The wendigo was in the area all along and we left before we had a chance to confront it," I said.

"How did Mr. Goodearl take it when he found out the horses he loaned you were killed by the wendigo?"

"He was naturally upset by the news. The FBI promised to reimburse him for the loss of his horses. But that doesn't make up for losing good animals," I said.

"The next day he provided us with more horses. We figured the wendigo was using the cover of the trees and brush in the creek bottom to hide its movements. We decided to cross over the creek so we were at the edge of the brushline looking outwards across open ground," Connie said.

"The area around the creek bottom proved to be an active area. Between two and three in the morning Connie detected somehow that the wendigo was nearby. We called by radio to Sid and John to come to our aid. We positioned ourselves only a few hundred yards apart for the night because we couldn't see very far through the trees and brush," I said.

"John and Sid came galloping to our location and tied their horses off just in time. The wendigo came at us from the direction of the creek, and it came very fast. Before we knew it the wendigo was nearly on top of us. All four of us opened up with our weapons at nearly point blank range," Connie stated.

"Yeah, I had an AR15 and two thirty two round clips with a bump stock that turned the AR15 into a fully automatic weapon. Sid had a shotgun loaded with rock salt. We all know that salt has an effect on supernatural beings. Connie had her Sig .40 loaded with teflon coated rounds that can penetrate bullet proof vests. Ben had his streetsweeper shotgun with a fifty round drum magazine. He had forty rounds of double aught buckshot and ten rounds of dragon's breath. We can thank the Great Spirit for the dragon's breath," John said.

"By the time I unloaded my first ten rounds of buckshot the others were out of ammo and relying on their backup weapons or reloading. Every round seemed to hit the wendigo center mass but it didn't seem to have any effect."

"After our talk about a demon and a wendigo being one and the same I had six Christian crosses on necklaces brought to us from Phoenix. We were all wearing them at the time of the altercation. The wendigo got within twenty to thirty feet of us and stopped suddenly as if an invisible force was keeping it a bay. It screeched something fierce. The volume was so loud that it bounced off of our chests and echoed off the trees around us," Connie said.

"After I fired off the first ten rounds My second ten rounds were the dragon's breath rounds. Dragon's breath are white phosphorus rounds. The flame shoots out of the shotgun barrel up to a hundred feet. It lights anything on fire that it touches and it lit the wendigo ablaze. The first round hit it square in the face from about twenty five feet away. I kept firing as fast as I could pull the trigger. Soon the entire being was totally engulfed in flame. It took off at a dead run for the creek. The four of us jumped on our horses and got the hell out of there."

"We heard the gunfire from where we were stationed in the farmyard and it sounded like world war three. We shot out of the yard in the Humvee and met them coming out of the edge of the creek bottom. They flew past us on horseback and we hung back behind them to provide cover with the armored vehicle," Virgil said.

"That's incredible guys! But if you had it ablaze and on the run why didn't you follow it and finish it off?" Bob asked.

"Well first of all the rock salt did seem to have a small effect on the wendigo. I could tell he didn't like it much. Second of all I fired all the dragon's breath rounds I had on me. We were down to secondary weapons and buckshot and the wendigo already proved to us it was ineffective at protecting us from it. So it was time to get the hell out of there and come up with plan B," I said.

"So have you come up with a plan B?"

"We have more dragon's breath rounds on their way and DumDum rounds. Dumdums are slugs that explode on contact and can tear out great chunks of flesh. At least it can when dealing with a normal animal and not a wendigo/demon," I said.

"I also have a grenade launcher on the way. I felt too exposed out there. Everyone else had long guns and all I had was my service weapon and a small backup," Connie said.

"Unfortunately in his infinite wisdom the director of the FBI saw fit to saddle us with a unit of Green Berets to help out with this problem," I said with distaste.

"Why is that a problem if they give you more manpower and greater firepower?" Bob asked me.

"It's because they don't think like we do Bob. They see, but they don't see the way Native Americans see. They smell, but they don't smell the same things we do. Things that catch our attention will go unnoticed by them. They hear but they hear the sounds of the city and not the sounds of nature. Some of them will end up being killed and there is nothing we can do to stop it because we were given no choice in the matter," I said.

"We have Greg the silversmith pouring small silver crosses for us. The wendigo has shown he doesn't like to be near crosses. We are going to dump out some of my buckshot rounds and load them up with pure silver crosses. Let's see if a belly full of silver crosses can't send him back to where he came from," I said.

"When are the Green Berets and your new supply of ammunition supposed to get here?"

"Everything will be here sometime tomorrow. We figure on being back out looking for the wendigo tomorrow night," Joe said.

"This whole story is fascinating," Bob said in awe.

"People are paying attention to our warnings and staying inside at night. Keep doing that and we'll let you know when it's safe to go out at night again," the sheriff said.

"The last person killed, Mrs. Hardwood was killed in town because people who live out of town aren't venturing out because of the danger the wendigo poses. A tactic it is starting to use is to go after livestock to draw people out of the safety of their homes. We told you this in the past but no matter what you hear outside you need to stay inside," Connie reminded them.

"Okay, we will now take calls from our listeners. Call in to KNAV radio if you have any information about the wendigo or questions for our guests," Bob said.

Bob answered the ringing phone. "This is KNAV, you have a question for our guests?"

"Should we all be buying crosses and wearing them?" asked a frightened woman.

"Wearing a cross we felt helped to protect us. But if you just stay inside at night so far that has proven to be an effective deterrent," Joe answered her.

"This is KNAV, go ahead, listener," Bob said again.

"If this thing only comes out at night. Why don't our street lights keep it out of town?" a man asked.

"That's a good question. The street lights are only on the streets. What if the wendigo is traveling through people's backyards and staying out of the light cast by the lamps?" Connie said.

"Okay, thanks for the answer."

"This is KNAV radio, you have a question for our guests?"

"Are you set on the area you've been hunting for the wendigo in the last couple of days or are you open to looking in other areas?" a man asked.

"Why do you ask that? Do you have information that might be of value to us?" Joe asked him.

"Well, I have a cupola on the third floor of my old house. I use it for a sunroom. I like to sit up there and read too. I also have a telescope to watch the sky at night with. Lately at night I've been seeing strange things and hearing strange sounds on a pretty regular basis."

"What kind of strange sounds are you hearing?" I asked, my interest on high alert.

"Well before a few weeks ago I've never heard this before but it sounds like this SKREEEEE, SKREEEEE! A couple of nights ago it was really bad around four in the morning."

We looked at each other with shocked expressions on our faces. The wendigo was traveling back and forth across his property.

"What strange things have you been seeing?" I asked, the excitement mounting.

"Just a shadow crossing from the creek bottom across to the desert beyond my fields."

"I hastily scribbled a note and held it up so Bob could read it. Bob read the note and nodded his head. "We are going to a commercial break to hear from our fine sponsors," Bob said before nodding to me to let me know we weren't broadcasting anymore.

"We are off the air now so we can have a private talk with you and not have the entire reservation listening in on it. What is your name?" I asked.

"It's Joe, Joe Brown."

"I know where he lives, Ben. He does have a room on the third floor of his house," Joe said.

"Mr. Brown, would it be alright with you if we came out and you could show us what's happening and where it's happening?" I asked him.

"Sure, I guess it would be alright. Anything to end the killing that's been going on."

"We are on our way and we'll be there soon," I said as we all got up and left.

"We will rebroadcast this at four o'clock so tell your friends to listen in," I heard Bob say as the door closed behind us.

We just about jogged all the way back to the sheriff's office to get our cars.

"Remind me next time to drive over to the radio station in case this happens again," Connie called out as she brought up the rear.

All six of us were going out to the Brown property. This was important and I wanted everyone to hear the homeowner first hand. We traveled in two cars. Joe jumped in with Connie and I and the other three officers took one of their cruisers.

"Point me in the right direction Joe," I said as I backed out away from the curb where I'd angled parked. Twenty minutes later we were going up the driveway. The homeowner was sitting on the front porch waiting for us.

"You got here pretty fast Joe. I see you brought the entire posse with you too."

"Good to see you again Joe. How come you waited until now to tell us about this?" the sheriff asked.

"Well sheriff, it's like this. When I first started to hear the noise I thought it was a mating pair of sandhill cranes. I actually had a nesting pair down by the creek last year and thought they might have come back. The sound this thing makes sounds a lot like a sandhill crane but it's ten times louder.

"I know what a sandhill crane sounds like too. They are loud and do sound similar to the wendigo but like you said, louder," I agreed.

"After listening in to your broadcast today I realized things weren't adding up for me."

"Why do you say that?" Virgil asked.

"Well, for one thing I was hearing it at night after dark. Sandhill cranes aren't night birds so that part of it didn't make any sense."

"You said you were hearing and seeing strange things. What strange things have you been seeing?" Connie asked.

"I was over by the creek bottom yesterday and there was a lot of damage in a fairly small area. Brush uprooted, large tree limbs snapped off of cottonwood trees. It was like something huge was in there having a temper tantrum. We haven't had any storms that could have accounted for the damage to my creek bottom. Also the damage was localized to a small thirty foot area."

"Can you take us to the area and let us see it for ourselves?" Sid asked him.

"Sure, but it's a bit of a walk. We have to cross over my hay field and walk about a mile beyond it."

I grabbed my shotgun from the backseat and carried it over my shoulder. The homeowner eyed the strange drum magazine on it.

"I don't go anywhere without this, just in case," I explained.

"I thought you reported it only came out at night?"

"We did report that but if he changes his patterns I don't want to be without this."

"The hay field was large, several hundred acres in size.

"So what made you decide to walk all the way over to where the damage is?" John asked as we walked through the knee high hay.

"It's because I've been hearing this thing just about every night and got curious. Two nights ago was the worst. That must have been the night he did all of this damage. He was so loud he rattled the windows in the cupola. It scared the hell out of me. I didn't know what it was but I knew it wasn't my nesting pair of sandhills. Then I listened to your news conference and instantly knew I needed to call you and tell you what I knew."

"We sure are glad you did Joe," the sheriff said.

We got across the hay field. The hay field had to have been more than a mile long. After crossing the field we entered the wasteland again. Like most of the reservation it was land that was left unreclaimed in its natural form.

"We have to go about another half of a mile yet."

"You said the wendigo rattled the windows in your cupola from over a mile away?" I asked as I looked all the way back at the house.

"Yeah, like I said it was loud and it sounded like it was extremely angry."

"He probably was. That was the night we hammered the hell out of him with every weapon at our disposal," John said.

"You even shot him with that thing?" Joe asked, pointing at my shotgun.

"The dragon's breath rounds are the only thing that kept us alive," I said.

"The crosses might have had something to do with it too, Ben," Connie reminded me.

"Yeah, they sure didn't hurt having them along," Sid agreed.

"We have to go into the creek bottom right here."

"How much further is it?" Virgil asked.

"It's just over this little knoll."

We walked over the knoll and the damage lay before us. Large bushes were pulled up by their roots and thrown a considerable distance. Tree limbs twice the size of my thigh were snapped off like twigs. The damaged area was about half the size of a basketball court but round instead of rectangular.

"If you would have never come looking for the source of the noise this would have gone unnoticed for years," the sheriff said.

"It takes a lot of strength to snap off a cottonwood limb this size," the sheriff said, giving a low whistle.

"It's a damn good thing you didn't go out at night trying to find out what that sound was," Sid said.

"Not love nor money would have gotten me out of my house after hearing it screaming and listening to your first radio announcement," Joe admitted openly.

"Do you mind if we set up in your cupola tonight to watch and listen for the wendigo?" I asked him.

"No, not at all. But I only hear him in the early morning hours between three and four thirty. I never hear him right after dark. So I don't know if he is traveling to and from wherever he is going to or just on his way back."

"It will be nice for a change. Being able to look for the wendigo and not be in danger by being out where he can get to us," Connie said.

"What do you guys say? Would the Navajo Rangers like to join us on sentry duty tonight?" I asked.

"Sure, it's like Connie just said. It'll be nice not worrying about surviving the night for once," Sid said.

"It looks like you and Virgil can stand down tonight and get a normal night's sleep," I said.

"I sleep with the phone a foot from my head. If anything important happens we need to act on right away, call me," the sheriff said.

"We'll be here right after suppertime Mr. Brown," Connie said.

"Just call me Joe, Mr. Brown was my dad and he's been gone nearly thirty years now."

"There is getting to be too many Joes around here," Connie said with a grin.

"There are too many Johns too," I added.

"Huh? There's only me," John Stillwater said.

"See, one too many," his partner laughed.

"You're forgetting John Goodearl, the rancher," I said.

"Oh yeah, but he isn't here in this room now. So how come all of you are confused?" John asked.

"Never mind. It's no fun if you're not going to pick up on being given a hard time."

We left for the rest of the afternoon. Looking at my watch it was already five o'clock. It was nearly time to eat before going back.

We got back to the Brown family home a half hour before dusk. We were met at the door by his wife who let us in.

"Joe is up in the cupola setting things up for you," she said.

We walked up the two flights of stairs and entered the small square room. Joe had brought up kitchen chairs for us to sit on. He was busy washing the windows to make sure they were clean for us.

"You didn't have to go to all of this trouble for us Joe. But the chairs are a welcome sight," Connie said with a small smile.

"It's no bother at all guys. I want you to have every opportunity to see and hear this thing for yourselves."

"Trust me Joe. We have seen and heard it, up close too!" Sid reminded him.

"If we hear it tonight we'll be able to tell you for sure if it's the wendigo Joe. Like Sid said we saw and heard it up close," I said.

We set our night vision goggles and FLIR units on a table in the corner for when we'd need them.

"I'll leave you be. If you need anything at all we'll be watching the tv set in the living room," Joe said before leaving.

"Have you had any more news on when the army is going to be arriving?" John asked.

"Supposedly sometime in the mid morning according to the director," Connie said.

John shook his head sadly. "I'm going to feel like we're saying hello to a bunch of men who have already died and don't know it yet."

"Tonight we'll try to come up with a way we can give them some protection from the wendigo," I said.

"Have them stay at the hotel, that would save them," Sid said.

"We've been ordered to use them and place them in the field if we go out," I said.

"That's a whole new term for use. Use them right to death!" John said as his face turned dark with anger.

"Yeah, I know," I said dryly.

"How many are they sending you?" Sid asked.

"I'm not sure the total number. For some reason I thought it would be eight of them. The director said he was sending a squad of Green Berets."

"I just looked it up on my phone and it says it can be any-where between eight and fourteen people," Connie said.

"So there will be at least eight and no more than fourteen?" Sid said.

"I think I have a plan forming depending on how many they actually send us," I said.

"Alright Ben, let's hear it," Connie said.

"If they send us eight I'll put two of the berets with you guys and two with Connie and I. The other four we'll station together halfway between our two groups. If they have four people all together to watch their six they shouldn't be able to be snuck up on."

"Now all we have to worry about is what they have for weapons. If they come with only M4 carbines they won't be any better off than I was with my AR15." John said.

"We also don't know if your director told them to be wearing crosses or not," Sid reminded me.

"If necessary we can take Joe's and Virgil's, they'll be fairly safe in the Humvee," I said.

"How far apart are we going to position ourselves tomorrow night?" Connie asked.

"We'll see what happens tonight and then look at the lay of the land tomorrow before deciding that," I said.

"One thing I did notice when we looked at the damage to the creek bottom. When we walked across the hay field I didn't see any trails where the wendigo was crossing the field. I saw areas along the edge of the field where deer were feeding thought," Sid said.

"I noticed that too. That means the wendigo is crossing to the creek bottom past the field through the desert waste land."

I looked at my watch and it was nearing three in the morning. I figured if the wendigo was going to make its present known it would be in the next hour to hour and a half at the most.

"SKREEEEE, SKREEEEE," the sound echoed from the creek bottom. By the time the sound quit echoing we had our night vision goggles over our eyes. We'd turned off the lights when it got dark so we would be able to see outside decently.

"Now that he mentioned it. The wendigo does sound like a sandhill crane only a whole lot louder," I said.

"Does anybody have eyes on it?" I asked the group.

"I don't see anything Ben. On the other side of the field the desert slopes down away from the field. Plus there are hills and dry creek beds and washes all through the area," Sid said.

"Yeah, the wendigo wouldn't have to be very far past the field to be invisible from here," John agreed.

"But we have a pretty high vantage point. We're thirty feet in the air looking downward. It must be using a gully, dry creek bed or ravine to stay hidden," Connie said.

"I wonder why it's crying out like that before it breaks from the cover of the creek bed. It doesn't make sense to me," I said as I scanned beyond the field.

"Yeah, it's almost like it's letting something know that it's nearby," Sid said.

"Maybe it's warning a hairy man that it's coming though it's territory and to stay away," John thought out loud.

"After seeing what's left of its victims I don't think it would worry about a hairy man," Connie said.

"It would be picking on something perhaps bigger than it is. Believe it or not Connie, hairy men have been reported to be as tall as twelve feet," John explained.

"Hairy man is a cryptid and the wendigo is a supernatural being. I'm not certain how the two would match up with each other. But I'm starting to think the smart money would be on the wendigo," I said.

We never spotted the wendigo that night. Like Connie said we had a very high vantage point but it managed to stay out of sight. It had to be using a feature of the terrain to stay out of sight of us. But why stay out of sight and then let us know you're there by calling out?"

Daylight came and we went out into the yard and stood talking to Joe the homeowner and his wife, Cindi.

"If it's alright with you, we'll be back later this afternoon with some reinforcements. We'll go out into the desert tonight and see if we can't end this," I said.

"You're going out where that thing is?" Cindi asked in shock.

"It's the only way to end this. It seems the problem isn't going away on its own," I said.

"You can come out whenever you need to Ben," Joe said as he shook our hands before we climbed into our vehicles and headed to the cafe to meet with the others for breakfast.

Our tired, sleepless group walked into the cafe to the welcome smell of coffee and bacon cooking. Joe and Virgil were already sitting at the table with two pots of coffee waiting for us. We filled our cups gratefully.

"Well, how did it go?" Virgil asked us.

"It's there alright. We heard it as plain as day. We never saw it though. It kept itself hidden in a feature out in the desert. It must be using a hill to hide behind or a gully to travel through," I said as I sipped my coffee.

"We told the director to have the Green Berets report to you at your office. We're going to try to get a few hours of sleep and don't want them pounding on our door to tell us they're here," Connie said.

"He never said how many he was sending, did he?" Joe asked.

"No but Connie looked up how many are in a squad and it said anywhere between eight and fourteen. I'm hoping for only eight," I said, sipping more coffee.

"Why is that Ben?" Virgil asked me.

"Because there would be less of a mess to clean up when these men are killed tonight," I said, not looking up at their faces.

"How are we going to place the men?" Joe asked.

"We came up with a plan but for it to help at all we have to wait to see how many are sent," Connie said.

Our food was brought out and we ate, all small talk was forgotten. The only thing I was thinking about at the moment was my bed.

We finished eating and pushed back our chairs. Virgil took a turn buying. "I'm going to be glad when the wendigo is gone and you two leave town. It's expensive having you around," he said looking at the total on the bill.

"They're supposed to be arriving this morning, Joe. We're making a quick stop at the silversmith and pick-up the crosses. When we get done sleeping we'll finish loading the shotgun shells before coming back into town," I said, yawning wide.

"Alright, go and get some sleep. I'll babysit the army when they get here. I'll wait until you come before we explain to their commanding officer what this is all about," Joe said.

"There are some smart officers in the military and there are some very stupid officers. We're going to find out what kind of officer he is," Virgil said with a grim smile.

"What do you mean by that?" Connie asked him.

"Because if he is a smart officer he is going to be shitting his pants when he finds out why he is here."

Chapter Twenty-One

"We only got four hours of sleep when we had to get up at one in the afternoon. Often when on cases the amount of sleep you got was dictated by what you had to do and when you had to do it. I needed to finish loading up the shotgun shells with the pure silver crosses and then we needed to get back to Window Rock and meet with the Green Beret unit before we had to go back out into the field for the night.

I got the shower first and after finishing went outside onto the deck to finish with the shotgun shells while Connie got ready for the day ahead.

An hour after I started I had all of the shotgun shells done. There were enough of the crosses to load twelve shells. I would keep six for myself and give the other six to Sid for his shotgun.

We angle parked in front of the sheriff's department. There were two more Humvees parked in front besides the one the sheriff borrowed from the National Guard. The army men were standing around their vehicles talking and waiting to get orders on what was going on.

We walked into the building. Joe was standing, talking to an army officer with captain's bars on his shoulders.

"Captain Baker, these are FBI special agents Ben Hawk and Connie Sanchez," Joe said as he made the introductions.

"I've heard a lot about both of you from the news," he said with a smile while shaking our hands.

"You don't know how much I wish you weren't here Captain," I said honestly.

"I don't think I understand sir," he said, looking confused.

"Wait a bit and maybe you will. Joe, are John and Sid around yet?" I asked him.

"No, they haven't checked in yet. They must still be in the sack getting some sleep after last night."

"Can you call them and get them down here right away so we can have a meeting with Captain Baker and his second in command?"

"Captain, why don't you have your second in command join us in the conference room. Once the two Navajo Rangers get here we'll fill you in on what's happening around here. I really don't think you're going to like it much," Connie said.

"Sergeant Wilson, could you join us please in the conference room for a meeting," The captain called out the door.

Ten minutes later the two deputies we were waiting for arrived and we got the meeting started.

"I'll be honest with the two of you. I fought with my director to try to keep him from sending you into this situation," I explained to them.

"Why would you do that sir?" the noncom asked me.

"Because even though you are highly trained Green Berets you are ill equipped to handle this situation. I'm scared some of you are going to die before this night is over."

They both got shocked looks on their faces and sat in stunned silence before the captain found his voice. "I can't imagine any situation that with all of our specialized training we couldn't handle.

"Maybe you will understand by the time we get done filling you in," Connie said.

The two army men looked at each other but didn't say anything, waiting for more information.

"We were sent here to the Navajo reservation because people have been brutally attacked and killed. Their remains were nearly totally consumed by the creature that did it."

"Well, they must have been attacked by a bear then," Sergeant Wilson said, looking less tense.

I put up the first picture Connie and I have ever seen onto the screen.

"Sure, I was right, it was a bear attack," the sergeant said with a relieved smile on his face.

"Look closer sergeant, have you ever seen a bear skin his kill before eating it?" Connie asked the shocked man.

"This next picture shows a different victim. This one was consumed in only twenty minutes. The body is seventy five percent gone. The next night, two more victims were eaten. Both of them are nearly gone. What can eat three people in two days?" I said.

"Well then, it must be a pack of wolves or coyotes doing it then. This much could be eaten if there were enough animals to feed on the body," the captain said.

"Wolves and coyotes don't skin their kills either gentlemen," I said as I watched their unease.

"We put a curfew on this town. This creature only feeds at night. No one is allowed outside of their homes from an hour before dark until an hour after daylight," the sheriff said.

"The night we put the curfew on we got a call of a stranded motorist outside of town a few miles away. Our officers were ordered to not leave their vehicles under any circumstances after dark. They drove out to where a mother and an eight year old girl were stranded. Their car ran out of gas. The officers drove past the car and spun around so they were facing back towards town. They could hear the creature nearby screeching loudly. They claim it was so loud they could feel it in their bones. When they were by the car they yelled for the mother and child to jump into the back seat. The mother tossed the child in and dove in behind her. She barely got away. The creature leaped for the open car door just as the officer driving spun his tires to get away. The beast missed his mark and slammed his hands down on the car as it evaded him," Sid said.

"This next picture is of the police cruiser that was damaged that night. The beast slammed its hand down once on the roof of the car and once on the trunk. He caved it in more than a foot," Virgil said.

"After daylight we drove out to the stranded car and had the local tow truck driver follow us. The creature returned to this car after missing his last meal and did this to it," John said as a new picture was put on the screen.

"I don't think you could do much more damage with a wreck-ing ball," the captain murmured.

"Did anyone see it though? Is there a description of the ani-mal?" Sergeant Wilson asked.

"The little girl was the only one who saw it. When her mother tossed her into the car she was facing the open door. She said it had a skull like an animal with no flesh on it. The skin was stretched tight across its head and its eyes glowed a bright red. She also said it had a set of bone white antlers on its head," Connie said.

"Well obviously that's just the wild imagination of a panicked little girl," the captain said.

"The next picture you'll see on the screen is a picture of an art masterpiece from the Louvre museum in Paris, France. There are several such paintings depicting this creature there. This one is titled Dante's inferno. After showing the girl this picture she agreed this is what she saw. This gentlemen, is a demon in the Christian world. It is also called a wendigo by Native American tribes," I informed them.

"This can't be right! This is a long way to go to pull off a prank on us. Who put you up to this?" Captain Baker asked as he looked around the table at the serious looks on everyone's faces.

"I don't think they're kidding captain," the sergeant said, looking at the same serious expressions on our faces.

"There is a lot going on here on the reservation. Since I got here I've seen a shapeshifter, a bigfoot and the wendigo and all within twenty five miles of each other," Connie stated.

"You saw a bigfoot? Come on, you don't really believe in that garbage do you?" Captain Baker said in astonishment.

"That attitude is exactly why I didn't want you to be sent here. You're going to be like babes in the wilderness. Putting you out into the field is going to be like ringing the dinner bell for this thing," I said unkindly.

"What Ben is trying to so eloquently say is you don't think like a Native American. You see but you don't see. You hear but only what you want your ears to hear. You smell but only the smells of the city and not the smells of the things that are most dangerous around you. This wendigo will be picking his teeth to remove your remains before you even know he is near you," John stated.

"You got the word of a little girl and nothing else," the captain said, ignoring the comments of his abilities.

"That's not exactly true. We did battle with it two or three nights ago," Sid said.

"See, and you're still here."

"We're jumping ahead of ourselves a little bit. Let's continue where we left off, Joe said.

"We received a call from a person known in town as the chicken lady. She supplies eggs for a lot of people. She said she saw a hairy man in her yard and it was stealing chickens from one of her coops. After it got light outside Sid and I went out to her chicken farm to investigate. We could see where the chickens were taken. There were feathers scattered everywhere. But the ground was too hard packed to pick up any tracks," John said.

"Now what is a hairy man?" the captain asked.

"It's what a lot of different tribes call a bigfoot," I said.

"We thought she might have misidentified what took her chickens so we went out to have a look. The lighting in her farm yard wasn't very good. We thought there might be a chance it was our creature she'd seen so we staked out the farm that night," I said.

"Sid and John were on one hilltop overlooking the creek bottom and Ben and I were on a different hill a couple miles from them. The sheriff and Virgil were stationed in the yard in the other Humvee you saw out front when you arrived," Connie said, taking a turn on the narrative.

"About three in the morning we heard a ruckus out by the chicken coops and called the two groups on the hilltops that something was happening. They were equipped with night vision goggles and FLIR units. After a few minutes they detected movement by one of the chicken coops. It turned out the chicken lady was right, it was a hairy man," the sheriff said.

"You actually saw a bigfoot!" the captain asked, turning his attention to Connie.

"One hundred percent true. I saw it on both the FLIR and the night vision goggles. In case you want to know I saw a shapeshifter too. It was a man running naked across the desert and when he got into some rocks he turned into a wolf," Connie said honestly.

"We're trying to get them to believe in us, Connie. The information overload isn't going to help us," I said.

"We figured the lady was right in what she saw so we called it a night. We'd borrowed horses from a local rancher so we took them back to the farmyard and tied them off right where the rancher left them for us the afternoon before. Around ten that morning we received a call about an angry rancher. He sent two ranch hands to pick up his horses only to find two of them dead and another one so badly injured it had to be put down," Joe said.

"The wendigo must have been in the area and attacked the horses after we left," I said.

"We forgot to mention the other dead livestock Ben," Connie reminded me.

"Oh yeah, when we found the dead couple some of their sheep and a cow and bull were also found dead. The bull was a huge animal and it had its neck broken cleanly. We had a veterinarian come out and look at the animals. All of them had broken necks. He says there was no animal on earth that could have cleanly broken the bulls neck like that. A bear or African lion might be able to kill it but there would be bite and claw marks on it. These animals didn't have any of that."

"What about the horses? The injured one that was still alive must not have had a broken neck," the sergeant said.

"Two dead horses, two broken necks. The injured horse had its head caved in just like the two cars were smashed in," Sid said.

"We promised to reimburse the rancher for the lost horses but that doesn't compensate for losing horses of this caliber." I said.

"The next night we went back to the chicken farm. The rancher supplied us with new horses. There was no way we were going to leave these unguarded like the last ones. For the night we decided to cross the creek bottom and set-up at the edge of the brushline facing outwards across the desert. We knew the wendigo was using the creek bottom for cover to conceal his travels. What we didn't know was he was using the creek bottom and traveling down it many miles," Virgil said.

"For this night we stationed ourselves only a few hundred yards apart so if either group was attacked the other could respond quickly. About two thirty or three o'clock in the morning Connie sensed the wendigos' presence and called the others to come fast. They got to us and tied off their horses just as the wendigo came out of the brush. By this time we'd already had a conversation and determined a wendigo and a demon were one and the same. This thing was straight out of the bowels of hell. We were all wearing Christian crosses around our necks for added protection," I explained.

"We'd discussed what we were going to carry for weapons. We decided a wide range of weapons was best because we didn't know by then what would work if anything. After all we are dealing with something evil, something not living. How do you kill a creature that's not alive? I was carrying an AR15 with a bump stock to make it fully automatic with two thirty two round magazines. Sid had a twelve gauge shotgun loaded with rock salt. In our culture we know salt is a protection from certain creatures and spirits. Connie was carrying her SIG .40 with teflon coated rounds that can penetrate a bullet proof vest and Ben had his streetsweeper shotgun with a fifty round drum magazine. He had it loaded with double aught buckshot and dragon's breath white phosphorus rounds," John said.

"Like I was saying the wendigo came out of the creek bottom and let me tell you it could easily outrun any deer you've ever seen. This thing is a full seven and a half feet tall with giant clawed hands and hooved feet. We opened up on it when it was within sixty feet of us. My first ten rounds were buckshot. By the time I fired off my first ten rounds the others were either switching to secondary weapons or reloading. The wendigo got within twenty or thirty feet of us and stood there screeching at the top of its lungs. We think the crosses kept it at bay. I got to my first dragon's breath round and hit it square in the face. Dragon's breath shoots out a white phosphorus flame up to one hundred feet out of the barrel and lights anything on fire that it touches. The wendigo didn't like getting hit in the face. I unloaded every one of those shells into it, all ten of them. He was burning from head to foot and he took off and ran back to the creek bottom. We jumped onto our horses and got the hell out of there," I said.

"We heard what sounded like world war three from the far-myard and took off cross country to help out if we could. We met them at the edge of the brush. They flew past us at a full gallop and we stayed behind them, guarding their rear. Once at the farmyard they tied the horses where we found them and then we stayed until morning and the horses were picked back up. We weren't taking any chances that more horses ended up dead," Joe said.

"The next picture on the screen Connie took of the wendigo as it ran away from us on fire," I said.

"There isn't anything in the picture but a ball of fire," the sergeant said.

"Yeah, we know. The wendigo cannot be photographed. If you look closely you can barely see the outline of the wendigo," I said.

"We now know where the wendigo is exiting the creek bottom and we plan on laying a trap for him tonight. But I have a lot of misgivings about your unit being a part of our plans," I said honestly.

"We can handle ourselves Agent Hawk," Captain Baker said with too much confidence.

"What did you bring along for weapons? I told the director your normal weapons would be useless against the wendigo."

"We have rifles with grenade launchers mounted underneath the barrels. Some are fragmentation grenades and some are incendiary grenades," the sergeant said.

"That's just great! So each of you will have a single grenade and then after that you'll virtually be throwing spitballs at it because Captain, your rifles are useless against the wendigo. You'll be nothing but a bunch of Barnie Fife's out there. You each only have one shot and then you're helpless," I said angrily."

"You did bring my grenade launcher with you didn't you captain?" Connie asked.

"Yeah, it's in one of the Humvees."

"So my one grenade launcher has as much firepower as your entire squad does?" Connie asked with raised eyebrows.

The captain sat glowering. "I followed orders and armed us accordingly."

"Were you even instructed to buy necklaces with crosses on them to wear for protection?" Connie asked.

"Nothing was mentioned to us about bringing them along with us," the sergeant said.

"That's just freaking great! Connie, come with me. We need to make a phone call. We'll be back in a few minutes," I said, getting up from the table. We went into Joe's office and shut the door for privacy.

"Ben, did the Green Berets get there yet?"

"Did you say Green Berets or fresh bait?"

"I'm not going down this path again. They are a highly trained military fighting unit."

"They are babes in the woods. I told you their weapons were no good so what do they bring with them? A single grenade each for their barrel mounted launchers!"

"They didn't buy crosses even after we told you the crosses probably saved our lives. Weren't you listening to us?" Connie added.

"I thought you were a religious man and believed in the bible. We showed you the evidence we were after a demon and you sent eight men to their deaths with no means of protecting themselves, WHAT THE HELL DIRECTOR!"

By this time I was yelling so loudly the door didn't keep the men in the conference room from hearing us.

"If you're so worried about it, then get them some CROSSES TO WEAR!," the director shouted back.

"We are going out in the field in two hours, TWO HOURS! Where the hell are we supposed to come up with eight crosses in two hours out here in the middle of nowhere?" I yelled angrily.

"You don't have any extra crosses they can borrow?"

"I can take the sheriff's and Virgil's because they're not going out tonight. But that still leaves us six short."

"How do you plan on deploying tonight?"

"I'll put two of the army men with Sid and John. Two of them are with Connie and me but the other four will have to be in a group on their own. I'm putting their commanding officer and his most experienced three men with him between The Navajo Rangers and us."

"So four of them may get protection from you and Connie and the two rangers wearing them?"

"We don't know for sure how this works. We don't know if each person needs to be wearing one or not," Connie said.

"It would probably be best if we don't put them in the field tonight until they have the needed crosses and better arms," I said.

"You have your orders, Ben. You will take them with you tonight!"

"You best be ready for the phone call in the morning telling you to come and clean your own mess up because these men are going to die!"

"I expect you to call in the morning with a report on your night's operation."

"Oh, you'll get a report alright!" I said as the director hung up on us.

We went back into the conference room, my face was dark with anger. The others were waiting for what I had to say about tonight's operation.

"We will go out as planned tonight. When we go out we will deploy Sid and John with two of the Captains newest men first. Then we'll deploy the captain with his three most experienced men. Then Connie and I will take the last two with us."

"Joe, can you have the rest of the army unit come into the conference room? You can give them the same talk we just gave to the captain and sergeant. I need to sit down with Sid and John and go over a few things."

"Sure, captain, can you bring your squad in and we'll go ahead and show them what we're up against," Joe said.

"The four of us went into the sheriff's office and closed the door for privacy.

"Sid, here are five dragon's breath rounds and five rounds loaded with silver crosses," I said, placing them on the desk in front of him.

"Thanks Ben. How do you think I should put them in my magazine?" Sid asked.

"You have an extended magazine on your shotgun, right?"

"Yeah, it will hold seven rounds in the magazine and one in the chamber."

"Load it so your first four rounds are silver crosses. Then make your last four rounds dragon's breath. Hopefully the crosses will do the job but if they don't we already know the dragon's breath will force it away from you."

"John, are you going to use the AR15 after the other night?" Connie asked him.

"The AR15 was useless. He shrugged my rounds like I was shooting blanks. I'm going to switch to a shotgun too. But mine will only hold six rounds and not eight."

"We'll fix you up with the special rounds too," I promised him.

"I was hoping you'd say that."

"The director ordered us to take the army unit into the field with us tonight," I told them.

"Yeah we heard. He just doesn't get it does he?"

"Can you give us his cell phone number? I'd like to send him a couple of pictures he hasn't seen yet. Maybe it isn't too late for him to listen to reason," Sid said.

"Yeah, I'll give it to you but he isn't going to like that I did it. But right now there is a better than fifty-fifty chance I won't be working there anymore once this case is over anyway."

Sid started typing away on his phone and showed me what he was sending before he hit the send button.

"Mr. Director, this is Sid Canyon of the Navajo Rangers. I am a member of the Navajo Reservation police department. These two pictures were never released. They show the total savagery of the wendigo. By sending these Green Berets unprepared into the field with us you are for all practical purposes committing their murders via the wendigo. We ask you to please reconsider and not send them out with us. Any deaths their unit suffers tonight will be considered a crime on your part and a warrant will be issued for your arrest. Please reply to this text message at once."

"Go ahead and hit the send button," I said with a tight grin, knowing my phone would be ringing almost instantly.

"What are you going to say to the director when he calls Ben?" Connie asked me.

"When he calls I'm not going to answer it and neither are you. We were out of range and didn't receive the message. Make him respond to Sid's text instead."

My phone started ringing and I saw it was the director and didn't answer. Connie's phone started ringing and she didn't answer either.

"I don't know if the director is going to text you or call you but when he does we aren't around. We went to look over the area where we are setting up tonight and can't get a signal in the area," I said, smiling grimly.

Sid's phone rang and he put it on speaker. "Officer Canyon, how can I be of assistance?"

"Put Ben or Connie on the phone right now!" the director yelled angrily.

"They aren't here. They went out into the field to plan tonight's operation. There is no cell phone service out there in the desert."

"What is the meaning of them giving you my private phone number!"

"We always trade phone numbers and other information when we work jointly on a case. If anything were to happen and we needed to contact their office we would need to know how to do it. We have their emergency numbers and they have ours."

"You threatened to have me arrested! Do you know who you are dealing with? I run the largest, most sophisticated law enforcement agency in the world!"

"That's the problem isn't it? You're too sophisticated for your own good. You won't listen to reason. You won't listen to people who have a much better understanding of what is going on than you do. You're pig headed and stubborn. We've been investigating supernatural beings and cryptids for decades but you, being in the mighty FBI, think you're automatically superior to us. Well I'll tell you something Mr. high and mighty director of the FBI, no one is above the law, not even you!"

"I want to talk to the sheriff!"

"He's busy right now. He is in the conference room seeing if any of your Green Berets want to make out new wills before tonight's operation. No, they are actually busy finding out the danger they'll be in tonight. If they have any more common sense than you, they will refuse to go out tonight."

"I'm the director of the FBI! You can't have me arrested for following protocol."

"Really? Show me in your handy dandy FBI field manual the part where it tells you how to deal with wendigos and demons."

"You know damn well there isn't a section on that!"

"Then how can you say to me you are following protocol?"

"I'm done arguing about this! Have Ben or Connie call me when they get back into town."

"They said they plan on staying out in the field and waiting for us to meet them. They aren't coming back before morning. If you want to change your instructions for the use of the Green Berets you'll have to deal with me," Sid said as the director abruptly hung up.

"Now that is one very angry man," John said.

"He's in over his head and floundering. He is unsure of himself and out of his element. So he is trying to bull his way through," I said.

"That's not a good way to operate if you're responsible for the lives of people," Sid said.

I could hear the meeting breaking up in the conference room. We stood in the doorway of Joe's office and watched as a group of very unhappy and scared looking Green Berets walked by without meeting our eyes.

The sheriff and Virgil came over by us and talked quietly.

"The further into the meeting we went the more uncomfortable and unhappy they became. Unfortunately if there is a fool in the group it's their commanding officer," Joe said.

"They didn't bring crosses with them either. Can you and Virgil give your crosses to the captain and the sergeant for tonight's operation? Neither one of you are going into the field so you won't be needing them. Right now we have no idea at all if everyone needs to be wearing a cross or if just having crosses in the group is good enough to have protection," I said.

"Sure, we can do it right now so we don't forget," Virgil said as he pulled his cross over his head. The sergeant and captain were still standing in the doorway of the building.

"Sergeant Wilson, Why don't you wear this tonight? You will

have more need of it than I will," Virgil said as he handed it over to him.

Wilson looked at the cross in the palm of his hand before slipping it over his head with a look of deep appreciation. "Thank you for this. You don't know how much it means to me to be wearing this right now."

"Trust me, I totally know having seen what the wendigo is capable of doing."

Joe handed his cross over to the captain. The captain put it in his breast pocket without saying a word.

"In a half hour or so we're going over to the cafe to get something to eat before we head out for the night. You and your men are welcome to join us," Connie said.

"We brought along our MREs. We can eat those," the captain said.

"The condemned should receive a decent last meal, captain," I told him quietly so as not to rub it in.

"You're not going to let off on that are you?" Captain Baker said as he looked at me angrily.

"Captain, it is my fondest dream that one of two things happen. One, either you decide to stay out of the field tonight, Or we don't run into the wendigo and everyone comes back in the morning alive."

"I have my orders Agent Hawk and you have yours." he abruptly left the building and joined his men.

"I don't know who is more stubborn Ben, your director or that Captain," Sid said.

"Sid talked to my director and learned first hand what a complete asshole he is when he doesn't have operational control of a situation," I said.

"Really, you talked to Ben and Connie's boss?" Joe said in surprise.

"Yeah, I told him I would put out an arrest warrant on him come morning if any of the Green Berets ended up dead tonight. He is putting them into a situation they can't deal with and any death suffered tonight would be considered a murder on his part."

"I don't think we can arrest the director of the FBI Sid. But I sure as hell would like to see the expression on his face when he gets the warrant."

We walked out of the building. The army men were talking quietly among themselves. As a group they stopped talking and looked at us expectantly.

"Have you changed your mind captain? Dinner is on the FBI if your men want a good hot meal," Connie said.

"Anyone that wants to go with them to the cafe is welcome to," the captain said with a sigh.

Everyone moved to join us except the captain. He let out another sigh before giving in and joining the group too.

"After we get done eating I want to take possession of my M320 grenade launcher. They did load it full of fragmentation grenades, right?" Connie asked the sergeant.

"I think every other round is a fragmentation grenade and the other four rounds are incendiary rounds."

"That'll work for me. You'll show me which end the grenades come out of too, right sergeant?" Connie said with a disarming smile on her face.

"Sure, it's simple enough to use. It's already loaded so you just have to know how to use the safety and then it's just a matter of pointing and shooting."

The army guys climbed into their two Humvees and we got into our car.

"When you use that grenade launcher Connie make sure the wendigo is far enough away from you. We don't want to end up eating our own shrapnel," I said.

"That would be a bad thing, right?" Connie said with a grin.

"That would be a very bad thing."

"The army unit occupied two square tables and the six of us sat around the round table we always sat around.

"Order whatever you want to eat tonight, the food is on us," I told the troops. The thought I voiced at the sheriff's office played through my mind again. The condemned men get their last decent meal.

Chapter Twenty-Two

"We finished eating and reluctantly it was time to pick out our spots to watch for the night. We stood by my car and we shook hands with Joe and Virgil before heading out to whatever was waiting for us tonight. I didn't like the way I was feeling about the situation but I didn't know of a single way out of it other than quitting the FBI on the spot. But what good would that do anyone? The problem would still exist and the wendigo would still be killing and eating people. The only answer was to meet the problem head on with the resources we had and hope for the best outcome.

Sid and John rode with us in our tahoe out to the three story house. The two Humvees full of Green Berets followed along behind us. We parked out of the way in the yard and were met by Joe, the homeowner.

"Tonight's the night, huh?" he asked as he watched the army men get out of the Humvees.

"For better or worse we hope to end this tonight Joe," I said. Nobody was smiling. We all knew the danger waiting out there for us.

"I plan on staying awake all night long in the cupola. If anything happens and you need assistance I will be awake and watching for you."

"I appreciate that Joe. Hopefully the night will go off without a hitch and this thing will end tonight." I didn't think it would at all, I was just kidding myself. There was no way this was going to end tonight without a hitch. We were placed in an impossible situation and we had no escape route out of it.

"Where is my grenade launcher?" Connie asked the sergeant.

"It's right here, Agent Sanchez," Wilson said as he handed the stubby barreled weapon with a drum magazine on it.

"That's what I'm talking about!" Connie said as she looked the weapon over with appreciation.

"Where are we going to set-up for the night Agent Hawk?" the captain asked.

"We have to cross this hay field. It's probably about a two mile hike to get to our spots," I said as I shouldered my streetsweeper. I had loaded the streetsweeper with the first five rounds being loaded with silver crosses. The next forty five rounds were five rounds of dragon's breath and the five rounds of DumDum and then I alternated them every five rounds until the magazine was full.

"Okay men, meet up with me!" I yelled out and gave a shrill whistle to get their attention. Everybody came over to where I was standing.

"You were all told to bring night vision goggles. Make sure you have fresh batteries in them before we head out for the night. Grab your weapons and grenades for the launchers. If you have a choice on types of grenades, I know from past experience the wendigo does not like white phosphorus. Do you have anything to add, Connie?" I asked my partner.

"We only have six crosses for the twelve of us so those of you that have crosses make sure to buddy up with someone who doesn't have one. Two people at each position will be wearing crosses. After dark those of you that don't have one make sure you stick tight to your buddy's side. We don't know yet if only those wearing crosses have protection or if an area around the person wearing the cross is protected but it's the best we can do for tonight."

"Turn your cell phones off and not on silent. Once we cross the hay field you'll need to keep your talking to a whisper. We don't know how close the wendigo is to where we will be setting up and we don't know how keen its hearing is," John said.

"Alright, grab your weapons and ammo and let's get moving. It's about a two mile hike to where the first team will be stationed," Sid said as he loaded his eighth round into his shotgun's chamber.

"That grenade launcher you have is a short little spud monkey

Connie," I said, eyeing it for the first time.

"It's plenty heavy though. I don't know how much eight grenades weigh but it must be a lot."

The Green Berets were ready to go and were milling around anxiously. I could see how uneasy they were, thinking about what tonight would bring.

I led the way across the hay field that ran parallel to the creek bottom.

"How far is this thing traveling at night when it goes out hunting?" Captain Baker asked.

"We don't know where its starting point is yet but it must be quite a few miles. Just from here to the chicken farm is five miles. From here to where it took the last victim in Window Rock is around fourteen miles."

"That means it traveled the night it went to Window twenty eight miles?"

"Yeah, and that's just to get to this point, not from where it started out from."

"That thing must really be able to move!"

"I'll tell you right now, it could outrun a mule deer."

We finished crossing the hay field and entered the desert. The terrain changed from hay to sand, rocks, cactus and sagebrush. A mile later we came to the first gully.

Sid, you and John will be stationed here. Captain, put two of your most inexperienced men with them," I said softly.

"Willy and Bob, you stay here with Sid and John. Stay alert and listen to the Navajo Rangers you are with. They've dealt with this thing before and have a better understanding of it than you do."

"Roger that Sir," Willy said.

"Copy that Captain," Bob responded.

We walked on another two hundred yards and came to a narrow ravine about forty feet across. "Alright Captain, this is your spot. Take your best three men and leave the last two with me."

"Tom and Jim, you two go with Agents Hawk and Sanchez, you other three will stay here with me."

"I looked at the two men he was sending with me and I saw

looks of relief on their faces. They didn't want to stay with their commanding officer. That spoke volumes to me about what kind of commanding officer he was. It bode ill of what the night could bring.

"Let's go. We have a ways to go to get to our spot," I said.

Our spot was a dry creek bed that was choked full of brush and cactus. It wasn't a spot I'd like to hike through but I wasn't a wendigo.

"It's still daylight out yet guys but once it becomes dark I want Tom to stick like glue to Connie and Jim, I want you to do the same with me. We will stay all together in a group for protection. I do not want to divide us up into pairs. There is safety in numbers."

"Yes sir," Both Tom and Jim acknowledged my message to them.

"I hope you aren't bashful Tom," Connie said with a grin to ease the tension they were feeling.

"What do you mean Agent Sanchez?" Tom asked her.

"I'm going to be so close to you that if you have to pee I'd be able to hold it for you. Call me Connie, not Agent Sanchez. By morning we are going to know each other real well," Connie said with a wink.

"Well hell, it looks like I got the wrong partner. Ben, no matter how close we get to each other I can hold my own," Jim said with a grin after he saw how red Tom's face was.

"You guys heard what Ben said in the farmyard. Willy, stay close to my side, especially after dark. Bob, you do the same thing with John."

"I'm going to be so close to you Sid that if you have to scratch your butt you'll be scratching the wrong one!" Willy said seriously.

"That's exactly how close I want you to be. Let's make it through the night alive."

"All right men, gather around. I want Sergeant Wilson deployed with Sanders on the other side of the ravine. Corporal Jacobs, you will be here on this side with me."

"Don't you think our defenses would be stronger if we stayed together in a group, Captain?" Sergeant Wilson asked.

"I'm in command here sergeant and I give the orders. Speaking of which, I don't need this damn thing!" Captain Baker said as he grabbed the cross out of his breast pocket and flung it into the rocks.

"What in the hell did you do that for!" Jacobs asked him, not believing he would do such a thing.

"I don't believe in all this wendigo, demon garbage."

"I would have taken it, I would have worn it!" Jacobs yelled in his face.

"It's in the rocks someplace. If you want it, go and find it."

"All that broken rock up there? I'll never be able to find it."

"Keep your voices down or the wendigo might hear us," Sergeant Wilson said quietly.

"Sergeant Wilson, hand me your cross," Captain Baker said, holding his hand out for it.

"You're not throwing my cross into the rocks like you did yours captain!" Wilson said angrily.

"Be a man sergeant, be a Green Beret!"

"Captain, do I need to remind you that the uniform code of military justice prohibits you from questioning and taunting a man about his religion. It is punishable by a reduction in rank and in more serious cases termination of your enlistment!"

"Fine, Keep your damn cross, but it won't do you a damn bit of good," Captain Baker sneered.

"What the hell has gotten into you! Have you ever heard the expression, there are no atheists in fox holes? I sure as hell hope you don't learn that lesson the hard way tonight."

Night fall came and I positioned our group so we were facing towards where the Captain was stationed with his men. The crickets were chirping, it was that time of year for them. In the far distance in the creek bottom I could barely hear the bullfrogs croaking up a storm.

"Connie, the homeowner, has only heard the wendigo in the early morning hours. Do you think that means he has a different travel route going to and coming from his destination?" I asked quietly.

"It's either that or it just isn't vocal when it goes out on a hunt. We got to stay alert just in case he comes ghosting through here quietly. Right about now would be when he becomes active," Connie whispered back.

"Aw hell, I have to pee," Tom declared uncomfortably.

Jim let out a snicker.

"Shut up Jim!," Tom hissed.

"Alright, let's go," Connie led him away fifty feet.

Connie heard him unzip his pants.

"Do you want me to hold it for you?" Connie asked as she grinned in the dark.

"I can find it in the dark by myself, thank you," Tom whispered tartly.

"What's taking you so long? Connie asked.

"Shhh, it's in here somewhere. Nevermind, I found it!" Tom said.

"See, you do have a sense of humor," Connie said, chuckling.

Connie and Tom came back and took their positions. We were all standing now on high alert. It was nearing the hour when we expected the wendigo to show itself. Tom, Jim and I were scanning the area with our night vision goggles and Connie was sweeping all around us with the FLIR looking for heat signatures.

"So how long have the two of you been Navajo Rangers?" Willy asked.

Only a little over a year for me but Sid had been doing it for what, six years?" John asked Sid.

"It's been almost seven years now."

"What do Navajo Rangers do? Are they like the Texas Rangers?" Willy asked.

"No, we investigate strange occurrences. Ghost sightings, hairy man encounters, shapeshifters and such. There are a lot of occurrences on the reservation. I don't think it's because we have more of that kind of thing here. I think it's because we are more in tune with our surroundings. That's one of the reasons Ben didn't want you here. You are out of tune with the surroundings so to speak."

"Do you really believe in all of that stuff?" Bob asked.

"If I didn't believe in it do you think I would be a Navajo Ranger?" Sid asked.

"We not only get a lot of reports but we've experienced a lot of strange things ourselves. Far too many to be naysayers. We take each report at face value and then investigate to see if we can come up with a reason for them seeing what they saw. Sometimes it's a misidentification but sometimes it's exactly what they saw. Take the egg lady for example. She said she saw a hairy man. We investigated the report and found it to be factual because the next night we saw the hairy man too." Sid said.

"A hairy man is a bigfoot, right?" Willy asked.

"It's one and the same. I could take you to a hundred different tribes and locations throughout North America and there would be fifty different names for the same being. With people seeing them from Alaska to Florida and from here to the pine barrens of New Jersey how can anybody say they aren't real. There are hieroglyphics depicting hairy man hundreds of years ago. You can't blame that on social media now can you?"

"You make a good argument about it, I'll give you that. But what about shapeshifters?"

"Ask Connie about shapeshifters. She chased one a week ago across the desert floor."

"Are you being serious right now?" Willy asked.

"They spotted a naked man walking across the desert at night when we were staked out. They thought it might be a missing ranch hand and gave chase. It saw them coming and took off running. By this time they were only a little ways behind it. It entered some rocks and out the other side sprang a wolf. Connie didn't believe in shapeshifters either. Ben challenged her to go into the rocks and find the naked man. After she did a thorough search she came out empty handed. Now she believes in shapeshifters." Sid said.

"We better settle down now and keep a closer watch. It's getting closer to the time when the wendigo started screeching last night," John whispered.

John scanned the area while Sid, Willy and Bob kept watch with their night vision goggles. Sid kept his attention in the direction of the Creek Bottom.

"I can't believe the Captain tossed his cross into the rocks, what the hell Sarge!" Corporal Sanders said angrily.

"Either the captain is an atheist or he is in denial of the information they gave us in town. There is no such thing as being too careful and I would have never tossed that cross away."

"Are you a believer, Sarge?"

"After what we saw and what was told to us, how can you not be a believer? I was raised in the bible belt. We went to church every Sunday and once a month the church had a potluck. My uncle was our minister in fact. I went to bible study most of my younger years. Yeah, I always believed Sanders. I just don't seem to make the time for it anymore. After we are done here I think it may be time for me to go back again."

"Would you mind much if I tagged along with you?"

"I don't know, how is your singing voice corporal?" Wilson said, grinning in the darkness.

"Not very good, how is yours?"

"Probably about the same as yours, we'll harmonize."

We were standing quietly paying close attention to everything around us.

"I don't like it at all Ben! Everything just went quiet. The frogs have stopped croaking, hell even the crickets have grown quiet," Connie whispered.

I keyed my handheld radio. "Pay attention, something is happening guys. The crickets and the frogs fell silent," I whispered quietly into the radio.

"10/4 Ben," Sid whispered back.

"Roger that," Captain Baker whispered.

For fifteen minutes all was silent. I was starting to think I gave out a false alarm when the wendigo announced its presence.

SKREEEEE, SKREEEEE, SKREEEEE!

The captain detected a quick flash of motion and turned towards the threat. Right now he would have given anything to have the cross around his neck. His last thought before darkness fell on him was that it was true. There were no atheists in fox holes. He triggered off a short burst before his neck was snapped and he fell lifeless. At least he wouldn't feel the pain of being eaten by a demon from hell.

Jacobs turned just in time to fire off his grenade. The wendigo was too close and if the grenade would have detonated he would have received a large portion of the blast. But anything would have been preferable to what was now right on top of him. He missed with the grenade and it sailed in the direction of the creek bottom where it detonated. It was as if a light switch had been thrown. One second he could see the wendigo and the next the lights went out forever.

Sergeant Wilson and Corporal Sanders saw the captain being attacked. They couldn't use their grenade launchers because they would have killed their own comrades. But by the time that thought went through his head it was too late, they were already dead. They hit the wendigo with small arms fire and saw it had no effect. The warning in town about small arms fire being useless rang in his ears. The captain should have kept his team together instead of separating them into pairs. If he would have kept them together nobody would have been in the line of fire.

The wendigo turned and looked across the ravine at the last two. His eyes glowing red as if lit like a pair of tail lights.

"SKREEEEE, SKREEEEE!" The wendigo gave a mighty leap and crossed over the ravine in a single bound. Its hip hit the sarge in the shoulder and he flew backwards and hit his head on a large rock and lay still.

Corporal Sanders fumbled with the safety on the grenade launcher. By the time he found it he was already dead, his lifeless finger on the switch.

The wendigo turned hungrily towards the unmoving sergeant. The moonlight glimmered off of the silver cross around his neck. The wendigo shrieked angrily, unable to cross the invisible barrier between it and the man laying still on the ground. It turned away and bounded in great ground eating leaps towards its lair.

"Everybody head for Captain Baker's location!" I screamed into the radio.

We couldn't run at night wearing the night vision goggles. It screwed up our depth perception. We would have to move cautiously and protect ourselves from being attracted too.

We got to the bloodbath at the same time Sid and the others did from the other direction.

The captain and one man lay half eaten on the other side of the ravine. On our side was a third man laying in the same condition. Sergeant Wilson lay in the rocks unconscious.

I was mad, I was livid! I felt like I was going to stroke out the way the veins in my neck were pulsing.

"We have one man on this side still alive," I called across to the others. I could see how this was affecting the army men. All of them were as pale as sheets. My warning time after time to the director kept playing back in my head as I crouched down by Wilson.

"He is still alive, Ben. I think he just hit his head on the rocks," Connie said.

"He had a concussion. We'll have to carry him all the way to our vehicles and get him to a hospital," I said.

"What about them?" Sid asked, nodding his head at the dead.

"There is nothing we can do for them now. We'll have to help the living first and then worry about recovering what is left of the remains later today." I said looking at the half eaten bodies. The bodies were more than half gone in only about ten minutes. I took photographs of the three and thought about my next conversation with the director. It was something I hoped he would remember his entire life!

Chapter Twenty-Three

We rolled the sarge over. The back of his head was a bloody mess from hitting the granite boulder. I took my tee shirt off and tore it into strips to bind his head to stop the bleeding. One of the Green Berets tore off his shirt to make a pad like a battle dressing to put against the seeping blood. He held his tee shirt tight against the sarge's head while I used my strips to bind it tight.

"We'll have to carry him the two miles to where our vehicles are parked," Connie said.

Two of us did double duty carrying extra weapons so hands would be free to transport the injured man. We did a fireman's carry. Every two hundred yards a new man would take a turn. It was slow work getting him back. It took three times the amount of time it did to walk out here. Finally two hours later we were back.

The ambulance was in the yard waiting for us. Connie called the homeowner, Joe and told him we would be needing an ambulance. We got the sarge onto the gurney and loaded it into the back of the ambulance. After finding out where they were taking him we stood back and watched it leave.

"Ben, none of this is any of your fault. You talked until you were blue in the face trying to talk him out of sending these men to their deaths," Sid told me.

"I know Sid, but it doesn't make this any easier to deal with."

"What are we supposed to do now, Agent Hawk? Both our commanding officer and our second in command are out of commission. We lost half of our unit tonight," Jim said.

"I don't know what is going to happen. For now I want you to go and check into the best western out on the highway. I'll call ahead and get you a couple of double rooms. The FBI will cover the cost of your rooms and meals."

"Can I give you my phone number? I want you to call us and let us know how the sarge is doing," Tom said.

"Sure, give it to Connie so she can put your number in her phone." My mind was spinning and I was having a hard time thinking about anything other than the men who lost their lives.

Connie jumped into our car and I spun gravel leaving the yard.

"I take it we're going to call the director and have a heart to heart conversation with him."

"Oh, yeah. It'll be more like man to weasel," I said darkly.

We pulled up in front of the sheriff's office. It wasn't daylight yet when we entered the office. We went into the conference room and I called the director and put it on speaker phone so Connie could hear.

"Agent Hawk, how did it go last night?" Washington was two hours ahead of us so the director was being driven into the office for the day.

"You wanted confirmation that these men were ill equipped to handle this job, you son of a bitch! Well you got it! Three dead and a forth one in the hospital." I said through gritted teeth.

The director opened his phone to messages and saw the half eaten corpses.

"That was done to them in only ten minutes! Are you planning on sending the wendigo another easy meal or are you finally going to start listening to us!"

"I don't understand why they failed," the director said while his head reeled.

"Yes you do, you were told and told and told over and over again! But would you listen to us? This is on your shoulders director. You are to blame for this and not us!" I said angrily.

"Now you have a mess to clean up. You have three half eaten bodies laying out in the desert in the hot sun. It's up to you to clean up your mess because we aren't going to be doing it for you!" Connie added.

The director was trying to think of a way out of the mess. The fallout could end his career.

"I'm going to have you recalled to Washington. Get on back to Phoenix and I'll have a corporate jet fly you back."

"Like hell you will! First of all you still have four Green Berets out here that are witnesses to your boondoggle. I put them up in a hotel and billed it to the FBI. Then you have three corpses of military men rotting out in the desert. They deserve a hell of a lot more than they got from you so far! Then you got me and Connie, we aren't coming back and leaving these people to fend for themselves. We were pulled off of vacation. We still have time coming and we are taking it."

The director's face went grey thinking about the position he'd put himself in.

"I'll send a clean-up team to retrieve the bodies and return them to their base."

"Make sure they do it in daylight or you'll be retrieving more bodies."

"Where were you and the others when they were attacked?"

"I was two hundred yards away. All of this was done to them before we could reach them. Hell, I think it was over in less than a minute."

"What about the four Green Berets still left unharmed?" Connie asked.

"Keep them at the hotel until they can be debriefed."

"That's political talk for brain washed Connie. They'll be forced to sign a paper stating that if they ever talk to anyone about what happened last night they'll end up in a prison somewhere and forgotten," I said.

"What are your plans for the rest of the day?" Director Burns said ignoring my comment as he thought about damage control.

"We are going to check on the injured man and then get some sleep. We've been up all night."

We drove to the hospital. The medical staff was busy doing a brain scan on him to check on brain activity. We were sitting dozing in the waiting room when the doctor came out to talk to us.

"You are the FBI agents that had him brought here?"

"Yeah doc, what can you tell us about his prognosis?" I asked.

"Well, brain function is normal as of now. We'll have to keep monitoring him for any changes. If there is pressure on the brain we'll have to drill a hole and relieve it. But for now we'll keep our fingers crossed and hope he wakes up on his own."

"Here's my card. If he wakes up or if there are any changes to his condition could you call us?"

"Sure, I'll do that," he said before tucking the card into the pocket of his lab coat.

I drove us back to the hotel. The green berets were sitting out front waiting for us, worried about their sergeant. They saw us pull in and walked across the parking lot to hear our update.

"The sergeant has a concussion. They did a brain scan and that was normal. They'll keep monitoring his brain function and wait for him to wake back up. If pressure on his brain increases they might have to drill a small hole in his skull to relieve the pressure. But for now it's a wait and see game," Connie told them.

"What about us, are we going out again tonight?" Willy asked us.

"No, you're going out days are over. You men should have never been out there in the first place," I said.

I could see the relief in their eyes. They didn't want to go out there the first time.

"So are we supposed to hang out here or drive back to our own base?" Tom asked.

"I was told to keep you here by the director of the FBI. He says you need to be debriefed before heading on back to your base," I explained to them.

"Besides that, you'll probably like to stick around for your sarge," Connie said.

"Did you check into the hotel yet?" I asked them.

"Yeah, but we could just as well camp outside in our tents," Jim said.

"Do you really want to camp outside with the wendigo still on the loose?" Connie asked them.

"I thought you said it wasn't killing this far away from where we were last night," Jim said.

"It hasn't, yet. But do you want to be outside if it decides to expand its killing field?" Connie asked them.

"I looked at my watch. "It's eight now so let's sleep until noon and we'll meet you in the hotel restaurant at twelve thirty for something to eat. So for now let's all hit the sack."

We met at the appointed time and ate a quick meal of burgers before I broke the news to them.

"We are meeting the recovery team at one thirty to recover your fellow Green Berets. Load up and come along with us," I told them.

"I thought you said this morning we were all done going out into the field?" Bob said.

"We are going out during daylight hours. The wendigo only hunts at night. We will be long gone before dark and besides we thought you'd want to be there to recover your buddies instead of letting strangers do it for you," Connie said.

"You're absolutely right Connie, we do want to be the ones to recover them," Tom said.

"Then let's load up and get moving. The four of you can follow us in one of your Humvees," I said as I signed for the check.

We got out to the three story farmhouse and the recovery team was standing by waiting for us.

As we got out of our car I saw the recovery agent in charge looking at his watch impatiently. After the night and morning we just had that irritated me considerably.

"Do you have a problem agent?" I asked him, not knowing his name.

"We were told to be here at noon," he said in an irritated voice.

"Well that's good then because you didn't keep us waiting for you to get here. We spent the entire night trying to stay alive and a lot of this morning on the phone with the director of the FBI. After that we finally found a few hours to sleep. So what have you been doing since yesterday morning?" I asked him from behind my sunglasses with an unhappy look on my face. He knew he pushed me too far.

"Sorry Special Agent Hawk. We just want to get this ugly business of recovering the bodies over with."

"So do we. These men are coming with us. They want the honor of carrying out their teammates. Let's get moving, we have a couple of miles to walk."

"Four men are going to carry out three bodies?"

"You'll understand better once we get to the killing field."

Once again we walked across the large hay field. Connie carried her grenade launcher and I had my streetsweeper.

"That's an awful lot of firepower to recover bodies with," the agent in charge said with a surprised look on his face.

"I didn't catch your name," I said.

For a second he thought about giving a flippant answer like, I didn't throw it but then thought better of it. "It's special agent Graham Peterson."

"Well Graham, when we get there all will be made clear to you," I said with a grim look on my face as I kept walking at a steady pace.

"You guys all have grenades in your launchers, right?" Connie asked the army men.

"You're damn right we do. I only wish we had as many as you do Connie," Tom said.

"We'll be out of the area before we will need them, Tom. I promise," Connie said.

We walked out into the desert and kept walking. We passed the spot where Sid and his partner were stationed last night. We got close to where the bodies were and flushed up three vultures that were feeding on the remains. They took off flying and the green berets in their anger over seeing their comrades being feasted on by scavengers, started firing on the birds, knocking one of them down.

"Cease fire, cease fire," I shouted.

"We don't want to advertise our presence here to anyone, do you read me?" Connie said, passing on the silent message. The wendigo wasn't known for coming out during the day. But why take unnecessary chances by ringing the dinner bell for it.

"You have two bodies on this side of the ravine to examine and another one on the other side," I said.

"What bodies? Everything is gone from the pecs on down," Gram said in awe.

The recovery team started to examine the bodies and take tissue samples along with DNA. It was slow work that took hours to do.

"What's this blood on this rock from?"Graham asked as he pointed to where the sarge was found lying.

"That was from the fourth victim. He is still alive and in the hospital in a coma," Connie told him.

I looked at the sky and saw how late it was getting. "You'd better wrap it up, Graham. We need to get the hell out of here," I said.

"I need at least another two hours to process the crime scene, Ben. We can't be rushed and do sloppy work."

"Well hell Graham, let me put it to you in another way. Do you see those bodies? That's what happens when you are out here after dark. This thing hunts at night and all of this carnage was done in only ten minutes. So now how much time do you still need?" I asked with raised eyebrows.

Graham looked around himself one last time. "Bag them, we're all done here."

"I was hoping you'd see it our way. Now you know why Connie brought along her bazooka."

"Also why Ben has his super sized Tommy gun," Connie added.

What was left of the remains probably could have been fitted in a single body bag but the evidence dictated they remain separated. Three of the green berets stepped forward to grab a bag each and carry their buddies' remains back to the farmyard. They placed them gently into the back of the recovery vehicle, stood back and gave their comrades a final slow salute before pivoting on their heels and walking away.

I gave Graham my business card and asked him to call me if they found anything useful that could help us out. He promised he would and then they drove away.

"What are we doing next?" Bob asked in the gathering darkness.

"We go back to our hotel and have a couple of much needed beers and eat dinner," I said.

"Copy that! I think we could all use a cold one," Tom said.

Connie called the hospital while I was driving to the hotel to find out how Sergeant Wilson was doing. She was told he was showing progress. The duty nurse said he was tossing and turning and mumbling in his sleep. She said it was a good indication he was coming out of the coma. I thought to myself he was having nightmares, and rightfully so.

We got back to the hotel and walked as a group into the bar and occupied a table before ordering two pitchers of beer. I leaned my shotgun against the wall next to me. By now the bartender knew better than to ask me to remove the shotgun.

Willy poured the beers and raised his glass. "Here's to our fallen comrades, may they find peace and reside in heaven by the side of our Lord."

"And now a toast to fighting men and lost brothers." Willy raised his pint of beer and we all raised ours to join in the toast.

"Here's a toast to fighting men and adventures alike! If you cheat, you may cheat death; if you steal, may you steal a woman's heart; if you fight, may you fight for a brother; if you drink, may you drink with me. Lady and gentlemen, here's to our friends and comrades who can no longer toast with us. Until we meet again, rest in peace my brothers!"

We all clinked glasses and bid them a final farewell in our hearts. Connie and I only knew them for a single day but they lost their lives fighting our demon, the wendigo.

After a few well deserved and needed pitchers of beer we moved into the dining room to eat dinner.

"What's on the agenda for tomorrow," Willy asked us.

"Well, first thing in the morning after breakfast we plan on checking on your sarge if you guys want to tag along. We talked to the hospital and they say he is showing improvement so we're hopeful he is awake in the morning and can talk to us," I said.

"We'd like to come along and check on the sarge. What time are we meeting for breakfast?" Tom asked.

"Let's make it seven. After we check on the sarge Connie and I have reports to file so that will take most of the day. There are a lot of reports to file, especially when there is a death. You guys will be free for the rest of the day. Go ahead and use the pool or go and look around the area. We'll meet you again at supper," I said.

"You're not going out again tomorrow night?" Willy asked.

"No, not all investigations are always in the field. There is research and resources that need to be checked in order to keep the operation as safe as possible," Connie said.

"It would be good if the sarge is awake when we visit tomorrow. He is the only one that can provide certain information for our reports," I said.

"Why is that Ben?" Bob asked me.

"It's because he is the only one left alive from his team. He can provide the details of what happened to the captain and the others," Connie said.

"I get it," Bob said as the entire group fell silent again thinking their own thoughts.

The next morning we met with our group in the lobby. "Good news guys, the sarge woke up," Connie said with a smile as she broke the good news.

"That's great, let's go and see him!" Jim said.

"Breakfast first guys. It's going to be a long day for us. Besides that the hospital will need time to feed and take care of the sarge first thing this morning," I said.

There was a bit of impatient grumbling but they understood and followed us into the restaurant. We'd found out the restaurant was open for breakfast on the weekends. After eating they followed us to the hospital.

"We're looking for Sergeant Wilson's room," Connie told the woman manning the front desk.

"He is in room 212," she said with a smile as her eyes followed the young army men in their desert camo uniforms.

We knocked on the door as we entered the room. Sarge was looking a little bit gray and a whole lot depressed over the events of two nights ago. He still didn't know everything that happened that night.

He looked at us hopefully and sat up a little bit straighter. "First, what day is it?"

"It's Saturday, you've been in a coma for over a day," Connie told him.

"My head feels awful but the nurse said she had to wait to give me something for it until the doctor has seen me."

"We need to get information from you about the night your group was attacked," Connie said gently.

"I need info too. Who else came out of it alive?"

"You are the only one to survive," Willy said gently.

"All three of them are gone?"

"It was awful, sarge! Not very much of them were left to collect," Tom said.

"Well, it looks like you were right on Ben. We had no business being out there. We didn't stand a chance when that thing attacked us. I would have never believed what it did physically was even possible."

"Tell us everything you can remember from the time we left you at that location until after the attack," I said.

"The captain blew up as soon as you were out of ear shot. He took his cross and threw it into the rocks. That really made the man that was going to be by his side angry. He told him if he didn't want the cross that he would have taken it. The captain told him if he wanted it he could go and find it. Corporal Jacobs looked everywhere for it but it must have fallen out of sight in the rocks."

"I knew he was stupid and stubborn but I didn't know how stupid and stubborn he was," I said.

"Then he separated us into two groups. He and Jacobs on one side of the ravine and us on the other side of it,"

"He separated his forces instead of keeping them together?" Connie said in astonishment.

"I fought with him on that too but he said he was in command and we had to follow his orders."

"After he tossed the cross I told him there were no atheists in foxholes and that made him mad too."

"So the only one wearing a cross was you?" I asked him.

"Yeah, I had the only one."

"So who was attacked first, the captain or you?" Connie asked him.

"It was the captain and Jacobs. We heard that awful screeching and then it was on us in a second before anyone had time to react. I wouldn't have believed it if I hadn't seen it. In a split second the captain was gone. Jacobs tried to fire his grenade but it sailed over the wendigos head. A split second later Jacobs was dead too. We couldn't fire our grenades at it in fear of hitting our teammates. Then the wendigo leaped forty feet across the ravine in a single bound and hit me in the chest with its hip. I flew backwards and the lights went out."

"After it hit you it took out your partner too. Did you see it consume any of your teammates?" I asked him.

"No, he must have done that after the attack was over. How long did it take you to get back to where we were?"

"Only about ten or fifteen minutes. He did all of that damage in less than ten minutes."

"He hit you and knocked you out. How was he able to do that if you were wearing the cross?" Connie asked him.

"He jumped all the way across the ravine in a single bound. Maybe he wasn't close enough to me to feel the effects of the cross when he jumped."

"That could be it, Connie. He was already airborne when he detected the cross and couldn't stop himself once he left the ground," I said.

"We know one thing for sure now at least. Everybody needs to be wearing their own cross to be safe from this thing," Connie said.

"What about the captain and the men we lost? Have they been recovered yet?"

"We went out and brought them back yesterday," Tom said.

"We'll leave you with your men so you can talk. We have things that need to be done today. Guys, we'll see you at the hotel around six?" I said.

"We'll be there," Willy said as we disappeared out of the room.

We got back to our hotel and my phone rang, it was Jeff Longbow.

"Ben, I finally have some information for you. Can we meet later on today?"

"Jeff, can we make it tomorrow morning instead? We're buried in paperwork. Three of the green berets were killed and we have to file the reports on the incident today."

"I'm sorry, I hadn't heard about that. The wendigo got them, didn't it?"

"Yeah, they wouldn't listen to us and had to send them here anyway. What a waste."

"I understand Ben. Should we say tomorrow morning at ten at my house?"

"We'll see you then Jeff and thanks for finding the information for us," I said before ending the call.

"We have a meeting with Joe's Uncle Jeff tomorrow morning at ten o'clock Connie," I informed her.

We both got our laptops out and sat on the deck in the hot desert breeze to do the reports. We both needed to do every report. The FBI was very thorough comparing reports to make sure the narrative of the event matched. Especially when loss of life was involved.

It was five o'clock before we finished with all of the paperwork. We read each other's reports to make sure they were in line with each other before we emailed them to headquarters and the desk of the director.

By now I was getting a stiff neck from leaning over my laptop. It was hard to see the screen out here in the desert sunlight. But I was too stupid to go inside where it was darker.

"The reports aren't word for word but they shouldn't be. Everybody has their own way of wording things," Connie said.

"I think we were too easy on the director though. We kind of let him off of the hook," I said.

"Yeah I know Ben. but a little cool down time before we see him in Washington might not be a bad thing."

We hit the send buttons and they were on their way to the director's office.

The director heard the ding announcing the emails being received. He saw they were from Hawk and Sanchez and opened them worried about how they would write up the reports. He sat and leaned back in his chair reading each report word for word. The reports were clear, concise and professionally done. The tension eased from between his shoulder blades. Maybe, just maybe this would blow over yet.

We went down stairs an hour early. Eight hours of doing paperwork had worn us out. The Green Berets weren't in the restaurant or bar. We'd checked on the way down and they weren't in their rooms either. A quick check showed us that both of the Humvees were in the parking lot. So that left us with two places left to search, the pool and the arcade. We found them in the pool swimming.

"Is it six o'clock already?" Tom asked, climbing out of the pool.

"No, it's only five but we got done early so we came on down," Connie said.

"We've been filling out reports on the deaths all day long and decided we deserved a cold one. When you guys decide to join us we'll be in the barroom," I said.

"Give us ten minutes to dry off and change and we'll join you," Willy's voice echoed off the tile from the other side of the pool.

The four Green Berets joined us ten minutes later. I could smell the chlorine on them from the pool.

"You guys look all done in," Tom noticed.

"There is only one thing worse to do than paperwork on people you worked with being killed," Connie said with a frown.

"What could be worse than that?" Tom asked her.

"Death notifications. There is nothing worse than telling a woman her husband was killed."

"Yeah, I can see where that would be way worse," Tom said, agreeing with her.

They told us the doctor visited the sarge while they were still there and he prescribed pain meds for him. The doctor said he would have to stay in the hospital for another day or two just to make sure he didn't have any brain bleeds.

"Are we going to be able to stay here until the sarge gets out and we can travel back to our base together?" Bob asked.

"I don't see why not. The FBI is going to want to debrief the sarge most of all so I would expect you aren't going anywhere anytime soon," Connie said.

"Where did you find swim trunks?" I asked them out of curiosity.

"They sell them in the gift shop. Saved us from trying to find a Walmart way out here in the middle of nowhere," Jim said.

"You guys are all set up for meals and drinks. Just give them your room number and the charges will be billed to it. From hour to hour we don't know where we'll be so after breakfast tomorrow morning we'll see you when we see you," I told them.

"Alright, we'll hang out at the hotel for the most part unless we're visiting the sarge," Tom said.

"Yeah, we shouldn't be too hard to find," Jim added.

We ate and parted ways. We didn't know what tomorrow would bring after meeting with Jeff but I had a feeling this case was going to ramp up.

Chapter Twenty-Four

We met with the Green Berets for breakfast as promised. They planned on going right over to the hospital to check on Sergeant Wilson.

"We have a meeting set for ten this morning with the guy who used to be in charge of the Navajo Rangers before he retired. From there we don't know where the case is going to lead us," I told them.

"Out of curiosity, can I ask you something?" Jim asked me.

"Sure, go ahead."

"Why do you carry your shotgun everywhere you go? You even have it with you in the bar and restaurant."

"I don't worry about getting attacked here, but twice now someone left rattlesnakes for us. I carry it with me so no one can screw around with it."

"You really think someone would be stupid enough to mess with your shotgun?"

"Two someones were stupid enough to toss a snake into our room and into our car, Connie was bitten. I don't want to need it, especially against the wendigo and have it go click when I try to fire it."

"What happened to the guys who tossed in the snakes?" Willy asked.

"I beat the hell out of them and tossed them in jail. They're now in Phoenix facing federal charges."

"We can't blame you for that. You look okay now Connie," Tom said.

"I got a dose of anti-venom and had to rest for a day, but I'm good now."

We finished eating and drove to the Sheriff's office to see if anything happened overnight.

"It was a peaceful night for a change Ben," Joe said.

"We have a meeting for ten this morning with your uncle. He says he has important information for us to hear." Connie said.

"It's nine thirty we may as well head over now," Joe said, looking at the wall clock.

We drove a few blocks to Jeff's home. He was sitting on the front porch waiting for us.

"Come on up and grab a chair," he invited us.

"What did you find that can help us?" Connie asked.

"These attacks have happened in the past. I was right about what I told you a couple of days ago."

"Really! Here on the reservation?" I asked.

"Yeah, but a long time ago. The last time was in 1900. The attacks went on for almost three months."

"We're only a little more than two weeks into the known attacks happening now. Does that mean they'll go on for another two and a half months?" Joe asked.

"I can't answer that."

"How many people were killed in the last series of attacks?" I asked.

"The total number of victims is unknown, Ben. You have to remember back in 1900 people were getting around on foot and horseback. Many of the deaths may have been undiscovered. But I can tell you the number of victims was more than eighteen."

"You said the last series of attacks was in 1900. Does that mean there were other occurrences before 1900?" Connie asked.

"Yes, from before we used the white man's written language. I found pictures painted on deer hides in the archives. There was a drawing of the wendigo attacking a village."

"Can you date how long ago the record of the event was painted?" Joe asked his uncle.

"I can't provide an exact date but I would guess it was from before 1800."

"How come the Navajo weren't aware of these occurrences? You would have thought it would have been part of your folklore and known by all," Connie said.

"Not so Connie. If it was thought the attacks were by an evil entity people would have been told not to talk about it or it would bring it back among the people."

"So then in a matter of a single generation all knowledge would have been erased. The only ones who would still know about it were the ones who lived through it and they were honor bound to not talk about it," I said.

"That's right Ben."

"So then the last time the wendigo walked the earth was 125 years ago. Is it safe to assume the time before that was another 125 years earlier?" Joe asked.

"I don't have that answer but you would have to be close to the right number of years."

"How did the villagers rid themselves of the wendigo in times past?" Connie asked.

"Nothing was mentioned about getting rid of it. I think after a certain amount of time it just went away on its own."

"We can't afford to leave it to kill at will for another two and a half months," Joe said.

"You already found out that Christian crosses can provide a level of protection. There are other ways of providing one's self with protection," Jeff said.

"What do you mean?" Connie asked him.

"Old ways, Native American ways. Ben, your grandfather was a healer?" Jeff asked me.

"He was a healer in the Oglala Sioux tribe for many years."

"We have healers, holy men and medicine men here too. I want to take the two of you to see one this afternoon. He should be able to help you in ways you don't know about."

"Alright Jeff, anything to help us win out against the wendigo," I glanced sideways at my unsuspecting partner. She didn't know yet what she was in for but I had a pretty good idea. I grinned behind my sunglasses and the grin went unnoticed by Connie.

"Good, it is all set then. I will let our holy man know we are coming this afternoon and to prepare for your arrival," Jeff said with satisfaction.

It was four in the afternoon and we were following Jeff's car to visit the holy man. We pulled off the road and drove for a mile on what seemed like an old wagon rut. The trail ended at a sweat lodge that was adjacent to a deep pool that was fed by a small series of three waterfalls. There were a dozen people in the water skinny dipping. Men and women and children alike were enjoying cooling off in the water.

"Ben, I feel like I'm invading their privacy," Connie said, red faced as she quickly looked away.

"I have a feeling you're going to lose your inhibitions," I said, grinning behind my sunglasses.

Connie was eyeing me suspiciously. An old man came out of the sweat lodge. He was bare-chested and his face showed a lifetime of desert life. It looked like a roadmap of cracks and creases but his eyes were bright and alive.

"You are the ones I've been waiting for, that Jeff Longbow called me about?"

"Yes, Ben Hawk and Connie Sanchez," I said.

"He told me you were doing battle with the wendigo, trying to rid our reservation of its evil presence."

"We're trying to but so far all we've been able to do is get three men killed," I said.

"Today we will see if we can't help you with discovering new ways of defeating it. Jeff said your grandfather was a healer in the Oglala Sioux nation?"

"Yes, I spent my summers with my grandparents in the Dakotas."

"You will be spending the night in the sweat lodge. When morning comes you will have the answers and information you need. During the night both of you will be visited by the Great Spirit and he will have knowledge that will be helpful."

"We can use all of the help we can get," Connie said.

"I need you now to become one with nature," the holy man said

"Huh?" Connie said in a shocked voice.

"He wants you naked," I told her with a grin.

"Huh?" Connie said again.

"Start stripping sister," I said grinning at her.

"Huh!?" Connie said looking around at a lot of people who would be able to see her nude.

"Connie, we don't get as hung up with being naked like you do.

When I was a boy I ran around naked at my grandparents house until I was seven or eight. If they made me put clothes on to go to town I thought I was being punished. I would have gladly waltzed into a store naked when I was a young boy," I said as I started stripping off my clothes.

Connie stood there frozen in place as she watched me strip to my bare skin.

"This better not be some sort of mean joke you dreamed up to get the better of me Ben!" Connie said as she pulled her shirt off over her head as her face grew red with embarrassment. Her other clothes soon followed and she was standing beside me naked for all of the world to see.

"Kind of liberating isn't it?" I grinned at her.

"Shut up Ben," she said, red faced.

"I must now prepare you for your meeting with the Great Spirit," the holy man said.

He had white paint on his left hand and placed it over my face. I closed my eyes so I didn't get it into my eyes. When he pulled his hand away there was a hand print covering my entire face. Connie was next and had his right hand covered in black paint. He proceeded to do the same thing to Connie's face he did to mine.

Next he put different colored streaks and stripes all over our bodies. Arms, legs, chests, backs and rear ends. As a final gesture he put a dab of black on each of Connie's nipples.

Connie jumped back in surprise. "Hey!"

"You are shy and timid of your own body and nakedness. These two dabs of paint will give you something to hide behind. When next I see you, you will no longer be afraid to be naked with others watching."

"You will enter the smoke lodge and stay in it until I come for you in the morning. Under no circumstances are you to leave the lodge. Sometime during the night ahead of you, you are going to both be visited by the Great Spirit."

"Why do we have to be naked when we are with him?" Connie asked.

"Certain things must happen to prove your worthiness to be in his presence. You must be naked before him to show him your willingness to meet with him on his terms. Inside the smoke lodge is a pot of water and a gourd dipper. You can drink all you want to during the night. You will find a bundle of sage inside. You can put small amounts into the fire for purification. You must also rub your bodies with it often to make your outer being as pure as your inner being. Finally, you will find willow switches inside to lash yourself and each other with. The red marks that are left on your bodies will show the Great Spirit your willingness to show penance for past transgressions. I will come and retrieve you in the morning. You can then bathe your tired and injured bodies in this welcoming pool of water."

"While you are inside greeting the Great Spirit I will be out here making each of you a talisman to help protect you from the wendigo. You must wear the leather pouch around your neck, for all time. It must always be worn from now until you are no more. To quit wearing it will bring on hardship and bad luck. I have worn mine for nearly seventy years.

"My grandfather wore one and set great store by it. The only time I can remember him taking it off was to replace the leather thong the small bag hung from."

"Your grandfather was indeed a wise man. Go now into the sweat lodge, the Great Spirit will be coming soon to teach you what you need to know to defeat the wendigo."

I raised the buffalo hide covering the doorway and motioned Connie in ahead of me.

"Why is it I think you knew what was going to happen when we got here before we got here?" Connie asked me accusingly.

"I had a pretty good idea when Jeff mentioned there being more ways of protecting ourselves than we know about. I guess you didn't notice me grinning at you when I thought of the surprise you'd be getting."

"Very funny Ben. I was naked in front of all of those people out there!" Connie said red faced.

"Well they were naked in front of you too! It didn't bother them so why is it bothering you?"

"Probably because it's new to me I guess."

I picked up the tightly wound bundle of sage and bent down to put a little bit into the embers of the fire. Connie picked up one of the willow switches and lashed me across my ass with more force than she should have.

"Damn it Connie, take it easy with that. You're not supposed to draw blood!"

"Opps, sorry Ben. I saw you bent over the fire and saw what a fine target your butt made. I wanted to make sure I got my lick in before you straightened back up again."

Connie hit me with the switch again and I jumped and covered myself.

"Connie, watch where you're swinging that thing! We might want to use it to have fun, after we are done with this case."

"Sorry Ben," Connie was grinning ear to ear. I could tell she wasn't sorry at all.

"So that's the way it's going to be, is it? Tit for tat? You hit me in the tat now I'm going to hit you in the tit!" I said as I lashed her across her breasts.

"Youch! Alright, I give, that's enough!" Connie squealed as she jumped around.

"No, you're right this is a lot of fun, repent you sinner!" I laughed out as I lashed her back, buttocks, legs and belly. I wasn't hitting her to draw blood or cause her undo pain. But in order to show the Great Spirit our willingness to show penance we needed to display welts meant to convey our desire to be better people.

"Youch! Ben, you can quit grinning now. You don't need to show so much joy in your work!"

"I'm sorry Connie but I like the way your boobs bounce when you're dancing around my switch."

"You like dancing? Start dancing funny boy!" Connie yelled as she started to lash me full of red marks. She was really getting into it. I had red marks in places I didn't think red marks could get to.

"Ouch, that's enough Connie! You're having way too much fun with that switch. Youch, I said enough!"

"You're right, Ben, I liked the way your little weiner was bouncing around as you danced too," Connie said, grinning ear to ear.

"Now let me rub your body all over with the sage. The holy

man said we needed to do that to make our outer being as pure as our inner being. We'll have to do it a few times during the night."

I took the sage and pulled out a handful so it was like a handful of hay or straw in my hands and rubbed it all over Connie's sweaty body. The use of the sage smeared some of the paint the holy man put on our bodies.

"Give me that sage, it's my turn to do you now," Connie said as she massaged my body with the sage.

"This stuff itches like rolling in the hay itches," I complained.

"The itching isn't going to go away until we can get into that pool of water tomorrow," Connie said.

"I'm really looking forward to that. It's really hot in here," I said.

"Do you really think we're going to have real visions of the Great Spirit Ben or do you think we'll just be hallucinating from a full night of this heat?"

"I guess you'll be able to answer your own question in the morning," I told her.

We were in the sweat lodge for several hours before it finally got dark outside. All we had for light in the sweat lodge was the glow of the embers in the fire. From time to time we added sage to the fire. The holy man was tending the fire from the outside of the lodge. Every now and then we used the switches on each other. It seemed the more we used them the less it hurt to be hit by them.

Water was streaming off of our bodies from the hours of heat. We took turns rubbing our oily bodies with the sage. That too quit itching the more we used it. Sometime after midnight we fell into a deep sleep.

In my sleep I started having a dream or was it a vision?

"Ben Hawk of the Oglala Sioux, you have summoned me. I can sense you have questions for me you need answers to?"

"Great Spirit, I am honored by your presence."

"I see you have presented yourself to me in the correct manner. You have purified your outer being with the sage and done penance with the willow switches. I know what you want to know but I'll let you in your own words ask me."

"Great Spirit, Is there a way of sending the wendigo to whence it came? Or are we doomed to failure and better off trying to avoid it?"

"It can be banned. You already know it does not like fire so fire is a great source as a weapon."

"Are a wendigo and a demon one and the same? Are they both from hell?"

"The wendigo resides in the bowels of the earth. I do not refer to it as hell but the place it resides in is very, very hot. The deeper you go into the bowels of the earth the hotter it gets."

"So you're saying a wendigo and a demon aren't one and the same? A Christian demon and a Native American wendigo are different beings?"

"That is not a question you need an answer to my Oglala Sioux child. You will gain knowledge of all of your questions once you are by my side for eternity. But today is not that day nor is tomorrow. Ask me just what you need to know and nothing more."

"I know wendigos are a part of Chippewa, Cree, Mohawk and blackfoot legend. Which tribe does this wendigo come from and why is it in the southwest instead of the cold of the far north from where it came from?"

"You are right, the wendigo is from the north. A wendigo can only become one by doing the most vile of deeds. Only greed and pure evil can produce a wendigo. For your purposes it is not important for you to know which tribe the wendigo was created by, but only that he is here. This wendigo has been on this earth for over four hundred years."

"What vile deed did the wendigo do to become one?"

"There was once a man who lived in a village. A village survives by everyone doing their part. There are women who cook. Some gather nuts, berries and other edible plants. The men hunt, fish and protect the weak and young. Even the old have jobs. Old women tan leather and make moccasins. The old men make arrows for hunting and defending the village. Everyone has what they need but not everyone has what they want."

"This man, Red Thunder, was caught stealing from others. He was greedy and wanted their possessions. He didn't want to work for these things but to steal the hard work of others. When he was caught he was forced to run the gauntlet naked while the men of the tribe beat him with clubs as he passed between them. "It took several weeks for him to heal enough to be of any use to the village."

"That doesn't sound like it would be enough to be cursed and become a wendigo."

"My tale isn't over yet. He was caught stealing a second time and banished from the village. Red Thunder, along with his wife and three children were forced from the village. He and his family left in shame and put their lodge up a dozen miles from the village he was banned from. As a village everybody works to feed the people. No one family can long survive on their own."

"For the first few months Red Thunder did alright. He was able to catch fish and small game while his wife did the cooking and gathering of edible plants. But then winter hit and it was like no other in anyone's memory. Many feet of snow fell. The big game animals herded up in the pine forests far from where their lodge was. They couldn't gather firewood and soon the lodge was cold. When it wasn't snowing, the cold from the far north came."

"That sounds like a hopeless situation to be in."

"It was a situation of his own making. Soon hunger was the only thing Red Thunder could think of. His youngest child died first, he was only two summers old. This is where the Vile, evil deed came into play. He ate his own flesh and blood. Nobody else in the family would partake with him and chose to die a slow and cold death instead. The first child only lasted him a week and then he killed the next one and then the next until all that was left to eat was his wife."

"What did his wife do to protect herself and her children?"

"There was not much she could do. She was cold and hungry and weak from not eating for many weeks, he killed her last."

"When spring came the people of the village went in search of Red Thunder and his family. They felt bad about banishing the wife and children and wanted to let them rejoin the village. They found his lodge and the bones of the dead were scattered everywhere. They could detect tooth marks on the bones and knew what had happened. Red Thunder was never seen again.

That was when he became a wendigo."

"My question wasn't answered Great Spirit, why is he here instead of the far north and why is it he doesn't like fire?

"He doesn't like the far north because he blames the cold and the snow for what he has become. He takes no responsibility for his own actions. He doesn't like fire because he is cursed and doomed to an eternity in the bowels of the earth where he must endure."

"But we don't go as far as to call it hell?"

"This is not information you need to succeed Oglala Sioux. Ask only the questions you need answers to in order to come out victorious."

"Do we have a pathway to victory?"

"Yes, I feel in my heart that where others have failed in the past you will come out victorious."

"I learned today this isn't the first time this wendigo had visited the Navajos."

"That is true, three times in the past he has cursed them with his presence."

"How did the others stop him?"

"They didn't stop him, my child. They endured him until his hunger was sated and he returned to the bowels of the earth. They did not have the weapons and the resources that you have in these times."

"You said his appetite was sated. Why does he even come back?"

"He has a hunger for human flesh now and comes back from time to time to feed his hunger. Once he is satisfied he returns to the bowels of the earth once more."

"So my weapons to defeat the wendigo are fire and ice?"

"I know of no weapon that is made of ice, my child. Your weapon to defeat the wendigo must be fire."

"There are tanks of liquid nitrogen that have a temperature of absolute zero. But I don't know how close we would have to get in order for it to be effective. I really don't want to get near it."

"As I just told you my Sioux warrior, fire should be your weapon of choice."

"If we defeat the wendigo will it be banished from the earth forever?" I asked hopefully.

"I cannot answer that question for it has never been beaten. But isn't it good enough to know the wendigo will never be seen again in your lifetime?"

"I don't understand, Great Spirit, why can't you tell me if it will never come back again?"

"Would you consider the wendigo to be a living breathing being or something walking this earth that is without a life? Can you totally banish something that was never alive in the first place since it became what it is?"

"I understand your answer now."

"I sense you are running out of questions for me Oglala Sioux. You are indeed a warrior and I take great pride in being able to help you banish the wendigo."

"I thank you Great Spirit for your help. And say goodbye until we meet again on the other side."

Ben returned to a deep sleep as the vision ended.

Connie tossed and turned in her sleep until the Great Spirit presented itself.

"It is a very rare occurrence when a person who is not of Native American blood presents themselves to me," the Great Spirit said.

Connie stared at him but didn't say a word.

"I sense doubt in your eyes and in your heart my child. You are wondering if I am indeed a vision or a hallucination from hour upon hour in the sweat lodge. Yet you have honored me by presenting yourself in the proper manner. You have rubbed yourself with sage to purify your outer being and flogged yourself to show your penance for past transgressions. "

"Are you really here Great Spirit or only inside my head?"

"Can I not be here and also inside your head, child?"

"Why the many hours in the sweat lodge if it isn't to produce a hallucination?"

"It is a part of your penance along with the flogging. You must first prove yourself worthy of a visit. "

"You have many questions to ask of me about the wendigo."

"Yes, I know it is a being from the north. I've found out that Chippewa, Blackfoot, Cree and Iroquois among others have stories about them."

"Yes many nations have tales in their past about wendigos."

"This wendigo was a blackfoot wasn't it?"

"What makes you think the wendigo was a blackfoot before becoming a wendigo?

"Because it has attacked and killed many people but the only one it took alive was Carl and Carl was a blackfoot.

"Ahh, the Oglala Sioux asked me the same question in a different way, but I refused to answer it. I didn't want to put any tribe in a bad light that was none of their doing. But you have guessed the truth on your own and I will acknowledge it as being true."

"Will we be able to rescue Carl from the wendigo?"

"No, it is too late for Carl to be rescued. The wendigo has been feeding him human flesh and casting spells and doing incantations meant to turn him into a wendigo. If Carl would have refused the flesh he might be able to be saved but he ate out of fear of the wendigo. So his fate is sealed. His transformation into a wendigo has already been started and cannot be stopped or reversed. You must vanquish him when you vanquish the true wendigo."

"Why is it even here? This isn't the far north. This isn't its homeland."

"I have told the Oglala Sioux, Ben Hawk the answer to that. You can ask him for the answer as to why it is here and not in the cold of the north."

"Are we going to be killed by the wendigo or are we going to be victorious over it?"

"I don't sense your death in the near future. I feel you will find a way of defeating it."

"Has it ever been defeated before now?"

"No one has ever found a way to defeat it."

"Then how come it isn't here all of the time?"

"When its hunger for human flesh is quenched it returns to the realm where it must reside for all time."

"So you're talking about hell then."

"I am talking about the bowels of the earth where it is very hot."

"You are the Great Spirit, are you also the Christian God?"

"You will not ask for answers to questions you do not need answers for at this time. All will be made clear to you on the other side when life is over."

"When I cross over to the other side will I be with you?"

"You are with Ben Hawk now. It would be a cruel thing for me to separate you after death. I would welcome someone such as yourself who has just honored me with open arms, my child.

"You keep calling me my child, am I?"

"Are you not a child of God?"

"But you just told me you weren't God."

"No, you asked if the Great Spirit and the Christian God are one and the same and I told you it was something you didn't need to know for the task at hand."

Connie's head was swimming by the non answer. "How can we possibly beat the wendigo?

"You have already found out the wendigo flees from heat. He must reside in the bowels of the earth when he is not among you. Your answer is to use a lot of heat, as much as you can find and muster."

"We have to know where we can find him during the daylight so we can surprise him and try to defeat him."

"Close your eyes my child and I will show you the way to his lair," The Great Spirit said as he waved his hand in front of Connie's eyes.

Connie's eyes drifted shut. "I take you now to the last place where the Wendigo killed, the ravine. We are now drifting upwards so we can look down upon the scene. Now we are floating over the desert heading away from the creek bottom. We have traveled perhaps a half of a mile from the ravine. "Do you not see his lair down below us my child?"

"What is that? What am I looking at?"

"It is a dugout log cabin with a sod roof. It is the same place he used the last time he walked on this earth. It was built by fur trappers in the mid 1800s to trap fir along the creek bottom."

"Why did they build it nearly a mile from where they were doing their trapping?"

"So they wouldn't be discovered by the people whose land they were invading and trapping the fir on."

"So the wendigo stays in the cabin during the daylight hours. Has it ever killed anyone during the daytime?"

"Only once when someone discovered the cabin and entered it to see what was inside."

"That would have been a very bad thing to have happened."

"Yes it was. I can sense now that all of your questions have been answered. You now know how to defeat the wendigo and where to find it in order to bring about its end."

"I thank you Great Spirit for your wisdom and kindness," Connie said with a smile.

"I sense you have become more comfortable with the skin you were born with since this experience has happened."

"I haven't thought of it but I guess you're right. Why should I be afraid to show my skin."

The Great Spirit smiled on her kindly. "Until we meet again in the hereafter I bid you farewell my child," he said as he faded away into nothingness.

Connie fell into a deep sleep and was only awakened in the morning by the holy man entering the sweat lodge.

"It is time to wake up and cleanse your skin," He announced, poking each of us with a staff to wake us up from a deep sleep.

I stood up and reached out for Connie's hand and pulled her to her feet. We walked out of the sweat lodge. The sun was showing us it was already almost mid morning. The pool of water already had its first visitors of the day splashing around in it.

"The holy man left us in the sweat lodge longer than I thought he would. Let's get into the water and cool our bodies off," I said.

We walked down to the water side by side. Only yesterday Connie would have been trying to find a way to cover herself up. But after the events of yesterday and last night she walked unashamed and joined the others in the coolness of the pool.

"What do you think now Connie? Was the Great Spirit a vision or a hallucination?"

"It was amazing and definitely a vision. We now know where the wendigo hides out during the daylight hours. The Great Spirit showed me the location."

"We also know how the wendigo came to be. How long it's been a wendigo and what it had to do to become one. I even know what his name was when he was alive."

"Oh yeah? But you don't know what tribe he was from. I guessed the right answer and the Great Spirit told me that I was right!"

"Well, what tribe was he from?"

"He was a blackfoot Ben, that's why he took Carl alive. He wants to make Carl in his own image."

"So we'll try to rescue Carl before we burn the wendigo."

"Carl can't be saved, Ben. The Great Spirit told me the wendigo was feeding human flesh to Carl and was casting spells and doing incantations to turn him into a wendigo. The Great Spirit said the transformation has already started and can't be stopped or reversed. Carl has got to die, Ben."

As we stood in the chest deep water we were busy scrubbing the paint off of our bodies while we talked. Connie turned around so I could do her back and her butt for her. It was plain to see the holy man had been thorough and generous with his painting.

I turned around so Connie could do my back and butt. "The Great Spirit said this wendigo has never been defeated and stayed until he had his fill of human flesh. He told me he has been around for four hundred years," I told Connie.

The wendigos hideout is only about a half of a mile from where the Green Berets were killed. He is staying in an old dugout trappers cabin. He stayed in the same cabin the last time he walked the earth," Connie told me.

"Well its days are now numbered because we have a weapon they never had in past times."

"What weapon is that Ben?" Connie asked as she dunked her head under water to scrub off the handprint on her face.

"We're going to use jellied gasoline on it," I said with satisfaction.

"Jellied gasoline, what is that?"

"Napalm Connie. We are going to bomb it with napalm."

Our body temperatures were back to near normal and the paint was all off our bodies. We climbed out of the refreshing pool and walked back to the sweat lodge and the holy man who was waiting for us. The sweat lodge was a hundred yards away. A curious young couple stopped us to talk with us. We all stood naked talking with each other. Before Connie would have been trying to hide herself but those days seemed to be behind us.

"Is it true you spent the night in the sweat lodge trying to communicate with the Great Spirit?" the young woman asked us.

"Yes, we were in the lodge for over fourteen hours," Connie told her.

"Did the Great Spirit appear before you?" the young man asked us anxiously.

"We both had visions with him before morning came and it was amazing," Ben said.

"You were very lucky that he appeared for you," the girl said.

"We have a common enemy, the wendigo. The great Spirit wants to rid the earth of its presence as much as we do. He cares very deeply for the Navajo tribe," Connie told them.

That message made them very happy. The four of us hugged and then they continued to the pool of water and we continued to the sweat lodge. Only yesterday Connie would have felt very shy about hugging other naked people but that phobia seemed to be over with.

The holy man stood by the sweat lodge waiting for us. In his hand were two leather pouches.

"These are your talismans that if put on must be worn for the rest of your lives. They will provide you with protection and prosperity. Do you accept these gifts in the spirit in which I give them to you," the holy man asked us.

"Yes, I accept mine," I said as I bent down my head to make it easier for him to put it around my neck.

"I accept mine too," Connie said.

Mine was on a short thong so it rode near my throat but Connie's was on a longer tether so it hung between her boobs.

"Why is mine on a longer piece of rawhide?" Connie asked.

"It's so If you want to wear jewelry you still can, and your pouch containing your talisman will be hidden from view. You can shorten it if that is what you prefer," the holy man explained.

"Okay, that's nice," Connie said as she felt the pouch around her neck.

"You may get dressed now, the ceremonies are over. I trust the Great Spirit paid you a visit and answered all of your questions?"

"Yes, the Great Spirit was very helpful to both of us," I told him.

"I wish you the best in your journey to defeat the wendigo. I have done all that I could to help you with your mission."

"I shook his hand gratefully and Connie gave him a big hug. Connie really was a changed woman. She hugged the old holy man while still naked, unaware and unashamed of her nakedness.

"It is as I told you it would be. I told you in the morning that your timidness over your nakedness would come to an end," the holy man said as he walked away with a half smile on his face.

Chapter Twenty-Five

I drove us back to the hotel. Even though we'd slept a few hours during the night we had in the sweat lodge we were still very tired. The coolness of the pool helped to revive us but the effects of the pool were wearing off.

"I'm for a few more hours of sleep Ben," Connie said while yawning.

"Hang on, I got a message from the Green Berets. Sergeant Wilson is being released this morning from the hospital. I'll text them back and tell them to book the sarge into a single room once they get back to the hotel," I told Connie.

"So, is it nap time or not?" Connie asked again.

"Yeah, I could go for a few hours of sleep. It's already going on noon. Let's take an hour just to take the edge off or else we'll be up half the night."

"Turn your phone off or it will be ringing just as soon as we're falling asleep." Connie said as she turned hers off.

We woke up almost an hour and a half later. I turned on my phone and saw I'd missed multiple calls from the same number. It was a number I didn't recognize.

I showed it to Connie. "Do you know who this is?" I asked her.

Connie looked at it and shook her head. "No clue."

I shrugged my shoulders and tried the number.

"Jim Collar speaking, is this Ben Hawk?" said the angry voice on the other end of the call.

I put my finger to my lips silently telling Connie to not talk. "Yes sir Mr. Secretary, what can I do for you?"

"You can start out by giving me some damn answers! I'm getting the runaround from your director!"

"Sir, give me five minutes to call you back. I want my partner

Connie in on this conversation."

"You got five minutes, Agent Hawk, I expect a call back," he said handing up.

"What was that all about?" Connie asked me.

"That was the secretary of defense. Our director seems to be giving him the runaround about the Green Berets he loaned him. He's calling us to get the answers our director won't give him. We need to talk before we call him back."

"You know the director is going to try to hang us out to dry to save his own ass don't you Ben?"

"I figured that's the way this is shaping out to be. We aren't going to lay still and become scapegoats for our director. This whole thing is his fault. We are going to tell Jim the truth. If the director can avoid the fallout he can do it on his own and not on our backs."

"We're on the same page Ben, call him back. You know how unbelievable this whole story is going to seem to him?"

"Yeah I know Connie. But we have his Green Berets to back our story up."

"How did he get our phone numbers anyway?"

"Our last case in Wisconsin when we borrowed his marine sniper/scout teams. He had our contact numbers, remember?"

"I forgot about that. Go ahead and call him back Ben."

'This is Agent Hawk returning your call sir. I have you on speaker phone. My partner Connie is listening in on the call."

"Thanks for the quick call back," Jim Collar said grudgingly. He was feeling agitated after two days of no answers from the FBI.

"What can I do for you? We haven't been in communication with Washington for a couple of days now."

"That makes two of us Agent Hawk. I called to get a sitrep report on my squad of Green Berets. I loaned your director to help you out on the Navajo reservation. He won't even take my damn calls!"

"Sir Connie and I are going to tell you about our op from the beginning. Trust me when I tell you, you're not going to like where the story takes you."

"Sir, about a week and a half ago we were called back to the office from vacation. It seems there were murders happening on the Navajo reservation, I said."

"That's federal jurisdiction, isn't it?"

"Yes sir, it is. But the tribal police departments don't normally call outside the reservations for help. They like to handle things on their own. But this was very different from normal circumstances. People were being killed and half eaten at the kill sights," Connie explained.

"That can be explained with wild animal attacks, can't it?"

"No sir, it can't. What wild animal do you know that will skin their kills before eating them?" I asked him.

"None that I know of," he said in surprise.

"Us neither. The sheriff of Window Rock, a man by the name of Joe Longbow contacted the FBI hoping we would be available to help figure this thing out. We were still on vacation and were called back to the office," I said.

"The sheriff claimed it wasn't ordinary murders but either a cryptid or a supernatural being that was doing the killing," Connie said.

"Come on now! Do you expect me to believe a bigfoot or something like that was to blame for the deaths?"

"No sir, we don't. We'll explain to you how this creature was way, way worse than any hairy man or bigfoot," I said.

"So the two of you bought his story and went out there to help him solve his problem?"

"We went just as fast as the executive jet could get us there. We armed ourselves the best we could before leaving. We didn't have any idea at the time what we would be facing or what we'd have to do to get rid of it," I said.

"Agent Hawk, you're of Native American descent aren't you?"

"Yes sir, half Oglala Sioux on my father's side."

"I just sent you a picture of the fifth victim, Mr. Secretary. As you can see the body is three quarters gone. This was accomplished in less than four hours. Later victims showed us it could be accomplished in only minutes," Connie said.

"Jesus, will you look at that! This was done in only minutes you think? I was right, it was a wild animal."

"No sir, it wasn't. Look closer at it. The body had been skinned." Connie said.

"There were multiple killings. Sometimes more than one day in a row. What could have an appetite large enough to eat that much day after day?" I asked him.

"Even a grizzly bear will take several days to consume a kill," Jim agreed.

"We were only there a day or two when we got a call that a couple were killed on their ranch. They were running a mixed herd of cattle and sheep. The couple were found butchered behind their barn in the high grass," Connie said.

"Both of them looked just the way the victim we showed you the picture looked," I said.

"Upon further investigation we found several sheep and a bull and cow were also lying dead. We called in a veterinarian to examine the carcuses to determine the cause of death. All of the animals had their necks snapped. Do you know what kind of powcr it would take to break the neck of a fifteen hundred pound bull?" Connie asked.

"We questioned the vet to find out what animal he thought would be strong enough to accomplish this feat. He determined no animal on the face of the planet could have accomplished it," I said.

"None? Not a lion or tiger or bear?"

"I'm not going to say oh my Mr. Secretary. Those animals are capable of killing a bull but not in the method used. There would be teeth marks or claw marks where it was grabbed and taken down. Only a fall off of a high cliff could snap the bulls neck." Connie stated.

"So then how were they killed?"

"Later in our investigation we determined the animals were struck by a massage clawed hand that was so powerful it would be like being hit by an anvil at a tremendous velocity." I said.

"How did you determine that?"

"Let us continue the narrative and you'll see."

"The next morning we got a call from the rancher on the Circle R ranch by the name of John Goodearl. He owns a ranch of maybe sixty thousand acres. He had a ranch hand assigned to riding the fence line to check for damaged fences. Normally it takes three days to make the circuit. He was overdue getting back to the ranch so the sheriff was called. I contacted the FBI field office in Phoenix and asked them to send us a helicopter so we could do an aerial search for the missing ranch hand. It got there the next morning and we followed the fence searching for him. They have two line shacks where the ranch hands will spend the night while riding the circuit. We found his horse in the corral at the second line shack. The door was busted off of the hinges and all of the furniture was broken and the man was missing but his horse was untouched,"

"We boarded the helicopter again and did a search and found his hat a few hundred yards away in the rocks. The man was never found."

"This is when our director contacted you asking you to send help to us. We asked him, we begged him to not send the Green Berets to us. We told him he was sending men to their deaths. We told him they were ill equipped to deal with something that was supernatural," Connie said.

"Connie, I think it was after we had the fight in the creek bottom that the director told us he was sending us the help we didn't want him to send to us, remember?"

"Oh yeah, my mistake Mr. Secretary," Connie said.

"They're one of the world's best fighting forces. Why did you think they couldn't handle themselves out there?"

Because they think like modern men, like city dwellers. They smell with their noses but they don't know danger when they smell it out here in the desert. They hear, but they wouldn't hear the scrap of a sharp claw on rock just before being pounced on. They see, but the movement of grass or the stirring of leaves just before being attacked would go unnoticed. They are not one with nature like I am," I explained the best way I could.

"You have agent Sanchez there with you and she can't do any of those things I would assume."

"No sir, she couldn't but she is a quick learner. Besides that she has been by my side the entire time we've been out here."

"The sheriff put a curfew into effect from an hour before dark until an hour after sunrise. This creature only hunts at night. If people stayed inside during hours of darkness they would be safe. He ordered his deputies to not get out of their patrol cars under any circumstances at night. That first night the curfew was in effect they got a call about a stranded car a few miles out of town. A woman and her young daughter were stranded and out of gas. The patrol car drove out to help. When they got there they could hear the terrible screeching of the beast that was killing everyone and it was close by. They turned the squad car around so they were facing towards town and told the women to jump into the back seat. She tossed in her eight year old girl first and dived in after her just as the beast tried to jump into the car. The police officer gunned the car and the creature just missed grabbing onto the door frame. But he did leave several huge dents in the roof and trunk of the car," Connie said.

"Did the officers get a look at the attacker?"

"No sir, all they saw was a blur. The woman was lying face down so she didn't see anything either but the daughter did," I said.

"What did she describe seeing?"

"A being seven to seven and a half feet tall. Huge hands with claws and hoofed feet. He had a skull of an animal for a head and it was lacking flesh and the skin was stretched tightly across it. It has bright red glowing eyes and the antlers of a deer on its skull," I reported.

"That must have just been the imagination of a very young girl."

"She described it as being similar to the monster in the movie Alien," Connie explained to him.

"The next morning we went out after daylight to retrieve the car with a wrecker. The creature must have been very angry. The windshield was smashed into the front seat. The hood, roof and trunk were almost smashed flat. I called the FBI field office in Phoenix for a forensics scientist to be flown out to our location. He arrived two hours later. He was able to take hair samples off of the windshield and examples of DNA," Connie said.

"Did you get the results of the test back?"

"Yes sir, the DNA showed twenty seven percent human and the other seventy three percent unknown. The hair sample wasn't in any known database," Connie told him.

"But that isn't possible. Could the DNA have been contaminated?"

"We asked that question too and the answer was no. This is possible if this is an unknown creature. But the creature is no longer unknown because we have identified it. Open up your computer and go to the Louvre museum website. Now search for masterpieces by Dante. Also look at other depictions of hell. Do you see a creature that resembles what the little girl saw?" I asked him.

"Yes, it's just like what the little girl described! But how is that even possible?" Jim asked in a shocked voice.

"Because that is exactly what she saw. Mr. Secretary, what the little girl saw was a wendigo. It's a supernatural beast of Native American legend. Tribes of the far north have stories of old about the wendigo. The Chippewa, Cree, Iroquois and blackfoot among others.

"How is that even possible? When those paintings were painted they had no knowledge of North American wendigos."

"That is absolutely correct. But they did have knowledge of the devil and demons from hell, didn't they?" I asked him.

"Are you trying to tell me that the devil and this wendigo are one and the same? That you're doing battle against the devil himself!"

"No sir, what we are saying is we are doing battle against a wendigo and we have determined it is the same thing as a demon. Just different names in different cultures. Are you beginning to see why we tried to refuse your help yet?" I asked him.

"This whole thing is mind blowing!"

"But wait, it is going to get way worse," Connie cautioned him.

"Do I even want to hear this?"

"You have to hear this sir. You need to hear the whole story and learn about the fate of your men," I said.

"The fate of my men! What, are they all dead?"

"No sir but you did lose some of them. Let us continue from where we left off on the story," Connie said.

"Allright, I'm listening."

"We received a phone call from the chicken lady. She lives a few miles out of town and raises chickens and sells her eggs in town. She reported a hairy man attacked her chickens and made off with a couple of them."

"The Navajo Rangers investigated the incident and found feathers all over the place. The hard packed ground made it impossible to see tracks."

"Thinking that at night with bad lighting in her farmyard she might have misidentified our creature for a hairy man we set up for the night to watch the area. We borrowed four horses from the rancher that lost the ranch hand. We had FLIR units and night vision goggles. Connie and I were on one hilltop and two Navajo rangers were on another one a couple of miles from us," I said.

"Refresh my memory but a hairy man and a bigfoot are one and the same?"

'That's right. The sheriff and a deputy by the name of Virgil were stationed in an armored Humvee at the farm. They called us about three in the morning and said that something was disturbing the chickens. We watched the yard with the night vision goggles and FLIR and finally detected the hairy man by the third chicken coop. We watched it as it went down into the creek bottom."

"Thinking she really did see a hairy man, we called it a night and went back to the farm and tied up the horses for the rancher to come and get. Sometime between then and daylight the wendigo attacked the horses. Two of them were killed outright and a third one was so injured it had to be put down," I said.

"The rancher couldn't have been happy about that."

"No sir, he wasn't. The wendigo was in the area the whole time and we didn't know it. This thing is fast, brutally strong, very intelligent and vicious in the way it does its attacks," Connie said.

"The next morning we got a call about an old woman being attacked right in town. This is the first victim that was killed in the town of Window Rock. Being a town person she thought it was safe for her to go into her yard and pump water before daylight. With the word getting out about staying indoors we feel the wendigo went into town in order to feed."

"We were putting information over the radio waves on a regular basis telling people what they needed to do to stay safe and so they were. That just meant the wendigo had to look harder for a meal," Connie said.

"Once again we called in the CSI tech to take samples for analysis. He is the one who mentioned the Dante paintings to us to look at. We were absolutely shocked at the close resemblance," I said.

"After the old woman was killed we met at the sheriff's office and discussed the possibility of a wendigo and a demon being one and the same. Could a wendigo and a demon just be different cultures' names for the same being? Were the Great Spirit and the Christian God the same but just different names for the same savior?" I asked.

"That's a very interesting surmise."

"I kind of lost track of time here. Somewhere along here we decided that if a wendigo and a demon were one and the same then Christian crosses might afford us some type of protection and we got six of them from Phoenix for us to wear around our necks," Connie said.

"We called the rancher again and asked to borrow more horses. We promised to stay with the horses this time until his ranch hands showed up to retrieve them. He agreed to supply more and had them at the chicken ranch for us late that afternoon," I said.

"This time we planned on crossing the creek bottom and posting on the edge of the brush looking outward. Instead of being a couple of miles apart we were only about two hundred yards apart because we wouldn't be able to see each other. The sheriff and Virgil posted once again as backup. About three in the morning I detected a threat and call the Navajo rangers to come to our location," Connie said,

"What tipped you off?"

"I don't know, some sort of sixth sense I've alway had. The Navajo rangers came as fast as their horses would go. They tied them off just before the wendigo appeared. It screeched so loud we could feel the bones in our chests vibrate. We all opened fire at once," Connie said.

"Now when we planned the night's mission we talked about what we were going to be packing for weapons. John had an AR15 with a bump stock and two thirty two round clips. Sid was packing a shotgun with an extended magazine loaded with rock salt. We know salt has an effect on certain beings but not always which ones. Connie had her SIG .40 with teflon coated rounds designed to go through a bulletproof vest. I had a twelve gauge streetsweeper with a fifty round drum magazine. It was loaded so the first ten rounds were double aught buckshot, the next ten were dragon's breath and the last thirty went back to buckshot," I explained.

"That's a wide array of weapons. I'm not going to try to understand rock salt though.

"Salt can ward off things like bad spirits. We were at that point still trying to figure out just what a wendigo was," I said.

"We all opened up at once. We put a tremendous amount of rounds into the wendigo with no effect other than to make it screech louder. We all ran out of ammo by the time Ben got to his dragon's breath rounds. The wendigo was within thirty feet of us by this time but something made him stop like an invisible wall. We figured afterward the only thing that made any sense was the silver crosses kept it at bay. Anyway Ben hit it square in the face with the first dragon's breath round and it didn't like it a bit. It let out a screech and Ben kept hammering it. The dragon's breath shoots a white phosphorus flame out of the end of the barrel up to a hundred feet. After the fifth round the wendigo was totally engulfed in flame. It turned away from us and ran back to the river bottom. Ben continued hitting it with the white phosphorus rounds."

"That's when I told everybody to get their asses into their saddles and get the hell out of there," I said.

"You had it on the run, why stop now?"

"Because I was out of the dragon's breath and we already knew the other weapons at our disposal were useless."

"We shot out of the river bottom headed for the farmyard. Hearing the gunfire the sheriff and Virgil met us with the Humvee and followed along behind us to offer some protection if it came after us. We got to the farmyard and sat in the Humvee waiting for the horses to be picked up the next morning," I said.

"Nothing you used bothered it other than the flame out of your shotgun barrel?"

"No, nothing! Can this thing even be killed? Does it even have a life, a beating heart? Does it breathe? At this point we didn't know yet."

"Why is it I think you found out what you needed to know?"

"We did find out what we needed to know but that's later in our story. We're still not sure if you need to know those details or not."

"I need to know everything, Ben and Connie. If I'm to put this entire story together I have to know every detail."

"After that night is when the director told us he was sending the Green Berets," I said.

"We knew conventional weapons were of no use. We told our director again and again, begging him not to send the Green Berets out here. We told him all he was doing was offering up an easy meal to the wendigo," Connie said.

"By this time you'd told your director you were dealing with a wendigo or a demon?"

"Yes, but first we questioned his spirituality. Was he a Christian and did he believe in what was written in the bible?"

"He told us he was a regular church goer and did believe in the bible. That's when we had him look at the pictures by Dante and the others to show him what we were dealing with. We told him conventional weapons were useless. We told him the silver crosses helped to protect us. We begged him to cancel the order for the Green Berets once again. But our demands fell on deaf ears,"I said.

"He called us and told us the Green Berets were being delayed in arriving by a day because of how far they had to travel. That afternoon we had another radio show to tell the listeners about new developments in the case and what to do to stay safe. We took questions and answers afterwards to help quiet fears and hopefully get a tip that would be helpful. That's exactly what happened. A caller called in to tell us he hears the wendigo early just about every morning traveling from the creek bottom out into the desert. We went out to investigate right away. The farmer walked us out across his hay field and into the desert where he thought it was crossing. The distance was over two miles. He had a three story house with a cupola on the top floor for reading and watching the stars. We asked if we could come back out and spend the night and he agreed," Connie said.

"Next we visited a silversmith and asked him to start making us silver crosses the size of a dime. I figured if the wendigo couldn't stand being near the cross I'd give him a belly full of them by draining the buckshot out of some of my shells and reloading them with the crosses," I explained.

"Sure as hell, about four in the morning we heard the wendigo screeching as it left the creek bottom and knew we'd found its travel route. Once it was daylight and safe to travel we left the farm to get some sack time. We asked the sheriff to meet the Green Berets and have them stay by the sheriff's office until we got up and met them."

"We had a meeting when we got to town with Captain Baker and Sergeant Wilson joining us. In the meeting were us, the sheriff, the Navajo Rangers, Deputy Virgil and the two Green Berets," Connie supplied.

"We explained to them in detail just how dangerous this mission we were on was. We were no longer calling it a case. We showed them photos of the dead and gave them a detailed report of the happenings since the wendigo first appeared. We explained to them why they were ill equipped to go on this mission. I told them they should go back to their base of operation. The captain refused saying he had to obey orders. Connie, send the secretary the picture you took of the wendigo."

The secretary opened the file. "There isn't anything in the picture but a ball of fire."

"You can just make out the outline of the seven and a half foot tall wendigo. The camera was unable to capture its image. It cannot be photographed," I explained.

"We asked the captain what he brought for weapons. All he brought was his normal weapons with grenade launchers mounted under the barrels. So each of them would be able to fire only a single grenade and then they would be helpless against the attacks of the wendigo. We asked them if they brought Christian crosses with them for protection and they said no one told them to," Connie said.

"So they would be going out into the field like Barnie Fife with only one bullet so to speak. No protection from the crosses that should have been hanging around their necks. We told them they were just setting themselves up to be an easy meal and they didn't belong in the field until they were properly armed and protected," I said.

"I could tell by looking into the sergeant's eyes he believed us and didn't want to go out that night, but he wasn't in charge. The captain reiterated they were going to follow orders. Even with all the evidence we showed them. All of the three quarter eaten people, they were still going to go out and throw their lives away like there was no value to them at all," Connie said.

"Connie and I went into the sheriff's office with the Navajo Rangers and once again called the director on the phone. The Navajo Rangers laid out the case to keep them out of the field. They told the director point blank these men were going to be killed. They threatened the director with murder charges if any of these men died because of his orders," I said.

"I take it he once again ignored your warnings."

"He got his back up and wouldn't listen to our pleas. I ended up calling him a dirty rotten son of a bitch and that these deaths were going to be on his shoulders and not ours. I told him Connie and I would still have to bear the memory of what he made us do," I said as I grew angry all over again.

"So all we had were six crosses total. At the time we didn't know if each person had to wear a cross in order to have its protection. Or if all you need to do is be near one to be protected by it. We made sure each group that was in the field that night had two of them. The Navajo rangers each had one cross and they were teamed up with two of the most junior Green Berets. Connie and I had two crosses and we were also teamed up with two junior Green Berets. We gave the last two to Captain Baker who put his cross in his breast pocket and Sergeant Wilson who immediately put his cross around his neck. We explained to them they needed to buddy up with a man who didn't have a cross to try to protect them. They needed to stay very close to each other,"

Connie explained.

"About two hours before dark we headed out to the three story farmhouse to post for the night. Connie had a M320 grenade launcher sent out for her use. It was loaded with both fragmentation and incendiary grenades. Why the Green Berets didn't have such weapons themselves was a gross mistake on the part of our director and whoever else was privy to what we said they needed for weapons," I said.

"It was a two mile walk to get to the area we needed to be positioned in. We dropped off the Navajo Rangers by a deep gully first. Then we placed Captain Baker and his team by a fairly narrow ravine. Finally we posted by a dry weed choked stream bed. We had the captain's team between our two more experienced teams," Connie said.

"Why did you pick those locations to watch?"

"We watched the night before from the third floor of the farmhouse and didn't see the wendigo. We heard him but didn't see him. So we knew from our high vantage point if we couldn't see him he must be using a feature in the desert to hide his travels, a gully, or ravine and so on," I said.

"Okay, I get it."

"All of the groups were equipped with night vision goggles and FLIR units to help detect the wendigo before he got close. Everything was quiet until around four in the morning. The wendigo started his screeching from the creek bottom as he left it and headed in our general direction. We were facing in that direction all locked and loaded and ready for him to appear. Suddenly there were screams of pain and terror coming from the captain's location. We heard the explosion of a single grenade and then small arms fire. I radioed the other group to converge on the captain's location. From start to finish the attack lasted way less than a minute. When we got there the wendigo was gone and three of your men looked just like the pictures we showed you earlier," Connie told him, finally breaking the news of his men's deaths.

"This...wendigo consumed three full sized men in the time it took you to respond and still had the time to vanish from sight?"

"Yes sir, that's what happened."

"Who was the lone surviving member of the group?"

"That was Sergeant Wilson. Remember, he was wearing the cross around his neck," Connie said.

"But you gave the group two crosses. Why was there only one survivor?"

"Maybe you want to ask the sergeant that question."

"I want you to give the full report. Afterwards I'll confirm the attack with the sergeant."

"We went there and the sergeant was out cold. He slammed his head on a granite boulder. The back of his head was bleeding badly. We put a dressing on it using our shirts and then carried him out to the vehicles where we had an ambulance waiting for him," I said.

"So the sergeant is in the hospital in a coma?"

"No, we got a text message this morning that he was being released. The other men of his unit went to pick him up. He should be back here right about now," Connie said.

"We called the director up to report on the mission. We told him he was responsible for the deaths of three men. I called him a son of a bitch again and a couple of other things too. He said he was scrubbing the case and calling us back to Washington. I told him to go to hell. I still had vacation time coming and that we weren't leaving these people to deal with this on their own."

"So what did he say to that?"

"He told me to keep the Green Berets in the hotel until they can be debriefed."

"So Anthony is trying to do damage control, is he?"

"I figured he'll come up with a paper for each of them to sign. If they ever talk to anyone about what happened that night they'll be dropped into a deep dark hole somewhere," I said.

"Those are my thoughts too. But he just lost that lifeline. I think Anthony's days are numbered, please continue."

"The rest of that day was spent doing reports. There is a ton of paperwork to do especially when someone is killed. While we were working on the reports Jeff Longbow called us asking for a meeting," Connie said.

"Please, refresh my memory again. Do I know who this person is?"

R.P. Deiss

"He is a retired Navajo Ranger with twenty five years of experience. He knows more about cryptids and supernatural beings than anyone else on the reservation," Connie explained.

"He offered to look through old Navajo records to see if any attacks like this have ever happened before. We told him we couldn't meet with him until about ten the next morning," I said.

"Jeff Longbow is the sheriff's uncle so we asked him to come along to hear what Jeff found out first hand. Jeff told us he had found evidence the wendigo attacked the Navajo reservation on two earlier occasions. Once in 1900 and once in the 1700s. The 1900 attack had sketchy documentation. We didn't know for instance how many died. You have to realize this reservation is huge. It's by far the largest reservation in the United States. Back in 1900 there were no cars here. Everyone got around on foot and horseback. There were no phones or electricity. Many of the deaths probably went unreported," Connie said.

"The earlier report was from before the Navajo used a written language. They had pictures drawn on deer skins but there was no mistaking the painting of the wendigo," I said.

"But why? Why here and why now?"

"Well sir, we're getting to the part where we have to decide if we want to share the information with you or not," Connie said.

"The two of you have me on the edge of my seat. I have to hear the rest. This is like reading a book and finding out at the end the last ten pages are missing!"

Connie and I looked at each other trying to read each other's minds."

"Out with it, I'm dying here!"

"First of all, we are talking about wendigos, demons, hairy man and shapeshifters. How much of this are you actually believing? We have to know before continuing on."

"I know the two of you from your last case in Wisconsin. I know of your reputation for finishing cases. I know there is much in the world that I don't know and understand. Do I believe what you are telling me? The short answer is yes, one hundred percent. But you never mentioned shapeshifters to me before now."

"Oh yeah, we did forget that part of the story. The day after

Carl disappeared we borrowed horses and staked out the ranch watching for the wendigo or any sign of Carl. Connie spotted a naked man walking across the desert floor towards some rock formations. We thought it might be Carl and that he was lost. We couldn't figure out why he would be naked. We jumped onto our horses and gave chase. He heard us coming and ran for the rocks. By the time he got to them we were only a hundred yards or so behind him. He disappeared into the rocks and a large wolf bounded out the other side and ran over the top of a hill. Connie poo pooed it being a shapeshifter and that the man was hiding in the rocks. I told her to go ahead and find him then. It shouldn't be too difficult to find a naked man in a pile of rocks. She came out of the rocks and became a believer," I said as I grinned at Connie.

"That's true, I saw my first shapeshifter that night."

"So are you going to tell me the rest or not?" The secretary asked impatiently.

Connie nodded at me. "Go ahead Ben, we told him this much."

"Jeff wanted us to visit with a Navajo holy man that afternoon. He knew we were getting protection from the crosses. But he said there were other ways of gaining protection we didn't know about."

"So we followed him to the holy man's location. He was a very old man that has lived in the desert his whole life. His face was a roadmap of creases and lines. He was standing there bare chested waiting for us. Next to him was a sweat lodge and a hundred yards away a deep pool of water fed by a cascading forty five degree series of small waterfalls," Connie supplied.

"What did the holy man want to do to help you?"

"He wanted us to spend the night in the sweat lodge and have a vision with the Great Spirit," Connie explained.

"Unbelievable! But did you do it?"

"Yes we did," I said as I grinned at Connie. But it didn't have the desired effect because she grinned back.

"The first thing the holy man wanted us to do was to get one with nature," I said.

"What the heck is that?"

"He wanted us to strip down naked and stand there outside in front of him for all of the world to see," Connie said.

"So you didn't do it, did you?"

"You bet your boots we did. Right there in front of God and everybody!" Connie said unashamed.

"You have to realize our culture is different to understand Mr. Secretary. When I was growing up and spending time with my grandfather in the Dakotas it wasn't unusual to see me running around their property without clothes on. If I had to put clothes on to go to town I thought I was being punished. We didn't mention either that the pool of water was full of people skinny dipping. No one even noticed us."

"So here we are totally naked standing outside in front of this holy man and he started putting paint on us to prepare us to meet the Great Spirit. First he put hand prints on both of our faces and then he used different color paints all over our bodies, and I do mean all over," Connie said looking at me.

"The holy man had no trouble seeing how uncomfortable Connie was with being naked in front of other people. So as a final gesture to Connie to help her hide her nakedness he put a dab of black paint on each of her nipples. He said it would give her something to hide behind until she lost her timidness and fear of being naked in front of others," I said grinning at the memory.

"Him doing that shocked me and I jumped back. He then explained there was sage in the sweat lodge. We were to put small amounts of it into the fire from time to time and we were to rub it over each other's bodies often to help purify our outer being. There were willow switches inside the lodge we were supposed to whip each other with to show penance for past sins and transgression. There was water to drink inside but nothing else. We were to stay in the lodge until morning when he came for us. During the night we would be visited by the Great Spirit and he would share his wisdom with us," Connie said.

"This is really amazing! So then you entered the lodge?"

"Yeah, I moved the buffalo hide so we could enter and we went inside. The light was pretty dim inside. I bent over to put the first of the sage onto the fire when Connie attacked me," I said as I eyed my grinning partner.

"He bent over the fire to put on the sage sir. It was too tempting of a target so I gave him a wack right where he lives! I had to get my shot in before he straightened up didn't I?"

"You mean you hit him right in his butt?"

"Yeah and with way more enthusiasm as I should have shown because later on I paid for it," Connie said as she watched Ben grinning back at her.

"So did you see the Great Spirit as promised?"

"We both did in the early morning hours," I said.

"It wasn't just caused by the heat? You actually had a real vision?"

"Well, let us tell you what we found out from him and you can decide for yourself. I found out the wendigo had been around for over four hundred years. I found out how he became a wendigo too," I said.

"How does a mortal man become a wendigo or demon?"

"He does it by doing the most evil, vile act imaginable. He was banned from his village for stealing, his name was Red Thunder. So his wife and three kids joined him and moved a dozen miles away. A family on their own especially in the far north has very little chance of surviving the winter without a village to work together with. They had a very harsh winter, the worst in anyone's memory. The snow was very deep and he couldn't find game or gather firewood. Soon their lodge was cold and there was nothing left to eat. The first child died, a two year old and he ate him. No one else would do such an evil thing as this. As the winter went on one by one he ate his family until only the wife was left and then he ate her too."

"That is just awful!"

"In the spring the villagers went in search of the family and found their lodge. There were bones scattered everywhere but no sign of the man who robbed them. He was never seen again."

"This was told to you by the Great Spirit?"

"Yes,"

"Then the Great Spirit visited me. He told me it was a very rare thing to have someone who is not a Native American summon him. He was pleased I presented myself in the correct manner, naked. He also said I had cleansed my body properly with the sage and that I had done penance with the switch to his liking."

"He told you all of that?"

"I also found out our wendigo was a blackfoot before he became the wendigo. He took Carl from the line shack because Carl was also a blackfoot and he wanted to make Carl in his own image."

"He can turn others into wendigos?"

"Yes he can according to what the Great Spirit told me. He must eat the human flesh the wendigo presents to him. Then the wendigo does incantations and casts spells. The Great Spirit told me Carl had dined on human flesh out of fear of the wendigo and there was nothing more we could do to save him."

"What is to become of Carl then?"

"He must die alongside the wendigo. There is no saving him. The Great Spirit also showed me where the wendigos lair is. We now know how to find him in order to send him back to where he came from."

"Back to hell?"

"The Great Spirit does not refer to it as hell. He refers to it as the bowels of the earth."

"So morning came and the holy man came for us way later than I thought he would. It was going on nine in the morning. He told us to go to the pool to cool off and bathe our injured, tired sweaty bodies," I said.

"So you walked to the pool a hundred yards away in front of everyone naked!?"

"Bare assed naked for all the world to see," Connie confirmed.

"Weren't you awfully self conscious walking all that way to the water in front of everyone?"

"Everybody else in the water was naked too. We washed each other's backs to get off the paint and cooled down in the water for a while before going back to where the holy man was waiting for us.

"As a footnote another younger couple stopped us to question us about being in the sweat lodge and if we actually saw the Great Spirit," Connie said.

"They stopped you and talked to you when you didn't have any clothes on? Wasn't that just a little bit awkward?"

"What makes you think they had clothes on? They were headed for the water too," I said.

"We got back to the holy man and he asked us if the Great Spirit had helped us in our quest to vanquish the wendigo and we told him yes. He presented each of us with a talisman to help protect us. They are hanging around our necks as we speak," Connie said.

"Okay, so what happened next?"

"There is no next. This happened last night. We were in the pool of water a couple of hours ago," Connie said.

"This just happened!" The secretary said in shock.

"Yep, you are now up to date on our activities," I agreed.

""Is Sergeant Wilson back at the hotel yet?"

"His teammates went to pick him up at the hospital, he should be back now," Connie answered.

"Can you get him to come to the phone? I want to hear his side of what happened to his commanding officer and the others."

"Sure, give me a couple of minutes to locate him for you," Connie said as she called the front desk and had them transfer her call to his room.

"Hello, Sergeant Wilson here."

"Sergeant, this is Agent Sanchez. Could you come to my room? The secretary of Defense is on the line and wants to have a word with you about the night you were injured."

"Yes ma'am, I'll be right there," he said in a surprised tone of voice.

A few seconds later there was a knock on our door and Connie let the sergeant in.

"Come out onto the deck. We have the secretary on speaker," Connie told him.

"Mr. Secretary, this is Sergeant first class Wilson, how can I help you sir."

"Sergeant, first of all, are you feeling alright after your time in the hospital?"

"I had a concussion and still have a nagging headache. The doctors tell me it will go away in a week or two. In the meantime I have pain meds to help with it. Thank you for asking sir."

"Agents Hawk and Sanchez have filled me in on what has been

going on out there. I want to hear your take on your unit's involvement. Don't forget to include what happened the night your unit was attacked.

"Yes sir. We got to the town of Window Rock on the Navajo Indian reservation late in the morning the day before the attack. Agents Hawk and Sanchez weren't there yet. They'd been out all night searching for this thing that was attacking everybody. They finally showed up sometime between one and two in the afternoon.

"This was two days ago?"

The sergeant looked at us questioningly and I held up three fingers.

"No sir, I'm told it was three days ago. You have to remember I've been unconscious."

"Okay sergeant, go on."

"The FBI agents asked the captain and I to join them in a meeting in their conference room. In attendance was Ben and Connie, the sheriff, the two Navajo Rangers and deputy Virgil. They told us what we were up against. They showed us pictures of some of the mutilations. They told us about their battle with it by the creek bottom. It was all amazing and mind blowing sir."

"Yes it is mind blowing isn't it?"

"Ben and Connie asked us what we'd brought along for weapons. When the captain told them they were not happy sir. They said all you have is one shot and then after that what the hell are you going to do to protect yourselves, throw spitballs at it?"

"They already explained to me why they thought you weren't prepared to go out with them."

"Then they found out we weren't told to wear Christian crosses either. They explained to us what we were facing was a wendigo or in other words a demon from hell. They said the crosses provided a level of protection we shouldn't go out into the field without. The captain argued we were a highly trained fighting unit and we could handle whatever headed our way. Ben and Connie told him he was full of shit sir."

"How did the captain handle being told he didn't know what he was talking about?"

"Not very well sir. His face got red and I could tell he was going to bull his way through no matter what."

"What else happened in the meeting?"

"Ben tried to explain to the captain some of the reasons he shouldn't go out that night besides being under armed and without crosses to wear. I said we don't use our senses like indigenous people do. We see with our eyes but we don't always see the danger that is lurking before us. We hear but we don't hear the whisper of the grass as the snake slithers through it. We smell but we don't recognize curtain dangers when we smell it. We think like city people and we are going to get someone killed."

"Did Agents Hawk and Sanchez actually tell the captain that men were going to die if he didn't listen to him and stay out of the field of operation?"

"Yes sir, point blank and right to his face. But he refused to listen to them. He just got angrier and angrier."

"Alright, continue sergeant."

"They only had six silver crosses but they exposed themselves and shared them with us. The Navajo rangers had two crosses and two of our most inexperienced men went with them. Connie and Ben had two crosses and two more of our men. Captain Baker received a cross and put it in his breast pocket. I got the last cross and put it around my neck and I was damn glad to do it too sir."

"Your captain didn't wear his cross?"

"No sir, he tucked it into his pocket. They explained to us they didn't know if each person needed to wear a cross to be protected or just be close to someone who was wearing a cross. They told us to make sure to buddy up with someone not wearing a cross and keep them very close to us to hopefully afford them some protection."

"What are your feelings about what you learned in the meeting sergeant?"

"I was scared sir. I've never been this afraid of a mission in my life. I know from the meeting we had and the evidence they were able to share with us that we were in way over our heads. We were dealing with something that might not be a living being, so how were we supposed to defend ourselves against it? If I would have been in charge we would not have gone out that night but I had to follow orders."

"After hearing the evidence myself, I wouldn't have wanted to go out there either, sergeant."

"Our meeting ended and we called in the rest of our team and they showed them the evidence so they would know what they were dealing with too. The Navajo Rangers and Connie and Ben went into the sheriff's office and I could hear them yelling at somebody."

"We called the director of the FBI again, Mr. Secretary and once again tried to get him to not send your men to what we felt was a certain death. We could have resigned on the spot and he would have still sent them out. We felt the best hope of protecting them was not to abandon them. The Navajo Rangers even threatened the director with murder charges if anyone was killed while he knew the risks of their involvement," I said.

"I see, go on sergeant, you were saying?"

"So we finished our meeting and the men went outside by the Humvees and Ben tried one last time to get the captain to see reason but he once again refused to listen. Ben told him they were going to the cafe for supper before heading out and the Green Berets were welcome to join them. The captain said we had MREs so we were good to go. Ben told the captain even in prison the condemned man got a good final meal. That, excuse my language sir, really pissed him off. He finally relented and let the men get a free meal courtesy of the FBI."

"What time did you head out to watch for the wendigo?"

"About two hours before sunset. We parked and it was about a two mile hike across a hay field and then a mile of desert before we left the first group in their spot, the Navajo rangers were watching over a gully. We went another two hundred yards and there was a ravine where the captain's team set up. I don't know how much further away Ben and Connie were."

"We were about the same distance as you were from the Navajo Rangers," Connie said.

"As soon as Ben and Connie were out of earshot the captain took the cross they gave him and flung it into the rocks."

"He did what!"

"He flung it into the rocks and then he ordered me to hand

mine over to him so he could throw it away too. I told him in no uncertain terms I wasn't giving it up. He told me to be a man, to be a Green Beret! I told him the uniform code of military justice forbids him from criticizing my religious beliefs or ridiculing me for them. I told him he could be demoted or kicked out of the military altogether. He got really angry at that too. I told him there were no atheists in fox holes and prayed that he didn't regret what he just did with his cross before morning."

"I'm starting to believe a failure of command is to blame for this."

"He divided his forces. He put me and one man across the ravine from him. The man he was with was pissed the captain tossed away the cross. He told him that he would have worn it. The captain said if you want it then go and find it. He looked for it but it was never found."

"I sense we are coming to the important part, go on sergeant."

"I believe the captain was unfit to command but we would have suffered losses no matter what he did sir."

"How so sergeant?"

"Like you said sir, we're getting to the important part so bear with me. Everything was quiet until nearly morning when the wendigo started to screech. Sir, you have never heard anything like it in your life. I was so loud I could feel it in my chest and it hurt my ears. We all turned as one to face the direction the sound was coming from. I saw a flash of movement and I do mean a flash. The wendigo's speed was unbelievable. First it wasn't there and then it was on top of the captain tearing him apart. The corporal stationed with him was next. Even though the thing was just about on top of him he fired off his grenade. He must have thought anything was better than being killed the way the captain was. But he missed with his grenade because of panic probably. It sailed over the wendigos shoulder and towards the creek bottom. The two of us that were left started hitting it with small arms fire. We couldn't fire our grenades because we would have been hitting our own men."

"You were injured but you were wearing a cross. How did that happen, sergeant?"

"I'm just getting to that sir. The ravine was all of forty feet across. He turned to me and my eyes locked in with his glowing red ones. He let out another terrible screech and leaped over the ravine in a single bound. Thinking back on it I think he could have leaped even further. It didn't look like the distance bothered him at all. Anyway he leaped across the ravine and his hip hit my shoulder and I flew backwards and hit my head on a rock. When I came too I was in the hospital."

"If the cross protected you, how did you get injured?"

"We figured when he first leaped he was too far away to feel the effects of the cross. But part way across he detected the cross and turned away. That's why he hit me with his hip instead of hitting me with one of his massive clawed hands."

"I saw the picture of the wendigo or demon that Ben and Connie think is an accurate depiction. I want you to describe it to me now."

"Sir, it was all of seven and a half feet tall. It had hoofed feet and huge clawed hands. Its eyes glowed an eerie red and I don't mean they were just red. It was as if there was a light bulb shining from behind them. His skull was inhuman. It resembled the skull of a bull or some other large bovine. It seemed devoid of flesh on its head and there was translucent skin stretched across it. The bone white antlers on top of its head were massive."

"Is that everything sergeant?"

"No sir, the captain was definitely unfit to command but we would have lost men even with a good commanding officer. Only those who were wearing crosses were safe sir. Even if the captain would have kept his cross on. Even if he would have kept his team together as he should have. Two men would have still died. We had no business being out in the field that night."

"I don't agree with you on that sergeant."

"Why is that sir?"

"Because a good commander would have listened to reason. He would have heard Ben and Connie and the others and kept you from going out there in the first place."

"Yes sir and now we have three funerals to attend. But we have orders to stay here until the director of the FBI can debrief us and get us to sign some sort of papers I think."

"Yeah, he's trying to get you to keep him out of trouble by

putting yourself into trouble. As of now his orders are rescinded. I want you to gather your men together sergeant and first thing in the morning head on back to your home base."

"What about the FBI director sir?"

"You don't need to worry about Anthony Burns, he needs to be worried about me. You're under my command sergeant. Just follow my orders and you'll be okay."

"Yes sir, thank you sir."

"Now Ben and Connie, what do you have planned for next?"

"We're going to end this and take the son of a bitch out and send it back to the bowels of the earth where it belongs!" I said.

"As of now I'm taking control of this operation. This isn't a criminal investigation and so it's outside the limits and jurisdiction of the FBI. As far as I'm concerned with the wendigo or demon or whatever else you want to call it, this is a case of national security and under my jurisdiction."

"We didn't see that one coming Mr. Secretary. Does that mean we are no longer on this case?" I asked him.

"No it does not. Your director borrowed men from me so now I'm borrowing the two of you from him. You are to continue your investigation. I will help you in any way possible. What can I do for you to ensure your success and bring this to an end?"

"I'm really glad you asked us that, Mr. Secretary. We need to reconnoiter the dugout log cabin the Great Spirit showed to Connie. We'll do that tomorrow during the daylight when it's safe. We'll have to position ourselves on the opposite side of the creek bottom so we don't accidentally run into it when it comes out for the night. Once we know for sure that is where he is staying we can make our move," I said.

"Ben, are you doubting what the Great Spirit shared with me?" Connie asked me with raised eyebrows.

"Not even a little bit, partner. But what's to say he didn't move on to someplace else?"

"The Great Spirit said he used the same dugout the last time he roamed the earth so I can't see him going someplace else other than back to the bowels of the earth."

"Even so, I want to see him coming and going."

"Whatever you say non believer," Connie said with a wink.

"I'm anything else but a non believer. Anyway once we verify his presence I'll call you back and plan the operation that will end this."

"I await your call, Ben and Connie. That was good work you did. What an amazing story. The sad part is I lost men that didn't deserve to die. I'm going to let you go now. I have your director to deal with now and he isn't going to like where this is going to be taking him," Jim Collar said angrily as he ended the call.

"Well that went about as well as it could have. Not only is Director Burns not giving the orders anymore. But we're going to be working with the one man that can give us what we need to end this.

Chapter Twenty-Six

The Secretary of Defense, Jim Collar had a number on his desk phone that went directly to the executive secretary of the President of the United States.

"Cindi, Jim Collar here. Is the president in his office?"

"Yes he is Mr. Secretary but he is just finishing up with a meeting."

"As soon as the meeting ends, have him call me please, this is urgent," Jim told her.

"Wait a minute Mr.s Secretary, the speaker of the house is leaving now. I'll ring the president for you."

"Mr. President, the Secretary of Defense is on the line for you and he says that it is urgent that you talk with him," Cindi explained to him. The secretary of defense was one of few people in the president's cabinet that could always count on getting the president's immediate attention.

"Jim, what's on your mind?"

"We need to have a face to face Mr. President. You might want the Vice President in on this one too. Also we Don't need any press listening in."

"Alright, get on over here. I'll have my secretary clear my calendar for the rest of the afternoon.

The secretary of defense called for his limo and told his secretary he would be out for the rest of the day.

"It took a while to get from the Pentagon to the White House. By the time he got buzzed into the Oval Office by Cindi the Vice President was sitting with the president waiting for him.

"Jim, sit down and tell us what's going on," the president said.

"Do the names Special Agent Ben Hawk and Connie Sanchez mean anything to either one of you?" Jim asked them.

"You remember hearing about them Mr. President. They're the ones who took out the serial killer in Wisconsin a couple of weeks ago," the veep said.

"Oh yeah, that was good work, good work! Didn't I hear when that story was breaking they only work on serial murder cases now?"

"Yes sir, you did," Jim agreed.

"So why are you getting yourself involved with FBI matters?"

"This is going to take a while to explain to you sir. So get comfortable for a long and fascinating story."

"Let's move over to the easy chairs then," the president said.

"Connie and Ben were called back from vacation. The Navajo police department had tribal members being brutally murdered and wanted Ben and Connie to help solve the case."

"So has it been solved?" The veep asked.

"No, not yet but they're getting close. Anyway they were shown pictures of slain tribal members that were half eaten." Jim showed them a photo on his phone so they would know how extreme it was.

"Wild animal?" The president asked.

"No sir, if you look closely you'll notice they were skinned first before being eaten."

"So it's a cannibal?" the veep asked.

"No, they instantly thought it was either a cryptid or a super-natural being of some sort. Ben Hawk is half Oglala Sioux and so he has deep beliefs in such things as this."

"So, I assume they went out there to investigate the situation?" The president said.

"Yes sir," Jim told them about all of the killings. As of now there were twelve of them that they knew of. He told them about the missing ranch hand and how the search only produced his hat. He told them how the murders were only being done under the cover of darkness.

"I think most killings happen at night so the ones doing it can get away with it without being seen," the veep said.

"They put a curfew into effect to keep people inside at night to keep them safe. The patrol officers were put two to a car at night for their safety and told to not under any circumstances get out of their vehicles. By now they knew it was a supernatural being and not a cryptid."

"What is the difference between the two Jim?" The president asked.

"Cryptids are like bigfoot or the Loch Ness monster. Supernatural beings would be like poltergeists and demons and such."

"How did they determine it wasn't a cryptid?"

"The police were called out of town. A woman ran out of gas a few miles away and she had her young daughter in the car with her. They went out to the location and found her. They turned the squad car around so it was facing back towards town and stopped alongside her vehicle. When they did this creature let out a screech that could be felt inside their rib cages. They cracked open the window of their car and yelled for the two to get into the back seat. The woman threw her daughter in first and then dove in after her. The deputy driving hit the gas to distance themselves from the creature. The creature leaped and tried to get into the back seat but missed. He severely damaged the squad car by slamming his hands down on it."

Jim showed the two of them pictures of the damaged squad car.

"I don't think you could do this with a sledge hammer," the veep whispered in awe.

"Did they get a good look at it?" The veep asked.

"All the police officers saw was a blur as it tried to get inside. The woman was laying face down after leaping inside. Only the seven year old girl got a good look at it."

"What did she describe it, as being Jim?" The president asked.

"She described a monster sir. Seven and a half feet tall. Hooves for feet and massage clawed hands. Its head looked like the skull of a bull and it didn't have much flesh on it. There was skin stretched tightly over its head. Its eyes shone a bright red and it had huge bone white antlers on top of its head."

"Clearly the imagination of a young girl," the veep said with an understanding smile.

"No it wasn't. By now they had a town hall meeting to warn everybody about the threat. They broadcast their message over the local radio station too. They along with the Navajo Rangers started doing night searches for it. The Navajo Rangers investigate unusual encounters. Bigfoot, ghosts, shapeshifters, anything paranormal and the like. They are the tribal experts on all things out of the ordinary."

"So far the two of you look like you're not doubting what I'm telling you," Jim said with relief.

"I know there are things out there beyond my understanding Jim. I've seen a few things in my lifetime to know better than to doubt the existence of cryptids or the supernatural," the president said.

Jim showed them a masterpiece depicting the demon the girl saw. "This is what the young girl saw."

"Is that the devil himself?" the veep gasped out.

"No sir. In Native American culture it is called a wendigo. It is from the far north. Tribes such as the Chippewa, Cree and blackfoot among others have legends involving this creature. In the Christian bible this is a demon. We now feel they are one and the same. They are just different names from different cultures."

"They're out there chasing an actual demon from hell?" The president gasped out loud.

"They call it a wendigo from the bowels of the earth but if you ask me it's the same thing."

"How is this possible? How can they defeat something that probably isn't a living being?" The veep asked.

"I don't think it's a matter of killing it but a matter of ridding the earth of its presence."

"There is a way of doing this?" the president asked.

"We think so sir. But now we're coming to the reason why I'm here to begin with. Anthony Burns contacted me and asked me to borrow some special forces to aid the FBI in this matter. He never mentioned wendigos or demons when he made the request. I let him borrow a squad of Green Berets. I sent eight men to aid him that were ill equipped to handle the situation. Ben and Connie begged him not to send these men. They told him he was sealing their deaths by sending them. He wouldn't listen and sent them anyway. I wasn't privy to any of this."

"So I took it, they went to the reservation," the veep said.

"Yeah in the meantime Ben, Connie and the Navajo rangers

had a gun battle with this thing. They found our religious crosses provided a level of protection from the wendigo. They went out with a vast array of weapons from AR15s to shotguns and handguns. The only thing that had any effect on it was Ben's dragon's breath shotgun rounds that shoot out a white phosphorus flame up to a hundred feet. It hated getting hit by it and took off in the opposite direction. But Ben only had ten rounds and they got the hell out of there before it came back hunting."

"So if they saw it face to face they verified that it was indeed a demon or wendigo?" The president asked.

"Yes sir. They once again called their director and begged him not to sacrifice my men for nothing but he wouldn't listen. They told him standard issued arms had no effect on it. They told him the crosses did help. But my men didn't get either message. They walked into a situation they had no chance of surviving."

"All of your men were killed, Jim?" The president asked sharply.

"Not all of them sir, but some of them died. Including their commanding officer, Captain Baker. Part of it was a failure of command on the captain's part. But most of it was Anthony's fault for not trusting and listening to his FBI agents in the field. This entire thing could have been avoided. My men could still be alive if the director of the FBI wasn't a total failure."

"That's pretty strong language Jim," the veep said.

"I had to get this information from the FBI agents in the field. He is stonewalling me every step of the way. I called him for a sitrep on the team I loaded him and he won't accept my phone calls. He is doing damage control to try to save his own ass. Never mind the men he got killed for no reason at all. Right now he has them staying in a hotel until he can personally debrief them and get them to sign papers saying if they ever speak of this night they will go to prison for a very long time. The person going to prison should be him!"

"So, is the wendigo still a threat?" the veep asked.

"Yes sir, he is. But Connie and Ben enlisted the help of a Navajo holy man. He put them naked into a sweat lodge for a full night. According to them they received visions from the Great Spirit. Not only do they know who the wendigo was originally, and that he's been one for over four hundred years. They know how to end it's time on earth and where it's hiding during the daytime."

"They spent the night naked together receiving visions from the Great Spirit?" The president asked, looking shocked.

"Out of respect for their privacy, I don't feel right about going into great detail on this part of the story in length. Just know the event wasn't sexual in nature in the least."

"Understood. So where do we go from here Jim?" The president asked.

"Tomorrow they are going to reconnoiter the supposed den of the wendigo to make certain it is indeed there. Then they're contacting me for supplies and support to send this thing back where it came from. I told them I was personally taking this mission over. I told them this was outside the jurisdiction of the FBI. I told them for the rest of this mission until its end they were working for me. Hopefully this will be over within the next two days."

"Cindi, call the director of the FBI and have him report to the Oval Office immediately," the president told his secretary over the intercom.

"Yes sir," Cindi responded.

"Now we sit and wait for him. The longer he keeps us waiting the worse it is going to be for him," the president said as the anger shone in his eyes.

It was an hour before Director Burns walked through the door of the Oval Office. He saw the president sitting with the vice president and the secretary of defense and instantly knew he was in deep trouble as his stomach dropped.

"What took you so long Anthony," the president asked hotly.

"My apologies Mr. President. I was in a staff meeting sir."

"Since when do staff meetings come before meetings in my office when I call for you?" The president asked hotly.

"I didn't get the message right away sir," he said as he tried to lie his way out of the situation.

The president could see right through him and knew he was being lied to. He hit the button on his intercom. Cindi, call the FBI director's secretary and ask her if she gave my message to the director right away or if she waited until his meeting was over."

Director Burn's face was drained of color. He knew he had been caught in a lie to the president.

The president's intercom buzzed. "Sir, she gave him the message right away and he wasn't in a meeting sir."

The director was sitting still as his face grew red. "You have my apologies Mr. President," he said stiffly while looking down.

"Your apologies aren't going to get it done this time Anthony. The secretary of defense has been telling us an interesting story involving you."

"Did you think I'd let you continue stonewalling me Anthony? Did you forget that I had Ben and Connie's direct phone numbers from the Wisconsin Case?" Jim Collar asked him angrily.

Anthony's face grew redder still as he looked down at the Oval Office carpet.

"You got my men killed and then didn't even have the decency of taking my call and telling me about it yourself! Then you sequester my men, My men! In a hotel so you could threaten them with arrest if they ever talk and get you into trouble? How dare you!" By now the secretary of defense was shouting at him hotly.

"Getting your men killed was a tragic accident. I should have had better people in the field," Burns said as he tried to throw Connie and Ben under the bus.

"You don't have any better people than Ben and Connie! They begged you not to send my Green Berets to their deaths, they begged you! You wouldn't listen to them even though they were the ones on site. They were the ones who had their fingers on the pulse of the situation. You just ignored them completely and threw my men's lives away like they didn't matter at all! Well they might not have meant anything to you, but you're going to find out they meant a hell of a lot to me!"

"What do you have to say for yourself Anthony? We all know this whole mess was on you. You couldn't be any more responsible for their deaths if you put a gun to their heads yourself and pulled the trigger," The veep said.

Director Burns sat saying nothing.

"Today is Monday. I want your resignation on my desk no later than quitting time on Friday. Jim is taking over the case at the reservation. He is going to be in charge of Connie and Ben for its duration. You are to have no further contact with them or anyone else on this case. As for the Green Berets still alive they have been ordered back to their base. You can forget having them sign any silence agreement. I will be calling the justice department to investigate what happened and decide if any further action is required by the department of justice."

"I am part of the department of justice," Director Burns said with a weak smile.

"You were a part of the department of justice, but not anymore Anthony. You can find your own way out. I'm sure it won't take as long for you to leave as it did for you to get here," the president said without sympathy.

Director Buns left the office for the last time without saying another word.

Chapter Twenty-Seven

"**S**ergeant Wilson, first thing in the morning you're to head on back to your home base. Do you mind if I ask you a personal question before you go?" I asked him.

"Sure, what is it?"

"What the hell is your first name?"

"Ha, ha, ha, It's Homer! He said grinning.

"Homer, no shit! Are you being serious right now?"

"Ha, ha, ha, No actually it's the same as yours, Ben."

"We'll meet in a little while for one last dinner down stairs and then after breakfast we'll see you on your way back to your base," I said.

"Can I ask you two for one last favor before we leave for home tomorrow?" The sarge asked us.

"I think you're all out of favors Ben," I said sternly.

"Seriously?"

"You're not the only one that can bullshit sarge. What do you want?" I said grinning at him.

"Can I give you my phone number? We really need to know if and when this thing is finally over with. We need to know for the men we lost, and for ourselves sir," the sarge said solemnly.

"Consider it done. Give me your phone number now and I'll put it into my phone so we don't forget to do it before you leave tomorrow," Connie said.

By five that afternoon we were in the barroom tossing down a few. The sergeant was sticking to cokes because of the concussion and the pain meds. It was a somber occasion with more toasts to honor their fallen comrades. We ate high off the hog that night with everyone ordering steaks with all the fixings.

We wouldn't be going out looking for the wendigos lair until early afternoon the next day so tonight was a night off. The Green Berets questioned us on what we did the day before when we ditched them. Connie told them the story in great detail enjoying the looks on their faces. She saw looks of shock, disbelief, wonder and excitement, sometimes all at the same time.

"Alright, I have my bullshit detector out and on high alert and I'm calling bullshit on your entire story! But you made it interesting," Willy said, grinning.

Connie looked back at him with raised eyebrows and didn't show him any emotion at all. She just stared at him silently, displaying her best poker face.

"Do you know the wendigo has been on this earth for over four hundred years?" I asked them.

"Do you know his name was Red Thunder before he became a wendigo?" Connie asked them.

"Did you know he became a wendigo after eating the flesh of his entire family. The evilness of the act is what turned him into the wendigo," I said.

"Did you know we know where to find him during the daytime now?" Connie asked.

"How did you find all of that out?" Tom asked us.

"By getting naked, going into the sweat lodge, whipping each other with willow switches and getting rubbed down with sage so the Great Spirit would think us worthy of his presence. Show them Connie," I said.

Connie stood up and turned around picking the back of her tee shirt up so they could see the welts from the willow switches on her back. Then I stood up and raised my shirt up to my armpits and turned in a slow circle so they could see the red marks all over my upper body.

"Is your whole body like this?" Bob asked in awe.

"Everything but our heads and necks," I said.

"I had Connie howling like a banshee when I was chasing her around in the sweat lodge hitting her with the willow switch," I said grinning wide.

"I had your voice up a couple of octaves too fella!" Connie shot back.

"Well, I'll be go to hell! The entire story is true?" Willy said in a shocked voice as he looked back and forth at us.

"Right to the last detail. It's a great place to go skinny dipping if you want to swim before leaving in the morning. We can park by the sweat lodge and the five of you can enjoy the hundred yard walk to the pool of water in front of a dozen or more people, " Connie said with a grin as she watched their faces start to glow red.

"I am forced to send my bullshit meter in for repair. Obviously it's on the fritz," Willy said.

"Tom, we got pretty close the other night when we were buddies. Do you want to go for a swim with me?" Connie asked with an evil grin. She wasn't quite ready to let them off the hook yet.

"No thanks Connie, I'll pass," Tom said as his face started glowing even redder.

"What's amazing to me is the lengths the two of you will go to in order to solve a case. No barrier is too wide, no wall is too high. I mean, having to get naked for all to see and then whipping each other!" The sarge sat shaking his head in wonder.

"We have people dying gruesome, horrible deaths. You lost three of your own men in the same manner. I will go to any lengths to solve and end this," I said.

"Losing one's modesty is a small price to pay to rid the earth of the wendigo," Connie added.

"It was more of a hang up for Connie than it was for me. When I was growing up in the summers at my grandparents place as a young boy I was bare ass naked more often than I was clothed. Connie had a little trouble crossing that barrier and being comfortable being naked in front of other people, especially strangers," I informed them.

"That might be Ben, but I did cross it."

"Yes you did Connie, and I was never happier to whip a bare butt in my entire life," I said grinning.

"That might be Ben. but I got in the first lick and it was a good one," Connie said grinning back at me.

"Yeah, that's true. You almost drew blood with that one. I bent over to put sage in the fire and Connie saw an opportunity to strike and hit me with the switch while I was bent over."

"In my own defense, I swung fast afraid he would straighten up before I got my lick in."

The five Green Berets were grinning wide at the story. Our steaks came and the small talk almost ended while we ate. We agreed to meet the next morning. They would follow us to the cafe in Window Rock for one last breakfast. It would be Monday and dining room in the hotel wasn't open for breakfast during the week. All they had was the continental breakfast.

We walked out the next morning and found the Green Berets loading their personal effects into the Humvees.

"Are we taking back your grenade launcher Connie? Jim asked.

"No way in hell! I'm not facing that thing without it. We'll give it back when I'm done with it."

"Alright with me. Are you guys ready to go and eat?" Jim asked us.

"Sure, eat first or go swimming first Tom?" Connie asked as she grinned behind her sunglasses.

"Ummm, eat first I guess," Tom said nervously.

"Okay then," Connie said as she grinned like a shark eyeing its prey.

We entered the cafe and sat down. The sheriff and his deputies weren't there this morning. After eating I paid for the meal and we met outside.

"You guys want to follow us to the pool?" Connie asked as she smiled wide.

"Damn it Connie, I forgot you can't go into the water until at least an hour after you've eaten. We have to leave for our base. Oh well, maybe next time," Tom said.

"Alright Tom, I'll let you off the hook but next time we're going swimming," Connie said as she gave him a hug.

After I shook all of their hands and Connie gave out hugs to everyone it was time for them to go.

"Remember to call me when this is over so I can let the others know," the sarge said.

"I promise sarge, you'll be my first call," Connie promised.

We watched as their Humvees disappeared down the road before climbing into our car. We drove to the sheriff's office and found him sitting behind his desk hard at work.

"Knock knock," I said before taking a seat in his office.

He closed his computer and leaned back in his chair. "What's new with you? How did the night in the sweat lodge go?"

"We found out all we needed to know in order to take out the wendigo Joe. We know who he was and where he came from. We know how long he has been here, over four hundred years. This is the fourth time he has returned here. We know how to defeat him and where he is hiding too," I said.

"So I assume you both had your vision and saw the Great Spirit?"

"It was an experience I will never forget," Connie said.

"Our FBI director is no longer in charge of this operation. The secretary of defense is taking over and our director is in the hot seat," I said grinning.

"How did this come about?" Joe asked us.

"Our director has been stonewalling the secretary of defense. The secretary has been calling our director for two days wanting to know about the unit he lent to us. Our director decided not to take his calls while he tried to do damage control. But he forgot the secretary of defense, Jim Collar, had our direct numbers from the Wisconsin case we just finished a couple of weeks ago. He was fed up with not getting any answers so he called us and we had to brief him on the operation," I said.

"How much did you actually tell him about it?"

"We gave him every detail of it," Connie said.

"Every detail?" Joe asked with a grin as he pointed at the talismans hanging around our necks.

"Yes, every detail. Is there no one who doesn't know about our escapades yesterday?" Connie asked in frustration.

"It's not every day people get a personal visit from the Great Spirit. We are the talk of the reservation for sure," I explained.

"Oh, I thought it was because of... never mind," Connie said.

"Connie, believe it or not you still have a hangup about being naked in front of other people," I told her.

"No, it doesn't bother me that I was naked with other people. I just thought other people were talking about it, that's all."

"Nobody cares, it's not like you're a supermodel you know," I said, grinning at her reaction.

"Hey!"

"Relax partner, I'm just pulling your leg."

"What's our next move?" Joe asked while laughing at Connie's reaction..

"We need to get together with the Navajo Rangers. We need to make a plan. I figure we'll head out at least a couple of hours before dark and set up near his lair. I want to watch him come and go tonight before making the final plan for his demise," I said.

"Now with the secretary of defense in charge we don't need to go through a middleman to get what we need to end this," Connie explained.

"So are you figuring to stake its lair out tonight and then tomorrow night lay in wait for it to come back and then ambush it?"

"That will all depend on how fast the secretary of defense can get what we need. It will either end tomorrow or the next day for sure," I said.

"You want to show me on the map where his lair is? Just in case things go bad for you tonight. I don't want to start all over again," Joe said as he pushed back his chair.

"You've been spending way too much time with us. You're turning into as big an asshole as Ben," Connie said while the sheriff grinned.

I walked up to the wall map and looked at it. "Right here is where the Green Berets were killed. If you follow this line straight away from the creek bottom another half of a mile or so Right here is the dugout log cabin," I said pointing to the spot.

"Only the top three feet of the cabin are above ground and it has a sod roof so it will be very difficult to spot from the sky," Connie added.

"Is spotting it from the sky important?"

"It could be, but we'll have to wait and see until after we recon the area," I said.

"From the three story farmhouse it looks like a two and a half to three mile trek to get where you need to be," Joe said as he looked the map over.

"Yeah, we'll have to spend the entire night out. I want to see it leaving and coming back just in case it takes different travel routes," I said.

"Where do you plan on setting up for the night?"

"Over here somewhere, on the opposite side from the creek bottom. We want to make sure we are totally out of his direction of travel," I said pointing at the spot on the map.

"It has to be taking different travel routes Ben,"

"How do you figure that Connie?"

"Because if he was taking the same travel routes coming and going the Green Berets would have had a run in with him when he went out hunting for the night and not on his return trip," Connie reasoned.

"Connie has to be right on this Ben. If it used the same route every time the army guys would have met with it just after dark," Joe said.

"I'm not just another pretty face you know," Connie said smugly.

"That's a fact!" I said, grinning again.

"Hey! You better watch it buster, I have a fresh clip in my SIG!"

"Jeez, I was just agreeing with you is all!"

"Uh huh, nice try sport!"

"Contact the Navajo Rangers for us Joe. Tell them to meet us at the cafe at four. We'll eat and then set up for the night. Tell them to make sure to bring their night optics and fresh batteries," I instructed him.

"Tell them to come loaded for bear too, just in case we run into this thing. Also tell them to not forget their crosses," Connie added.

I was standing looking at the map again. "What's this over here?" I asked the sheriff.

"It's a smaller community of about thirty people."

"Is it under the curfew order too?"

"Yes, everything in this county is, why?"

"I'm thinking it's not too far for it to go to get there. What if it heads there looking for an easy meal first. The creek bottom runs right alongside this little town. From there it can drop into the creek bottom and follow it almost all the way to Window Rock. So it goes hunting here first and then makes a circuit towards town. Then back to where it left the creek bottom and ambushed the Green Berets on its way to its hideout."

"There are a lot of small spreads along there too. One man cattle and sheep operations to look over. That must be how Kyle and Sandy Cloud were taken. Their place is right over here," Joe said.

"You'd better send out some deputies to that small town and knock on everybody's doors. Let them know we now think the wendigo is traveling either through or close to their town every night. Reiterate the importance of staying inside when it's dark out," Connie said.

"Call Bob at the radio station and have him announce it over his radio station too," I said.

We met with the Navajo Rangers at the prearranged hour at the cafe. The sheriff joined us for supper. Virgil was busy with notifying the people in the small town of the danger that was nearby.

"When we go out there tonight there will be absolutely no talking at all. Turn your phones off. The last thing we're going to need tonight is a phone call coming in when we're within earshot of it. We don't know how acute its hearing is so we aren't taking any chances," I said.

"Maybe it can't hear at all. I don't remember seeing any ears. But I'm betting it can do pretty much everything well," Sid said.

"I didn't notice any ears either. But the wendigo is a whole lot of ugliness to take in all at once. Maybe with looking at all of him we just didn't notice them," Connie said.

"How on earth did you find its lair anyway?" John asked us.

"The Great Spirit showed it to Connie," I said matter of factly.

Sid started looking around the cafe.

"What are you looking for?" Connie asked him.

"The hidden cameras, we're on candid camera or some other show like that, Right?"

"Ben and Connie spent a night in the sweat lodge paying homage to the Great Spirit. My Uncle Jeff set it up with our holy man," Joe explained.

"You mean the two of you spent the entire night there and he appeared before you?" Sid asked us in awe.

"How was it?" John asked eagerly.

"It was simply amazing," Connie said.

"Yeah, we have the whip marks to prove we were there," I said.

"That means you were....oh...." John said with a surprised look on his face.

"Don't knock it if you haven't tried it," Connie grinned.

"The two of you aren't even members of the Navajo tribe and you're willing to do this for us," Sid said gratefully.

"We'd do anything, anything at all to end the savage murders happening here," I said simply.

"Yeah what's a little lost modesty? I shed that when I shed my clothes," Connie said with a grin.

We ate then drove out to the three story farmhouse and parked. We walked on an angle across the hay field so we came out in the far left hand corner of it. We walked straight out into the desert from there for a half of a mile before turning ninety degrees and straight away from the farm.

"Stop here for a second. Is everybody's phones powered off? I don't mean on silent, I mean off," I whispered as everyone checked their phones to make sure.

"Are we close?" I asked Connie.

"Yeah, very close. Let's creep up to the top of this sand dune and look over the other side. When we get close to the top drop down and crawl the rest of the way on your bellies," Connie whispered.

We crawled the last thirty feet through the hot desert sand before we could see over the top of it.

Connie hit me on my shoulder. "Ben, look, it's right there. The logs in the back are nearly all the way covered up by blowing sand. But you can still make out its shape. When the Great Spirit showed it to me it was from the other side of it and from there you can see the top few logs," Connie whispered.

It was a good thing we brought water bags along. Before morning we'd need them. For now we would go without any water. I was fearful of how accurate the wendigos' sense of smell was. Cattle could smell water from a couple of miles away. The wendigo had a skull similar to that of a bull. But could it smell water as far away as a bull? I wasn't willing to take that chance.

The dark of night couldn't come fast enough. The desert heat was wearing everyone down. It was one thing to be standing and having it beating down on your head. It was quite another thing to be laying prone and having it bake your entire body. Finally darkness fell and I slipped my night vision goggles over my eyes. We'd agreed one person would be without them just in case the wendigo appeared close to us. The person not wearing the goggles would be responsible for warning the others.

It was a half hour after dark when the wendigo appeared in front of the dugout. It glided silently away, not making a sound as it traveled in the direction we thought it might, towards the small town.

Once the wendigo disappeared in the distance we took a chance and drank some of the water to ease our parched throats. The night passed slowly. I was laying on my back looking up at the stars to ease the tightness in my back from laying on my belly for so long.

My watch showed it was nearing four in the morning. The wendigo must appear in the next hour or it would be daylight out. I motioned the others to be on high alert as we waited tensely. Connie had her grenade launcher by her side with the barrel of it sticking just over the top of the dune. John had switched to a shotgun after he found out how useless his AR 15 was against the wendigo. He was loaded with Dragon's breath and dum dums. Sid had four dragon's breath rounds and four rounds bearing the silver crosses. My first six rounds were silver crosses followed by alternating dragon's breath and dum dums.

"SKREEEEE, SKREEEEE!" The wendigo shouted as it came out of the creek bottom.

We all waited with bated breath for it to appear over the slope where the Green Berets were killed the other night. Suddenly it was in front of us headed straight for the dugout. It seemed to glide along more so than walk. I could see through the night vision goggles it had made a fresh kill. It was carrying part of a human torso. The wendigo had to turn its head sideways to get its large antlers through the doorway of the dugout.

We lay there for twenty minutes to make sure it wasn't coming back out before sliding back down the sand dune. We walked away a half of a mile before I stopped so we could all talk about what just happened.

"It's what we surmised in the sheriff's office. The wendigo is heading in the direction of that small village before entering the creek bottom," Connie said.

"We'll need to contact the secretary of defense once we get back to the office. I have a shopping list of military grade weapons and equipment we'll need to end this," I said.

"What time are we coming back out tonight if we get the equipment we need in time?" John asked.

"I figure midnight or so. The wendigo should be long gone and on the hunt. So we shouldn't have to worry about running into him as we position ourselves for the ambush," I said.

"Where are we going to be setting up?" Sid asked.

"You and John will be on the sand dune where we just spent the night. Connie and I will be on the other side of the dugout, off to the right in that brushy area behind the small hill."

"So we'll be on the east side and you'll be on the west side?" John asked to confirm it.

"Yes, don't come down that sand dune until after shit hits the fan. I don't want to accidently barbeque you in the process," I said.

"Well hell, we would appreciate that Ben," Sid said dryly.

"Let's go and meet in the cafe for some breakfast and I'll break down what we're going to do in detail," I said as the four of us started walking again.

We turned our phones back on and I looked at mine to make sure I hadn't missed any calls.

"Why don't you guys call the sheriff and Virgil and have them meet us for breakfast so they know what's going on too," Connie said.

It took us a while to walk back to our cars and drive into town. By the time we got there the sheriff and Virgil were waiting for us Joe brought his Uncle Jeff along too. I hadn't thought of that but Jeff was a big part of our success and deserved to know what was going on too.

We sat with them at our normal table and poured coffee into our waiting cups.

"So tell us? Did you locate the lair of the wendigo or didn't you?" Jeff asked impatiently.

"Yeah, he was right where the Great Spirit showed me he was," Connie said.

"So our holy man was helpful to the cause then?" Jeff asked with a grin.

"We couldn't have done it without his help and the guidance of the Great Spirit," I said.

"That was a good idea you had. You were right, there are more ways of gaining protection than the one we were using," Connie said.

"So in order to see the Great Spirit I'm told you need to do certain things to make yourself worthy," Jeff said, acting innocently.

"You mean like being whipped?" Connie asked as she showed them the fading marks on her back."

"So you did the full Monte?" Jeff asked with a grin.

"The full Monte?" It suddenly dawned on her what Jeff was saying.

"I watch movies, you know," Jeff said as he sipped his coffee.

"You already know that, don't you? It's hard to keep anything around here secret you know," Connie grumbled.

"That lipstick camera in the sweat lodge helped. I was watching you on tv with the tribal elders and the chief. The next time you do this though we'll have a pay per view event. We could make a bundle!" Jeff said with a wide grin after seeing the look on Connie's face.

"Huh? You were watching us all night chasing each other with the willow switches!" Connie asked in shock.

"Ha ha ha, I'm just kidding you. How did I not know? Not only did I talk to the holy man the next day but I also talked to a few of your swim buddies. I was anxious to find out if my suggestion worked or not."

"Now that was funny as hell Uncle Jeff," Joe said as he and the others laughed out loud at Connie's reaction.

"After spending fourteen hours in the sweat lodge the pond

was a very welcome reprieve from the heat," I said while grinning at my partner.

"We were right yesterday Joe. The wendigo is heading in the direction of that small village before going down into the creek bottom. When it came back it went right through the area where the green berets were killed," I told him.

"So do we have a plan of attack planned yet or not?" Virgil asked.

"I'll tell you what we're going to do. After breakfast we'll all go back to your office and give the secretary of defense a call and ask for help," I said.

"Sounds good," Joe said as the waitress, Sadie came over to take their orders.

"This is going to be our shopping list. I want four military grade com units. They have to be able to communicate with each other at least two miles away. We will be a lot closer to each other than that. But I don't want to take a chance of having bad reception. We have to have clear communications with each other. I need a military grade laser to paint the target with."

"What do you mean by paint the target?" Sid asked.

"We use the laser to paint the target so a smart bomb can be dropped on it with pin point accuracy."

"Dropped on it from where? And what kind of a bomb?" Joe asked in surprise.

"We are going to use napalm, jellied gasoline. It will be dropped on target by fighter jets."

"If the wendigo doesn't like heat this should give him a real hot foot," John said with a grin of appreciation.

"We'll need a military grade communication device to communicate with the fighter jets. Also I want two flame throwers, one for each team."

"Would flamethrowers even bother it after having napalm dropped on its head?" Jeff asked.

"Hang on, I'm not done yet. Sid, your shotgun will be loaded full of silver crosses, all eight rounds. John, you'll be the one with the flamethrower but bring your shotgun along too. Your shotgun will be loaded with dragon's breath. Use the flamethrower if it gets too close to use then switch to the shotgun. After you fire off your silver crosses reload with the DumDums."

"We're going to be too far from the cabin to be effective, Ben," Sid said.

"Once the napalm is dropped on the target that will be your cue to move in closer to the dugout. But stay far enough away from it so you get your shot at taking out the wendigo before it's on top of you."

"That shouldn't be a problem. The heat from the napalm should keep us from getting too close," John said.

"Connie and I will be where we told you we would be hiding until it is in the cabin. We will stay there until the napalm hits it. Then we'll run in closer too. My shotgun will be loaded with silver crosses first, eight rounds. After that I'll be alternating between dragon's breath and DumDums."

"Oh Jeff, just an FYI for you. The wendigo had been here a total of four times. It has never been defeated in the past so this will be the first time it has. It's over four hundred years old," Connie informed him.

"Wow, I figured three times for sure but I couldn't find any records of a time earlier than the late seventeen hundreds. If we defeat it does that mean it can never come back again?" Jeff asked.

"The Great Spirit didn't know for sure because it has never been defeated before. But his question to me was, we'll never see it again in our lifetime and isn't that enough?" Connie explained.

"Connie, your primary weapon will be the grenade launcher. It is loaded with both incendiary rounds and fragmentation rounds. If the wendigo gets too close to us to use the grenades then use the flamethrower instead. We don't want to catch shrapnel from our own grenades.

"If Jeff is switching to his shotgun, if the wendigo gets too close. Why am I switching to a flamethrower for the same reason?" Connie asked me.

"I have fifty rounds in my shotgun. He is never going to get that close to us. Besides that you'll have to quit using the grenade launcher at a further distance than John would have to quit with his flamethrower."

"I hope the napalm is the right answer," Joe said.

"It had better be, because I'm all out of ideas. This is what the Great Spirit told us to use against it."

"Did the Great Spirit ever tell you why the wendigo is in the southwest instead of in the north where he came from?" Jeff asked us.

"Yes he did. The wendigo hates ice and cold. He blames the winter weather for what he became instead of blaming himself. He was trapped one winter by deep snow and by spring he'd eaten his entire family. The evilness of that act is what made him a wendigo, He avoids the cold of the north now," Connie explained.

"Lucky us," Jeff said angrily.

Our food came and we ate before heading over to the sheriff's office as a group. We went into the conference room and I called the secretary of defense and placed my phone on speaker so everyone would hear the conversation.

"Mr. Secretary, this is Ben Hawk. I have you on speaker phone. Listening in is the entire team helping on the hunt," I said.

"Good morning everyone. I'm hoping you have good news for me Ben."

"We have confirmed the location of the wendigo's lair. It is exactly where we were shown it to be by the Great Spirit."

"That's excellent news! What do you need me to provide for you to end this?"

"I'm glad you asked. Do you have a pen and paper handy to write this down?"

"Hang on a sec. Alright Ben I'm ready."

"I need four military grade com units with a minimal range of two miles. I need a military grade laser for painting targets. Add two flamethrowers. I also need a military grade communication device to communicate with the fighter aircraft I need you to supply us with," I said.

"What armament do you need on the aircraft?"

"Napalm bombs sir, smart bombs because you won't be able to see the intended target from the air, it's camouflaged. I'll paint the target so your plane knows where to drop the ordnance. After they fire bomb the target it will be our job on the ground to make sure the wendigo stays inside the fire. Make sure it has more than one bomb. We might have to call in a second air strike on the target."

"Okay, I have everything. How soon do you need these?"

"The sooner you can get them to me the sooner we can end this,"I said.

"I'll have an Apache helicopter fly these into you today. I'll have it there at three this afternoon if that's soon enough for you. Where should the helicopter land?"

"Have him land next to the truck stop. It should be easy to find from the air. One more thing Mr. Secretary. The communication device you loan us to communicate from the air should have a range of at least twenty five miles."

"That shouldn't be a problem as long as you maintain line of sight with the plane."

"Good, I want the fighter to maintain a pattern twenty five miles away so the wendigo isn't spooked. We will fire bomb the wendigo just after daylight tomorrow morning. We'll make sure the wendigo is inside the cabin and settled down before calling in the air strike. We will have friendly's stationed to the west and east of our target. The fighter must drop its load from the north to the south to keep our ground forces out of harm's way."

"What do you want to use for call signs for you and the pilot of the airplane?"

"The pilot will be Archangel and I'll be the vengeful one," I said as the anger crept back into my voice over our losses.

"That sounds pretty appropriate Ben. Is that everything you need for now?"

"Yes sir, hopefully by morning we can report we were successful."

"Go get that son of a bitch! Good luck everyone," the secretary said as he hung up.

I looked at the others sitting around the table listening in on the conversation.

"Now what?" John asked.

"Now we go and get some sleep. I'll see everyone back here at two thirty so we can go and meet up with the helicopter." I said as everybody pushed back their chairs and got up.

Connie and I drove back to our hotel and showered before sleeping. We had an abundance of sand on our skins from hours of laying in the desert. I put the do not disturb sign on the door and pulled the drapes closed to darken the room as much as possible. Connie called the front desk and asked them to wake us up at one in the afternoon.

I slept fitfully. The events of last night and before kept my mind racing nonstop. Finally I might have slept for an hour but no more than that. The phone rang with our wakeup call. I lifted the receiver and dropped it back down on the cradle to stop it from ringing. I looked at Connie as she sat up in bed and she didn't look any better than I felt.

"Trying to sleep was a real waste of time," I said.

"Tell me about it. The only good thing about it is we get to try again before we go back out again later on tonight," Connie said with a yawn.

We drove back to the sheriff's office and joined the others in the conference room.

Joe looked at us as we came in through the door. "I thought you said you were going to get some sleep," Joe said while grinning.

"Shut up Joe," Connie grumbled.

"It doesn't look like Sid or John had much better luck," I said as I looked at the others who would be going back out again tonight.

"Sleep was a real waste of time," Sid admitted.

"Hard to sleep when my mind is on facing the wendigo in the near future," John added with a yawn.

"Coffee, I need coffee," Connie muttered.

"We have to wait for the helicopter anyway. Let's stop in the cafe and get some coffee, in to go cups. We can drink it while we wait for the equipment to arrive," Joe said.

"That's the best idea you've had since we got here," Connie said, as she turned back around and headed for the car.

The five of us walked into the cafe and were met by Sadie the waitress at the counter.

"What can I get for you dears?" the older woman asked us.

"Five coffees in to go cups," Joe said.

"Nectar of the Gods," Connie said as she sipped her coffee with her eyes shut.

In the far distance I could hear the wop, wop, wop of the approaching helicopter. We watched as a small dot slowly grew bigger and ten minutes later landed next to us.

There were a couple of techs along to show us how the radio equipment and flamethrowers worked. Once we knew how to open the valves on the flamethrowers and to ignite the napalm that would flow out of the nozzle the other tech, a radioman showed us how to use the com units and the radio we'd need to contact the fighter jet with.

"What about the laser unit?" Connie asked the radioman.

'Oh yeah, that's right here. You throw this toggle switch to power it on. Then it has sights on it like a gun has. Just aim it like a gun and point it at your target then pull the trigger. The important thing is you have to keep the trigger pressed until the bomb hits your target or else the smart bomb won't know what to hit, got it?"

"Got it!" Connie said as she looked through the laser's sights.

We walked away from the helicopter so the sand wouldn't blow into our eyes when it took off.

"Sheriff, can we store this equipment in your office until we need it later on tonight?" I asked him.

"Sure, no problem. When do you plan on heading back out again?" Joe asked us.

"We'll meet here at your office at midnight. It's only a ten minute drive to the farmhouse and another hour walk to where we have to get to. So we should be on station no later than two in the morning. That should get us set up in place two hours before the wendigo reappears," I said.

"Sheriff, this morning when the wendigo went back to its lair it was carrying a part of a carcass. Has anyone been reported missing?" Connie asked.

"We haven't received any calls about killings or missing people. But that's a real problem out here. There are a lot of remote areas and a lot of sheep herders and cattlemen who work alone. We might not know for several weeks who is missing," Joe explained.

"If my count is right, the one last night brings the total to thirteen. But like you said there might be others out there we don't know about yet," Connie said.

"What's next?" John asked as he set down a flamethrower in the sheriff's inner office.

"Get some food into you and meet back here at eleven thirty," I said.

"Virgil and I are going to post at the farmhouse in the Humvee. After all of this we don't want to miss the final show," Joe said.

"That's fine Joe but you have to be careful. Any sounds or light might attract it to you instead of where we're expecting it to go. Then you'd be a target and it would come back into its den from a different angle. If that happened it might accidentally run into us where we are hiding and waiting for it," I explained.

"I understand and the last thing we want to do is screw things up this close to the finish line. Tell you what, we'll be watching from the third floor of the farmhouse instead and we'll make sure there are no lights on up there," Joe said.

"That would be a lot better and a lot safer for those of us out there laying the trap for it," I said.

Connie and I went back to our hotel and ate an early lite supper. I didn't need anything heavy in my stomach for what lay ahead. I just had a BLT and a coke and Connie went with a chicken salad. Sleep came a little bit better this time around. Our minds were eased by the fact we had the supplies we thought we needed to send the wendigo back to the bowels of the earth. We left a wake up call for ten that night. After getting dressed and driving back to Window Rock it was nearing the pre arranged meeting time.

We got to the sheriff's office and found everyone already there waiting for us.

"I called the homeowner and told them we needed to use his third floor room again. He'll be up waiting for us to get there," Joe told us.

"We may as well head out then. Let's shut off our lights a mile before we get to their farm lane. The last thing I want to do is to attract the wendigo to us with our headlights if it isn't out of the area yet. Also shut your car doors gently. We don't know how acute his hearing is and we don't want him to hear us in the area," I explained.

"Yeah, I wouldn't want to meet it halfway to the dugout in the dark," Sid agreed.

The six of us piled into two cars for the trip to the farm house. I shut off my lights long before getting there and I saw the sheriff do the same thing with the Humvee.

We got out of the cars and gathered around the back of the Humvee where our equipment was.

"Be careful lifting out the flamethrowers. The last thing we need to do is clank one of the tanks on the side of the vehicle," I said in a low, soft voice.

John and I shouldered the heavy flamethrowers. We each put in our com units and activated them. Connie grabbed the laser unit and I grabbed the radio set for communicating with the aircraft.

"We should have asked for a fifth com unit so we knew when it was happening," Joe whispered.

"Trust me sheriff, you'll know when the shit hits the fan. From here you should have a ring side seat," I told him.

We headed out across the hay field single file and then across the desert floor. By the time we got to the spot where Connie and I would part company with the Navajo rangers it was one thirty in the morning.

"Stay behind your sand dune until I give the word to get closer. The secretary of defense never indicated to me if he was sending one plane or two. We'd hate to have you move up closer and have a second bomb dropped when you weren't expecting it," I whispered to them.

"Yeah, we'd hate that too. Good luck and we'll see the two of you when this is over with," Sid said as they moved away from us.

We set up behind our small hill. The sage brush on the hill gave us better concealment.

"Ranger one, com check," Connie whispered into her tiny mic.

"You're coming in loud and clear," Sid whispered back.

I pulled my watch out of my pocket and saw it was two thirty. "Ranger one, make sure your phones are powered down," I whispered. It was something we forgot to do before heading out.

"Roger that," came the whispered reply.

It was nearly four in the morning when I contacted the aircraft on our other radio. "Archangel, this is vengeful one. How do you read me," over," I whispered.

"Vengeful one, this is the archangel, you are coming in five by five, over."

"Maintain your holding pattern. I will be calling for your bomb run within the hour. Standby after making the run in case a second bomb run is necessary, Over."

"Roger that,"

I turned off the radio to make sure it didn't make a noise the wendigo could hear.

A half hour later we could hear it coming from the creek bottom. "SKREEEEE, SKREEEEE!" The wendigo screeched as it made its way to the dugout and went inside of it.

"We won't call in the air strike until it is daylight out," I said.

"We think you should call it in right now Ben," John whispered back.

"Why do you think that?" Connie asked.

"For two reasons. One, the wendigo will be backlit from the fire and we'll be hidden better in the darkness. Two, with you using the laser the aircraft doesn't need to be able to see the target as long as you can see it well enough to hit it with the laser," John said.

"That's good reasoning, keep your heads down and we'll call in the air strike," I whispered.

"I have the laser powered on Ben. I'll hit the dugout when you say so," Connie whispered.

I powered on the radio. "Archangel, this is the vengeful one. Commence airstrike, drop your ordnance from the north to south. We have friendlies east and west of the target, over,"

"Roger that vengeful one. ETA to target in just over one minute. We are turning and burning, over."

"Roger that! Okay Connie, light up the target." I watched as Connie hit the dugout with the guided bomb laser.

"Target acquired, bombs away," The jet roared past us as the bomb fell towards the dugout. There was a tremendous ball of fire seventy five yards long and reaching into the sky sixty feet.

Five seconds later a second jet screamed overhead and another napalm bomb hit dead center.

"Holy shit!" The sheriff declared as the clap of the explosion echoed through the farmyard. They could easily see the towering flames from the bombs over two miles away.

"Okay, move in closer," I yelled into my mic. It was no longer necessary to remain quiet.

"SKREEEEE, SKREEEEE, SKREEEEE!" The wendigo screamed out.

"I can't believe the wendigo is still alive Ben!" Connie yelled out as she ran behind me as we advanced on the dugout.

"It probably wasn't alive in the first place. But we already figured on that."

I heard Sid's shotgun being fired rapidly from the other side. I could hear the woosh of the jellied gasoline being sprayed on the wendigo by John.

"We forced it back into the fire! I would have thought the wendigo with a barc skull for a head couldn't show any emotion but it did," Sid yelled excitedly.

"I could have sworn I saw pain and anguish painted on its face," John added.

"Watch it guys, It's probably headed in your direction," Sid warned us as he fed DumDums into his magazine.

"SKREEEEE, SKREEEEE!" the wendigo screamed as it came out of the inferno and leaped in our direction.

I started hammering it with my rounds containing pure silver crosses and I could see the anguish on its face, mostly around and in its glowing red eyes.

"Hit it with the grenade launcher before it gets too close to us Connie! I screamed out.

Connie's first grenade was an incendiary round and hit it right in the chest. The grenade exploded into a white phosphorus ball of fire that blew the wendigo off of its feet and backwards twenty feet. I was through my silver cross rounds and I was now hitting it with DumDums and dragon's breath rounds.

The wendigo was back on its feet and I could tell that it was really pissed off. "SKREEEEE, SKREEEEE!" It screamed out even louder than before.

"Hit it again Connie!" I said as my first DumDum round hit it in the chest. Connie's next round was a fragmentation grenade. The concussion of the explosion made our ears ring. Once again the wendigo was thrown backwards. This time it landed back into the jellied gasoline inferno.

"SKREEEEE, SKREEEEE, SKREEEEE!" It screamed out as it once again leaped out of the fire at us. By now I was pounding it as fast and as hard as I could with the DumDums and the dragon's breath.

"I've had enough of this!" Connie screamed out as she went into rapid fire mode. She hit it with another incendiary grenade that knocked it off its feet again. Then before it could regain its feet, she hit it with a fragmentation grenade. The wendigo seemed shaken and instead of leaping to its feet it was on its hands and knees. Connie hit it with another incendiary round. It flopped down on its face and she hit it with another fragmentation grenade. The wendigo started crawling towards the fire to escape and Connie hit it with another incendiary round. By now the wendigo was actually crawling into the fire and Connie hit it with another fragmentation grenade that propelled it out of sight into the fire.

I looked sideways at Connie. "Temper temper!" I grinned with relief.

"Move back guys we're calling in another airstrike to make sure this is over with."

We ran back to where the radio was. "Are you guys out of harm's way? Connie yelled into her mic.

"Yeah, go ahead and hit it!" John yelled out.

"I have the target painted, Ben!" Connie said as she held the laser steady.

"Archangel, this is the vengeful one. Hit the target once more. We want to make damn sure this is over with!"

"Roger that vengeful one, target is acquired!"

"SKREEEEE, SKREEEEE!" Screamed out the wendigo from inside the blaze.

"Now that is one unhappy wendigo," Connie stated as she turned the valves of the flamethrower on.

The first bomb hit dead center followed closely by the second one.

"Wowowee, now that is a nice fire for a weenie roast!" John called out from the other side of the fire.

"Get a little bit closer and you can have one," Connie laughed out.

"SKReeeee, SKreeeee, Skreeee, skreeeee, eeeee, eeee, eee, ee...."

"I do believe this whole thing is over with guys," Sid said with a smile of relief.

I think when we heard its screams fading it was returning to the bowels of the earth," I said almost in disbelief.

"Just to be safe I'm staying right here until the fire goes out to make sure the damn thing is gone," Connie said.

The Navajo rangers walked over to our side of the fire and we sat on our sand hill and watched as the fire burned down.

"What the hell was going on over here?"

"Connie knocked it off of its feet twice with her grenades and it kept getting back up. I think it pissed her off. She went into rapid fire mode and every time it started to stand up she hit it again and knocked it flat. It was trying to crawl back into the fire for safety when she hit it the last time."

"You're just lucky I asked for the grenade launcher or the wendigo would have had us for lunch. By the way, I'm out of grenades. I fired all eight of them."

"I have two thoughts on that. First of all, I told you before this was over that you'd want a bazooka. And secondly, we had the protection of our crosses."

"That's true Ben, but if it would have escaped it would have gone on killing."

We sat there for a few hours and waited for the fire to burn down to just a few hot spots before we entered the area and kicked it around with our feet.

I found the burnt brittle bones that must have been what was left of Carl but nothing else.

"Well I guess this is a wrap. We can head on back to Washington now and tell the director where to stick our badges," I said as I shouldered my shotgun for the walk back.

"We better turn our phones back on and let the sheriff know we're still alive," Connie said, having forgotten we had them off.

"We can see that you're still alive," Joe said as he walked up carrying a shotgun.

"We expected you guys back a few hours ago. When you didn't come back we went looking, wondering what happened to you," Virgil said.

"With all of the excitement we forgot to turn our phones back on, sorry," Connie said.

"What the hell was going on here? It sounded like world war three!" Joe said.

"Connie started hitting it with grenades and it wouldn't stay down so she went into beast mode," Sid said.

"So is it all over with finally?" Joe asked us.

"Yeah, we sent the wendigo back to the bowels of the earth. We found the bones of Carl too so it is totally over," I said.

"Ben and I will be heading back to Washington tomorrow morning."

"Not so fast guys. The tribe isn't done with you just yet," Sid said.

"What are you talking about Sid?" Connie asked.

"The tribe will be having a celebration tomorrow night and the two of you are going to be a big part of it," Joe said.

"But first, I think we need to visit the radio station and tell the good news to the people. We need to let them know they are no longer living in fear," Virgil said.

We loaded up the weapons into the back of the Humvee and then told the farmer the threat was over with. The wendigo has been banished from the earth.

Chapter Twenty-Eight

T he six of us walked up the stairs of the radio station unannounced and walked into the sound proof booth.

"I interrupt our programming for an unscheduled announcement from the team hunting for the wendigo," Bob said.

The chairs we'd used last time were stacked in the corner. We set them up in front of Bob and sat down.

"What new developments do you have to report?" Bob asked us.

"We have the news the entire tribe has been waiting for. The threat is over and the wendigo has returned to the bowels of the earth," the sheriff said.

"The curfew has been lifted and everyone can return to living a normal life," Virgil said.

"This isn't the first time the wendigo has been here. The wendigo was over four hundred years old and has been here four times in all," I said.

"How can you know that Agent Hawk?" Bob asked.

"Because that's what the Great Spirit told me when Connie and I spent a night in the sweat lodge."

"The two of you spent a night in the sweat lodge and received visions from the Great Spirit?" Bob asked in shock.

"We wouldn't have been able to solve the case without the Great Spirit's help."

"Oh, and the Great Spirit wants the Navajo people to know that you are loved by him," Connie added.

"You saw the Great Spirit too?"

"Do you want to see the whip marks on my back to prove it?"

"No, that's alright. In modern times it's a rare thing for people to spend time in the sweat lodge and receive visions. It's an unheard of thing for a non native to do," Bob said.

"Tomorrow night at dusk we will be having a celebration in the ceremonial bowl to celebrate the wendigo being vanquished. We are expecting a big turnout by the tribe for the powwow," Joe said.

"No more living in fear. I expect to see many fires burning tonight and many people enjoying an evening by their backyard fires. Celebrating with their families and friends," John said.

"So what are you going to do now that you don't have a case to work on anymore?" Joe asked us.

"Well, it's nearly noon. I thought we'd go and get a little shut eye. Why don't all of you meet us at our hotel at five for a celebration. The FBI is buying," I said.

"I like your thinking Ben," Joe said.

"We have one more thing that needs doing yet, Ben," Connie said.

"What's that?" I asked as Connie pulled out her phone.

"Sergeant Wilson? This is Connie Sanchez. It's over, Sarge, the wendigo has been destroyed."

"Are you serious? How were you able to do it?"

"We hit it with napalm smart bombs, grenades, flamethrowers and pure silver crosses loaded into shotgun shells."

"Thank you everybody for bringing this to an end. "I'll let the others know. Our dead will be able to rest in peace now," Ben Wilson said gratefully as Connie hung up.

"Let's go back to Joe's office. We have to make one more phone call to the secretary of defense and let him know it's over," I said as we got into our cars for the three block ride.

We sat in the conference room and I put the phone on speaker mode and hit his auto dial button.

"Ben, how did it go last night?" Jim Collar, the Secretary of Defense asked.

"Sir, I have you on speaker phone and our whole team is present. We are happy to report we were successful. The wendigo is no more."

"Now that's great news people! Congratulations to everybody who was involved. Was it as hard to get rid of as you thought it would be?"

"Mr. Secretary, it was touch and go. For a while there I didn't know if we'd be successful or not. We hit it with a flamethrower, shotgun shells loaded with silver crosses. Connie hit it eight times with grenades and your planes dropped four napalm bombs on it. It wasn't gone until after the last two bombs were dropped. We stuck around until after the fire went out to make sure it was gone."

"Are you ready to come back to Washington then?"

"No, sir, not yet. We've been told by the tribe our presence is requested for a celebration. We'll be back on Friday."

"I'll make sure your plane is standing by in Phoenix waiting for you. Great job everybody!" he said as he ended the call.

"Now we can go and get some sleep. See all of you in our hotel bar at five?" Connie asked.

"I'm on patrol tonight," Virgil said unhappily.

"No you're not, I just gave you the night off. This day is worthy of a celebration Virgil," Joe said.

We got back to our hotel room and showered before sleeping. Once again we had sand everywhere from laying down in it for hours on end. Plus we smelled of napalm. Four thirty came and our phone alarm woke us up.

We walked into the bar and the others were there ahead of us drinking a beer. It was the first time we'd seen them out of uniform.

"It's about time you guys showed up," Joe said with a grin.

"Yeah, we were the ones who had to travel this time and you're still the last ones here," Virgil laughed.

"You guys are early," Connie said.

"My old dad used to tell me that if you weren't ten minutes early then you were late," John said.

This was the first time I was in the bar and I wasn't carrying my shotgun with me. Now that the case was over with, I didn't have to worry about anybody messing around with it.

The bartender came walking over to our table with two new pitchers of beer. "Is what they're saying on the radio true? The wendigo is finally gone?"

"Yep, we guarantee that it's gone for good," Connie grinned.

"The manager told me to tell you that your pitchers of beer are on the house tonight and to thank you."

"Did you hear that Virgil? Our beers are on the house!" Sid said with a grin.

"You guys have to drink responsibly though. You have an hour's drive home," I said.

"Oh yeah, we forgot to tell you that part. We got hotel rooms for the night and charged it to your account," Joe said with a grin.

"You did say the FBI was treating and we knew you wouldn't want us to drive," John said happily.

We had surf and turf for supper. Everyone was in a happy mood. If we were going to celebrate we were going to do it right. All of us had spent many days not knowing if we were going to survive the battle with the wendigo. This was a huge relief and the weight of the world was off of our shoulders finally.

We wound down the celebration around eleven. Even though we were having way too much fun we knew we had more responsibilities tomorrow with the tribal celebration and the barrage of questions we'd have to field.

The next morning we checked out of our hotel. We knew we'd have to stay one more night for the Navajo celebration. But we'd check back into the motel in Window Rock for one night.

The six of us drove back to the cafe for breakfast. The cafe was in a festive mood. Everyone was smiling and coming to our table to congratulate and thank us for getting rid of the wendigo.

After breakfast we drove to the sheriff's office. As we went through town everyone was honking, waving and smiling at us. So much for being treated like an outsider like when we first got here.

"What's on the agenda for today?" Joe asked us.

"We have to meet up with an army helicopter at one this afternoon to return the equipment we borrowed from them. We also have to check back into the motel for tonight. Tomorrow we'll say our goodbyes before leaving for Phoenix and then on to Washington," I said.

"You won't need to check into the motel, Ben. The tribe has a special surprise in store for the two of you."

"We're not staying another night in the sweat lodge Joe!

Although it was quite an experience, once was enough," Connie said.

"No, no, nothing like that. Trust me you're going to enjoy this."

"Good because I've had all the surprises I can stand for one case. Shapeshifter, hairy man, and wendigo. About the only thing we haven't seen are werewolves, thunderbirds and chupacabras," Connie said.

"We have all of those here too, plus ghosts and skinwalkers. If you want to stick around for a while we can maybe show you some of them," Joe said with a grin.

"Maybe next trip Joe," Connie said trying to figure out if he was pulling her leg or not.

"We'll have to return the Humvee tomorrow after the powwow tonight," Joe said.

With nothing to do the day dragged on. But finally it was time to return the equipment. We loaded everything into the back of the Humvee and drove over to the truck stop.

We watched as the Apache helicopter came in for a landing before getting out of the Humvee so we wouldn't get sand in our eyes.

"Everything you loaned us is here. You'll have to have the armory clean the grenade launcher. I used up all of my grenades," Connie told the pilot.

"I'll let them know. Did you accomplish what you set out to do?"

"Yes we did, mission accomplished thanks to you loaning us the military grade equipment," I said.

The pilot climbed back into the Apache helicopter and soon the blades were turning slowly. We hurried back to the Humvee and climbed in as the blades gathered speed.

We had some time to waste before we needed to join Joe and the others to go to the powwow so we went into the few shops in town and browsed. We stopped into the silversmith that made our crosses for us and Connie bought a silver and turquoise necklace and I bought a silver and turquoise men's bracelet to wear on my other wrist.

"If we would have checked into the motel we could have taken a nap," Connie complained.

"If you're bored we could always go back out into the desert looking for more cryptids."

"That's funny Ben, you're a regular comedian!"

Out of boredom we ate an early supper and lounged around drinking cokes. Finally it was time to meet up with the sheriff.

"We followed him to their ceremonial bowl. There was wood already laid for a fire. The crowd was already gathering. Many of those here were wearing ceremonial dress.

Connie and I along with Joe, John, Virgil, Sid and Jeff entered the bowl.

"The two of you are to sit here," Joe said pointing at our seats. The others sat on both sides of us.

"Okay Joe, what the hell are you up too?" I asked him.

"Sid put the idea into my head. Remember when we were eating in the cafe not long after your night in the sweat lodge where you were visited by the Great Spirit? Sid made a comment after seeing your backs. He said, wow it's amazing what you're willing to do for us and you're not even one of us. Do you remember those words?" Joe asked me.

"Yeah, I remember him saying that."

"Well, it put an idea into my head. He was right, you weren't one of us but you should be. Tonight the two of you are becoming part of the Navajo Nation."

"I'm humbled, that's a great honor Joe, thank you."

"Yes, that is a great honor and I'm thrilled," Connie said with a smile on her beaming face.

"Oh crap, Connie!" I said to her out of the corner of my mouth.

"Oh crap, what?"

"When a new Navajo comes into the tribe it's born naked out of the mother's womb. We are coming into the tribe. They'll be expecting us to join the tribe in the same manner, naked!"

Connie looked at the crowd forming. "Huh?"

"I'm serious Connie! We're going to be paraded around the ceremonial bowl wearing nothing but a smile!"

"Huh?" Connie said again in shock.

I grinned at her and started laughing. "That was way too easy."

"Ben, the case is over with. You can quit being an asshole anytime now!" Connie said as she jabbed my ribs with her elbow.

The others were listening in and laughing at Connie's expense.

"Hopefully they'll give you a good name like Petunia," I said, grinning.

Connie didn't say anything but I received another elbow as her acknowledgement of my comment.

"After the way you paraded around between the sweat lodge and the pond you ought to be used to it by now," Jeff said, grinning.

"Fifteen people seeing you naked is a lot different than fifteen hundred Jeff," Connie said.

"You'll have to let us know what's happening as it happens Joe," I said.

Some tribal members used lit torches to light the fire. Suddenly a bass drum started to beat slowly and rhythmically in the background. The sound of the drum bounced around the inside of the bowl. Down the hill came a single file of men wearing ceremonial headdresses.

"That's the chief in the lead and the tribal elders following him," Joe whispered.

I saw one of the tribal elders was the holy man who we met at the sweat lodge.

The solemn looking group walked slowly around the inside of the bowl. Keeping step with the beat of the drum. Suddenly the drum became silent and the chief was standing right in front of us.

"Stand before me Ben Hawk and Connie Sanchez," The chief said, his face covered in paint with the light of the fire reflecting off of it eerily.

Connie and I stood up next to each other and faced the chief.

"You have shown your bravery and done much for the Navajo Nation. You helped the tribe rid the reservation of the wendigo. You have earned the right to join our tribe and become one with the people."

The holy man stepped forward and painted our faces with multiple colors and then stepped back.

"From this day forward your names will be entered into the tribal rolls as members of our tribe. Now you must be given tribal names of honor. Ben Hawk, your tribal name will be Red Hawk. A keen-eyed, sharp-talloned, swift bird of prey. Connie Sanchez, your white streak in your hair reminds me of the white plumage on the head of the bald eagle. Your name shall be White Feather in honor of the bald eagle. A majestic, regal and noble bird that fears nothing. Now your tribe will dance before you to honor your acceptance into the tribe."

Connie and I sat back down. "That's just great!" Connie growsed.

"What's wrong now?" I asked.

"The chief just named me white feather. Now I can't get rid of the white streak in my hair or I'll offend our tribe."

Connie saw a couple of porta potties off to the side. "I'll be right back," she said.

I watched her leave and turned back to the dancers and listened to the beat of the drum.

"Can I have a word with you?" Connie asked the holy man.

""What can I do for you White Feather?"

"Red Hawk has been giving me grief ever since the night in the sweat lodge, even though I'm over being naked in front of others. Here's what I'd like you to do...."

Connie went back to her seat and sat waiting for what was going to soon happen to Ben.

Soon the holy man walked up to Ben. "Rise before me, Red Hawk. In celebration of your rebirth into your new tribe I need you to become one with nature and dance before your new tribe!" The holy man said solemnly.

"Huh?"

"I said raise before me and become one with nature!"

"Huh?"

"Hoooooo, Heeeeee, Waaaah, ha ha ha ha ha Weeeeee! Oh my sides hurt, oh I can't breathe," Connie laughed as she fell out of her chair and onto the ground. "He said strip brother!" Connie said with delight as the tears ran down her face.

"You too White Feather, you too must become one with nature!"

"Huh?"

"You must show your pride in yourself and in your new tribe!"

"Huh?"

"You heard him White Feather! Now see what you started! Start stripping, sister!"

Joe and Jeff were laughing so hard they couldn't breathe.

The holy man was grinning wide. He winked at Connie before turning and walking away.

"Hey, that last part wasn't funny you know!" Connie shouted after him. I could see his shoulders shaking as he walked away from laughing.

It was nearly eleven before the celebration ended. The wendigo was no more.

"Follow me Red Hawk and White Feather," The holy man said as he took a torch and led the way out of the ceremonial bowl. In front of them stood a teepee made out of buffalo hides. Exactly like the lodges of the plains Indians used for centuries.

"Wow, this is amazing!" I said with appreciation.

"This is a lodge of honor. To honor your accomplishments for the tribe this is your lodge for tonight," the holy man said before taking his torch and walking away.

They entered the teepee. There was a battery operated lamp giving off a dim light. In the corner sat a pallet with a bear skin on it for softness.

"This bear skin feels wonderful, Ben," Connie said as she rubbed her hand on it.

Connie turned around to look at Ben. In a few brief moments he'd stripped naked and his manhood was saluting her.

"The case is over with now Connie so guess what time it is?"

"Oh! "Connie said as she worked fast to rid herself of her clothes.

Like we said at the beginning we never had sex while on a case. We felt we didn't need the distractions. Mistakes happen when people are distracted. In our profession people could die if that happened.

"Oh, this bear skin feels wonderful against my bare skin Red Hawk."

"I got something else that will feel wonderful against your bare skin White Feather," I said lustily as I covered her body with mine.

Oh, Red Hawk the talisman is working wonderfully! I'm feeling very lucky," she whispered breathily into my ear before groaning with delight.

"You are about to feel even luckier White Feather."

We got up the next morning as the sun shone through the walls of the lodge and had sex again. "The teepee doesn't have a shower White Feather, so now what?"

"That's easy, Red Hawk. Let's go for a nice refreshing swim."

We walked back through the ceremonial bowl and to our vehicle and drove to the pond. The pond already had a half a dozen people enjoying the water. We quickly shucked our clothes and tossed them into the back seat before walking to the pond and joining the others.

We still had the face paint on from the ceremony the night before so we scrubbed that off first. Everyone there knew who we were even without the face paint and the faint lash marks still criss crossing our bodies. They all wanted to talk to us about the night we'd spent in the sweat lodge. They were eager to learn what we'd experienced. It was a very rare thing in these modern times for someone to willingly suffer through the ordeal in order to talk to the Great Spirit, and that seemed sad to me.

"How long were the two of you in the sweat lodge?" Asked a woman in her thirties.

"It must have been about fifteen hours or so, Right Ben?" Connie said.

"That would be my guess," I agreed.

"Both of you actually experienced visions?" asked her husband.

"No doubt about it. When we first went into the sweat lodge Connie thought having to spend so many hours in the heat what we would experience would just be hallucinations. But she doesn't think that anymore, do you Connie?"

"Not a bit. It was a real life experience. Ben learned from the Great Spirit how long the wendigo has been a wendigo. He learned how he became one and what we needed to do to rid you of it," Connie explained as the group around them grew.

"Connie learned where we could find him, where his lair was. She learned what tribe he came from too. Without the help of the Great Spirit we'd still be hunting for him. Trust me when I say that would have been very dangerous."

"The Great Spirit said he has been on this reservation four times in the last four hundred years. He also said it has never been beaten before," Connie added as she dunked her head underwater.

"We heard what you had to do in order to send it back. Why did it keep coming back in the first place?" A tribal member in his fifties asked us.

"He had a taste for human flesh. Eating human flesh is what turned him into a wendigo in the first place. Once he's had his fill he would return to the bowels of the earth until his hunger for it returned decades later," I said.

"Can it ever come back again?" Asked a woman in her twenties fearfully.

"I asked the Great Spirit that exact question. He said he did not know because it didn't have a life and it has never been beaten before. But he assured me we would never see it again in our lifetimes and wasn't that good enough for now," Connie said.

"The Great Spirit gave us a message to share with the Navajo people. He said to tell you that he still loves the Navajo people very, very much. He will see all of you on the other side in the afterlife," Ben told the group. Men were smiling and women were tearing up at the news.

I looked up at the sun and saw it was time to meet with the others for our last breakfast together. "We need to get moving."

Everyone in the group hugged or shook hands and the group parted for us so we could wade ashore. At the end there must have been twenty people in the group. I was sure word of what the Great Spirit told us to tell them would spread like wildfire.

We got back to the car and I started to rummage around.

"What are you looking for Ben?" Connie asked me.

"Our towels, you did bring some from the hotel didn't you?"

"Oops, I guess I forgot to, sorry," Connie said, slapping her forehead.

I grabbed my phone and called Joe.

"You guys are meeting us for one last breakfast in a half hour right?" He asked me.

"We'll be there but we might be running a little bit late," I said as I eyed a sheepish looking Connie.

"Why, you stayed in the ceremonial teepee last night didn't you?"

"Yeah, but the teepee didn't have a shower so Connie and I decided to join the others and use the pond this morning. The only problem is we didn't bring any towels. So we're just standing here next to our car like a couple of dumb asses while the wind and the sun dry off our naked bodies."

"Now that's funny as hell Ben. I'd bring you some towels but by the time I got there you wouldn't need them anymore," Joe said as he laughed over the phone.

"How is Connie dealing with having to stand around naked?"

"Why don't you ask her? She is standing here next to me with a shit eating grin plastered on her face."

"Hi Joe, nice day to sunbathe isn't it? Woot, woot, ha ha," Connie laughed out.

"I'll let the others know and we'll see you when you get here," Joe said as he hung up, still laughing out loud.

With the desert heat and wind it didn't take too long to dry off. Twenty minutes later we were dressed and headed to the cafe.

"Cops being cops, you know they're going to pull something don't you?" I asked Connie.

"Yeah, but I don't really care. The wendigo is gone and the water was great. Also, the look on your face when you had to stand there naked was hilarious!" Connie said, grinning wide.

We entered the cafe and saw a table full of grinning cops. "We got a going away present for you. His and hers matching fig leaves," Virgil laughed out holding up a couple of cottonwood leaves.

"One size fits all," grinned Sid.

"They're only good until fall and then they'll fall off," laughed John.

"I gotta say, that's funny. You guys actually used your imagination. Did you visit the local Walmart and buy your imagination on sale?" Connie asked them.

We finished our breakfast and knew it was time to hit the road. Everyone was sad we were going.

"You two know you'll always, always have a home to come

back to here. I don't think we could have come out on top without the two of you," Joe said sincerely.

"It was a two way street guys. If Jeff hadn't sent us to see the holy man and get our butts literally whipped. We wouldn't have come up with the answers we needed," I said.

We were standing out by our car saying our final goodbyes. Connie was starting to tear up. I reached out to shake Joe's hand.

"A hand shake isn't going to do it my brother," he said as he gave me a bear hug. We all ended up hugging.

"You guys have our cell phone numbers. If anything comes up give us a call. But I think we got this thing beat," I said.

"The tribal council is already talking about having a yearly wendigo festival. You know carnival rides, music, dancing and good food. They're thinking about having a three day event every year to celebrate.. The final night will be a big powwow. It could end up being a real tourist attraction once word gets out. We'll already starting to field calls from news agencies about it," Joc said.

"They're planning on even having a parade and they want you two to be the grand marshals the first year. I'm thinking you'll be coming for it every year so this isn't goodbye. This is, we'll see you again next year," Jeff said.

"We'll definitely be here for it guys," Connie said as she cheered up considerably at the news.

"Give us advanced notice about the dates of the events so we can make sure to be on vacation," I said as I climbed into our car for the return trip to Phoenix.

We settled in for the several hour ride back to our waiting corporate jet. Connie called Colin and told him the case was over. If he and Brian wanted to see us one last time we would be boarding our plane in three hours. Next Connie called our pilot to let him know we would be ready to fly back to Washington in three hours.

"I never dreamed the case would go in the direction that it did Ben," Connie admitted.

"I told you before we left Washington where this thing was going to go but you didn't believe me."

"Why should I believe you? You're not right very often you know," Connie said, grinning out the window.

"The main thing is we came out on top. All of our body parts are still intact and where they belong."

"Yeah but not for the Green Berets, Ben. They had to pay a terrible price just because our director wouldn't listen to us. It was a real shame Captain Baker was just as stubborn."

"That's another conversation we need to have. I can't see myself staying with the FBI and working for him. He lost my respect when he sentenced those men to their deaths. I refuse to work for someone I have no respect for or trust in," I said, getting angry all over again.

"So what are the plans then?"

"I don't know, we could always write a book on our adventures."

"You don't seem to me to be the book writing sort. You're more of the private security force kind of guy."

"Alright partner, what do you say we start our own company. There are tons of high profile people in Washington that need protection. Our names are well known and word will get out quickly that we are in business."

"Alright Ben, let's do it. I never want anyone to order me to get men killed again. From now on we're the ones calling the shots," Connie said as she fist bumped me.

We got to the airport and Colin and Brian were standing next to their car waiting for us. I pulled up next to them and handed the keys for the car over to Brian.

"Mission accomplished I hear," Brian said as we shook hands.

"Yeah, it was touch and go for a while but we won," Connie said.

The flight crew loaded out stuff into the aircraft while we said our farewells.

"We want to thank both of you for making sure we got what we asked for while on the case. Without your help more people might have died," I said.

"We were glad to do it, Ben," Colin said.

"Did we ever get any more results on the DNA testing?" Connie asked.

"Nope, unknown for the hair sample and part human for the DNA sample," Colin said.

"Yeah guys and we did promise you some answers before we left town. Sorry we don't have time to do it over beers like we promised you. Connie, show them the painting from the museum on your phone."

Connie brought up the painting depicting a demon and showed it to the two shocked agents.

"This is a wendigo in Native American folklore. In the Christian faith it is a demon. It is what was terrorizing the Navajos. We had to perform air strikes among other things to send it back to the bowels of the earth," I said.

"So you see guys, you'll never have its DNA or matches for the hair sample. The wendigo was originally a human several hundreds of years ago before it did something so evil it became what you see," Connie said.

Both of their jaws were left hanging open.

"We know when our legs are being pulled. We aren't rookies you know," Brian said.

Neither one of us looked like we were kidding. "Okay then, explain your test results to us?" I said.

"You're not kidding?" Colin asked.

"Not everything on this earth can be explained. This is just one of many examples of that," Connie said.

We boarded the plane and looked back at the still confused agents. Sometimes it was fun to blow people's minds, I thought as I found my seat for the take off. Four hours later we were on final approach for Andrews Air Force Base.

We got into our car and neither one of us were talking. We were both thinking our own thoughts about the meeting we were about to have with our director.

We parked in our own private parking spot for the first and last time before riding the elevator up to the director's office.

"Is the director still in?" I asked as I exited the elevator.

"Yes. he knew you were flying back and told me to let you in as soon as you got here." She hit a hidden buzzer under her desk and unlocked the door.

We walked into Anthony Burns inner sanctum. The director had his back to us and was standing looking out over the Potomac River.

We both tossed our credentials onto his desk and turned to leave without a word.

"I've made many mistakes during this case. Please have a seat for a moment."

Connie and I looked at each other before sitting down.

"I was in over my head and tried to bull my way through it. I and I alone are responsible for getting three good men killed."

"We warned you, we begged you not to send them and you wouldn't listen to us. We thought we had your trust and that hurt most of all," Connie said.

The director turned around. I was shocked to see he looked to have aged twenty years in the two weeks we were gone. He sat behind his desk with a sigh and saw our badges sitting there for the first time.

He looked sad and tired as he rubbed his face. "Please, pick them back up."

"We're sorry sir but we can't work for someone who doesn't trust us. Who won't heed our advice and wantonly tosses away human lives," I said.

"You won't be working for me anymore. The president has demanded my resignation by the end of today. I don't know who is going to be replacing me long term or in the interim."

"We don't plan on quitting twice. Whoever gets the job can call us if they want us back. If it's someone we think we can work with we might decide to come back. But if it isn't we plan on starting our own security firm," I told him.

"I'm honestly sorry if this is how our relationship ends," the director said.

"I truly hope you have success in your future. But for that to happen you'll have to trust and have faith in those around you," Connie said.

The director stood up and offered me his hand one last time. I hesitated before shaking it. I could see the pain in his eyes that wasn't there two weeks ago. If nothing else the director definitely felt remorse.

Connie and I walked out of his office without looking back. As we entered the elevator I was thinking about our future. Perhaps we could open an agency that handled cryptids and supernatural beings, I thought as I looked sideways at Connie and grinned crookedly.

The End

~ * ~ * ~ * ~

I hope you enjoy reading this book as much as I enjoyed bringing the characters within its pages to life. May we share many more adventures together.

About the Author

I am a Vietnam vet having served on an ammunition ship in the closing days of the war. I was a radioman with a top secret clearance. I learned my typing skills on the keyboard of a teletype.

I am a three term commander of an American Legion Post and designed our local veteran's memorial. I also spent 19 years in our local boy scout program helping eleven boys reach the eagle scout rank while scoutmaster.

I live in a small Wisconsin town with my wife. I have two married step-daughters and six grandkids.

I have written books in several genres. Supernatural, thriller, historical fiction and mercenary adventure. I am currently working on my ninth book.

~ * ~

Other Books by R.P. Deiss

The Spirit Warriors: *A Spirit Warriors Adventure – Book 1*
Return of the Piano Man: *A Spirit Warriors Adventure – Book 2*
Double Trouble: *A Spirit Warriors Adventure – Book 3*
The Doomsday Event: *A Spirit Warriors Adventure – Book 4*
Dead Men's Isle: *Sea Demons – Book 1*
The Cuban Connection: *Sea Demons – Book 2*
Payback Time: *Sea Demons – Book 3*
Apache Crossing: *Sea Demons – Book 4*
Oak Island: *The Adventure Begins*
Copperhead
Sidewinder (A sequel adventure to *Copperhead*)

Connect with Rick at:
RPDeiss@gmail.com

Facebook: R.P. Deiss Books
http://facebook.com/pages/Rick-Deiss-
Books/300158563484156

~ * ~

Made in the USA
Monee, IL
06 May 2025

16858214R00184